Three Bedrooms
in Chelsea

CASTLE HOUSE
FARM
061 395 139

CLOUNION HOUSE
061-396-657

OUNRR VEN
069 63 400

LACE OB BAWN
061 396 443

Books by Liz Ireland

HUSBAND MATERIAL

WHEN I THINK OF YOU

CHARMED, I'M SURE

THREE BEDROOMS IN CHELSEA

Published by Kensington

Three Bedrooms in Chelsea

LIZ IRELAND

KENSINGTON PUBLISHING CORP.
http://www.kensingtonbooks.com

STRAPLESS BOOKS are published by

Kensington Publishing Corp.
850 Third Avenue
New York, NY 10022

All Kensington titles, imprints, and distributed lines are available at special quantity discounts for bulk purchases for sales promotion, premiums, fund raising, educational or institutional use.

Special book excerpts or customized printings can also be created to fit specific needs. For details, write or phone the office of the Kensington Special Sales Manager: Kensington Publishing Corp., 850 Third Avenue, New York, NY 10022. Attn. Special Sales Department. Phone: 1-800-221-2647.

Strapless Reg. U.S. Pat. & TM Off.

ISBN 0-7582-0543-0

First Kensington Trade Paperback Printing: June 2004
10 9 8 7 6 5 4 3 2 1

Printed in the United States of America

A big *danke* to Mom, Dad,
Marlen Curry, and Fred Herschbach
for their German first aid.

Chapter 1

UZBEKISTAN OR BUST

"Edie! You'll never guess—the *Times* is sending me to Tashkent!"

Edie Amos stared at her boyfriend, Douglas, as he quivered with excitement in the doorway of their apartment. It was eleven o'clock on a Friday morning. Douglas *never* came home this early.

"Sending you *where?*" She worked late nights slinging fettuccine Alfredo at tourists in the theater district, so she suspected she was still partially asleep and hadn't heard him correctly.

"Tashkent, Tashkent," he said, bobbing on his heels like a little kid about to pee his pants.

"Tashkent . . ." Geography was one of those holes in her education. She had gone through school at the tag end of that blissful window when educators didn't want to stuff too many facts into kids' heads. Part of that generation of Americans condemned to blunder around Trivial Pursuit boards in vain pursuit of the blue pie wedges. "That's in . . . ?"

"In Uzbekistan. Isn't that fantastic? It's like my life's big dream has finally, finally come true!"

Give the guy another moment, and he would break into highlights from *Man of La Mancha*.

From the rapturous glint in his green eyes, Edie was certain Douglas expected her to receive his incredible news with grace and selflessness. With shared joy, even. And Edie did make a valiant attempt to curve her lips into some semblance of a smile.

But she couldn't. She just couldn't. Her lips had gone as numb as the rest of her.

Uzbekistan? *Uzbekistan* was Douglas's big dream?

Apparently she had missed, or maybe just forgotten, a conversation somewhere along the way . . . the one in which her boyfriend confided that his *life's big dream* was to travel to remote former Soviet bloc countries. She couldn't remember Douglas ever mentioning big dreams, period. Or even middling ones. She'd assumed that living here in New York in this apartment with her was his dream.

"Can you believe it?" Douglas, flushed with happiness and so animated that he was practically tap-dancing in front of her, was completely oblivious to her lack of enthusiasm. "I get to leave on Sunday!"

He might as well have doused Edie with ice cold water, which wouldn't have been a bad idea in any case. She was floored. She felt like all those cartoons featuring a guy walking down the street who has a piano drop on him. Emotionally she was just two legs sticking out from under a Steinway.

"This Sunday?"

"Of course!"

Of course. In his eyes she could see him mentally ticking off the list of things he had to attend to in two short days. Laundry. Phone calls. Packing.

Girlfriend dumping.

He ruffled her hair as he skipped past her on the way to their bedroom. Her heart sank. *Their* bedroom. This was the first bedroom, the first apartment, Edie had ever permanently shared with a guy.

Well. She'd *thought* it was permanent.

"I bought my e-ticket before I left the office," Douglas chattered as he scanned the closet for his bags. "Dontcha *love* the Internet?"

She stumbled after him, trying to process it all. *Don't panic,* she told herself. *Don't jump to conclusions.* He hadn't said anything about breaking up. Going to Uzbekistan wouldn't necessarily be fatal to their relationship.

"When are you coming back?"

He twisted around with a look of astonishment. "Edie, don't you get it? I'm being transferred."

"Transferred?" *That* sounded fatal. Her voice rose. "Why didn't you tell me?"

His eyes dilated in surprise at her reaction. Apparently, the fact that she wasn't sharing his Uzbek bliss was finally beginning to penetrate his cranial matter. "Because I didn't know. How could I? This is all a big surprise to me. The guy who was there had a heart attack, and he's flying home for a triple bypass."

"So this is just temporary."

"They're not sure. It's sort of up in the air."

Up in the air? That made it sound as if he could be gone forever. "Uzbekistan . . . it's so far. . . ." She would have to rustle up an atlas. And what she didn't know about the political situation there could fill an encyclopedia. It *sounded* uncertain. . . .

She would also have to start skipping "The E! True Hollywood Story" and flip over to the news a little more often.

"Why are they sending you there?"

His jaw dropped. "It's just one of the hottest places in the world at the moment, that's all."

"Dangerous, you mean," she said, hysteria rising in her throat.

"Not really. Not yet. What with the rebel groups gathering on the border with Turkey . . ."

Her breath caught.

"There's political instability, but no real violence," Douglas said with a shrug, already sounding like a seasoned pro. If it were possible for a voice to swagger, his did. "A good journalist knows when the danger's serious enough to require him to pull out."

The key word in that sentence being *good.* It wasn't that Edie doubted his prowess. Douglas just didn't have that much experience . . . didn't speak the language . . . hadn't even been out of the country as far as she knew, except to go spend a week in the Caribbean each February. Why were they sending *him?*

Why my boyfriend? she thought selfishly. For the past few months, whenever Edie had thought of her future, Douglas had been in it. Now he was just blithely leaving New York. Leaving her.

They hadn't been dating long, but their relationship had

seemed so solid. A month ago she had agreed—at his invitation—to move into his apartment, which she'd had the sneaking suspicion he'd rented with an eye to having her share with him. It was preposterously big for a bachelor, an argument he had used to wheedle her out of her matchbox-sized Brooklyn efficiency. It hadn't taken much arm-twisting, of course. She had thought it was so romantic that he wanted to share his life with her.

"I never knew you wanted to go to Uzbekistan."

"It's not Uzbekistan particularly," he said, shifting his feet. "It's the opportunity to be a foreign correspondent. It's what I've always wanted."

"Since when?" The question exploded out of her. "When did you decide this was what you wanted? Last month you were talking about trying to find a job on local TV news."

He clucked. "That was just a whim."

He *always* had whims. "And this isn't?"

He turned impatiently and put his hands on her shoulders, almost as if to give her a firm shake. "Edie, this assignment is a plum—and it just dropped in my lap! I hate the idea of us being separated, too—I'll miss you like all heck—but this is too good an opportunity to turn down."

Like all heck. Edie wanted to cry. Half the time she found his leftover Iowa farmboy phrases irritating, but now they seemed so cute. Now he would be off saying "like all heck" and "dollars to donuts" in a country where no one could appreciate how sweet they were.

"I hate the idea of your leaving."

He leveled a disappointed gaze on her. "I can't believe you're being like this. Do you think that if *you* got a big acting opportunity to make a movie somewhere far away that I would try to discourage you? I wouldn't dream of it!"

"You wouldn't?" she asked. "Not even for a second?"

"Of course not. I'd *encourage* you."

His eagerness to send her packing on this nonexistent movie shoot didn't strike her as flattering. And the difference was, a movie wrapped in a few months, tops. Whereas this new assignment of his sounded completely open-ended.

But deep down she knew he was right. She was being ungenerous. She just felt so resentful—of his job . . . of Uzbeks . . . of the way he was so happy about something that made her feel as if she were about to go into cardiac arrest.

His hands dropped from her shoulders. "Anyway, it's not like we're married."

"No." They hadn't even gotten around to buying a couch yet. Now the odds of them ever being joined in wedded bliss were probably even significantly lower than the odds of them ever getting a Jennifer convertible sofa for the living room.

It was almost too much for her to take in. They had met at a bar in the East Village four months ago. From the first night, Douglas had pursued her with an intensity that had overwhelmed her. It was the first time she'd actually felt courted. The guys she had known before Douglas were more interested in hooking up and then moving on than settling down. But they had mostly been actors. Douglas, with his stable career, his farmboy background, Jiminy Cricket enthusiasms, and general togetherness had bowled her over. She'd thought she was so lucky. She'd finally thought she was getting it all together.

Now it was all falling apart again.

"Hasn't our relationship meant anything to you?"

He stared at her with unveiled impatience. "How can you even ask that?"

"Because you acted as if it meant everything. You acted as if this was something permanent. You even begged me to give up my apartment to move into this place!"

"I never begged."

"Yes, you—" Okay, maybe he hadn't. "Well, you *asked*."

He tossed an empty, flaccid-looking canvas duffel down on the bed. "Because we were together, and it would be more economical."

Her breath caught. "You mean it was all about *economics?*"

He rolled his eyes. "Edie, c'mon. You're going nuts here. Of course being with you has been special. But we're single, and this is part of the reason we *are* single—so we can jump at opportunities like this. Both of us."

He sounded so rational. Too rational. What about love? It seemed foolishly late to ask, but didn't he love her? "I never saw this coming. What am I supposed to do now?"

"Just do what you always do. Stay here and try to light a fire under that career of yours."

She crossed her arms. There was sarcasm in his voice when he talked about "that career." Which really wasn't much of a career at this point, she had to admit. But lots of actresses didn't flit right up the ladder of success. Most everyone's career suffered little stumbles along the way.

"What about the apartment?" she asked.

He sent her a perplexed gaze. "What about it?"

"This place is twenty-one hundred a month. I can't afford it on my own." She really couldn't afford to pay half, if truth be told. Already she was passing over things, real life necessities like cool new shoes and those yummy double lattes at the Last Drop, so that she could pony up her ten fifty at the first of the month. And that was with Douglas footing most of the bills. On her own, she was really going to be straining the limits of her bankbook.

"You'll survive," he said.

Would she? she wondered. When she moved in with Douglas a month ago, she'd felt so hopeful. She had thought they were going to spend happy years together in this apartment, furnishing it, gathering memories. She had thought they were building toward something.

And apparently they had been. Toward this. Toward having the man she thought she was in love with pat her on the back and say *you'll survive.*

She would be on her own again. All the things she had taken for granted—the couple things—weren't going to be there for her. There would be no ready person to eat dinner with, no more phone calls in the middle of the day just to ask how she was, no more snuggling on Sunday mornings.

Worst of all, she would have to move.

Was there anything worse than moving? In the past five years she had moved three times, always from one fleabag efficiency to another. Without fail, she longed to escape before her things were moved in. Before she'd moved in with Douglas, she had been living in a postage stamp Brooklyn efficiency that smelled as if something large and mammalian had died nearby—like, maybe in the apartment down the hall. (The peculiar odor made her only too happy not to get chummy with her neighbors.)

And now she was being thrown out into the rental jungle once more. She wanted to weep. Suddenly she felt an almost fanatical attachment to this apartment. It was a two-bedroom—sprawling by Manhattan standards—that the landlord, in typical sleazy landlord fashion, had advertised as being in Chelsea. It was really midtown. It was above an Indian restaurant named the Tandoor Express and reeked of curry, which was a big improvement over dead animal smell. And there was a balcony off the living room that you could actually stand on.

Not that it was perfect here. With the restaurant downstairs came bugs. The battle against roaches was as fierce as it was futile. And the landlord, Bhiryat, hadn't glued down the linoleum in the kitchen or bathroom, so the flooring sort of slid around beneath their feet and curled up next to the walls. Several of the light plugs didn't work and there was no cold water in the bathroom sink, and there was no hope Bhiryat was going to fix anything.

The smell, the bugs, the landlord . . .

She *loved* this place.

It was so big, so open. The apartment building had been built pre-1920s and actually had a livable floor plan, unlike all the railroad flats and chopped-up brownstones people put up with in this city. The front door opened onto a rectangular living room, which was set off by a beautiful period light fixture and gorgeous double doors leading onto a tiny iron balcony. At the end of the room there was an odd space that seemed to have been a large closet. Some earlier tenant had taken the doors off, though, and now the space just stood gaping open, like a missing tooth. The only purchase Edie and Douglas had made together so far was a cheap screen from Chinatown to cover the gap. Next to the gap was an archway leading to a galley kitchen. Moving back counterclockwise between the kitchen and the front door were a bedroom, a bath, and a slightly smaller second room.

Edie's first few days there, she had been like one of those

caged animals reintroduced to the wild; she'd huddled in the bedroom or the kitchen, unable to grasp that all this was hers. It was the first place she'd lived in Manhattan that had seemed like it could really be a home—her home. Even if it was, technically, Douglas's. She'd had big plans for it.

And now she was going to have to move out? The thought of leaving the balcony and the two bedrooms and the ten-foot ceilings made her breath come in gulps, like a beached fish.

"Where am I going to go?"

"What are you so gosh-darned panicked about?" Douglas asked. "You must have some money saved up."

"Oh, sure. I'll just dip into that big 401K I've accumulated from waiting tables for five years."

He rolled his eyes. "Edie, I know you're supposed to be an actress, but do you have to overdramatize everything?"

She was *supposed* to be an actress? "Don't hold back with the wounding comments today, Douglas. Really. I can take it."

"I just don't see what the big deal is. Just stay here."

"The big deal is, you're leaving me here and my name isn't on the lease."

"Talk to Bhiryat."

"But he'll want me to sign a new lease, and if I sign a new lease, he'll raise the rent."

"Okay, *don't* talk to Bhiryat," he huffed. "I'll give you some money . . . I need to store my stuff anyway, and this would save me the hassle of moving it and renting a storage space."

"So you'll be coming back?"

"Sure." He turned back to his packing and muttered, "Eventually . . ."

She flopped onto her back on the bed.

"For Pete's sake, Edie. I'll be back. Have a little faith."

"I can't believe you're just leaving," she said, hating the break in her throat as her words came out. She was beginning to sound so like a dumped girlfriend.

"But I'm not leaving *you*. You understand that, don't you?" He reached out and rubbed her tense shoulder, and she closed her eyes. Douglas could be oh-so nice. She squeezed her eyes shut as if to block out thoughts of the lonely days and nights ahead.

"This isn't a breakup," he said, "it's just that you and my job are temporarily incompatible."

He could also be oh-so full of shit.

But lame as the rationalization was, her brain managed to latch on to it as if it were a lifeline. It was something, she supposed, not to be dumped outright. And she didn't want to be a pill. He couldn't refuse a great assignment that had just fallen into his lap. This was part of his job.

For the next two days, "this isn't a breakup" became her mantra. She embraced the explanation that she and Douglas's job were just having a temporary compatibility problem, and disseminated it to all her friends and loved ones. She and Douglas had several reassuring rounds of wild farewell sex. Saturday night she got roaring drunk at an impromptu bon voyage party for Douglas at the apartment, and cried tears of gratefulness when he presented her with a check for his half of three months' rent to help her out while he was gone.

And then, on Sunday, he stepped onto a plane and flew out of her life.

Chapter 2

The New Yorker
Four Times Square
New York, New York 10036

April 10, 2003

Danielle Poitier
1818 Travis Circle
Amarillo, TX 75762

Dear Ms. Poitier:

Thank you very much for submitting your story, Kappas Are Such Ho's!, *to The New Yorker. Regretfully, as was the case with your eleven previous submissions, we found this story not quite strong enough for our needs. I am therefore returning the manuscript herewith.*

I showed your work to an editor here, Mr. Picard, and though he was impressed by the (presumably intentional . . . ?) surreal tone, he pronounced the story's subject matter a trifle juvenile. Interest in sorority girl literature among The New Yorker read-

*ership is, on the whole, limited. He suggested that for examples of
what we publish, you should read our magazine regularly or
simply go to your library and check out a collection of John
Updike.*

Sincerely,

Jennifer Poon
Editorial Assistant

Chapter 3

AUF WIEDERSEHEN,
FRANK

When Greta Stolenbauer walked into what she sincerely believed was her apartment, she found a petite brunette wearing not a stitch of clothing standing by the open refrigerator, her shapely silhouette backlit by the tiny light next to the milk. Hearing Greta, the girl whirled on her bare heels. Her eyes popped open and her hands, one clutching a bottle of iced green tea, crossed over all her naughty bits in a futile attempt at modesty.

"Mein Gott!" Greta exclaimed. *"Entschuldigung!"*

The girl continued to stare bug-eyed at her, and Greta realized that she probably had blurted out German.

"I mean . . . excuse me." Greta backed out the door into the hallway and slammed the door shut. She sank against the hallway wall; her heart was hammering against her ribs.

This was a first. Bizarre things tended to happen when she was drunk or hungover, but cold sober Greta had never walked into a stranger's apartment thinking it was her own.

Weird! She'd been so sure, too.

. Maybe she was experiencing one of those delayed trips they always warned about in high school scare films—films with titles like "Party Till You Die" and "Dead is Dead," which she'd barely understood because she hadn't spoken English her last year in high school, when she had first arrived in the United States. That had been one of the oddest things about her new country at first. The schools here seemed to be all about drugs—adults lectured about them in class, and in between classes kids distributed them at their lockers (proving once again that there was no such thing as bad publicity). As a teenager, Greta had indulged in all sorts of stuff, all in the name of assimilation.

So that was probably what was going on here—just a slight brain twitch. She was experiencing a delayed reaction to something. It had been ages since she'd been that stupid, of course. She hadn't touched anything since she'd left rehab eight years ago.

Well. Anything but alcohol.

Although, come to think of it, last night at Malatov's there *had* been that bizarre-looking guy at the bar, the one who resembled an anorexic Vin Diesel. She wouldn't have put it past him to have slipped something into her drink.

She closed her eyes as she squatted in the hallway, trying to breathe normally and get her bearings. Trying to backtrack to where she could have gone so wrong. This evening she'd left work, caught the subway, changed trains, gotten off, walked five blocks, opened her door, walked up two flights . . .

Her eyes blinked opened and she peered at the door she'd just scurried out of—3A.

She and Frank lived in 3A.

Details were coming back to her now. That had been *her* Picasso print from the Berlin Museum on the wall. And *her* couch being used as the divider between the living room space and the kitchen space. Come to think of it, that had been *her* iced green tea that naked chick had been in the process of stealing.

She glared at the door. *Son of a bitch!*

Why did everything have to go sour on her all the time, and so fast? She'd only been with Frank for two months. Of course, she had suspected he was cheating on her right along. But she thought he would be afraid of her enough not to let himself get caught in the act. Damn it! What was the point of being five foot ten, blond, and fierce if you couldn't even intimidate your boyfriend?

A quarter hour later she was at the Bitter End, nursing a Dewar's. She fished a few cubes out of the glass, wrapped them in the napkin coaster, and placed it over her sore hand. (Frank's jaw had proved surprisingly bony.)

Now what was she going to do?

The eternal question. Greta had been alternately worrying about what she was going to do and trying to escape worrying about anything since she was seventeen years old.

Seventeen. Or, as she thought of it, the year everything turned to shit. Losing your parents, especially both at once, was probably terrible at any age. But she was beginning to wonder if losing them at seventeen might not be the worst possible time. She had been in a rebellious stage that year. Her father had been talking about sending her away to school, but her mother, the more stoic parent, had insisted that Greta would grow out of whatever demon had possessed her . . . and that sending her away would only make things worse.

Greta wished she could call up more happy memories of them, but she couldn't remember any exceptionally tender scenes of family closeness. It wasn't that she hadn't been a happy kid, doing all the usual kid stuff, but her parents were busy people; they were friendly, even funny, but not particularly demonstrative. Her father owned a music store, and her mother worked there, too. They didn't dote on Greta or shower her with affection as she enviously imagined other parents would an only child. When Greta made good grades, they took it as a matter of course. *"Soll ich Dir ein Ehrenmal setzen?"* her father would ask sarcastically when Greta pointed out a good grade from school, hoping for praise. ("Shall I erect a monument to you?") When she messed up, of course, she was punished.

The day they died she was in the doghouse. She had wanted to stay in Munich while her parents visited friends in the country, but she had stayed out too late one night and was told that they would not leave her alone in the apartment until they could trust her. All during the gloomy drive, she had seethed in the backseat, arms crossed, refusing to speak to them except in grunts and operatic gestures of teenage disdain. She kept her eyes pointedly trained out the back passenger window at the rainy countryside, so she hadn't seen what happened. She only pieced it together later, in the hospital. An oncoming car swerved into their lane.

Their car skidded, spun, and collided head-on with a car that had been traveling behind them.

And that was the end of her family.

If there was a heaven, was that picture of her, pouting and rude, ingrained in her parents' minds for all eternity? It was in hers; she'd been dipped in formaldehyde at her worst moment. No matter where she went, that vision of the kid with her arms crossed in the backseat, slumped and glaring out the window, followed, haunting her. *Why couldn't I have said one nice thing to them?*

Maybe some people, better people, would have viewed the accident as a transformative experience. After the accident her aunt in Cleveland took pity on her and invited her to live, but two years with an unhinged teenager had nearly been poor Aunt Lotte's undoing. When Greta was twenty Lotte sent her to rehab (the first rehab) and suggested her niece might be happier on her own.

Since then, Greta had been stumbling around searching for a place where she would be comfortable in her own skin. She was beginning to wonder if she would ever find it. She'd moved so often she felt like a human ping-pong ball.

A girl named Jenna, whom Greta had called from the apartment, came into the bar a few minutes later and hoisted herself onto the next stool. She had green streaks in her black hair and more metal sticking in her than your average pincushion. Greta was proud that she herself had limited herself to a few earrings and a navel ring . . . though she *had* gone on an ill-advised tattoo jag a few years earlier. Jenna sported eyeliner that made her look like a raccoon, but Greta was also something of an eye pencil dervish herself on days when she wasn't working.

She usually just ran into Jenna at clubs, and had almost been surprised to find her home number in her wallet. Surprised and relieved. Jenna was still a kid, and she definitely wasn't a brain, but she knew a lot of people.

Her ringed eyes zeroed in on Greta's swollen knuckles. "What the hell happened?"

"I punched Frank."

Jenna gasped. "*What?* Why?"

"A naked midget was wandering around our apartment when I got home."

"No shit! You mean a girl?"

"Would I be so frenzled over a boy, do you think?"

Jenna flinched a little. "Frenzled? What's that?"

God, she hated English sometimes. And it was irritating that people who had never learned a second language themselves could be so nitpicky with tiny errors. "*Frenzy*," Greta corrected after hunting for the word. "Would I be so in a frenzy over a boy?"

"Well . . . I don't know about a frenzy," Jenna said, "but it would really explain that thing Frank has for Ashton Kutcher movies."

"This was a definite girl," Greta said.

"What a dick!" Jenna's pierced brow puckered. "Like, how small was she?"

Greta shook her head. "Not a real midget. I was just using a figure from speech."

"Ohhhh." Jenna nodded. "So you actually fought with Frank?"

"*Ja*," Greta said, somewhat proudly. Whatever she was, no one could call her a wimp. "We went one round. When I left he had the little birdies twittery over his head, like in the cartoon."

"You go, girl."

Greta took a swig of her drink. She felt morose. "Sure, go and find another place to stay."

"That shouldn't be hard."

"I have no money."

"*That's* hard," Jenna agreed. "But not impossible."

"Frank better be leaving my furniture alone. He hurt the furniture, he will die."

Jenna laughed. "You and that junk of yours! I can't believe you've dragged it along with you all these years."

"Where I go, it goes."

Jenna's black-polished nails tapped the waxy wood of the bar. "Okay. So that means you need space. My place is out, of course." Jenna lived with her boyfriend in an efficiency. "Except if you need a place to crash for the night."

"Thanks."

She snapped her fingers. "What about Asgarth?"

Greta moaned. "*Nein.*"

"Now don't go spitting *neins* at me. Why not? He's crazy about you!"

"Sure, and you can emphasize the crazy. Asgarth is a lunatic." He was a biker, he was loud, and he had dreadlocks. If Greta were queen of the world, the first law she would dictate would be a prohibition against white guys trying to look like Bob Marley.

"Poor old As!" Jenna said. "I think you should give him a chance. I'll bet *he* wouldn't cheat on you."

"He's *crazy*. Nuts. Two weeks ago he parked his motorcycle below my window and sang at three A.M."

"A serenade?"

"With old rock songs." Asgarth had to be the last Lynyrd Skynyrd fan left on earth.

Jenna's nose wrinkled. "So I guess his crooning schtick didn't win you over."

"Frank called the police."

Her friend sighed. "Still . . . it *was* sort of sweet of As, don't you think?"

Greta shook her head. She was beginning to wonder if Jenna was really such a friend; apparently she would foist Greta off on anyone. But then, Jenna was still at that stage in life where it all seemed like one big party ahead. She didn't know that someday you were going to want to stay in one place, and maybe not go out so much, and regret having gotten so many tattoos. She didn't know what it was like to be pushing thirty.

"Widerlich," Greta said.

"Huh?"

"It was obnoxious. And as for living with him, thank you, no. I am not so desperate as that."

Jenna frowned. "Oh, man, I'm not so sure, Greta. You've crashed with practically everybody else."

That she had. Ever since her move from L.A. she had bounced from one place to another, all over the five boroughs. She never seemed to be able to stick in one place for very long. People said she was difficult, which was such a load of crap. Just because she wasn't a loser, a cowering little sheep like everyone else, did that make her a bad person?

What she needed was her own place, but she was so short on

cash. She made good money, but it always seemed to disappear on her. Of course, her pitiful finances might have something to do with the fact that she went out all the time . . . but what else could she do? She never felt comfortable anywhere. If she stayed home, she'd just be sitting around someone else's cramped apartment, feeling like an intruder, which is pretty much what she'd felt like for years and years. She was beginning to believe she was one of those persons who didn't belong anywhere in the world.

If only things had been different. If only . . .

She lifted her hand to summon the bartender for another whiskey.

Jenna sighed. "It's a shame. Asgarth is the only person I know whose place could fit all your furniture."

Greta's ears perked up, and she swiveled toward Jenna. "What?"

"He's got that loft in Red Hook. Haven't you ever been there?"

"No . . ."

"He got it from an uncle who died. It's, like, huge."

"Really?"

"Oh yeah, baby," Jenna said, gulping down the rest of her beer. "And it's completely empty, except for As's sculptures. He creates really cool things out of old Harleys. Still, even with his work and all, the place is practically empty. There's an echo."

Greta stared sightlessly at her swollen hand. She was always making plans . . . probably because the previous plan never seemed to work out. Frank had been a plan at some point, and look how *that* had turned out. Same song, over and over. When she'd lived in Cleveland with her aunt and uncle, she'd had a million different plans, from Plan A to Z-6. The same thing had happened in Los Angeles, and for the little hiccup of time she'd spent in Phoenix. Now here she was, working on yet another. Moving in with Asgarth.

If this didn't work out, she didn't know what she would do. Something even more desperate, probably.

Chapter 4

OLD FRIENDS

"**I** never liked him."

Edie's jaw dropped. Her friend Aurora was talking about Douglas. "You never told me that!"

"How could I have told you?" Aurora asked, pulling a Dunhill from its box and tapping it. She'd spent the last two months in England making a movie, and now was smoking only English cigarettes. "You acted like you were so in love with him."

"I *was* in love with him." As the words left her mouth, Edie flinched. "I mean, I am. Still."

"Hmph." Aurora leaned back and regarded Edie with her cat-shaped green eyes. Aurora was stunningly pretty, the kind of woman men gawked at without even realizing it. She had a heart-shaped face with a nose that seemed to be chiseled right out of the plastic surgeon's manual, and long, thick dark hair. Small wonder Hollywood was beginning to take notice.

"You were so sneaky about it all," Aurora said. "The moment my back was turned, you moved in with him!"

"I don't remember sneaking."

"I was in Minneapolis, remember? Making that HBO thing . . . with Susan Sarandon. When I came back, the deed was done. You'd given up that cute little place in Brooklyn."

Cute place! "It was a vermin-infested dump that smelled like I had Jeffrey Dahmer living next door."

Aurora frowned. "Oh, right."

"I *love* my apartment. Our apartment, I mean. Douglas is coming back."

It was just the end of April. To the extent that she was temperamentally able, Edie was practicing positive thinking. The three months' rent check probably meant he was just going to be gone for three months, right? If that was the case, she shouldn't even begin worrying until mid-May.

Doug even called her . . . occasionally. Unfortunately, when he did call, it was usually to tell her how great his new life was. How exciting. How he was traveling all over in his free time and meeting all sorts of fascinating, sophisticated people. And had she read his articles?

He'd promised to send a rug, though. That meant he was thinking about hearth and home, didn't it?

Aurora and Edie had been freshman roommates at NYU, and even though they really couldn't be more different, they were adept at sizing up each other's moods. Aurora knew she was a wreck inside.

"You're better off without him."

"But I'm not without him, exactly," Edie insisted. "He's coming back."

She kept repeating this fact for Aurora, but she might as well have been talking to the Scooby Doo chia pet on the coffee table that Aurora kept flicking her cigarette ashes on. Aurora collected the oddest crap. Edie never understood it. "I don't know what it was about him," Aurora mused, as if Douglas were not only gone but dearly departed. "Maybe it was the way he referred to women as 'gals'—that always gave me the creeps. Also, he always seemed to be on some kind of kick. Remember when he decided to take up the oboe?"

Did she remember? Last week Edie had been reduced to tears when she found herself gazing lovingly at the oboe, which was still in their closet. She held back a sniff now. "I remember."

"He even signed up for lessons. Like he was going to become the next . . ." Aurora frowned. "Well! I don't even know of a famous oboe player. Do they exist? Maybe Douglas thought he'd be the first."

"He gets very enthusiastic about things," Edie said wistfully.

"Yeah, and he went out and sprung for that expensive oboe, took one lesson, and just dropped it."

"Actually, it's his impetuous nature that gives me hope. This business about his wanting to be a foreign correspondent could be like the oboe."

Aurora exhaled a cloud of smoke. "I'd be more worried that *you're* the oboe."

Edie froze. Oh, Lord. Stuck on a closet shelf and forgotten. This gave her a whole new angle to obsess about.

"Forget him—I met a guy you'd *love*," Aurora gushed. "He's a lighting designer. Well . . . assistant lighting designer. I think you guys would really hit it off."

The idea tempted Edie for a flicker of a moment; not that she would ever cheat on Douglas. Neither of them had breathed a word about dating other people while he was away. Still, there was something rugged and sexy about those lighting guys swaggering around in their tight jeans and boots, rigging up klieg lights from high above the stage and handling asbestos cables. They were the Marlboro men of the theatrical world.

But she wasn't really tempted. "I *told* you, Douglas is coming back."

"Oh, sure. Coming back with a Christiane Amanpour clone on his arm. You can't trust those randy journalist types."

"Unlike staid, buttoned-down actor types," Edie joked.

Aurora didn't bat an eye. "That's why you should forget Doug the lug and jump on my lighting fellow! His name is Mizlov and he's incredibly hot."

"I don't care about hot."

Aurora laughed. "You are so full of it. Everybody likes hot, and hot and foreign is especially cool. Mizlov is from the Czech Republic, and he's without consort at the moment. And the last thing he went out with was a real hag, in my opinion. He'd go for you in a big way."

"Great. I'm a step up from a hag."

"You know that's not what I meant."

Edie nodded. It wasn't. Not really. It was just so hard when nothing was going right for her to take advice from a person who seemed to have the world on a string. Someone had sprinkled fairy dust over Aurora: her career was catching fire, money was starting to pour in—she'd even had to go to an investment counselor.

Back when they were first starting out, things had been different. Right after college Edie had had a string of good luck. It seemed flukish now, but she had landed a few really juicy parts while Aurora with her Lara Flynn Boyle looks was doing local commercials for coat factory closeouts and fly-by-night technical schools. Somewhere along the way, though, the pendulum had swung, and now Edie watched from the shoreline as her friend sailed off every few months to ever more prestigious movie shoots.

These days Edie felt lucky when her agent sent her on deodorant ad auditions. Under different circumstances she would have thought she needed a better agent. That was the actor's customary gripe. Unfortunately, she and Aurora had the same agent.

But she was happy for Aurora . . . and she couldn't help thinking that knowing someone with good luck might make that luck rub off on her, too. Anyway, she had known from the start that an acting career would take perseverance . . . and patience. It was just that everything seemed to be going wrong all of a sudden. She hadn't had an acting job since Christmas. And now she felt so alone.

But she shouldn't let Douglas's absence get her down like this. And she shouldn't be testy with Aurora, who had always been there for her.

Except when she was gallivanting off with Susan Sarandon, a rebellious little corner of her brain meowed.

"Thanks for the offer," Edie said, striking a diplomatic tone, "but I think I need to give it a little more time before I throw in the towel on Douglas."

Aurora smiled. "Who's talking about throwing in the towel? Why not just do some old-fashioned cheating?"

"I can't. Especially not while I'm staying in his apartment. Our apartment."

Aurora's brows drew together. "Can you afford that place now?"

"Douglas left some money . . . I've got enough to last me till summer."

"*Summer?* Summer's not far off! And when Douglas doesn't come back, what will you do? Give up the apartment?"

Edie had spent many sleepless nights chewing over just that possibility. Douglas had left her in emotional and financial limbo. All she could do was just try to hang on to what she had—the apartment and her firm belief that Douglas would be back. Someday.

Aurora touched her forearm. "Look. I'll probably be working on that Adrian Lyne project in June." Her next role was a good secondary role in a thriller. "Do you want to borrow my place while I'm in Toronto? You could stay as long as you want. I'm so busy now the place is just standing empty half the time."

Edie shook her head. If she moved into Aurora's, there was a chance that she might end up actually living with Aurora, and even as a temporary measure that would be a disaster. They hadn't lived together since freshman year . . . with good reason. Aurora's clutter drove Edie up a wall. Even now Aurora seemed never to have grasped the concept of picking up after herself; her apartment was always like an archeological study of how her life had been since the maid had last been there. Clothes heaped wherever she'd felt like shucking them. Various cosmetics and diet soda cans stood forgotten on tables next to plates and bowls that were empty except for the cigarette butts that had been stubbed out in them. Aurora had thrown out all her ashtrays two years ago when she'd decided to give up smoking. In the end, all she had really given up were the ashtrays.

Edie just couldn't abandon her place. It seemed like the one stable thing in her life—this wonderful big place that was really like a home. She intended to cling to it like a shipwrecked soul clinging to jetsam on the open sea, no matter what. "If push comes to shove, I can always get a roommate."

"Oh no!" "Horror-stricken" best described Aurora's expression. "Thank heavens I came back from England in time! Think, Edie, *think*. Think of all the kooks you'll have to sift through. And the worst part is, you'll end up living with one of them!"

Edie didn't need to be reminded of the danger of roommates. She'd had several awful ones in college (she was staring at one of them right now). "But this would be different. This time I would be picking *them*. I can be patient and wait till I've found a good match."

"Doesn't matter," Aurora declared flatly. "Everyone is weird. Even the people who look nice have hidden annoying habits that will drive you nuts within weeks. Plus, you're a neatnik!"

"I am not."

"Yes, Edie, you *are*. No one could live up to your standards. How come you can stand to live in that big, empty apartment? I'll tell you. Because it's easy to keep clean."

"We were going to get furniture."

"Uh-huh . . ."

"Anyway, Douglas didn't think I was hard to live with. We got along fine."

"For a month," Aurora reminded her brutally. "Then he left."

Edie felt as if she'd been sucker punched. Unfortunately, Aurora was just pointing out the naked, brutal truth.

"People just weren't made to live together long-term," Aurora went on.

"Oh, come on. Look at married people."

"Exactly! Look at them. Ninety percent can't even make it through a party without jumping down each other's throats. And I'm convinced that the other ten percent are just putting on a good show."

"But some married people *do* stay together," Edie pointed out.

Aurora flicked an ash authoritatively. "For the *health insurance*. If it weren't for sharing health insurance benefits, marriage would probably disappear in this country altogether." She leaned forward. "*That's* why we'll never have socialized medicine here. Our entire social order would fall apart."

Edie laughed. "Okay, but your doomed-marriage theory doesn't apply in this case. I'm just talking about a roommate. And since it's my apartment, *I'll* be the one with the claim on the place. I'll be in control. I won't have to put up with a freak if I don't want to."

Aurora had skepticism written all over her face.

"Besides, this is all just speculation," Edie said. "Douglas's name is still on the lease. His stuff is there. I know he's coming back, it's just a question of when."

"If his name is still on the lease, it's going to make living there and renting a room to somebody else a little dicey," Aurora told her. "Especially if he comes back after you've got a roommate. Would you be comfortable booting the poor renter out?"

"Well . . ." Edie wrestled with this dilemma. She had never been in a position to decide someone's fate before. "Would you?"

"Oh, sure!" Aurora chimed without so much as a second thought. "I'd put her ass on the street *tout de suite*."

"Nice," Edie said.

"But that's me," Aurora said. "*You're* the one who agonizes over these annoying ethical quagmires."

It *would* be a quagmire. But like the wise man said, she would burn that bridge when she came to it. "None of this really matters," Edie said. "How long can a guy stay in Uzbekistan? Douglas will probably be back before the end of the month."

Aurora released a long plume of smoke. "You know him better than I do. . . ."

Chapter 5

**The New Yorker
Four Times Square
New York, New York 10036**

May 18, 2003

*Danielle Poitier
1818 Travis Circle
Amarillo, Texas 75762*

Dear Ms. Poitier:

Thank you so much for your most recent submission, My Fucked-Up New England Family. *Though the general theme of the story seemed more appropriate for our readership than your previous submissions, our fiction editor felt the quality of the story just was not up to our high standard in this competitive fiction market. Therefore, with sincere regrets, I am once again forced to return your manuscript to you.*

I might add that I showed the story to Mr. Picard, who suggested your story, despite its ambitious subject, revealed a rather limited—I believe the word actually used was shallow—*life experience. For instance (this is a quibble, of course) Long Island is generally not considered an island in the tropical paradise sense of the word.*

Best wishes for your writing endeavors, which I now feel quite certain I will be seeing more of in the near future.

Sincerely,

Jennifer Poon
Editorial Assistant

Chapter 6

PUSH COMES TO SHOVE

Geppetto's was an Italian restaurant in the theater district that catered to the Broadway ticket-holder crowd and anyone else who didn't know better. The owner tried to combine a serious eatery with theme-park décor, so that tourists from Iowa could eat their chicken parmigiano in Sicilian fairy-tale surroundings, with Perry Como and Andrea Bocelli floating in over the sound system. The walls were bare brick, the floors pine, and from the raftered ceilings hung marionettes featuring Pinocchio characters. Rustic shoemaker junk—including old shoes, which Edie had always found particularly unappetizing—stood on shelves drilled into the walls. Wine bottle candleholders graced the checkered tablecloth–covered tables. Portions were large.

Edie supposed she should be grateful that the manager, Larry, didn't make the waitstaff dress like Italian peasants. Or puppets.

But frankly, she was having a hard time working up an attitude of gratitude about anything right now. It was the end of May, and Douglas's phone calls had trickled to a halt. She was going to have to do something drastic. Soon.

As the last customers were lingering over their cheesecakes and cappuccinos, Edie cornered Sam, a friend and fellow waiter. They had been at NYU at the same time and since leaving the bosom of the university had stayed in contact. It was one of the mysteries of the universe why Sam, who bore a passing resemblance to Rupert Everett, hadn't found more success in New

York. Edie suspected someday he would wise up and go to Los Angeles. The movie cameras would love him.

In the meantime, she was glad to have him here. It was Sam who had given her the heads up about this job waiting tables a few months ago.

"Do you know anyone who needs a room to rent?" she asked him.

Sam nearly dropped a tray of cannoli. He swooped down on her with dramatic concern. "Father in heaven! You aren't taking in *roomers*, are you?"

She laughed. His over-the-top reaction would have been appropriate had she announced she had a fatal disease. "It's okay. I just need money, and I've got that big apartment. . . ."

His face didn't change. There was only more pity there now. "Oh, Edie. Edie. No."

She rolled her eyes. "What's with everyone? Aurora gave me the same reaction. But *you* have a roommate."

"That's what I mean! Look at my life and *learn*. I am an object lesson in why *not* to get a roommate."

"What's the matter with Louis?" Edie had met Louis once or twice, and he seemed like a nice guy. The oddest thing that she could see about their living situation was that Louis was straight and Sam was gay, but that didn't seem to bother either of them or their social lives at all. "I *like* Louis," she said.

"It's not Louis, it's the state he's in."

"Did something happen to him?"

"Yes—he fell in *love!* With a lady bond broker. It's so awful, I can't tell you."

Edie tilted her head, trying to sort this out. "Wait . . . are you saying love is awful, or the bond broker is awful?"

"It's the combination. Believe me, she's a perfectly lovely person—except, perhaps, for having Margaret Thatcher's taste in day wear. Even *that* doesn't really bother me. The problem is this: Love plus Suzanne the bond broker equals extremely noisy sex in the *room right next to mine.*"

Edie frowned. Louis seemed like such an unassuming, quiet guy. He was a dramaturg, for heaven's sake. Hard to imagine a sexy beast of a dramaturg. "What could they be doing in there?"

Sam lifted his hands. "I don't want to think about it."

"Have you complained?"

"Complained?" Sam laughed. "I've walked into their bedroom clutching my head and screaming."

"Oh."

"Then the next night is always just as bad. I don't know what the problem is. The woman has serious volume control issues."

"Why don't they go to her place? If she's a bond broker, I'll bet she has a nice apartment."

"She does. In White Plains. Louis won't leave Manhattan. He said it took him twenty-two years to get out of Nebraska. Now he has a terror of dying in rural America."

"White Plains is rural America?"

"*You* explain it to him."

Edie shook her head in sympathy.

"I'm just warning you," he said. "Sure, you think you'll find this perfect, quiet, considerate roommate. But all it takes is cupid's arrow to turn your life into a nightmare of irritation and insomnia and Suzanne's zesty, kittenish squeals."

Edie sagged against a shelf with an old high-button boot on it. "What on earth am I going to do?"

"Toss Doug's stuff into storage and find a nice overpriced studio somewhere."

The trouble was, you could hear things through the walls of studio apartments, too. (And smell things, she couldn't forget . . .) Part of her dreaded giving up complete privacy, but the other part of her felt as if now, in this apartment, she was finally living like a human being. Her life when she had moved in had seemed so perfect.

Silly her. She had forgotten that when life was perfect, things could only get worse.

N one of the other people she asked were any more forthcoming with roommate candidates than Sam had been, so the first week of June, Edie paid her landlord the last of Douglas's money and took out an ad in the *Village Voice*.

* * *

ROOMMATE WANTED:
Sunny Chelsea! Big bdrm in great apt. Lots of space/light.
Share bath/kitchen/lvrm $1050.00 + 1/2 bills; Fem preferred,
nonsmkr, no pets; refs. req'd. Call Edie

She packed all of Douglas's remaining stuff into boxes and stacked them against the wall in the alcove in the living room that looked as if it had once been a large closet.

The extra bedroom, the one she would be renting out, they had been using as a sort of office. Now Edie squeezed the small desk and chair into the corner of her own bedroom. It was really lucky that she and Douglas hadn't had time to go furniture shopping. With minimal effort on her part, the spare room was completely empty and the place looked move-in ready. In fact, the apartment looked open, inviting. She had even sold her old futon couch after moving in, since she and Douglas were going to buy a real couch. All that was in the living room now was a television set on some crates and a chair Douglas had salvaged from the street.

After her ad ran, the expected parade of dubious contenders came traipsing through her life. Though she had specified that women would be preferred, several men called on the ad. The first was a good-looking guy who claimed to be a successful banker, and though Edie was tempted to simply rent the room to him and get it over with, in the end she couldn't understand why a successful banker would need an apartment share. Either he was a habitual liar and wasn't successful at all, which made him undesirable, or he had a serious problem handling money, which made him doubly undesirable. Or maybe he was actually a successful banker but had a psychotic desire to live in close quarters with a lone woman in lower midtown, which made him completely unacceptable.

Another man came through who seemed like he might work until he just happened to mention that he was in the middle of divorce proceedings and would have occasional weekend visits with his three children, ages seven, five, and two.

After that, she decided to consider only single women, and excluded even the man who claimed he was in the process of changing gender. Close only counted in horseshoes.

She received calls from a performance artist (a deal killer in itself), some chick whose thick accent made her sound like Anna Nicole Smith, and a woman who was receiving outpatient care from Bellevue. A very sane sounding legal secretary in her thirties got Edie's hopes up, but at the last minute decided she didn't like the place when she saw that she would have to share a bathroom, which she said—somewhat creepily—would not work for someone "with her needs."

Almost a week crawled by, and anxiety settled in. Would she have to spend months opening her door to oddballs? Would she ever find *anyone* to rent her damn spare room?

Edie was snatched from the jaws of despair when a woman named Greta Stolenbauer called her. There was something about the woman's voice—husky, no-nonsense, its German accent seeming to bespeak a comfortingly Teutonic decisiveness. You vill rent it! that voice trumpeted.

She liked the idea of renting to someone foreign. It made her desperation suddenly seem more exotic. And though she knew she shouldn't make hasty generalizations, weren't Germans supposed to be very clean and orderly? And good with money?

In person, Frau Stolenbauer seemed even more promising. She arrived at the apartment at exactly one o'clock on the dot—punctuality could not be oversold, Edie decided—and she was an impressive sight. She wore, rather surprisingly, a black blazer over mint green surgical scrubs that accentuated her tall, pointy build. Sturdy—that's how she looked. Not to mention, those scrubs gave her an air of medical authority. Her hair was so blond it was almost white, and it was cut short and moussed back, sort of like David Bowie in his "Let's Dance" period.

Lesbian, Edie thought. She didn't care. She felt fairly certain she could assure Sam this one wouldn't be a kittenish squealer.

"What do you do?" she asked her.

"I am dental assistant," Greta announced. "Very good at my work."

She said *verk*. However long Greta had been in this country, she hadn't seemed to have gotten the letter *w* licked yet.

Edie was only a little disappointed with the answer. Given Greta's Annie Lennox–joins–"ER" looks, she'd been envisioning companionable evenings hearing dramatic life-and-death surgery tales. Dentist offices didn't exactly spark the same kind of excitement. But it was easy to believe that Greta was good at what she did. This Amazonian creature combined with a sharp metal object would make short work of tartar.

Greta marched around the apartment three times, which didn't take that long. There wasn't much to look at, really, since the place was empty, but Greta seemed to enjoy throwing open cabinets and peering curiously into the rooms other than the one she would be renting.

Edie couldn't help noticing the woman's gaze lingering on the curly-edged linoleum and the indelible brown stain of indeterminate origin on the kitchen wall. But her attention was most drawn to the living room. The bare living room. Edie was embarrassed now at how naked it must seem.

"I haven't lived here long," she explained.

Greta nodded.

She felt as if she were holding her breath. *Please, please take it.* She desperately wanted to rent the room to this woman. She really didn't want to have to interview any more freaks.

Finally, Greta spoke again. "This is not Chelsea."

Edie, lifting a page from the sleazy landlord handbook, had fudged about the location in the ad. "Well, it sort of is."

"Bull crap. This is midtown."

"Oh, well . . ."

"On your balcony I could stand and spit in Penn Station."

She looked like she just might spit on Edie, who was cowed by the slightly staccato rhythm of that husky voice. "I guess technically you could say—"

"But I like."

Edie sagged with relief. "You do?"

"*Ja.* Very much. It's not what I expected, though. It's spatial."

"I beg your pardon?"

Greta looked at her as if she were mentally defective. "Spatial. Big," she translated impatiently.

Edie nodded. "Oh, *spacious!* Yes, your bedroom's ten by twelve. And the rest of the apartment has plenty of room for both of us. We could—"

"Too big," Greta declared.

Whatever else Edie was about to say died on her lips. *Too big? Too big* did not exist in New York City. Even though the place felt roomy, they were still talking less than five hundred square feet. Maybe in Tokyo that would be considered too big. In Hong Kong or Calcutta it might be considered sinfully huge. But in New York it was considered a lucky find. For twenty-one hundred a month, you might even say a miracle. Worth putting up with the constant smell of curry and the critter problem that accompanied living above a restaurant.

"You say to live here you will charge me one thousand and fifty dollars?" Greta asked.

Edie slumped. "You can't afford it." She'd known this was too good to be true.

"No, the price is entirely rational," Greta countered in her Marlene Dietrich voice. "But why do not you rent this third room and charge seven hundred dollars?"

"What third room?"

Greta pointed to the screen.

Edie squinted. "Charge someone to live in *that?* It's little more than a closet. In fact, I think it was a closet, originally. It's almost as small as the bathroom! Besides, I don't *want* two roommates."

"It would be much more economic."

Suddenly, Edie began to understand. She had heard of this happening. A person rented a room in an apartment and didn't mention that he or she had a significant other or a relative who would be living there, too. Maybe Greta already had someone in mind for the closet.

She stiffened defensively. She was on guard now. "I don't have anyone else to rent it to." She left the door wide open for Greta to suggest someone. To which Edie intended to give her a categorical no. She wasn't going to be the odd woman out in Greta's love nest. She wasn't going to be invaded. The whole point here was that *she* was going to be in charge.

Greta just tilted her head. "Really? Too bad."

"Do you have a significant other?" Edie asked her.

"No."

"Because I work late nights, and I need quiet during the . . ."

Her words tapered off as Greta pulled out her pocketbook and produced ten one hundred dollar bills and a fifty. Nothing like cash to silence piddling objections and doubts.

"You have no animals," Greta observed.

"No," Edie said as she ruffled the bills. It was amazing. She'd gone from rags to comparative riches in five minutes.

"*Gut!*" Now that Greta was in, she showed more enthusiasm. She took one more turn around the room. "Also I like balcony. *Fantastisch!* I can smoke there."

Smoke. Edie's heart sank even while her fists clenched reflexively around all that money. It was going to kill her to give it up. "Maybe you didn't read the ad carefully. I specified nonsmokers."

"This is not a problem. I will smoke on balcony only."

"But—"

Greta's startling blue eyes fixed on her, and Edie's mouth snapped closed. "It will work out good. You will see."

It vill verk! Edie couldn't seem to form any words to the contrary. She feared that Greta could have flashed those eyes at her and persuaded her to do just about anything.

"Oh, and you are almost forgetting," Greta said, twisting around to pull something out of her shoulder bag. She unfolded a piece of paper and handed it to Edie. "My references."

Edie took the paper, feeling a little foolish. The references had completely slipped her mind. Not that Greta didn't seem like a pretty safe bet. Or, rather, the cash in hand felt like a pretty safe bet.

"Some of the numbers listed are businesses," Greta told her. "I am sorry, but a few of them did not want for me to give out their home numbers."

"Mm." Casually, Edie began to scan the list, but just the first name made her breath catch. When she could speak, her voice was a helium squeak. "You know Rudolph Giuliani?"

The only other person who had bothered to bring references had put her grandmother at the top of the list.

Greta nodded. "Yes, he is a patient at the office where I work. A very nice man. He helped me once when I was having problem with immigration. Wasn't that kind?"

"No kidding! And—" She looked down at the next name.

Jesus. She couldn't believe it. The second name on the list was

Lauren Bacall! In fact, the whole sheet of paper was like a Who's Who in Manhattan. Kofi Annan! She cleared her throat. "Okay, well . . . I'll just give a few of these people a buzz. . . ." She wished Greta *had* listed her grandmother. She was a little intimidated by the idea of phoning celebrities.

"I see you, then." Her new roommate made a move for the door, then turned back, slapping her forehead like a first year student at the Academy of Dramatic Arts. "I forgot almost to tell you. I need to move in soon."

"How soon is soon?"

Greta glanced at her watch. "Four o'clock."

Edie gulped. That *was* soon. Then again, Greta had paid in cold, hard cash, so Edie didn't have to worry whether the check would clear. She just had to worry about what this woman did that made her carry around wads of cash. *Drugs* was the conclusion her brain immediately leapt to. She was illegally renting a room to a chain-smoking lesbian crack dealer.

Although how many crack dealers were personal friends of Rudolph Giuliani?

"Great!" she chirped. "See you at four."

Rudy and Lauren weren't in, so Edie spent the rest of the afternoon cleaning. The apartment was already spotless, but Greta's *ich-bin-ein*-neatfreak gaze had made Edie feel the urge to give the place a good second scrubbing. Which is what she was doing at two-thirty, when the door buzzed.

Edie frowned as she snapped off her soapy Playtex gloves and clomped down the steps to the ground floor. The intercom hadn't worked since she moved in, and Bhiryat the landlord didn't appear inclined to fix it. Or anything else, for that matter.

When she opened the outside door, a girl with button brown eyes, clear skin, and pearly white, desperately straight teeth loomed right in her face. "Hi!"

She had a heavy Texas accent, though, so the sound came out closer to "Ha!"

Edie drew back. "Hello," she said doubtfully.

The girl just kept on smiling. In fact, she appeared almost top-heavy with teeth, like Hilary Swank. She either came from a fantastic dental gene pool or else her parents had made some orthodontist very rich. Something about her oozed money. Probably the designer clothes. And the flawless skin. And the chunky stones dangling from her ears, which honest to God looked real. Real what, Edie wasn't certain.

"I'm Danielle."

"Uh-huh . . ."

A little of the brightness in that Pepsodent smile dimmed. "Danielle Poitier? I'm here about the room?"

"Oh!" Damn! *Danielle on Tuesday at two-thirty.* She had forgotten all about the Anna Nicole Smith person. "I'm sorry—right after I talked to you this transsexual called and knocked you out of my memory. That's no excuse, I know. I should have written it down."

"Oh, well, that's okay," Danielle drawled obligingly. "You know I'm here now, at any rate."

"Yeah, but the thing is, the room is rented now."

A crestfallen expression clouded Danielle's face. "Already?"

To Edie, it seemed like she had been looking for people forever. "I'm very sorry."

At that juncture, she expected little Danielle to toddle off, but the girl stubbornly planted herself.

Edie's gaze darted toward the restaurant door. The last thing she needed was for Bhiryat to come out and discover her interviewing people. She hadn't told him that she was renting rooms. She was afraid that would make it seem to him that Douglas was gone and that he could present her with a new lease.

"Can I at least look at it?" the girl asked.

"Look at what?"

"The room."

"It's *rented.*"

"The person you rented it to might change her mind."

"She gave me cash."

"I can pay you cash, too!" Danielle assured her.

Edie had to give the kid points for persistence. Although maybe she was just uncommonly dense. "Yes, but I don't need your money, see, because the room has already been paid for."

"But if you needed a backup, I would be a real good bet." Her voice took on a more desperate, keening tone. "See, I'm living at a hotel—the Alexander Hamilton residence hotel? Do you know it?"

Edie shook her head.

"Consider yourself lucky!" Danielle exclaimed. "It's so ghetto, you'd die. My room is total scuzz and I'm pretty sure the guy next door is a paroled rapist or something, because he cracks his door and leers at me every time I come out of my room. I sure would like to move somewhere permanent, with no pervs."

Edie didn't know what to say. "No" didn't seem to be doing the trick.

"Please, won't you reconsider? I have references!" She started digging through her handbag.

Edie waved her hands. "I'm sorry—"

Danielle snatched a piece of paper and pressed it into Edie's hands. "They're great references. The governor of Texas would personally vouch for me."

Edie couldn't help checking. Sure enough, there was the Texas governor's phone number. Also listed was an ex-senator. Poor Danielle. A few hours earlier, Edie might have been impressed.

She attempted to hand the piece of paper back to her. "There are other people looking for roommates in the city."

Danielle flapped her hands in frustration. "I know, but damn it, I keep arriving after the rooms have been rented. I seem to have my timing all wrong, or maybe I just don't understand the way things work here. I'm from Texas. Amarillo." *Amarilla* was how she pronounced it.

"I'm sorry." Danielle sniffed, and Edie realized too late she made it sound as if she was sorry the girl was from Amarillo. "I didn't mean . . ."

Danielle waved her hands. Tears streamed down her face, though Edie could tell that the girl was trying to fight them off. When words finally exploded from her, they came out in a quavering whine. "That's okay! Never mind . . . it's just . . . you see, I've been in the city for one whole week and it seems like nobody wants to talk to me. This is the longest conversation I've had with anybody except this guy who chatted me up at Union Square. I told him all about how I was from Texas and what I was doing here—I want to be a writer, see—and I thought he was really friendly until I realized he was just a homeless guy wanting a buck from me. But even that was okay because it was nice to have someone to talk to."

Danielle had to stop and dig through her purse so she could find a tissue and blow her nose. Edie looked away awkwardly as the young woman honked noisily into the Kleenex.

"I'm sorry," Danielle said, sniffling, "I know New York is filled with nice people and I just got here and I have to give it time, but I feel s-s-so lonely!" Her shoulders began to shake, and she stamped her foot as if to hold off another weeping jag. "I swear I'd live *anywhere* just so long as I could be around people I could talk to again!"

She sank onto the stoop, and the few people shuffling past on the sidewalk turned to gape. Edie stared down at the neat part on the woman's scalp. Jesus. What was she supposed to do? Did she look like she was running a halfway house for displaced Texans?

The image of the Chinatown screen flashed through her mind.

Did this girl really mean that she would live *anywhere?*

She *did* look desperate.

Not that it was a good idea . . . renting to one person when she didn't even have the lease in her own name was dicey enough.

Except when wasn't extra money every month a good idea?

She cleared her throat. "Look. I've just rented the room to a really nice woman—a German lady—but *she* suggested that the place was big enough for another person. See, there's this tiny little room . . . more of an alcove, actually, that—"

Before she could even finish, Danielle sprang to her feet and threw her arms around her. "Oh, thank you thank you thank you! I'll never forget this. The minute I saw you I knew you were a kind soul."

Edie felt uncomfortable being on the receiving end of all this gratitude. She wasn't really certain she wanted Miss Cutesy-poo here living with her, and she certainly wasn't sure Danielle and

Greta would hit it off. But now that Danielle had complimented her soul, she felt as if she should at least show the woman the screened-off matchbox space they were discussing.

"Come on up, then. It's on the second floor." Danielle was apparently part boa constrictor, because it was a job prying her loose. "You'd better take a look before you decide."

"I know I'll like it! I just know it!"

"It's a little on the small side."

"Cozy!"

Edie grunted. "Yeah, *very* cozy."

She was half expecting Danielle to come to her senses the minute she got a load of her five-by-eight cubbyhole. Instead, the woman rushed into the tiny area and threw her arms out like Julie Andrews on that Austrian mountaintop. From the joyous look on her face you would have thought that there was an endless vista of living space all around her, but as she threw out her arms and twirled, her hand clunked against the doorless doorframe.

They both winced at the crack of bone against plaster.

"How much?" Danielle asked, gingerly rubbing her hand.

Edie hesitated. Greta seemed to have been suggesting splitting the rent three ways. But tempting as that was, Edie's conscience just wouldn't allow her to charge little Nell from the country here seven hundred dollars to live in a place the size of a refrigerator box. She and Greta would just have to pay a little more.

"Five hundred dollars." If Greta didn't like it, she would just have to lump it.

Realistically, though, Edie couldn't imagine actually working up the courage to tell Greta to lump anything.

"Five hundred dollars?" Danielle asked, aghast. "A *month?*"

Edie frowned. "Yeah . . . what'd you think?"

"I'm paying more than that at the hotel for a furnished room. With bugs!"

"This place has bugs, too," Edie assured her.

"Yeah, but you've got a kitchen and a bathroom with a real door. And the balcony! It's pure luxury. I'd feel guilty paying a dollar less than six hundred."

She wanted to pay *more*? She really had just fallen off the turnip truck. "Listen, Danielle, you shouldn't feel guilty. And you shouldn't insist on paying a penny more than what people ask you."

"But I want you to feel like you're getting something out of my being here. Otherwise I'd just be leeching."

Only in New York could you have leeches paying you five hundred dollars per month. "This room is tiny," Edie told her. "Even by Manhattan standards. After you put a twin bed in here there won't be room for anything else, and I still need to get these boxes out." Douglas's boxes were stacked up against one wall.

"Oh no—I need those!"

Edie wasn't sure she'd heard correctly. "You need boxes filled with someone else's crap?"

Danielle nodded eagerly. "See, I'm a writer . . . I think I told you that . . . and the minute I walked in I thought I could use those. I don't have any furniture, but I thought I could sort of stack those up and make a little desk for my notebook computer."

"Oh." Weird. But Edie couldn't see any harm in it. "Well, if you're sure."

"Oh, I am!" Danielle reached into her Kate Spade handbag and pulled out five hundred dollars in cash. Most of the money was in small bills and she was a slow counter, so it took awhile. But when the last ten dollar bill was placed in Edie's hand, she beamed triumphantly. "There!" She seemed thrilled to be parted with her cash.

Edie couldn't believe it. All this money was coming her way and she hadn't done a damn thing. No wonder people became slumlords.

"Can I move in now?" Danielle asked eagerly.

Edie thought nervously of Greta. She really should ask her permission about this, but then, she didn't know how to contact her. Unless she could get her a message through Rudy. . . .

Then again, this whole arrangement was really Greta's idea. Why wouldn't she agree? Especially after she got her two-hundred-and-fifty-dollar refund from Danielle's share.

"I guess."

Her new roommate hopped and clapped like a cheerleader. "*Yay!*" "I just need to go by the hotel and get my stuff. I'll buy a bed on the way back."

"A bed? Won't you need help with that?"

"No, no. Don't worry, I've got this all figured out. I don't want to be any bother to you." Danielle darted toward the door. "See you in about an hour!"

Goodbye, privacy, Edie thought, seized by a sudden panic. She didn't even know either of these people. "Wait!" She caught Danielle just before she dashed out. "What did you say your last name was?"

She might write it down somewhere for her parents to find in case her body turned up in the basement one day.

"Poitier. It's on the reference sheet."

Oh, right. Poitier. "As in, Sidney?"

"That's right," Danielle said, then quickly added, "not that we're related or anything."

"I didn't think so."

Danielle tilted her head. "Didn't someone write about that?"

"About what?"

"A guy pretending to be Sidney Poitier's son. Only as it turns out, he's not."

Edie nodded. "Oh, right. *Six Degrees of Separation.* It was a play."

"I only saw the movie." Danielle brightened. "See? If I'd been here, I could've seen the play, too. I should have come to New York ages ago!"

She scampered out the door, leaving Edie feeling slightly uneasy.

That guy who had been pretending to be Sidney Poitier's son . . . didn't he turn out to be some sort of con artist?

Edie pondered this fear for a moment before shaking it off. She didn't have time to worry about a psychotic Texas girl robbing her blind or putting poison in her Snapple. She only had one hour to get duplicate keys made.

Chapter 7

LIFE EXPERIENCE

Danielle swung out of the doors of Bed Bath and Beyond feeling like she could conquer the world. Her oversized shopping bag held her first adult piece of furniture—an Aero inflatable bed—and now she was going to move into her very own room in her very first Manhattan apartment. Hot damn! Could life get any better?

Her dad said she wouldn't last a week in New York, and here she was on Day Eight. A survivor.

Yesterday she'd had her doubts. She had felt restless staring at the stained, yellowed walls of her hotel room, which reeked of stale cigarette smoke and something sour she couldn't put her finger on. There was a hint of rotten fruit, but she had the sneaking suspicion it was the remnant odor of the hundreds of unfortunate souls who had stayed in that room before her. All the smells were amplified in the warmth of the afternoon. Plus the room was mildewy, since she kept showering because there wasn't any air-conditioning. (There was nothing but a flimsy cotton curtain between the bedroom and the bathroom, so the whole room was really like the bathroom when you got right down to it.)

Nights she would just gape up at the bulb overhead, wondering what the Sam Hill she'd gone and done with her life. Maybe she really had gone crazy, just like her parents said. Dumping Brandon Sutter—the best fiancé a young woman could ask for, she'd been assured—quitting a decent paying job, leaving a comfortable home for a stinky, hot, mildewy room . . . At face value, these were not the actions of a sane woman. A sane woman apparently would have jumped for joy at the opportunity to settle down at the tender age of twenty-three and grow prematurely middle aged in West Texas.

The problem was, no one at home seemed to be able to take into account the fact that she wanted something more. Something that she felt distinctly foolish admitting aloud . . . yet surely she wasn't the only one in the world who longed for it. She wanted a little excitement.

She was a writer. Well, *wanted* to be a writer. Writers needed excitement, didn't they? (Unless they were crazy, reclusive poet types, but that really wasn't her bag.) She had started scribbling out of boredom after she got out of college and moved home. Those stories had saved her from going insane, and the amazing part was, she was pretty good. Everyone she gave them to said they were really entertaining.

She'd begun to realize that she wasn't going to be happy as Mrs. Brandon Sutter. All the excitement Brandon wanted he could find on a golf course or in the bleachers of the Nascar track on a Saturday afternoon. But everybody loved Brandon. Her best friend back home, Bev, had wept when Danielle had called a halt to the engagement. *Poor Brandon,* everyone had said. *Have you lost your mind, Danielle?* For weeks afterward her parents had moped around the house looking like the dog had died.

Meanwhile Danielle had skulked guiltily around Amarillo, feeling as if she were going to explode if she didn't get away. She'd been writing furiously in the evenings. Then, when she'd gotten that letter from Jennifer Poon—the one telling her she needed more life experience—the solution had seemed obvious. She wanted to be a writer. She wanted excitement. She belonged in New York.

It had seemed less obvious when she was in the mildewy room, waiting sleeplessly for the garbage trucks to start their unholy beeping at around five A.M.

But now . . . what a difference a day made! Persistence, apparently, really did pay.

Everybody back home had warned her that she was going to get lost in the big city, and it *was* a little overwhelming. But mostly it overwhelmed her because she didn't yet know where she was going to fit into this big honeycomb of concrete and people. The city pulsed with an unfamiliar energy that she was dying to be in sync with.

Now she had her own place . . . well, her own *corner* of a place. She felt like her foot was in the door.

Her new room, of course, was even tinier than her hotel. Even smaller than her walk-in closet back in her parents' house in Amarillo. But the rest of the apartment would be heaven! There was a big living room, and a kitchen, and a bathroom with a genuine door, and a little balcony, even. She didn't know about this Greta person, but Edie seemed real nice. It was going to be fun living there; like being back in her old college apartment at UT. It wouldn't hurt to have an apartment of ready-made girlfriends.

She hurried back to her room and grabbed her stuff, triumphantly checked out of the Alexander Hamilton, and flagged down a taxi just like people did in the movies. That's what this felt like—like she was in a movie. She leaned back against the springy seat that, oddly enough, had that hot vinyl smell of her granddaddy's old Chevy pickup back home, and sighed contentedly. So what if she was in a strange, big-ass city where she didn't know a soul and had paid a total stranger five hundred dollars to rent the world's pokiest bedroom? All those old clichés flooded through her mind as she thought about her new life and her new little room in Edie's apartment: *These were the best years of her life. The world was her oyster. Size doesn't matter.*

She hooted, earning a quizzical rearview glance from her turbaned cabdriver. She trilled a wave at him with her fingers. To her surprise, he laughed and nodded, almost as if he understood. Like there was a bond between them. They were both immigrants—she from Texas, he from . . . well, wherever he was from.

Or maybe he was just used to lunatics riding in his cab.

One thing at that moment was crystallized in her mind. This

was where she belonged. New York City. She vowed that in six months she would have a swinging social life, including a cool boyfriend (she'd seen so many hotties just walking down the street), and most important, that she would be a published writer.

Of one thing she was dead certain: She was *never* going back to Amarillo.

Chapter 8

MOVING IN

"This is the nicest place I've been since I landed in New York." Danielle hopped up and down enthusiastically on her newly inflated bed. It resembled an oversized blue swimming pool raft. Edie had folded up the screen and leaned it against the wall for Danielle's move-in, expecting that a girl like her was going to need every square inch of space. But, amazingly, everything Danielle owned fit into the cubbyhole, no problem.

Edie eyed the single bag and the powerbook lying on top of the boxes. "What were you in Amarillo? A street person?"

Danielle stopped bouncing and sent her a quizzical stare.

"You don't seem to own much," Edie pointed out.

"Oh! That's on account of I sort of got out of town in a hurry. My parents were dead set against me leaving Amarillo. Especially after Dad had used his influence to get me that internship at a law office."

Influence? Sounded like he'd made someone an offer they couldn't refuse. Edie thought briefly of the gushing conversation she'd had when she had called the governor. Actually, the person doing the gushing wasn't the governor himself, but the governor's assistant chief of staff. Now that she thought back on it, the guy had seemed almost *too* enthusiastic. "What is your dad—the Amarillo mafia?"

Danielle struggled to her feet. "Lord no, he's just a judge. But he knows a lot of people."

And he apparently ran around twisting arms to get his dippy daughter internships. Lovely. "I hope he doesn't come here and try to influence me to get you to leave."

She laughed. "You don't have to worry about that. Daddy always says he'd sooner go to hell than to New York City." She shook her head. "I don't see it myself. Anyhow, since I don't have any clothes, that means I'll get to shop for some. Which is great, because I love to shop and I hear New York has some really great places."

"That's the rumor."

"Don't you like to shop?"

"I'm not sure anymore. The last time I had disposable income was back during the Clinton administration."

"Oh." Danielle looked sorry for her, then turned away and breezed over to the window. "None of the other apartments I arrived at too late to rent had balconies. This is pretty neat."

"Yeah, it's keen." As soon as the words were out of her mouth, Edie shook her head. What was wrong with her? Every time she opened her yap she sounded like a sarcastic bitch.

Not that Rebecca of Sunnybrook Farm here noticed. Honestly, the kid hadn't stopped enthusing since she walked through the door. Her room was *super cozy*. The kitchen was *incredibly nifty*. She'd even gone into paroxysms over the bathroom door, and then kept staring back at the bathroom fondly, as if it were some kind of novelty. Edie was fairly sure indoor plumbing had made it to West Texas, at least in the houses of judges with influence, but you wouldn't have guessed it from this girl's reaction.

"What is this?" Edie asked, looking into the open lid of a cardboard box on the bed.

If Danielle minded her shameless snooping, she didn't show it. "Oh! That's my gas mask." She crossed back and gave Edie a demonstration, putting it on. She looked like a science fiction creature who had just come from Saks Fifth Avenue. "Dad bought it for me in case I ever wanted to take the subway."

"*In case?*" Edie couldn't imagine getting around any other way. Money had been tight for so long, throwing money away on cabs just didn't make sense to her.

"Don't you have one?" Danielle asked her.

"Uh . . . no."

She pulled the mask off her head and tossed it back to the bed peevishly. "He's so paranoid! I *told* him that nobody was wearing these, that I'd just look like a freak."

"I wouldn't worry about looking like a freak on the subway." Edie picked up the mask. "Besides, these days, you never know . . ."

"Try it on if you want," Danielle said.

Edie did. It felt heavier than it looked, and the fresh rubber smell would probably asphyxiate you if the gas attack didn't.

"What do you think?"

Edie tilted her head. "It does give you a sort of invincible feeling." Sort of a like a scary modern security blanket. Who knew? After Armageddon it might just be Danielle and the cockroaches.

"My parents think I've made the mistake of my life, leaving Texas." Danielle sank onto her raft. "Are you from here?"

Edie shook her head. "Massachusetts."

"Boston?"

"Springfield." When Danielle showed no recognition of the name, she added, "It's where Dr. Seuss came from."

She hadn't thought Danielle's expression could get any brighter, but suddenly she was grinning as if Edie had just turned into Horton the elephant himself. "No kidding! So when did you move to New York?"

"College."

Her eyes lit with envy. "Your parents let you come to college here?"

"Sure. I got into the Tisch School at NYU. I was a theater major."

Danielle hopped up again. Talking to her was giving Edie motion sickness. "You mean you're an actress?"

"I try to convince myself of that while I'm waiting tables."

"Have you ever been in anything?" Danielle asked. "Anything I would have seen?"

"Just a few off-off-Broadway things, and a commercial or two," Edie said modestly. But of course she couldn't resist adding, "I also had a featured part in a soap opera, but that was a while back."

Danielle sucked in her breath. "Which one?"

Edie savored this moment. She always knew she could count on a big reaction. " 'Belmont Hospital.' "

Danielle clapped her hands over her cheeks. "No f-ing way! My whole family watches that! Well, at least my mom and my grandma. Grandma used to make me watch it at her house over tuna salad sandwiches at lunch. Who did you play?"

"Adelaide Harris."

The hands slid down her face, leaving a puzzled mask. "Who?"

"Dr. Wayne Harris's niece."

The confusion didn't go away. "But I thought Wayne Harris was the only child of the Harris Cosmetics fortune."

She was obviously way behind. "But you know how Wayne's father was always angry that Wayne wanted to be a heart surgeon and not head of the cosmetics company? Well, last year the father revealed that he'd had a love child by a cocktail waitress. She was my mother."

"The cocktail waitress?"

"The love child."

"Oh. I never heard about this."

"I wasn't on for long. Wayne's evil fiancée tampered with the brakes of my car and I drove off a cliff before I was even on the show for a month."

Actually, her character had only really been on for two and a half weeks. But they'd kept her in a coma for another two weeks.

"That's awful!"

"It was for me. I was making twelve hundred a week. I had health insurance, even." Thinking about "Belmont Hospital" too much gave Edie a heavy, depressed feeling. Her little success had been so short lived. Her ship had come in, but she'd been washed out to sea before she could climb aboard.

"I'll bet my mother remembers you," Danielle said. "She watches 'BH' religiously. She'll be so impressed when I tell her that I've got Dr. Wayne Harris's niece for a roommate!"

"His late niece."

"Well . . . at least you were on something everybody's heard about."

Edie nodded. An unknown actress in this town was lucky to get periodic work. But of course she couldn't help comparing her own sputtering career to Aurora's, which seemed to be set on an ever-upward trajectory. She was going to be killed by Ray Liotta in a major motion picture. Who knew where *that* could lead?

"I'm hoping something exciting will happen to me while I'm in New York," Danielle said.

More amazingly, she said it with a straight face.

Edie cleared her throat. "Really? What kind of excitement, exactly?"

"Oh, you know—I want to get a story published, and maybe have a few torrid love affairs. All the stuff you read about. My life has just been so deadly dull. You wouldn't believe how close I came to becoming Mrs. Brandon Sutter, Junior League goddess."

"You were engaged? I thought you were just out of college."

"Oh, I've been out of college for a whole year. Not that it mattered—Brandon and I were high school sweethearts. We were prom king and queen, if you can believe it.

"Well, it was actually sort of a scandal, because Brandon was going out with my friend Bev at the time, but shortly thereafter they had a falling-out and then Brandon was my boyfriend through the tag end of senior year and then off and on throughout college. Then my parents lured me home, and it seemed everybody else went back to Amarillo, too, and life just kept plodding along as if there were a pattern and we were just scissoring along the lines, just like we were supposed to. Everybody was settling into their jobs and pairing off and preparing to mate like there was no other world out there to explore. It was just so stifling sitting around and trading gossip about the same old people I'd known since kindergarten, I finally just couldn't take it anymore. So I bolted."

Edie was amazed. Danielle didn't look like a woman who would be the one to break out of her Peyton Place world; but apparently she was the Allison MacKenzie of Amarillo.

The doorbell buzzed for an extra long time, as if someone were leaning on the button.

"That's probably Greta," Edie said, getting up. She felt a moment of trepidation. Sure, Greta had *said* the place could stand another roommate . . . but did she really mean it? And how would she feel about Edie already having found one without consulting her?

Oh, screw it, Edie thought. If Greta didn't like the setup now, Edie could always just rent the big room to Danielle.

She marched downstairs, torn between her impulses of ownerly defiance and groveling apology. The moment she opened the door, however, she was faced not with Greta, but with the arm of a couch. A hulking, bearded red-headed guy poked around the huge piece of furniture at her. "Watch it!" he shouted.

Edie flattened herself against the wall as two men began to muscle the couch through, regardless of what she had to say about it. "Wait! Is Greta . . . ?"

The Viking bobbed his head toward the street. "Back there."

Not that Edie could see out. Even when the couch cleared her, she only got a fleeting glimpse of pavement before another guy swung toward her with a wardrobe. It was a massive piece, with a large mirror and a marble top. "Watch your head!"

She yelped and pancaked herself against the wall again. For some reason, she hadn't imagined large pieces of furniture moving in, but Greta seemed to have enough for an entire house. It was all heavy, dark mahogany. The men cursed and huffed up the staircase with their loads, and pieces of plaster pinged through the air as the corner of the wardrobe took out a chunk of wall.

"Be careful!" Edie shouted.

"Sure, okay."

After the wardrobe and the mirror and the marble cleared the two downstairs doors, a stream of people who had been backed up behind them on the sidewalk started to parade through. Guys with holes in jeans that were held up with thick black, silver-studded leather belts. Guys who looked like they hadn't shaved for two weeks. Women pierced all over the place, with hair in any hue besides anything that resembled a natural hair color, and none of whom were wearing a top that actually managed to cover their navels. They were all lugging shopping bags and pillowcases stuffed with clothes and sheets and towels. Single file they trudged wordlessly up to the second floor, like a column of slacker ants.

One of them, a tall, short-haired blonde wearing a tight black leather skirt over lace leggings and some sort of netting that was supposedly an excuse for a shirt, did a double take as she passed. "Hey, Edie!"

Edie, still flattened against the wall, blinked. At first she thought she was seeing things. *"Greta?"*

A deep laugh rumbled out of the blonde, and she said in that accented, low voice. "Did you think some other person vas moving in?"

It certainly looked like it. Edie had to force herself to stop gawking. This woman in no way resembled the businesslike dental technician whom she'd met a few hours ago. Dark eyeliner made her eyes appear almost frighteningly blue. A dragonfly tattoo decorated the bicep of one of her long, thin arms. On the other was some kind of birdlike totem figure. A ring stuck out of her navel.

From behind, Edie was nearly knocked over by a lamp-wielding, green-haired goth girl. "Watch your head!" the creature belatedly snapped.

Edie let her pass and then joined the freak train up the stairs. A little healthy outrage was pumping through her now that it was all becoming clear. Greta had purposefully misrepresented herself. In essence, she had lied. She certainly hadn't mentioned a word about furniture. No way was all that stuff going to fit in Greta's bedroom!

"Greta!" she yelled over the lamp. Greta turned a heavily eyelined gaze toward her. "I need to talk to you . . ."

Greta sighed and turned, dropping her pillowcases and glaring down at Edie with impatience. *"Ja,* what is it?"

A lightbulb flashed on in Edie's mind. Maybe she didn't have to make a big scene about the furniture and Greta's changed personality. Maybe if she told Greta about Danielle, Greta wouldn't want to move in. "There's been a slight hitch."

"Hitch?"

"A problem. Something's happened," Edie translated.

The woman practically snarled at her. "You said it was okay to move here now. Four o'clock."

"Uh . . . yes, I did." She took a deep breath. Here went nothing. "But remember how you said the apartment could stand another person . . . ?"

Greta nodded slowly. *"Ja,* sure. I said that."

"Well, the truth is, I rented the alcove to some girl from

Texas." As the new scarier Greta glared silently down at her, Edie explained in a nerved-up voice, "She seemed so desperate, see . . ."

"That is what you call a hitched?" Greta let loose a husky laugh. "Whew, you scared the crap from me. I thought I am going to have to moved back with Asgarth."

Edie took a few seconds to untangle the sentence. "Asgarth?"

"My ex."

"Oh!"

"He's bad news," the green-haired girl in front of her said in a voice very Jersey. "He *seemed* so nice but turned out to be a real ass. Look at that bruise on Greta's face."

Greta tilted her head, revealing a bluish cheekbone. Edie had seen it before and assumed it was just part of the look she was going for. "He *hit* you? Oh my God! That's terrible!"

"Ha!" Greta snorted. "You should see the shape *he's* in."

As Greta and her friend clomped up the stairs, Edie sagged against the wall. This was awful.

"Don't vorry," Greta yelled down at her, laughing raspily, "I lost him on the Brooklyn-Queens expressvay."

Another man muscled through and clamored down the stairs for a second load. Edie had to dart right to allow him room. How could she get rid of Greta now? Not only was the woman intimidating, she apparently had a wacko ex-boyfriend; it would be like throwing a battered woman onto the streets. She already had a pity-case taking up residence in her living room. Now this.

She staggered up the stairs, squeezing out of the way of several more people who were on their way down, apparently for a second load. How was it all going to fit? When Edie pushed her way into the apartment, the place was cramped with living room furniture and people trying to figure out how to shove the wardrobe through the too-small doorway into Greta's bedroom.

At the edge of the swarm, Danielle was hopping and making eager, helpful suggestions. "I think we're gonna have to take the door off its hinges!" She called it out several times before anyone paid any attention to her.

Surprisingly, she was right. Edie hunted around the apartment for a hammer, then handed it to the Viking, who seemed to be in charge now.

That's just the trouble. I'm not in charge anymore. Aurora was right. The idea of being able to stay in control with a room-mate—never mind two of them—had been a delusion. Now her Maginot Line had collapsed and the occupation had begun.

The sofa that was pushed in the middle of the room was an old-fashioned heavy oak piece with ornately carved legs and wood along the back of the seat, which was upholstered in a dense gold velvet. There was a matching love seat. Two tables had appeared, along with a standing brass lamp and two lamps that had incredible rose patterns painted on the pottery. Douglas's street chair was squished into a corner to make way for two wood-framed armchairs covered in burgundy brocade.

Greta stood beside her, surveying the setup.

Edie, still fuming, turned to her. "You never mentioned furniture, Greta."

"You never mentioned no furniture, Edie."

Damn it. Should she have? Did you have to spell out every little thing for people?

Of course, having furniture wasn't a crime. The apartment had been empty.

Edie forced herself to ask, almost pleasantly, "Did you meet Danielle?"

Greta eyed their roommate, who was hovering right over the guy trying to get the door off its hinges. She was chattering directions . . . or maybe just chattering. "*Everybody* has met her."

Edie bit her lip, searching for something else to say. "Your friends seem very efficient."

"I was hurrying to get everything moved before Asgarth got home. When he sees I am gone, he'll be fumed."

Fumed. Edie guessed she meant steamed. She didn't like the sound of this guy. "He doesn't have this address, does he?"

"Hell no," Greta said.

That, at least, was some comfort. He sounded like the kind of guy who would come murder them all in their beds.

The door came off and the wardrobe went through. Much arguing ensued over where to put the bedroom things. Along with the dresser there was a matching double bed, two bedside tables, a maple chest, and a rocking chair. Figuring out how to position everything so there would actually be a pathway through it all was a challenge. But finally the work was done and all the people seemed to flood out the door as quickly as they had come in.

When the front door finally shut on the last mover, Edie looked down. A plastic animal carrier was sitting in a corner. She hadn't noticed it. "What's that?"

"Oh, that is Kuchen," Greta said nonchalantly.

"What—" Edie didn't get a chance to finish.

"*A kitty!*" Danielle squealed. She skipped over to peek through the barred door. "Kuchen! How cute!"

This was the limit! Edie decided she absolutely had to put her foot down. "Greta, I can't have cats."

"Why not?"

"It's in the lease." Not that the lease was *her* lease. . . . "The landlord would have a fit."

"So ve don't tell him," Greta said. "That is okay with me."

Danielle opened the little door and the fattest cat Edie had ever seen waddled out. "Kuchen!" she exclaimed gleefully. "I *love* kitties!"

Marvy.

Kuchen was a giant ball of a calico with odd tabby markings splotched here and there, and big amber eyes. Edie blinked in amazement. The cat had to weigh twenty pounds at least. She looked like a fur-covered basketball with a tail attached. Had Greta thought she could just sneak *that* by her?

"Greta, I told you no cats. We talked about this."

"No, you said you had not already an animal. And I said that was good. Because Kuchen does not get along so vell with the other cats."

"You didn't say a word about Kuchen," Edie argued.

"Is that true?" Greta thought for a moment. "You may be right."

"Greta, *no cats*."

Though looking at Kuchen, it was hard to think of her as a cat, exactly. Most cats, when introduced to a new environment, would dart under the nearest piece of furniture and hover there for about a week or so. Kuchen, on the other hand, had ambled to the

middle of the living room and plopped herself down in the spot
where the sun was slanting through the balcony doors. She rolled
over on her back like a lazy old hound dog and let Danielle pet
her spotted tummy.

"Kuchen is a roly-poly little sweetie!" Danielle cooed.

Edie sighed impatiently. It wasn't that she didn't like cats; she
did. But she felt like she was being railroaded here.

Greta hesitated for a moment, then caved in. "Okay, don't
vorry. Tonight I take her to the shelter."

A jolt bolted through Edie's spine, and even Danielle stopped
petting Kuchen to stare, appalled, at Greta.

"An animal shelter?" Danielle asked, aghast.

"Sure," Greta said. "That is the place I should take animals
when she is unvanted, *ja?*"

"But you must have a friend who would take her!" Edie said.

"Who?" Greta looked genuinely puzzled.

As if the apartment hadn't just been filled with people helping
her pack and run!

"I don't know. *Somebody* must want her," Edie said.

Kuchen was cute, after all. Awfully cute. Take away ten pounds,
and she looked just like the cat Edie had owned when she was a
little girl. Chewy. Her heart sagged at the memory.

"Nobody I vould trust," Greta said.

Edie fixed her with an amazed stare. She would trust the over-
crowded animal shelters over her own friends?

Greta shook her head. "She is very, very old, this cat. Also, I
think she has bad heart. Last year she had a bad sinking spell."

A pained sigh gushed out of Danielle. "Pooooor Kuchen!"

Edie felt her shoulders slumping. Great. An ancient, obese cat
with a heart condition. Take her to the Humane Society and she
would jump right to the head of the euthanasia queue.

She *did* look an awful lot like Chewy.

She sank onto the couch Greta's movers had brought in. "All
right. We'll keep Kuchen. But the landlord can't see her. It's the
guy who owns the Tandoor Express downstairs. In fact, he really
shouldn't see too much of you two, either."

It was a cinch that he had seen all that furniture coming into the apartment, though. She would just have to tell him she bought some stuff secondhand. Luckily Bhiryat knew her and Douglas's apartment was practically empty.

Greta crossed her arms. "You didn't tell the landlord you are letting your rooms?"

Edie shrugged sheepishly. "Well, no. See, there used to be someone else living here . . . the guy whose name is actually on the lease . . ."

"*Ach so!*" Greta interrupted, laughing raspily.

"What?" If Greta wanted to be snide, Edie wished she would be snide in a language she could understand.

"I see! You were dumped."

Edie's cheeks stung. "No, I wasn't. Douglas is a journalist, and he had to go to Uzbekistan."

"Cool!" Danielle exclaimed. Then she frowned. "That's sort of around Asia someplace, isn't it?"

Another of the blue-pie challenged.

"This Douglas," Greta said, clearly not impressed with his journalistic credentials. "He is coming back when?"

"I'm not sure. Between his job, and my own work here in New York, our lives are just really incompatible right now."

Greta snorted.

Edie had never felt so close to punching someone. She was beginning to sympathize a little with the crazed ex-boyfriend. "He won't be in Uzbekistan forever."

"You must be really sure of him if you are renting your apartment out to strangers," Greta observed.

Edie gritted her teeth. How on earth was she going to stand living with this woman?

"*Greeeeeeetta!*"

The howl from the street broke everyone's focus. The three women ran to the balcony, though Greta hung back, only peeking out through the corner of a windowpane. "Shit!"

"*Greeeeeeetaaaaa?*"

Down below, a massive Harley-Davidson with glaringly bright chrome was illegally parked in the loading zone in front of the restaurant. Next to it stood a man in black jeans and a leather vest. His face was red, and his eyes looked unfocused; maybe even slightly mad. Ropes of dark brown hair hung over his shoulders.

Edie swallowed and ducked back inside. "Asgarth?" she asked Greta.

This was all they needed!

Greta waved a hand in dismissal. "He'll go away."

"He looks like a Hell's Angel or something," Danielle observed.

"He just likes motorcycles," Greta said. "He's harmless, really."

Harmless? "Greta, he punched you!"

She showed Danielle the bruise on Greta's face and Danielle was outraged. "We should call the police right this minute and turn that bastard in!"

In a flash, Greta grabbed Danielle in a grip that looked as if it might snap the Texan's twiggy little arm in two. "No police."

And she said it like she meant it.

"*Greeeeeeetttta!!!!*"

Terrific. Edie felt like weeping. She had a police-phobic roommate and a pissed-off violent biker creep to deal with now. She staggered toward the couch again, nearly tripping over Kuchen, who was flopped on her tailbone calmly cleaning herself. The freakishly fat animal looked like a giant feline Buddha.

This was all a huge mistake. Aurora had warned her, Sam had warned her . . . How could her friends have been so right for once? Edie suddenly found herself longing for tiny vermin-infested efficiencies with serial killers living next door.

Greta paced across the room, obviously still mulling over the Asgarth situation. "Eric must have told him, that bastard."

"Eric?" Edie guessed, "The red-headed guy who was here?"

"He is Asgarth's best friend. They don't get along."

Edie didn't even try to figure that out. "Well, why did he tell him where you were? Wasn't it obvious that you were trying to get away?"

"It is not Eric's fault. Asgarth probably made him talk." She shook her head ominously. "He's very, very good at that."

Edie and Danielle's gazes met and held.

"How on hell am I going to get out of this building now?" Greta muttered, glancing in irritation at her watch.

"You're *leaving?*" Edie's voice rose in despair.

"*Jawohl!*" Greta said, as if the question was a stupid one. "I planned to go out tonight."

"Out?"

Greta looked as Edie as if she were uncommonly dense. "To clubs. It's Tuesday."

She said it as if Tuesday had some significance. As if everyone waited for Tuesday to go clubhopping.

"But . . ." Just as Edie was about to point out the problem, Asgarth let out another of his howls. Substitute "Stella" for "Greta" and you'd have Marlon Brando in *A Streetcar Named Desire.*

Greta clucked as she sifted through a fringed leather bag for a lipstick. It went on a sort of red-black color.

"Cute purse, Greta!" Danielle chirped.

Greta shot her a look of disgust. "Asgarth makes my plan difficult now. Is there a vay out the back?" she asked Edie.

"There's a door at the end of the hallway on the ground floor, but it's an emergency exit. Opening it triggers an alarm," Edie warned. "Anyway, the door just leads to a little dead-end brick patio area. You'd have to climb over a brick wall to get to the alley."

"Excellent!" Greta exclaimed, heading for the door.

Edie couldn't believe it. She was actually leaving?

"Wait!" Edie tagged after her. "When will you be back?"

"Tomorrow. It's no problem."

Not for you, maybe, Edie thought, boiling. *She* wasn't going to be stuck here with the crazy biker boyfriend screaming at her all night.

"Don't vorry over Asgarth," Greta said, as if Edie were being somehow babyish. "He cannot scream forever."

She turned and clomped down the stairs in her heavy lug-soled boots.

Edie went back into the apartment. Danielle was peeking out the balcony window again. "He's still there," she informed Edie.

"*Greeeeeeettttttaaaaa!*"

"My God, he sounds more desperate," Danielle said.

The emergency alarm went off downstairs. Greta had escaped.

If only I could. Impotent rage rose in Edie's chest, and she let out a strangled howl of her own.

"What's the matter?" Danielle's eyes were wide with alarm.

What was the matter? *What was the matter?* Was this girl utterly clueless?

"Greta is the matter! Everything is the matter!" Edie lashed out. "She came here this afternoon looking so together. I kid you not. She had on this tidy green scrub suit and she handed me these references . . ."

The thought of that reference list made her cringe. How on earth could she have thought this woman knew Lauren Bacall? How could she have been so gullible? "You saw her. She's a lunatic! Did you notice how nervous she was when we said something about calling the police? She could have spent half her life behind bars, for all I know." She harrumphed indignantly. "I wouldn't be surprised to find out that the accent is all a fake, too. She's probably not even from Germany!"

Danielle's lips turned down. "If she was trying to make a play for your sympathy, she wouldn't put on a fake German accent. Who feels sorry for Germans? She'd probably pretend to be from Central America . . . or Africa."

"Danielle, she's a giant albino! She could hardly expect to pass as a starving Somalian."

"Well, it isn't her fault that her boyfriend turned violent," Danielle retorted with surprising spunk. "You couldn't very well turn her out."

"Right," Edie said. "I had no choice. That's just what makes me fume. I feel obliged to her for some reason. Meanwhile, she skips off to go nightclubbing—because it's Tuesday, whatever that means—and leaves us here with Mr. Psycho."

Edie picked up her cordless phone. If she called the police, she was going to have to think of something to tell them. Right now she couldn't think where she would even begin.

Danielle shot her a sympathetic look with her doelike brown eyes. "Edie?"

Edie was looking at Danielle, but she was lost in thought. She wondered if Asgarth would believe that Greta didn't live here if he heard her telling the police that. Maybe he would think that Eric guy had given him the wrong apartment number.

"Edie?"

"*What?*"

"I sure am sorry about all this," Danielle said.

Edie's lips twisted. "Thanks."

"But I want to assure you that *I* don't have any crazy men that will be coming after me." Danielle bit her lip. "Except maybe Brandon."

Great. Once she got rid of the Hell's Angel Stanley Kowalski, she'd have to deal with the Lone Star brigade. Edie blinked at Danielle's earnest little face and wondered suddenly how long it would take for that peaches-and-cream complexion, those copious teeth, and the drawling little voice to drive her stark stirring mad.

Chapter 9

CALLING KOFI ANNAN

Brandon Sutter never did come after Danielle. He just called. Called and called. Sometimes several times in a day. The parents checked in frequently, too. There was also a flurry of calls from friends in Amarillo; Edie heard messages left on the machine drawling that the caller had just phoned to "see how Dani was settlin' in."

After a week, Edie's nerves jangled every time she heard the phone. She hated the sound almost as much as she hated the sight of the Harley parked outside her building. The calls usually started coming in at nine, which, given the time difference between Texas and New York, meant that those Amarilloans were always up-and-at-'em with the birds. Considering the fact that Edie worked nights at Geppetto's, sometimes till one, this was just too damn early.

Edie used to think of Texans as cowboys, big-haired women, and Willie Nelson–type country music stars. But when Edie visualized Texas now, she just saw a state populated by people with permanent crooks in their necks from being on the phone all the time.

Exactly one week after her roommates had moved in, Edie awakened to ringing and crawled bleary-eyed out of bed. The clock read nine-thirty. It was no use hoping she could get back to sleep again. She shoved her feet into her slippers and stumbled out toward the kitchen.

Stretched out on Greta's couch, Danielle was arguing with someone on the phone. "...*No*, I am *not* gonna get mugged! I don't think people even get mugged here anymore, Brandon. It's safer here than in Austin, and you weren't worried about me while I lived there ..."

Edie nearly tripped over a phone book that had been left lying on the floor and then just managed to sidestep Kuchen, who had planted herself right in the kitchen entrance. Kuchen enjoyed lying flat in the middle of an open surface so that her body could spread out and achieve ultimate mass. Whenever the cat moved, her fur-covered flesh seemed to roll with her like a waterbed mattress.

Having survived the mini–obstacle course, Edie groaned at the mess before her. Cups littered the counter, which obviously hadn't been wiped down since she had done the chore herself yesterday. Crumbs and half-moon stains from coffee mugs were everywhere on the orange Formica. And someone had left a bag of chips *open!* Looking at the open maw of the crinkly bag made her shudder. No telling how many bugs had been feasting there. No doubt the cockroach kingdom had already spread the word that apartment 2A was the breadbasket of the building. At this moment there was probably a weevil diaspora heading up from the Tandoor Express's basement storeroom.

She attempted to blinker herself from the horror of it all and lurched for the coffeepot. One good thing about Danielle: she always seemed to have some sort of beverage brewing.

When she turned back to the living room with her cup, Edie felt a wave of shock to see what had become of her pristine apartment. Even after a week she wasn't used to it. Greta's heavy furniture seemed to have displaced all the airiness from the room. The place looked overstuffed ... and none of the stuffing was hers. She had even agreed, after much arguing, to let a giant Picasso print be hung on the wall, even though it was of one of those portraits of a woman with a monstrous head—she seemed to have two noses and uneven eyeballs that didn't match. Edie didn't dislike Picasso, but she had never imagined something like this on her wall.

That was the weird part about it all. It felt like Greta had burst into her life, crammed the apartment full of furniture, left her fat pâté-goose of a cat with them, deposited her bike-riding lunatic of an ex-boyfriend on the sidewalk downstairs . . . and then disappeared. Edie had seen Greta only a few times since the day she moved in. Their schedules weren't at all compatible, although Danielle said that *she* barely saw Greta, either. And Danielle was here all the time, except when she ventured out to shop.

Edie supposed she should just be grateful that it wasn't Greta that was home too often, given the fact that they never did hit it off on the few times they had spoken. She had to wonder what Greta was doing all the time, though. Could a woman really go out that much?

"Why don't you call Bev?" Danielle was saying into the phone.

Edie eased herself onto Greta's love seat, which sent up a flurry of Kuchen fur. Neither the Dustbuster nor the Eureka canister could keep up with the amount of hair that cat shed. Just when Edie had thought she'd sucked it all up, another little cloud of it would float out from a corner or under the coffee table.

"You don't have to fall in love with her. Just go to a movie or something." Danielle rolled her eyes at Edie and made a yakety-yak gesture with her hand. "What do you mean *what would you talk to her about?* You've known her since you were in kindergarten! I'll bet you didn't have trouble talking to her then." She laughed and shook her head. "I'm not hearing this. I gotta go. Brandon, I love it here and you gotta stop pestering me. Y'hear?" The smile melted from her face. "Oh, for heaven's . . . no! Well, if that's the way you're gonna be, okay!"

She punched the off button of the cordless headset with an emphatic poke of the index finger, the modern-times equivalent of slamming down the phone.

"Can you beat that guy with a stick?" Danielle asked her. "He says he thinks Bev's irritating!"

"Is she?"

"Well, yes, but he's not supposed to tell me that. She's my best friend." Danielle sighed. "Or she was. I haven't heard from her in ages."

Edie knew for a fact that she'd just spoken to Bev three days ago, so apparently Danielle was now judging time as if she had the life expectancy of a fruit fly. "Why don't you call her?" God knows, the woman had her ear to the horn most of the day anyway.

"No . . . I don't want folks back home to think I don't have anything better to do."

Edie sipped her coffee and tried not to stare at the shopping bags trailing away from Danielle's screened-off room. All day long she was either typing or talking, except once a day when she would run out and buy something. It was weird. She'd just bolt out the door, and come back an hour or so later with a new shirt, or a pair of shoes, or a hair dryer. Danielle told Edie that she had come to New York to find excitement, but Edie wasn't certain she was going to find it at Macy's. (A pair of socks and a lot of aggravation was all Edie had ever found in there.)

"Who called earlier?" she asked Danielle. Once upon a time, *her* friends and *her* agent had called *her* at *her* apartment, but those days now seemed to belong to a fog-shrouded past, like Vanilla Ice.

"That was my dad. He told me he'd find me an even better job if I went back to Amarillo."

"What was your job before?"

"I worked in a law office. They called me a paralegal intern but mostly I served coffee."

No wonder she was so adept with warm beverages.

"He's worried now that I don't have enough money," Danielle said. "He says that I'm going to have to pinch pennies or something, but I told him that the allowance he gives me is more than enough. I wish they would stop worrying about me!"

Edie had to rewind. *"Allowance?"*

Danielle seemed taken aback by Edie's reaction. "Sure. Haven't you ever had an allowance?"

"Yeah—when I was twelve. It was five dollars a week!"

"Oh, come on," Danielle said. "What kid could survive on five dollars a week?"

Edie couldn't help cutting another glance at those shopping bags. Judge Poitier was obviously shelling out substantially more than five bucks.

"Okay, okay," Danielle said, her mouth forming a hint of pout. "My parents *baby* me. Totally. That's why I had to get away—to get a measure of independence."

Financially subsidized independence—what a concept! Edie couldn't decide whether she was scornful or simply awestruck. She was actually living with a person whose size-six-and-a-half feet seemed never to have touched the ground. Danielle didn't just have the world on a string, she had it dangling from a gold chain. And she complained about feeling *stifled!* Edie couldn't quite grasp it all. All of Danielle's troubles seemed like luxury problems, but to her they were obviously real.

Cute as a bug, beloved by all, rich . . . Edie wondered whether she could ever learn to actually like this person. Yet she couldn't bring herself to dislike her, exactly. It would be like hating fuzzy puppies, or the Easter Bunny.

The phone rang again and Danielle picked it up so quickly that Edie barely saw her hand move; she was like one of those quick-draw gunslingers in old westerns. She immediately began babbling to a friend on the other end of the line.

Edie got up and sauntered back to the kitchen, maneuvering around Kuchen this time as nimbly as the latter-season Dick Van Dyke stepping around the ottoman. It bothered her that her agent, Noel, hadn't called her with anything in weeks. She needed to call him up and remind him that she was still drawing oxygen.

She opened the fridge in pleasant anticipation of what was becoming the highlight of her day: eating her leftovers. Geppetto's might not be a five-star restaurant, but it was still better than what she could do herself, and it had the added benefit of being free. Last night there had been a tiramisu surplus, so she would be feasting on something decadent this morning.

But when she reached toward the white take-out box, it was lighter than she remembered. She opened it and gawped at what was nothing more than a little hacked-up wedge of cake and cream. There wasn't even an entire ladyfinger visible. Her face felt hot, and her hands trembled. She felt violated.

In symphony with her emotions, the bone-rattling emergency

alarm went off in the hall. Bootsteps clunked up the stairs and a second later Greta let herself in. Her usually pale cheeks were red and she was sucking in air in heaves. Much as Edie herself was.

"I had to come in back door!" Greta said.

Downstairs the front door slammed open. They could hear the landlord charging through the hallway to see what had set off the alarm, which suddenly stopped. "Who keeps doing this thing?" the disembodied voice yelled in frustration.

Edie glared at Greta. "How did you get through the emergency door? It's locked."

Greta shrugged. "Locks open." She looked into Edie's eyes, then frowned. "Is something wrong with you? You look like a rabies animal."

Edie poked her tiramisu box toward Greta. "Look!"

Greta peered at it, then back at Edie. "So?"

"*So?*" Edie parroted. "That's all you have to say?"

Greta's brows beetled. "What do you want that I should say?"

Danielle, obviously sensing trouble, had begged off the phone and was now hovering behind them. "Edie?"

Edie didn't take her eyes off Greta. "I want you to apologize for eating my food!"

"For—?"

"For being a thief!" Edie exclaimed.

Something tapped on her shoulder. It was Danielle.

"Edie . . ."

"Just a minute," Edie snapped. "I want to know why Greta thought she had the right to eat my tiramisu."

"I didn't!"

Edie laughed. "Right! Then who did?"

"I did," Danielle admitted sheepishly.

Edie nearly dropped her box. "You!"

"I'm sorry," Danielle said.

Greta sneered triumphantly. "I was not even here last night or this morning."

"I got up early and had the munchies," Danielle explained. "I shouldn't have done it, I know. I was going to go get you a treat this morning for your breakfast . . . only you got up earlier than you usually do." Tears filled her eyes. "I'm soooo sorry."

All the indignation seeped out of Edie; she couldn't light into distraught, apologetic Danielle, who looked like she might grab a butter knife and perform some Japanese-style exercise in contrition right there in the kitchen.

Edie tossed the box onto the counter. "Don't go over the top about it, Danielle." She glared at Greta instead. "What are you doing here, anyway? Aren't you supposed to be at work?"

Greta looked offended. "What is this, the fifth degree? Please to remember that this is my apartment, too."

As if she needed to be reminded!

Greta was looking around distractedly. "I came back only for my wallet, and now I am late." She tore around the apartment, searching under couch cushions and then running into her room and flapping the covers of her unmade bed. She lit a cigarette, and smoke swirled in her wake.

Edie flapped her hands. "Greta!"

Greta clucked her tongue and stubbed it out.

"Your *wallet?*" Edie asked. "You mean you were out all last night and you didn't have any money or ID?"

"*Ja*—so stupid, right?" Greta spotted it on her crowded dresser. When she laid her hands on it, she tossed it up in the air and closed her bedroom door behind her. "This is good. Now I won't have to come back after I get off on Dr. Hanff."

Edie and Danielle exchanged confused glances. Greta was either screwing her boss or she had mangled yet another preposition. Edie shook her head, guessing the latter.

"You mean you're disappearing again?"

Greta turned on her way to the door. "What does that mean?"

"I mean, you pay rent but you don't live here."

"So? I do not steal your food, either." She smirked at Danielle. "Unlike Danielle Steele, Junior."

She left, and for a few seconds, Edie and Danielle stared at the closed door. A couple of moments later, the alarm went off downstairs. While the clanging continued, Edie reached for the phone and then grabbed a well-worn sheet of paper.

"What are you doing?" Danielle asked.

"I'm calling the United Nations."

Danielle squinted at her. "Because of Greta?"

Edie handed Danielle the worn reference sheet as someone picked up the line.

"May I help you?"

Though it was probably just a switchboard operator, Edie straightened as if she were visible to that businesslike voice. "I'd like to be connected with the secretary general, please."

"Mr. Annan's office?"

"No, Mr. Annan himself."

There was a pause. "I can connect you to his office."

Edie sighed. This was going to get her nowhere, she knew. She'd been through this drill before. "All right, thank you."

The rigmarole she went through with the next disembodied voice was frustratingly similar to what she went through with Rudolph Giuliani's people. She asked for the man, was put on hold, was asked to leave her name and number, and then was cut off.

When Edie beeped off the phone she was still fuming.

A knock at the door startled them. Danielle hadn't heard anyone coming up the stairs. She and Edie gaped at each other in momentary panic. Had Asgarth finally found the right apartment?

"Who is it?" Edie called out in a high, thin voice.

"Mr. Bhiryat Singh, your landlord."

Danielle remained frozen, but Edie exhaled in irritation. "Jesus wept! This is all I need." Executing a drill she had only practiced in her mind, she tucked Kuchen like a football under her arm and dashed her over to Greta's bedroom. "Be with you in a moment, Bhiryat!" She shut Greta's door, then started snatching up felt mice and catnip toys and chucking them to Danielle to stow behind the screen.

The relay over, she shot a stern glance at Danielle. "Just follow my lead," she directed in a stage whisper. Then she slid over to the door and threw it open, greeting the landlord as if he were a long-lost friend. "Bhiryat! Hi! Come in."

Bhiryat shuffled across the threshold. The Indian man was wearing a white collarless shirt with embroidery down the front, starched and pressed black pants, and black street shoes shined to a high polish. The only untidy thing about the smallish man was the sweat beading at his temples.

His perpetually worried eyes were fixed on Danielle.

"You want some coffee?" Edie asked him.

"No, no . . ."

Edie followed his gaze and then let out a trilling sound. She pranced over and surprised Danielle with a big hug. "Bhiryat, have I introduced you yet to my cousin Danielle? She's from Texas!"

Bhiryat politely extended his hand. "I am very, very pleased to meet you."

"Danielle just moved to New York and we're letting her stay here until she's settled in."

Bhiryat picked up on the "we" immediately. "Is Douglas back, then?"

Edie's lips turned down in a dramatic frown. "No, darn it, he's still playing at being the roving journalist. But he thought it would be very good for me to have Danielle here while he was away. He worries about me being alone, you know."

The fictitious statement of Douglas's concern apparently appealed to Bhiryat's old-world sentiments. "Oh yes. I often worry about all you single women, living all by yourselves in this big city. You must be careful, you know."

"We certainly try to be."

Bhiryat cleared his throat, getting to the crux of what had brought him up here. "But now I must tell you that I am very concerned about the strange doings here."

Edie let out an irritated huff. "You mean that alarm?"

"Yes. Someone is using the emergency exit," explained Bhiryat in his precise, clipped Indian cadence, "which is a door only to be used in emergencies."

"I know." Edie was able to inject a believable ferocity into her voice. "I'd like to strangle whoever's doing that."

"Strangling will not be necessary, so long as they stop. I am going to post a notice on the door this afternoon."

"That's a fantastic idea," Edie said.

"Such strange goings-on!" Bhiryat exclaimed. "Twice I have called the police about this motorcyclist on my sidewalk."

Edie frowned. "The guy who keeps screaming?"

"Yes! But they say they cannot arrest him. They can only issue a ticket for parking illegally."

Danielle and Edie clucked sympathetically, and Edie started edging the man toward the door. "Well, you just keep pestering the police, Bhiryat. They'll have to do something eventually."

"All the time he screams for this Greta," the landlord said. "She must be new to the street. This has never happened before."

"With any luck, she'll be gone soon," Edie said.

"I hope so."

When he was finally gone, Edie shut the door and crossed back to the phone book.

Danielle went over to open the door for Kuchen, who waddled out, looking perturbed at having been confined to quarters.

"Who are you calling now?" Danielle asked Edie. Anyone would think the woman didn't see the point of talking on the phone.

"I'm going to try that second number again." Edie glanced at it to refresh her memory.

"Lauren Bacall?" Danielle asked on a gasp. "You can just call somebody like that?"

"If you've got their phone number, you can."

You could *call* them, but you couldn't speak to them.

Edie got the same person at the same agency who had blown her off the last time she called. After a frustrating few minutes telling the person that it was *very important* that she reach Miss Bacall, she was cut off.

She sat back.

"Why are you calling all these people?"

"They're Greta's references."

Danielle laughed. "For real?"

"She said for real—but it's all a big lie. Everything about that woman is a lie. Did you see what she was wearing on her way to work? Black jeans—with holes in the knees. Have *you* ever seen a dental technician with her navel ring showing? For that matter, have you ever seen a tattooed dental tech?"

Danielle shook her head. "No, but I guess New York's different that way than in Amarillo. Back in Amarillo my dentist wore

Justin cowboy boots, but I bet you wouldn't see that here." She frowned in puzzlement. "If you don't think Greta knows any of those people, why are you so het up on calling them?"

"Because I want just one of them, just one, to tell me that he doesn't know Greta and has never even heard of her."

"Why don't you just tell Greta you think she's full of hooey?"

Hooey. It was just the sort of word Douglas would have used. Edie felt a pang. Why didn't he call her? Why had he left her in this situation in the first place?

"Edie?"

"I want proof, damn it, so I can prove she's a liar. I want to get her out of my hair."

"But she's not in your hair. She's hardly ever here."

"But when she *is* here, she annoys me. I've got her furniture crammed in my home, her cat shedding all over creation, and her cigarette smoke stinking up the place. Besides, even when she's not here, I worry that she will be. I haven't been at peace all this week."

Naturally, Danielle took this statement personally. "Are you tired of me, too?"

"No, no, you're fine," Edie lied, punching in Rudolph Giuliani's number. Though she did suppose at this point that Danielle was the lesser of two evils. "Just don't eat my breakfast again."

"I'm sorry," Danielle said. "I just took one bite to see how it was, and then I couldn't stop. I just didn't know I'd lose control that way."

Edie frowned. She could sympathize with that sentiment! For the past two weeks she'd felt on the verge of coming unglued.

When someone answered the phone, she snapped to attention and shut out Danielle again. "May I speak to Rudy, please?" she asked, hoping a casual tone would get her further this time. The guy on the line wasn't buying it. Mr. Giuliani was out of town on a speaking engagement. He was *always* out of town on a speaking engagement (or had been for the past week). The ex-mayor was apparently talking himself hoarse.

"May I leave him a message?" Edie asked. "It's urgent."

Chapter 10

GRETA AT WORK

Greta knew things had gone very wrong when she woke from a deep sleep and saw the faces of her coworkers, her boss, and her next patient looming over her. She was lying in a dentist chair and squinting up at their stunned and, in the case of Dr. Hanff, angry expressions. Groggy panic overtook sleep. She may have even gasped. It was like a nightmare, except for the unfortunate fact that it was really happening.

She bolted up, bumping her shoulder against the swiveling instrument tray that she had been preparing before she decided a nap was in order. A little paper cup of fluoride tumbled to the linoleum tiles. From the horrified look on Dr. Hanff's face, you would have thought she'd just knocked liquid gold off the instrument tray.

"I'd like to speak to you in my office," he said.

It was that sort of day. And believe it or not, this was an improvement over how it had begun. *Gott*, what a morning! Somehow, she had wound up in an apartment building in Sheepshead Bay, Brooklyn. Luckily—if she could actually use the word *lucky* in this instance—when she'd come to she'd been leaning against the apartment door out in the hallway. Which would indicate that she hadn't actually gone into a stranger's apartment.

Or maybe she had, and then she'd been kicked out. Which would have been even more humiliating if she had been able to remember it. Perhaps it was just as well that she'd blacked out.

At seven A.M. a guy wearing jeans, heavy boots, and a tool belt had come charging out and nearly tripped over her.

"Hey!" he'd said, catching himself on the banister. "You okay there?"

Like this happened to him a lot.

She'd mumbled back at him in German, which satisfied him enough to send him trotting off to work. He'd turned back to her on the staircase. "I sure enjoyed that tangerine!" he'd said with a parting wave.

That last sentence had made no sense to her whatsoever. It still didn't, and she'd had five hours to mull it over. *Tangerine?* Was that a new euphemism for something kinky, or had she really given him a piece of fruit?

Of course, a strong possibility existed that he hadn't even said tangerine at all. She might have heard wrong. When she was tired the English language tended not to function with one hundred percent accuracy, coming or going.

Who *was* that guy? Some guy she'd danced with? Had she made out with him? And if she had made out with him, why had he apparently locked her out of his apartment?

She had stumbled off to work, where she changed into the clean pair of scrubs she always kept there in case she didn't make it home, which was most nights now. And she had spent the rest of the morning wondering what the hell she was doing to herself. No sleep, the increasingly pointless nights out, fleeing from one boyfriend to another, one apartment to another, one city to another . . . She was caught on a downward spiral, and she couldn't seem to get off because she didn't want to go back to her apartment, the land of the annoying people.

Okay, maybe Edie and Danielle weren't really annoying. But Greta didn't feel like she belonged in that place. The apartment share had been something born out of desperation. She had thought being around normal people would make her feel more normal, but it had the exact opposite effect. They treated her as if she were a freak or something. Edie, especially. From the moment she moved in she'd been complaining about mess, and smoke. As if her nasty, bug-ridden apartment was hot stuff to begin with. And then there was the other morning, when she had accused Greta of being a thief!

The apartment made Greta want to stay out as much as possible, which meant she was going out too much and waking up in strange hallways in Brooklyn. And then dozing off at work.

"I don't need to tell you that I can't tolerate having assistants napping on the job," Dr. Hanff told her when they were seated solemnly in his office. "Especially not in front of patients."

"I did not know a patient was coming in so soon," Greta said carefully. "Terri usually buzzes me to bring them back."

Dr. Hanff's lips thinned into a grim line, almost to the point of disappearing altogether. "She buzzed you, but you didn't respond."

Why, then, did Terri bring the patient back?

Greta felt her cheeks flame up, and she hardly ever blushed except when she was mad. Her job was the one thing she was actually good at, and now she had screwed that up. Yet she couldn't help wanting to climb up on blame mountain and point a finger at Terri. "I do not know what happened."

He narrowed his eyes at her. "Are you sober?"

She feigned offense. "Of course!" And as far as she knew, she was telling the truth. She had slept it off in that stranger's hallway, she was fairly certain. Now if Dr. Hanff had asked her whether she was hungover, that would be different. . . .

She made the heartfelt promise *never* to do anything like that again. She would have to be careful of even yawning in the future, she knew. These people would be watching her like hawks. The moment she left Dr. Hanff's office and stepped into the hallway, she ran into Terri, the office receptionist, whose perky efficiency always drove her to drink even on her best days.

"Awake yet?" Terri asked her.

"Of course," Greta said. Why *hadn't* the receptionist informed her that her patient was here? "I don't understand the fuss. I was only closing my eyes for a short time."

"You were *snoring*."

Damn. "I just—how do you say it?—nodded off."

The receptionist smirked. "Oh, sure. It could have happened

to anybody. I put Mr. Attar in your bedroo—excuse me, I mean your usual treatment room."

"*Danke*," Greta said through gritted teeth, seething as she headed back to her patient. She hated Terri. *She* belonged at the apartment in Chelsea. Greta could just envision Miss Snake Terri and Miss Grand Inquisitor Edie buddying up in a big way.

Mr. Attar watched her nervously as she struggled into her latex gloves. Poor man. He obviously thought he was about to let a lunatic into his mouth. "Bad day?" he commiserated.

"Very bad." Though she wasn't about to tell a patient that she'd woken up in a doorway. *That* wouldn't instill confidence. "I'm very, very sorry to have kept you waiting."

He chuckled. "You might not believe this, but *I've* fallen asleep on the job before."

But he was an accountant. She didn't know how people crunching numbers all day could stay awake anyway.

He reached into his breast pocket and pulled out a pen, then reached into his wallet for a business card to write on. "I'll give you the address," he said, scribbling.

"The address for what?"

"My AA group."

Greta stiffened. The guy thought she was an *alcoholic?* Was he insane?

"Never mind that." She clipped the paper bib around his neck and reclined him so far back, he was one degree away from standing on his head. She would have said something sharper to him, but she liked Mr. Attar. He was one of her few patients who didn't come in every six months and kid her in a bad German accent he'd learned from watching Arte Johnson and old WWII movies, or ask her if she'd ever seen "Hogan's Heroes."

"What's the matter?" he asked. "It's just a place to meet people with similar problems."

"I would not belong there."

She didn't belong anywhere in the whole world. There was no one in the world who cared about her. Except maybe Asgarth. If she died tomorrow, the only person who would show up at her funeral would be a Harley-riding lunatic.

She was not a sentimental person. She didn't buy into love and forever. And yet . . .

And yet occasionally she felt that if she could just find *someone*. Someone who would make her feel like she belonged.

Mr. Attar would not be put off. Fighting gravity and the blood rushing to his head, he reached one long arm over and placed the business card with an uptown address scrawled on it onto the side table, next to the magazines.

"Manhattan?" she asked.

"It's convenient to work for me," he explained.

But she didn't live near the Upper East Side. So that was that. Aside from being entirely pointless, going to an AA meeting up there would be a big inconvenience. She told herself that if she ever changed her mind, she might look for something closer to her apartment. This was New York—support groups were as common as newsstands.

Mr. Attar's card stayed next to the magazines all day. She forgot to put it into a drawer at the end of the day, even. She dismissed the conversation from her mind.

And yet, somehow, after Greta finished work for the day, she caught the wrong train home and found herself in a strange building uptown, in a basement room filled with alcoholics.

Chapter 11

THE HOOEY HITS THE FAN

Poor Edie. She looked like hell.

At the sound of a door opening around noon, Danielle poked her head around the screen in time to see her come stumbling out in her oversized men's pajamas . . . probably left over from that boyfriend who dumped her who she never talked about. Her light brown hair was mussed and there were sheet wrinkles on her face. She hadn't quite gotten off all her makeup the night before, and a clump of mascara gave her brown eyes a seventies rock star look.

"Mornin'!" Danielle grinned, trying to chirp some pep into her roommate.

Moaning, Edie sank onto the couch—Greta's couch, Edie always called it—but she couldn't really get comfortable. Kuchen's considerable girth was spread across the center cushion, making stretching out impossible.

After a moment, Edie looked like she was starting to come into focus. Her brow puckered. "Is that . . . singing?"

Danielle nodded. Asgarth was in his usual place near the Tandoor Express. "He started about fifteen minutes ago. I can't make out what he's actually singing, can you?"

"I'm not sure, but . . ." Edie's face tensed in concentration. ". . . I think that's Lynyrd Skynyrd."

"Who?"

"I guess that's before your time." Edie frowned. "Come to

think of it, it's before my time, too. I shouldn't have to know who that is."

"Do you think he's trying to serenade Greta?"

"I don't know," Edie said, obviously as mystified as Danielle was. "I can't imagine why he would think any woman would be won over by 'Freebird.' "

"It's really lame that he can't take a hint. I mean, it's pretty obvious Greta's not interested in him."

Edie burrowed into one end of the couch, burying her head in her hands. She obviously still wasn't quite up yet. "I heard the phone ring," she said. "Any message for me?"

"No, that was my mom. I hope she didn't wake you." She looked over at her nervously. "Would you like a muffin?"

Edie grunted.

Danielle trotted over to the kitchen. She had told her parents not to call so early in the day, since Edie was an actress and had to work the night shift at her restaurant. But that just seemed to make them even more suspicious of the life she was leading. They seemed to think that just by living in New York City their little girl was in imminent danger of being killed by terrorists or seduced by sexual deviants.

Her parents, she realized with something like shock, were not very worldly people. In Amarillo she had thought they were sophisticated. They subscribed to the *Atlantic Monthly* and ate Thai food. Her father was published in legal journals. But when it came to her and her future they were *so* provincial. They seemed to want to revert back to some pre-1960s soda fountain utopia when girls stayed home till they were married. Honestly.

"Mom did say I should expect a surprise," she told Edie as she handed her a muffin on a plate.

"Thanks," Edie said, sniffing the muffin. She put it on the coffee table. "Is she sending more money?"

Danielle shrugged. "I have no idea. My poor mom! She's got empty nest syndrome, big time."

Edie frowned. "It's a little late for that. You went off to college, didn't you?"

"Oh, sure, but you know parents. They always assume you're coming back."

"Mine didn't," Edie said.

"My mom's always been a little bit of a worrywart with me." Peggy Porter would never understand how her daughter could give up a rich fiancé who had a golf score in the low nineties and had owned his own boat since he was twenty.

"I warned them that this would happen," Danielle said. "After college I wanted to stay in Austin, but they threw a fit until I agreed to come home for a while. They said Austin was too far away. Sure, it's seven hours away from Amarillo, but then, so's *everything*. Except Lubbock." She sighed. "They just didn't understand that my interests weren't the same as theirs. I wanted to be on my own—get life experience. If I did what they told me to, I wouldn't have anything to write about except lawyers and judges and law firms. Who cares about that?"

Edie coughed. "John Grisham does okay."

"Oh yeah. Him."

Edie reached out and poked the lid off the top of the box with the gas mask in it. "What's this doing here?"

"I thought maybe we should keep it out in case of emergency."

"Mm." She grabbed the mask and twirled it absently. "Must be nice to be a writer. You're more in charge of your own destiny than actors are."

"My destiny seems to be more rejection letters from Jennifer Poon at the *New Yorker.*"

"Yeah, but you can get back on your powerbook and try again. When an actress gets rejected there's not a lot she can do but wait for the next audition, which could be for anything from a feature film to a laxative commercial."

"You could start up your own company," Danielle suggested. "Put on your own show."

"What? Like Mickey Rooney and Judy Garland? Do you know how much *putting on your own show* costs in New York?"

"Oh." Edie could get a little touchy on this subject. People were so funny about money.

Edie eyeballed the muffin again. "Where did you get this?"

"From the kitchen. Greta made it."

Greta had actually been home some in the past week.

"I just found them in a container on the kitchen counter,"

Danielle said. "She had scrawled 'you can eat' on a paper bag and left them."

Edie took a tentative bite and then made a face. "That's awful!"

"Isn't it?"

"That's about the worst muffin I've ever tasted."

"I know," Danielle said. "I ate three of them. I don't know when she made them. Must've been yesterday when I was at Bloomie's."

"I noticed a few shopping bags." Edie kept staring at her muffin. "What flavor is this supposed to be?"

"Bran, I think."

"Is bran a flavor?" Edie asked. "Isn't that like saying they're flour flavored?"

Danielle shrugged. "I can't help you there. Personally, I never bother to make anything myself unless the main ingredient is chocolate."

"Greta should probably avoid making anything, period."

"How did your audition go yesterday?" Danielle asked, changing the subject.

"Oh, fine," Edie said gloomily. "Broadway, British import. Jeremy Irons is the star. Actor's Equity says they have to hire a certain number of Americans for the show, so they've set aside a few bit parts. And even for those they'll probably want names."

Danielle was amazed to find herself in a world where people threw around big names like Jeremy Irons and Actor's Equity, whatever that was. It gave her a little thrill. Truth be told, even having crazy, mysterious Greta stomping around occasionally seemed sort of exciting to her.

"What makes you think *you* won't be a name someday soon?" Edie leveled a "get real" look on her.

"Or maybe you're already more of a name than you know. You were in 'Belmont Hospital' and even I've heard of that."

"A soap," Edie said dismissively.

"So? I bet soaps are great exposure for an actress! You can't let yourself get discouraged. I know something about getting discouraged, believe you me. I sent off my short story to the *New Yorker* weeks ago and I haven't heard a word back yet, even though I sent them a new self-addressed stamped envelope with my updated address. I know the chances are good that I'll be rejected, but I intend to keep plugging. . . ."

Someone buzzing at the door interrupted them, which was probably just as well. Her pep talk didn't seem to be having much of an effect.

Edie was still in her pajamas, so Danielle volunteered to go downstairs to the door. Their visitors were two young men in dark suits. They were staring at something about ten feet away. Asgarth, Danielle assumed.

"Is that Lynyrd Skynyrd?" one guy asked the other, amazed.

While they were talking it over, Danielle took a moment to size up the two men. Who were these guys? She would have said they were hot, except they were a little too straight arrow for hot. In fact, there was something a little scary about them.

The finally turned their attention to her. "Edie Amos?" one of them asked.

Danielle shook her head. "Edie's my roommate."

"We'd like to speak to her." In unison, they flashed badges at her. "FBI."

Danielle froze. Oh, God—just like in the movies! And one of them was a dead ringer for a young Tommy Lee Jones. (Sort of like he looked in *The Eyes of Laura Mars*, only this guy had better skin.)

But she realized it didn't matter *what* they looked like. They were G-men. Danielle's knees knocked noisily. She didn't know what in tarnation to say. She was fairly certain that Edie wasn't a criminal, but should she tell these guys that?

Or should she bar the door and tell them to come back with a warrant?

On second thought, the FBI probably didn't do things like warrants. On the silver screen they were always more kick-in-the-door types, inclined to open fire on the first person who crossed them.

Danielle didn't intend to cross them. She stared intently at their jackets, wondering if they were packing heat.

"C-come in," she spluttered, caving in. Then, to make sure they didn't think she was Edie's conspirator—in whatever it was they wanted her for—she added, "I just moved in. Really. Just two weeks ago."

They looked like they couldn't care less about her. Which was a relief, she supposed as she scampered up the stairs ahead of them. She skidded into the apartment—though not so fast as to make the FBI guys think she was going to pull a fast one—and called out casually, "Oh, Edie? FBI's here!"

Edie rocketed off the couch, still in her pajamas. For some reason she had decided to fool around with the gas mask, which was over her head. "What?" she asked, her shock muffled by the mask.

Danielle didn't have time to explain; the men in suits were right behind her, flashing those badges again. They seemed a little taken aback by finding their interviewee in survivalist gear and pajamas.

"We're FBI, Ms. Amos. We need to speak to you alone."

Off came the mask. Danielle was all set to disappear when Edie reached out and clutched her arm tightly. *Don't you dare*, her look said. "I'd prefer it if my friend Danielle stayed."

"I'm just her roommate," Danielle reminded them quickly.

They considered this a moment, then assented to the request. "Ms. Amos, we're here to speak to you regarding a security matter reported to us by the offices of the secretary general of the United Nations."

Edie's face went scarlet. "They reported me to you?"

"They said they had been receiving harassing phone calls from you." The guy who looked like Tommy Lee Jones flipped open a small spiral notepad. "They said you have called eight times in the past two weeks, each time mentioning a German woman by the name of Greta Stolenbauer. Is this information accurate?"

"Sort of," Edie said, her voice strained. "I *did* call, but I certainly wasn't harassing anyone."

"They seemed to think you sounded like a suspicious character."

"*Me?* Oh, for Pete's sake!" Edie tried to explain what had happened with Greta. Danielle thought she kept a pretty cool head—she even produced written evidence in the form of her original printed ad from the *Village Voice* and Greta's reference sheet.

The two FBI guys eyeballed the documents soberly. Then Tommy Lee Jones squinted out the balcony window, clearly perplexed. "You call this Chelsea?"

The other guy seemed more taken with the references. He laughed. "You believed this?"

Edie looked shaken and offended. "No, of course not! I just wanted to get proof that she was lying. All Kofi Annan had to do was tell me he'd never heard of Greta Stolenbauer."

"Ma'am, Mr. Annan is a busy man."

"He obviously had time to call *you*," she said, growing huffy.

The guy turned to his partner and pointed at the reference sheet, grinning. "Look—Rudolph Giuliani."

The partner looked up at Edie. "You call him, too?"

Demoralized, Edie nodded.

The two men sniggered. "Great! We'll probably be getting a call from his people soon."

Edie herded them out of the apartment. When she stomped back up and closed the door behind her, her face was beet red. "No wonder this world is in such a mess! Wasting government resources investigating innocent people!"

"But they didn't know you were innocent," Danielle countered.

Edie looked irritated with her . . . or maybe with the entire world. She spun quickly, scanning the apartment for a moment before she spied the phone book on the floor next to an armchair.

"I put it there for Kuchen," Danielle explained. "She looked like she was having trouble jumping onto that chair."

Edie grumbled distractedly as she flipped through the massive book. "God knows we need to make sure there's not a square inch of the apartment untouched by fur."

"*Greeeeeeeeeetaaaa!*" Asgarth yelled outside.

Seeing the door open sometimes set him off.

"Who are you calling?" Danielle said over the noise.

Edie flipped through the phone book with frantic movements. She looked like she would rip some pages out before she finally found what she needed. "Aha! Here we go!"

"*Greeeeeeeeeetaaa!*"

Danielle tilted her head. "Here we go where?"

"Damn!" Edie's mouth screwed up in displeasure. "There are two Dr. Hanffs, DDS."

"You're looking for Greta's Dr. Hanff? What for?"

"Because I want to confront her, that's what for," she said.

"Why don't you just wait for her to come home this after-noon?"

"*A*, because I'm too pissed off to wait that long, and *B*, because I want to see if she really works as a dental assistant, or if she made *that* up, too."

To tell the truth, Danielle sometimes wondered if Edie weren't a little crazy herself. Or maybe there was just something about Greta in particular that made her go slightly mad.

"The FBI!" Edie railed, frantically scribbling down info. "I'm going to have an FBI file because of Greta's lying. Well, I'm going to tell her that I have proof now that she rented this place from me under false pretenses and that she'll just have to leave. *I'm* the one in charge here."

"But what about the money?" Danielle asked. "I thought you rented the place out because you needed to share the rent."

Edie waved her hand. "She can have her money back. I'll scrounge up enough by the first of next month. Somehow." She jotted down numbers and addresses and slammed the phone book closed. "Now, here's the strategy: I'll go check out one dentist, and you can go find the other one."

"Me?"

A light brown eyebrow arched at her. "Why not? Are you busy?"

The question seemed a little snide to Danielle. But Edie was right—she *wasn't* doing anything really important. "Where would I have to go?"

"I'll give you the closest one. He's on the Upper West Side, which is a straight shot up on the train."

"The train?"

Edie leveled a stare at her. "The subway."

Danielle shifted uncomfortably. "Oh."

"Surely you've heard of it. It's where all those staircases on the street lead to."

"Well, of course I've *heard* of it. That's what the gas mask is supposed to be for, remember? I just haven't ridden it yet," Danielle said.

Edie looked as if she'd been hit by a stun gun. "How have you been getting around?"

"By cab. It's so convenient."

Edie clasped her hands to the sides of her head. "Danielle, you're wasting money. You've got to learn to use the subway, and this will be a good trial run. I'll even go with you to Penn Station. You just follow the signs that have the blue circle with the A in it."

"Where are you going?"

"Somewhere in Queens . . . but don't worry about me," Edie said. "When you get to Dr. Hanff's office, just ask if Greta works there and come right back, okay?"

"Okay," Danielle said. It sounded simple enough.

In fact, it sounded like a lead-pipe cinch.

Chapter 12

NOT IN KANSAS ANYMORE

It began as an odd prickling sensation when she realized that the subway train hadn't stopped for a very, very long time. Danielle strained to remember the last fuzzy, mumbled announcement she'd heard; the loudspeakers on the train sounded like old Vietnam-era walkie talkies. Half the challenge was trying to pick out the human voice amid the static.

Had the guy said *bridge?*

Bridge would indicate a river had been crossed, wouldn't it?

Prickling doubt turned to panic.

Every time the doors opened, a rush of stuffy heat blew into the over-air-conditioned car, making her skin feel clammy. Edie had told her that she'd only be on the train for a couple of stops. Something was wrong. The train stopped at someplace called High Street. And then the disembodied voice said that word again. She heard it distinctly this time. *"Brooklyn Bridge."*

Damn! She knew she was directionally inept, but could it actually be that she wasn't even on the right island anymore?

One woman got off. Danielle considered following her.

All the things she associated with Brooklyn rushed through her head. Mobsters. Crime. A defunct baseball team. Coney Island. John Travolta in *Saturday Night Fever.* Crime.

She cut a sidewise glance at the odd smattering of humanity slumped in seats around her. They *all* looked like criminals. The doors slid closed, and the train lurched out of the station.

Danielle's gaze darted frantically around the car. There was a subway map on the wall next to a door, but there also was a guy sitting in front of it who looked like he hadn't bathed yet this millennium. For a face, two bloodshot eyes and a broken nose peeked out of a sea of scraggly gray-green facial hair. A battered grocery cart stuffed with garbage bags stood sentry in front of him. There was no way she was approaching that guy, even to get to a map. There was probably no way she could get near him anyway. Judging by the empty seats around him, he seemed to be emitting his own protective shield of body funk.

Meanwhile, the train kept racketing along, taking her God knows where. She knew she was on the right train. This was the A train. The very train Edie had pointed her toward. But what had happened to Columbus Circle? How had she missed it?

The train squealed to another stop, and the loudspeaker crackled again with more unintelligible words. All she could make out was "Jay-*static*, Burr-*static* Ha." Could *anyone* understand what that person was saying?

She stared at the door in a panic. If she got off now, Lord knows where she would find herself. Yet quite a few people were filing out, so chances were this was someplace big.

She bolted off the train so close to the last possible moment that she could feel the sliding doors almost nip her in the ass.

At first she felt a palpable sense of relief just to be on her own two feet and stationary again. Then she squinted toward a sign on the other side of the tracks. "To Manhattan," it read.

So it was official. She *was* in Brooklyn. Lost.

She stumbled after the crowd down the platform toward the exit sign until she came to a map. From Penn Station, the station where Edie had left her, she followed the blue line of the A train going the wrong way until she found the stop that said Jay Street. Yup, she had screwed this up royally.

What a pain. She was going to have to get on another train and then go all the way up to Columbus Circle—if she could find it—and then hunt down Dr. Hanff's address. Who knew how long all that would take? Meanwhile, she was starving. She thought back and realized she hadn't eaten anything today but those three muffins and an itty-bitty sandwich for a midmorning snack. Oh, and a banana. And one of those little packages of Oreos she'd picked up at the deli.

Her stomach rumbled. There was bound to be food around here somewhere. And how could she leave Brooklyn without stopping to take a peek?

When she finally climbed out of the subway, she was almost blinded by the afternoon light bouncing off the sidewalks. There was a plaza across the street, but Danielle followed the flow of people traffic onto something called Court Street and walked a few blocks until she arrived at an intersection, Atlantic Avenue, where it seemed that the world abruptly changed.

This place felt . . . well, it felt like a different country. All around her, signs were in Arabic. The people on the street and standing in doorways of the groceries and restaurants and foreign video stores were mostly Middle Eastern. Even the smell of the place was exotic. Spicy aromas emanated from the stores and restaurants. She'd eaten Middle Eastern food a few times in Austin and loved it, but here . . . well, who knew which place was best?

Not to mention, she was beginning to feel a little awkward. A few people had gazed at her as if she was a piece of foreign matter on their sidewalk. "Lost Anglo" was probably written all over her.

And then she spotted somebody. A tall, male somebody. It would have been hard to miss him—in this crowd he was practically a human beacon. He was approximately her age, lanky, with coppery red hair that reached almost to his shoulders. As opposed to the men around her, who were generally dressed in slacks and dress shirts, this guy wore the familiar young guy uniform of baggy jeans and a Gap T-shirt. He was lugging a thick, old-fashioned suitcase, which he maneuvered carefully through the door of a little kabob house.

He, Danielle decided at once, would be her guide.

She made a dash after him, following him into the restaurant. Immediately, though, she questioned her guide's taste. The interior resembled an old Arby's that had fallen on hard times and then reopened as an ethnic eatery; not promising. Cheap paneling in two different wood veneers covered the walls, and a few Formica tables were pressed between the window and the counter.

Two middle-aged men worked behind the counter. One was chasing some onions over the top of a hot grill with a spatula, and the other was idling next to a hunk of meat turning on a spit. The tiny air conditioner whirring at the top of one of the windows was no match for all that cooking. The place was steamy.

"Hey," the coppery-haired guy said to the man at the counter. "I'd like a falafel sandwich and a Pepsi."

The man nodded, and turned as if to give a mute repetition of the order to his compatriot at the grill. The man then took the red-haired guy's money and turned a raised eyebrow in Danielle's direction. "And you?"

"Oh! I'll have a falafel sandwich and a Pepsi," Danielle said. "Please."

At the sound of her voice, her guide swung around. She looked into his face and saw a dusting of freckles clustered around his long, straight nose. Nascent laugh lines crinkled at the corners of his gray-blue eyes when he smiled at her.

"You're a long way from home, aren't you?" he asked.

Now how the Sam Hill had he figured that out so quick?

"West Thirtieth Street," she said.

He laughed. "You sound like you're from farther south than that."

Doh! He meant her accent. People always thought she sounded funny. "I'm from Texas, originally." But right now even Chelsea felt far, far away.

"Another refugee."

"Refugee?"

"From the South. I'm originally from North Carolina."

He tilted his head at her curiously and she felt herself, foolishly, blush a little under the steady gaze of those gray eyes. They moved from her face down her outfit—a new skirt and blouse ensemble she'd picked up at Barney's. He stared at her clutch handbag, which was a vintage Chanel she'd stolen from her mother's closet last year. And then finished off by taking in her new Jimmy Choo slings, which she was inordinately proud of, having bought them on sale for forty percent off. Except that she hadn't had a pedicure since she'd left Texas, and as her mother would say in that disapproving tone of hers, her toes were disgraceful.

The guy behind the counter shoved two red, white, and blue paper cups of Pepsi toward them. In the steaminess of the restaurant, the cups began to perspire over their hands the moment they picked them up.

"Let me guess . . ." The red-haired guy said, attempting to size her up. "Hunter College?"

She frowned at him, utterly uncomprehending. "No. I graduated from the University of Texas."

"And you've come to NYC to find fame and fortune as an actress," he guessed.

"Um, no."

"Model?"

She laughed. "I'm five foot three."

"Oh." His expression went slack. "So much for my snap judgments. You're going to have to tell me your life story, I guess, because I'm obviously not doing too well on my own."

By unspoken agreement, they migrated to a table. "There's not much to tell. I haven't had much of a life," she said when they were seated. "I graduated a year ago, and then I went to work for a law firm in Amarillo. I decided to come here before my parents drove me stark stirring mad."

"How long have you been in New York?"

"Two weeks."

"Two weeks! You're still fresh off the boat. Are you staying with friends, or did you find a place?"

"I didn't know anybody when I moved here, but I found a place with two roommates."

"Two," he repeated. "That sounds grim."

She laughed. "I love it! My roommates are really nice—well, at least one is. Edie. She's an actress."

One of his brows quirked up. "And the other one?"

"The other one is Greta. She's a little peculiar—even scary sometimes. But maybe that's just because I don't know her too well."

"Or maybe she's scary."

"Anyway, it beats living with my parents. They wanted me to stay in Amarillo for the rest of my life and marry their best friends' son. I was engaged to him, but I don't know . . . after almost a year I started feeling oxygen deprived. Before my mother could throw herself into wedding prep, I panicked and broke off the engagement. And then I came here."

The guy shook his head. "You call that not having much of a life? It sounds like 'The Young and the Restless.' "

"It didn't seem that dramatic, really, except right at the end, when I left. The rest of the time I just felt I was being groomed to become my mother. I was even learning how to play bridge."

"Bridge is a good game to know."

"If you're in a nursing home, or in my old life."

The counter guy slapped down two waxed paper–wrapped pita logs in front of them and they dove into the chore of unwrapping. They sat quietly munching on their sandwiches for a moment (the food was fantastic) and trying not to look at each other. Danielle searched for something to say, which usually wasn't a problem for her. Her father always told her that she chattered like a monkey. But she had never chased a stranger into a restaurant before.

An odd thought occurred to her. "I don't know your name."

He swallowed. "Wilson."

"Wilson, like the president?"

"Or like the volleyball in *Cast Away.*"

"Don't you have a first name?" she asked.

"That's it. Wilson. Wilson Pickett."

Pickett. Like the charge. "Oh, I see. Do people call you Will?"

"No. Just Wilson." Wilson—he didn't look like a Wilson, in her opinion—was smiling at her. "What's your name?"

She shook her head. "Danielle Poitier."

"That's a pretty name."

"It ought to be. I picked it out myself."

His eyes narrowed. "You use a fake name?"

"Well, partly."

"What's your real name? Lula May Barnes?"

She laughed. She hadn't known many guys who could toss off *Breakfast at Tiffany's* references. She wondered if that meant she reminded him of Audrey Hepburn, and felt a sort of thrill just at the possibility. Audrey was so sophisticated. "My real name's Porter, but I think Poitier sounds better, don't you?"

He squinted, and those little creases jumped back into view. "It reminds me of Sidney Poitier."

"Exactly," she said. "Distinctive. I'm hoping my name will be worth something on its own someday. I'm a writer."

His eyes twinkled. Actually *twinkled*. He was so cute! "And your fake name will be worth something when you're published?"

"Of course. That's my goal. And if changing my name helps get me noticed, I figure it's worth it, right?"

Wilson seemed to agree with her, but she was beginning to wonder if he was that type of person who simply looked like he was with you all the way, while he kept his negative thoughts to himself.

She sucked down some Pepsi. "Are you going back to North Carolina today?"

He straightened. "What makes you ask that?"

"Your suitcase," she said, pointing down to the case next to the table.

He barked out a laugh. "That's an accordion."

"Oh." Now that she looked at it more closely, it *was* a little misshapen for a suitcase. "I thought you were a tourist."

"Disappointed?"

"No . . ." She sighed. "Only I thought if you were a tourist, you might have a map."

"A map? Are you lost?" he asked, surprised.

She let out a West Texas hoot. "Lost? I tell you what! A bloodhound couldn't find me in a week of good weather."

"And you were going to ask a *tourist* for directions? Do you have any concept of what a feeble idea that is?"

"It seemed sensible fifteen minutes ago. Mostly, though, I just wanted something to eat. That's why I followed you in here."

"You followed me?"

"Sure."

"Just because of my accordion case?"

"Not entirely." She frowned. She couldn't very well tell the guy that she followed him because he was beanpole tall and had red hair. You never knew when a guy would take offense at being called a human beacon. "Like I said, I didn't even know that was an accordion. What are you doing lugging one of those around for?"

THREE BEDROOMS IN CHELSEA   95

"Making money," he answered. "I play in the subway when I'm low on cash."

Her breath caught. A street musician! Was that fabulously boho, or what? "People give you money?"

"Enough to make it worthwhile calling in sick for a day if I don't have any ready cash and payday is still a ways off. I have to be choosy about the places I go, though. Brooklyn Heights is pretty good because there's not so much competition and a lot of rich people live here. I play 'The Happy Wanderer' and 'Lily Marlene' fifty times and by lunch I've got enough to eat on for the week." A chagrined look came over him. "Well, if I don't eat much."

Rich people? She turned a baffled gaze out the window at the bustling street of immigrants. *"Here?"*

"A few blocks away is some of the priciest real estate in Brooklyn," he told her.

"Oh. I didn't know."

"As far as being lost in New York, you could have done worse. Much worse."

She was beginning to feel like she lucked out just meeting Wilson. Not that he was all that good looking—not in the way she really went for. But he was friendly. *Cute*, like she said.

"What do you do when you aren't a subway musician?"

"Since I dropped out of graduate school I've been working as a legal proofreader."

How dull was that! The nine months Danielle had clocked in at the law office in Amarillo had dragged by like nineteen lab monkey years. "Are you interested in law?" she asked, almost afraid of the answer.

"No. I just like the money I make there."

Phew. "What school did you drop out of?"

"Juilliard."

Her mouth was hanging open, but she couldn't help it. These famous names gave her a jolt every time. They seemed to give even mundane things a certain cachet. People from all over the country wanted to go to Juilliard, and now here she was casually having lunch with one of its discards.

"Don't look so appalled," he said. "It's making me self-conscious."

"I'm not appalled. I'm impressed!"

"By a music school failure?"

"No, by the fact that you were there." She looked doubtfully at the accordion case. "Were you studying to be a virtuoso accordionist?" Did such a thing exist?

He nearly spat up his Pepsi. "Piano. The accordion's just for fun. Also, I couldn't haul a piano down into a subway."

"That's true. But if you enjoy music so much, why did you drop out of Juilliard?"

"It took me about three weeks in New York to figure out I don't have what it takes to be a concert pianist. I won a lot of contests when I was an undergrad—I went to all the right clinics in the summer. But I'm just not that ambitious. Professional musicians need to be very focused, especially when they're first starting out. When you walk down the halls at Juilliard, you see the laser intensity in people's faces. Music is what they live and breathe. But I'm interested in other things. When I found myself slipping out of practice rooms to go loaf around the Museum of Natural History, I knew I'd probably made a mistake."

"It doesn't mean you wouldn't be good."

"No, but it's not a good sign for a future in the profession. So I called it quits and decided to have fun for a year. I'm saving money, though, so I can go back to grad school in the fall."

"Studying what?"

"History."

The word hung awkwardly in the air. *History?* He was going to trade the romantic, exciting life of a professional musician to . . . ? "What can you do with history?"

"Teach," he said, warming to the discussion. He leaned forward. "I want to teach high school."

In response, she felt herself recoil slightly. Oh, this poor man! She felt an almost overwhelming pity for him. Teaching history. In high school. If he had said his ambition was to go to work in a rock quarry, she wouldn't have been any more flummoxed. Didn't he remember teachers in high school? Their bad shirts, their used cars, their enslavement to a system that most people couldn't wait to get out of?

"Are you all right?" he asked.

"I'm fine." She took a quick gulp of her drink. "I'd like to hear you play the piano someday." Maybe she could convince him he was making a serious mistake.

He laughed dismissively. "Pianos aren't easy to come by in this town. Tell you what, though. I'll take you to the promenade instead."

"The what?"

"The Brooklyn promenade. You'll love it. It always pops up in movies."

Danielle hesitated. And not, as her parents would have hoped, because she sensibly didn't trust this person she had only met by chance a half hour ago, who could be an axe murderer for all she knew. Though of course he wasn't. Even her father, who had the idea lodged in his head that every other person in New York City was a psychopath, would have taken one look at Wilson and liked him. He reminded Danielle a lot of guys she'd met at UT. After all these weeks of feeling like a foreigner in this strange city, it was nice to meet a guy who seemed as familiar as an old boot.

But she suddenly remembered that she was supposed to be looking for Dr. Hanff. Talking to Wilson had made her forget about that entirely. "I'm supposed to be someplace around Columbus Circle."

He seemed almost impressed. "Wow. And you live on West Thirtieth? You did get lost, didn't you?"

"I just went the wrong way on the A train," she said defensively. "That could happen to anybody, couldn't it?"

"It could . . ."

But his tone implied that it usually didn't.

"If you're going to be condescending, I'm not going anywhere with you," she said. "I think I made a perfectly understandable error."

His jaw sawed doubtfully. "You might have guessed that if you were going to the Upper West Side, you should have known you wanted to take the *uptown* train."

"Why?" she asked. "There's something above the Upper West Side, isn't there?"

"Well, yeah. An entire state."

"There! See? Some people have to go *downtown* to get to Columbus Circle."

He sent her an even stare, perhaps assessing her odds for making it where she needed to go without his aid. Apparently they weren't very good. "Tell you what," he offered. "I'll give you a tour of the promenade, and then I'll escort you back to Columbus Circle myself."

"Oh, but—"

"It's not out of my way," he assured her. "I live in Morningside Heights."

He said that name as if it should actually explain everything to her, when of course it didn't. It didn't even mean as much as the Upper West Side. At least she'd heard of that in Woody Allen movies.

"Thanks, but I'm just going to take a cab," she said.

His jaw dropped. "All the way up there? That's crazy!"

Crazier than wandering around Brooklyn with a stranger?

Wilson didn't appear to be of a mind to argue over the matter. When she picked him as her guide, she had unwittingly chosen very wisely. He stood and picked up his instrument case. "I'll make sure you get where you need to be, Danielle. I promise you." He gallantly held out his hand for her.

And with surprisingly little hesitation, she took it.

Chapter 13

COFFEE JITTERS

Caffeine was such a feeble drug. Greta had never understood what the big deal was. A hit of it picked you up for a little bit, sure, but from the way people slurped it down in this city you'd think the stuff was as addictive as heroin.

She wobbled on chunky-heeled boots over to an uncomfortable metal chair next to an empty table. Coffee shops seemed so claustrophobic, everyone sitting either in tight little conspiratorial duos or hunched over their cups with a book or a newspaper. Or even worse was the guy over in the corner with a computer, tapping away—how sad was that? He couldn't even just sit and unwind, like she was doing.

She took a deep breath, but instead of relaxing her, it just seemed to give her irritation more oxygen. Why did coffee shops tend to have precious names? The Last Drop, this one was called. An eye-rolling name. She felt irritated by it, and by all the DKNY yuppie caffeine addicts around her in for their evening fix.

What pathetic, desperate people there were in this world. Really, it amazed her sometimes.

Her hands shook as she grasped her café au lait and brought it to her lips. She took a long drink of the strong coffee and allowed the caffeine to disperse through her system. The day had seemed interminable, and now she had to face a long evening at home. Home. It was weird to think of that apartment as her home now, but it was. At least the way everyone's schedules worked out, she usually only had to deal with one roommate—Danielle. The Minnie Mouse from the South.

God, she didn't want to go back there.

She couldn't call up any of her usual acquaintances, because they would just want to go out to a bar or something. She noticed they hadn't called her up recently, either. She'd told Jenna about going to the AA meeting, and Jenna had reacted like a carnivore confronted with a newly minted vegetarian. Maybe word had spread.

She needed to think of something to do to pass the time. A hobby. Reading, maybe. She could read English novels and improve her language skill.

Ach! That sounded so boring. She sucked down half a cup of her coffee, put down the cup and planted her elbows on the table, burying her face in her hands. She had to go back to the apartment sometime, though she wanted to put it off for as long as possible. She dreaded a scene, but knew there would be one. After what had happened this afternoon, there would have to be.

Why the hell had Edie appeared at the dentist office? Greta wasn't buying that bit about the toothache, no matter how infected her root had turned out to be. Edie had been spying on her, she was sure. She wished she'd gotten a chance to talk to her, but when Edie had arrived, she'd been with a patient and wasn't free to talk.

Later, it was Edie who wasn't free to talk.

A wicked little grin touched Greta's lips. According to the receptionist, Terri, Edie had come in asking after Greta; when Terri informed her that she couldn't speak to Greta, Edie complained of some vague tooth pain and said she'd just come by to make an appointment. Wasn't it lucky that Dr. Hanff had an opening?

When Greta had left the office, Dr. Hanff was still performing a little impromptu oral surgery on Edie, who, to Greta's glee, had turned out to be a white-knuckle patient. She had been sweating like a maniac through her root canal.

After a few moments, her grin faded. In three months, she was going to turn thirty. Somehow, soon, she had to grow up. Had to. Which meant that no matter how much she wanted to flee this city and her screwed-up life for somewhere new, she had to stick. She had to make something work. Really, she should be thanking her lucky stars for Edie and that stupid apartment. It was her one little toehold on stability.

Her hands itched to reach into her bag for a cigarette, but that was pointless. You couldn't smoke in New York anymore. The whole place had turned into a city of hand-slapping nannies. She got up and ordered another café au lait.

She had to give up smoking anyway. Not just because smokers were being driven underground like crack addicts, but because she sometimes couldn't breathe. That was a little troubling. She supposed eventually she would have to give up everything that was bad for her and enjoyable, which made her wonder what she was going to do for the rest of her life. *Jog?*

Maybe she should just go to a taxidermist and have herself stuffed and planted on a stool at Dr. Hanff's. They could even set her mouth in a manic grin and she would finally fit in at the office.

Gott. What she wouldn't do for a shot of something strong. Just to take the edge off.

Something she'd heard at the meeting came back to her: Every day you don't drink is a day you don't drink . . . or something like that. People at that place spewed pat phrases all the time; they were all fluent in bromides. Normally she would have laughed at them, but while sitting in a roomful of people who were being so grimly honest they made sense. It was only when you thought about them later, alone, that what they said seemed flimsy.

She drummed her nails on the counter as she waited for her coffee. Hobbies . . . hobbies . . .

Maybe she could take up something healthy. Some kind of exercise that wouldn't be overly monotonous and punishing, if such a thing existed. She thought about getting a bike, but you could get killed riding a bike in the city. Yoga? No running involved in that . . . but those yoga people tended to be into all that annoying spirituality stuff. She'd have to learn what a chakra was.

Maybe she should focus on eating better. That was it. She could cook. The apartment had a good kitchen; she'd made those incredible muffins just yesterday. And there was that channel on television that was all about cooking. She could learn to cook healthy things and that way she wouldn't even have to worry about exercising.

Or she would feel so good she would *want* to exercise.

Greta was carrying her cup carefully back to her table when Edie winged through the door of the coffee shop.

"I *thought* that wath you!" Edie said, her words slurring slightly from the lidocaine. People at nearby tables looked up to stare, and no wonder. There was something wild in Edie's eyes.

Greta groaned. This was all she needed.

"Do you have the intention to follow me about for the rest of our lifes?" Greta growled at Edie in passing on her way to her chair. She sat down quickly, trying not to let her roommate see her ruffled.

"Thith is *my* neighborhood, if you'll recaw."

"Really? You own all of Chelsea now? That is very good. Next time I want a cup of coffee, I will ask your permission where to go."

"I'd be happy to tell you. Believe me I would."

There had been some kind of sarcastic double meaning in that, but Greta hadn't caught it.

Uninvited, Edie flopped down in the chair opposite her.

"Please join me," Greta offered sarcastically.

"I don't know what *you're* tho mad about!" Edie said.

Greta leaned forward. "I'm mad because you followed me to work. Why? What right have you to stick your nose into my life that way?"

"Greta, the FBI came by the apartment today."

That name made her freeze. She couldn't even laugh at the fact that Edie had said *apawtment*. Was there something wrong with her immigration? She was certain she was up to date. . . . "For me they were looking?"

"No, for me. See, it seems that I kept pestering Kofi Annan about a woman he had never heard of. Had no idea. Get it? The name 'Greta Stolenbauer' wasn't ringing Kofi's bells." Her voice rose sharply. "They thought I was some kind of a nut!"

Greta deflated with relief. "*Gott sie Dank!* You had me worried."

Edie's mouth dropped open. "I had *you* worried? Jesuth wept,

Greta—I had G-men in my apartment interrogating me! Because *you* lied."

"I am sorry for that, but I could not think of any references."

She was still gaping at her as though she were a circus freak. "That's it? You jutht made them up?"

"I asked advice of my friend, and she suggested if I named famous people, no one would call them. So we found an Internet site on how to get in touch with famous people."

Edie bridled in her chair, clucking wordlessly and tapping her fingers. Finally, she released a theatrical sigh. "Thith isn't working, Greta. You need to find a new plathe."

Greta was torn between laughing and crying. She was being kicked out of her apartment by a woman who sounded like a cartoon character. "Could we not talk over this later? I have a headache."

"*You* have a headache?" Edie practically shrieked. "What about me? Half my mouth is dead. That damn drill is thtill ringing in my brain. I'm dehydrated from thweating tho much."

"Would you like a coffee?" Greta asked.

Edie looked tempted for a moment, then slumped. "No." She sighed. "I'd just dwibble all over mythelf."

"The paresthesia will not last," she told her.

"The what?" Edie asked.

"The numbness."

Her roommate's pout looked all the more spectacular because of her saggy lip. "Then I'll pwobabwy be in pain. Dr. Hanff better not be a butcher."

"He is very able, I think."

"He's certainly eager!" Edie said, rubbing her numb jaw.

"He pays better than the man I worked for before."

"He ought to, for what he charges!"

"*Ja.* He is expensive."

Edie slumped back and crossed her arms. "How on earth did my life get thith way?"

"I ask myself the same thing," Greta said.

"What'th the matter with you?"

What wasn't? "I'm not sure. I was just considering having myself stuffed."

Edie laughed. "Like Twigger."

"Who is Twigger?"

"A horth."

"I have never heard of him," Greta said.

Her roommate shifted, looking more uncomfortable. She didn't speak for a long time, until Greta frowned impatiently. "The thing is, Gweta," Edie said, "you've got to move."

She was shocked at how sharply the words hit her. Even if she didn't like being there, she *needed* that place. If Edie kicked her out, where would she go? She had no more plans. No ideas for plans, even. She just felt burnt up. Or out. Whatever.

"You are so mad because of a few references?" she asked Edie.

"It's not only that . . ."

"I don't *want* to move," Greta said.

"But I want you to."

Greta would love to have seen a photograph of them in that moment. Numb and number—a snapshot of mutual irritation. "If you wish that I should move so much, I must go, of course," Greta said, sighing. If she had to, she had to. "But in that case, I want returned the money I gave to you."

"Of cour—"

Edie's words broke off and she bolted upright. She looked furious. "Your money!"

"What ist wrong?" Greta asked, alarmed.

"I jutht gave thix hundred dollars to Dr. Hanff!"

Greta couldn't help it. She chuckled. In fact, she tossed her head back and brayed with laughter. People stared, but she didn't care. She never did. "This is funny. You spy on me at work in hopes to find I am a liar, right?"

Edie's mouth popped open, but she didn't deny it.

"And now you have hole in your mouth and your bank!" Greta laughed again, completely alone. Edie was just glaring at her. "Now you are stuck."

"Thtuck," Edie said, defeated. "Cwap."

Chapter 14

THE TEMPTING OF DANIELLE

Before Danielle saw her roommates, she heard them. Outside the front door, all hell broke loose. A fight erupted between Edie, Asgarth, and Greta involving language that made Danielle's cheeks turn pink. Then the front door slammed and Edie's footsteps rushed up the stairs.

Danielle braced herself.

A key jammed in the lock and Edie flung the apartment door open. When she saw Danielle, she rolled her eyes in exasperation. "*Goddamn it!* You'll never believe what that—" Three steps into the apartment, she froze. Her eyes cut from Danielle to the tall older gentleman standing in the middle of their cramped living room.

"Thorry," she said. "I didn't know you had company."

Danielle tilted her head. What was up with Edie's voice? What had happened? Her heart sank a little at the state she was in. She was hoping at least one of her roommates would make a good impression. But Edie looked hammered and from the sounds of things out on the street, Greta had picked this of all moments to finally confront Asgarth.

"This isn't company," Danielle told her. "I mean, this is my dad. He's the surprise my mother was telling me about!" She tried to make it sound like it was a *pleasant* surprise. "Dad, this is Edie."

Her dad was an impressive sight—tall, with iron gray hair, and steely eyes that stood out all the more because his skin was Coppertone dark from playing tennis outdoors three times a week. He held out his hand to Edie. "Pleased to make your acquaintance."

Edie's face marched through several expressions—surprise to embarrassment to airline hostess cheerfulness. "It's nice to meet you, too!"

The cramped living room seemed to shrink around them. The place had actually seemed big to Danielle, especially after her week at the Alexander Hamilton residence hotel, but having her dad standing there critically eyeballing each square foot made her feel as foolish as if she'd moved onto a subway grate in Times Square. He could see none of the charm in the old plaster walls and the pressed tin ceiling, and the balcony that you could even sort of sit out on if you were careful. All he saw was peeling linoleum, the strategically positioned roach motels, the tiny bathroom with rust stains on the porcelain, and the Jabba the Hutt cat stretched out in the middle of it all.

"Dani," he'd scolded when she showed him her room. "That's not even a proper bedroom, honey. You're being cheated!"

He didn't know the half of it. She'd told him she was only paying four hundred dollars a month. A lie, but it was one of those necessary lies that are forgiven because you tell them to save people pain.

For a solid hour, ever since she'd returned from her great afternoon with Wilson in Brooklyn and found her father standing on her stoop, she had been treated to her father's low opinion of her life decisions. He had touched on everything, from her choice of singing "Material Girl" at the vacation Bible school talent show when she was eight to bugging out on Brandon last month.

"Now Brandon's going out with Bev Darcy," he'd informed her gravely.

The news lapped over her in a wave of surprise. "*Bev?*"

Her dad grunted.

"But that's great!" Danielle had exclaimed, meaning it.

Her father had glowered at her, not at all pleased with all that Sutter money dropping into the lap of some other family. She'd tried to explain that she *wanted* Brandon to go out with other women, to get on with his life just as she was doing.

But her father was not in a mood to listen. He was cranky. The cab ride from LaGuardia had cost him a king's ransom. His hotel was an airless dump. He was hot, tired, and not the least impressed with Danielle's adopted city. When he was so closed minded, how could she make him understand what it meant for her to be doing what she wanted and making her own way?

Well. Making her own way with his help.

She had hoped that Edie would be able to help her schmooze him a little. Edie was presentable, and pretty, and he had been mildly impressed when Danielle told him about the role on "Belmont Hospital." But Edie was clearly not at her best just now. It wasn't just her cursing and lisping, either. Her clothes looked wrinkly, there were sweat stains on the underarms of her blouse, and her hair had obviously not been combed since before they had both left to find their Dr. Hanffs.

"Would you like thomething to drink, Judge Poitier?"

"Porter." He frowned, correcting her with an annoyed flick of a glance at Danielle. "No, thank you."

Edie gazed in confusion at Danielle, who shook her head and rolled her eyes as if to say *I'll tell you later*: "Dad came to see how I was settling in."

"How nice!" There was something Eddie Haskellish about the bright tone she assumed now. "We all love Danielle."

Like there was a Danielle fan club in the building.

At that moment, the door banged open and Greta marched through. "Did you hear that? I finally got us rid from that asshole!"

The white-faced alarm on their faces registered at once, and she stopped short, blinking at this stranger in their midst.

"Dad," Danielle said, hitching her throat, "this is Greta. Greta, this is my father. He's here from Texas. Just came to see that *everything was fine here.*"

"Oh." Greta stood stock still.

"Pleased to make your acquaintance," the judge said formally.

Greta ducked her head. "Likeways."

"Well!" While Danielle spoke to her dad, she tried to pretend that she didn't see the bug-eyed expression that he was eyeing Greta with. It was the same look on Raymond Burr's face when he first spotted Godzilla. He'd always disliked short short hair on women. She didn't know his views on tattoos, but she could guess. "Dad, you've seen the apartment and met the roommates. What say we go tie on the old feedbag? I've hardly had a bite to eat all day."

"There's a steakhouse near my hotel." Her dad turned politely to Greta and Edie. "Would you two ladies care to join us?"

"No thanks," Edie said. "My mouth is thore."

"What happened?" Danielle asked her.

Greta snorted with laughter.

Edie shot her a hostile look before answering Danielle. "Root canal."

Danielle's jaw dropped. *"What?"*

"I found Dr. Hanff."

Judge Porter broke in. "I'm sure Edie wouldn't want to chew on a steak right now."

"No," Danielle agreed, depressed. "Greta?" She pleaded Greta with her eyes. Anything would be better than sitting alone with her disapproving dad through a long steak dinner.

Greta, of course, had no mercy. "No, thank you."

"That's all right, Danielle," the judge said. "Truth is, I sort of wanted to speak to you in private."

Danielle felt her shoulders droop. As if she hadn't known that all along. He certainly hadn't flown out all this way for a Circle Line boat tour.

Her father took her arm and propelled her toward the door. Danielle indulged in a last glance at the apartment, and at her roommates, who were watching her departure like schoolkids during recess watching a classmate get dragged away to the principal's office.

Edie sent her an encouraging look. "Have a good time." And, checking to see that the judge wasn't watching, she mouthed, "good luck."

Over sirloins at Smith and Wollensky, Danielle and her father chitchatted about his flight, about people in Amarillo, about the weather. She knew what he was doing. Sure, he was *talking* about the MacMahons down the street cutting down a hundred-year-old live oak tree to put in a Jacuzzi, but what he was really doing was plotting his strategy in his head. And if Danielle became distracted by chatter about Jacuzzis and the differences in the weather in Texas and New York and let her guard down, so much the better.

"Dad," she said, trying to interrupt his plotting time by jumping right in. Better to cut his argument off at the pass anyway. "I know you thought my apartment was a dump."

"Now I never said *dump*."

"But it's not. It's really not. In fact, for New York, it's really nice."

"Of course," he agreed. "By New York standards, I'm sure it's perfectly acceptable."

She wasn't doing too well. "You probably *hated* Edie and Greta."

He thought for a moment. "Edie seemed real nice."

"She is," Danielle said. "She's been *very* nice to me. And even Greta—she's a fascinating person. She knows Rudolph Giuliani."

Well . . . a bit of a lie.

Okay, a flat-out lie.

Her father smiled patiently. "It's nice that you've been making friends, Danielle—"

"I have! I even met a really nice guy today. You'd like him."

"I'm sure I would," her father answered in a voice that said he thought that about as likely as him liking gangsta rap. "I'm sure you'll do fine here. You're very able. But—"

"No buts, Dad. I'm never going back to Amarillo."

"Don't say never, Danielle. You might actually come to the realization that you want to go home, but that 'never' you uttered will hold you back. You'd stay just out of pride."

"But I won't come to that realization," she said. "I know I won't. I like it here. I'm going to get valuable life experience, and soak up culture, and meet new people." She remembered that most of the people she had met so far were makeup counter clerks and dressing room ladies, but brushed that aside. That had just been her orientation phase.

Her father looked more doubtful than ever. "You can do all that in Amarillo."

"No, I can't."

"Why not, for pity's sake?"

"Because at home, I'm perpetually sixteen."

"Nonsense!"

"It's true."

Her father's gray eyes practically glowed in his red face, and he sawed on his steak with new energy. For an endless awkward stretch the two of them chewed and chewed and avoided each other's eyes. Still, Danielle knew she was right, and knew he knew it; she had come out the winner of the argument. She had stood her ground, and won.

Which made her suspicious. She *never* won arguments with her dad.

Her father put down his knife and fork and took a long sip of wine. "I saw Buck Hossney the other day."

"Who?"

"You know, my old friend from high school who owns all the car dealerships."

"Oh." This was a weird thing for him to bring up now. "Are you and Mom getting a new car?"

"Not exactly." He released a long, regretful sigh. "I told Buck to order up one of those bitty cars you like so much. You know—the tiny car from that awful movie starring that little fellow I can't stand."

Austin Powers? Danielle practically levitated out of her chair. *"A Mini?"* She felt faint. Her father had always made her drive around in her mom's cast-off Ford Explorers. Said they were safer. Maybe they were, but they made her so prematurely soccer mom-ish. And now here he was, telling her there was a Cooper Mini out there with her name on it!

"Baby blue with the white top," he said. "That's the one you wanted, wasn't it?"

The one she'd wanted, craved, prayed for. "Oh, Dad!"

He was smiling. "It'll be waiting for you in the drive when you come home."

The words sank in, and her elation evaporated. "But I'm not going home."

"It'll be there for you if you do," he repeated.

Her heart hitched in her chest. Damn! She couldn't believe

this! He was trying to bait her home with a stupid car . . . and it was *so* working.

She *was* sixteen around him.

She wanted that car. She didn't even care that much about cars, but this one was different. It was so little and stubby and sweet. She'd pined after it like she'd seen women pine after babies. She squealed and felt a squeezing pain in her chest whenever she saw one on the street. *If I could just have one of those*, she would think, *I would be a complete person.*

Her fingers tapped on her thigh under the table, a nervous gesture she feared her father's eagle eyes could detect, even through a layer of wood. She closed her eyes for a moment to gather her thoughts, but all she saw was herself at the wheel of that perfect baby blue gumdrop of a car.

Amarillo was a nice little city, when you came right down to it. *No!*

And wasn't it comforting to be in a place where your family had lived for three generations? She had history there.

You are not going to cave in!

Family was important, too. Maybe when you were young you were apt to lose sight of that. . . .

Danielle! Snap out of it! It's only a car.

Her father's voice penetrated her thoughts. "Danielle?"

Her eyes blinked open. Her decision was firm, but her voice was tremulous. "Maybe I can drive it at Christmas?"

His disappointment was palpable. "Don't be stubborn."

"Dad, why can't you understand this? I need to learn to be independent. Really independent. That's not something I can trade for a car. You and Mom have been spoon-feeding me all my life. It's time I got out on my own and tried to make do for myself."

Her father took another sip of wine. "Sink or swim, you mean?"

Could it be that she was actually getting through to him? "Yes, *exactly.*"

"You sound like you really mean it."

"I do."

Not another word was spoken until they ordered dessert. And

then only nervous smiles passed between them as they stirred their coffees and waited for their sweets to arrive. Her steak must have looked bigger than it actually was, because Danielle was absolutely famished. When the waiter set a wedge of chocolate cake in front of her, she practically fell face first onto the plate.

"I guess I've been a little unfair to you, Danielle."

"Mm?" She scarfed down a mouthful of cake; it was really good.

"We've coddled you. You see, your mother . . ."

Uh-oh. Here it came—the guilt trip.

"Well, never mind what all your mother went through. The miscarriages. It was heartbreaking. By the time you came along, we had fair nigh given up hope."

She winced. "Dad . . ."

"You shouldn't think of that, though. Even though having you has meant everything to your mother and me. Everything."

Her eyes stung. "Everything is too much," she said. "For anyone."

He appeared to give her argument serious thought. "You're right. And by the same token, I shouldn't have tried to *give* you everything. It wasn't fair to you. And I'm going to try to make amends for that now, if you'll let me."

He'd lost her.

"I'm going to give you what you really want," he said.

Her heart leapt. Was he going to let her have the Mini anyway? *Here?* It would be a perfect car for New York City!

But where would she park it?

"Complete freedom," her father said.

There had to be garages in Manhattan. Maybe she could rent a space . . .

"Danielle?"

She blinked at him. "I'm sorry, Dad. Were you saying something about freedom?"

"I said, you can be on your own, like I was when I was your age. Free to make your own way, earn your own money, pay your own bills."

No mention of the Mini. She choked up chocolate crumbs.

Apparently, the car was out of the picture. "Dad . . . Are you trying to say you're cutting me off?"

"That's a harsh way of putting it. I prefer your take on the matter—I'm giving you your financial freedom."

She didn't know what to say.

"You know your mother and I will love you unconditionally, no matter what. And if there's ever any little thing I can help you with—advice or whatnot—you let me know."

"Advice." She felt as if she were on fire. Her allowance . . . her credit cards . . . those little extras he slipped her when she wanted to take a trip . . . Could he really be cutting off *everything?*

She looked into those steely gray eyes and knew the answer. Of course he was, the old cuss! He knew her better than anyone. A week without her Discover card could result in complete psychological collapse. Turn off the money and she would go crawling back to Amarillo like a man dying of thirst trying to get any little drop coming out of the spigot.

Or she might have . . . until now.

Edie had said she hadn't received an allowance since she was twelve. Wilson was playing accordion in the subways. And Greta . . . God knows what she was up to. She looked as if she had been cut loose from any responsible parental entity ages and ages ago.

If those folks could survive, so could she.

She really could.

She squared her shoulders. "Okay, Dad." Then, to ensure he didn't think he was scaring her, she added, "Thanks."

"Don't forget, you'll always be welcome back home in Amarillo."

She smiled.

"Would you like something else?" her father asked her.

"Oh yes," she said, "I'd like to get some stuff to go."

Better fatten herself up as much as possible while Daddy was paying, she thought. Starvation was just around the corner.

Chapter 15

PEACE SETTLEMENTS

Edie paced around the apartment, mostly from her bedroom to the distressingly empty refrigerator to the bathroom medicine cabinet. As her mouth denumbed, it became apparent that the demon dentist Hanff had taken a jackhammer to her jaw. Edie had called in sick to Geppetto's, which she now regretted since she realized she couldn't really afford to see her income dwindle. She still had another visit to the dentist for this tooth, and how would she pay for it if she didn't work?

Also, chances were that Judge Poitier . . . or was it Porter? . . . was going to collar his little darlin' and drag her back to Texas, so she could say goodbye to Danielle's five hundred dollars.

God, what a day! Danielle driving her crazy, G-men, going to Greta's office . . .

That office had been what threw her. The place where Greta worked was an aggressively bland dentist office, with Air Supply piped in over an unseen audio system, and *Highlights* magazines fanned out on tables for the patients, and a little poster of a bear cub hanging upside down from a tree underneath the caption "Hang in there!" Even after the receptionist—a smiley, nosy woman—had assured Edie that Greta worked there, Edie still hadn't been able to believe it. It was like imagining Snoop Doggy Dogg as a regular on "Sesame Street." So she'd asked for an appointment . . .

And then the terror had begun.

She sighed.

"Why don't you sit down?" Greta finally said without looking up.

She and Kuchen were parked on the couch in front of an old movie. The two were so stationary they seemed to be gathering dust. The last time her perambulations took her past the couch, Edie felt the urge to poke Greta to see if she was still alive.

"I can't sit down," she said, throwing an annoyed glance at the television. *To Have and Have Not* was on. "Besides, I've seen that one a million times."

"It is very good, I think. Humphrey Bogart was oddly good looking. And the woman with him is very funny. Like a cat."

The woman with him? Was Greta trying to yank her chain? "Don't you know who that is?"

"No, I started watching in the middle."

Irritation percolated inside Edie. "That's your old buddy, Lauren Bacall."

Greta leaned forward. "No kidding!" A sharp laugh escaped her.

Edie let out a strangled yell.

"Vat is the matter?" Greta asked her. "You act like you are sitting on tacks."

Forget the fact that Edie's tooth was throbbing; just being around Greta needled her nerves. "I'm waiting for Danielle to get back. Don't you understand? Her dad is probably trying to get her to go home with him."

Greta nodded. "To Texas."

"Yes! We were a big help, both of us cursing and me with my flop sweats and Barbara Wawa voice. You fighting with your boyfriend out on the street."

"Ex," Greta reminded her. "And I got rid of him, didn't I?"

"I don't know. Did you?"

"I told him that the FBI came by today looking for him. He won't be back here again."

Edie frowned. "Why would he think the FBI would be looking for him?"

Greta shrugged noncommittally.

Great. "Maybe Danielle's father was right to come after her. He can save her from the likes of us."

Greta blinked at her for a moment, then swung her attention back to the screen. Lauren Bacall was singing her last song.

Edie couldn't believe it. "You don't even care, do you?"

"What?"

"That Danielle might have her arm twisted into leaving New York."

"This is better, maybe," Greta said after some thought. "Danielle in New York City is like a little lamb in the woods."

"Babe," Edie corrected.

Greta looked startled. "What?"

"The phrase is *babe* in the woods."

Her blond brows drew together. "Babe . . . as in *baby?*"

"Yes. 'Babe in the woods.' It's a common English expression."

"Why would there be a baby in the woods?"

"Why would there be a sheep?" Edie countered. "Sheep live in meadows."

"Sheep makes more sense than baby."

Edie couldn't believe they were even arguing about this. "Greta—"

"*Ja*, okay, whatever. You are the big English expert." Then, under her breath, she muttered, "*Dumpfbacke.*"

Edie had no idea what that meant, but it didn't sound flattering. She sighed, trying to get her temper under control. "The thing is, Danielle wants to stay here. In New York."

"But she is better off with Daddy and Mommy, perhaps."

Slowly, Edie sank onto the love seat. "I'm not so sure. Didn't her dad seem a little overbearing to you?"

"Perhaps."

"Think about it. They're even doing their best to suffocate her from two thousand miles away."

Greta laughed.

"What?" Edie asked her.

"You lisped a little just then, like this evening. 'Thuffocate.' You sound like Daffy Duck."

"Greta, I was talking about Danielle! This is serious."

Her roommate actually weighed the situation for a moment. "You ask me to cry tears for a girl with the whole world on her feet? Well, okay. I have some sympathy, sure. But she is still better off than some." Her jaw set so tightly it twitched. "There are people without parents, rich or poor."

"Oh, sure. There are people with all sorts of problems. But that doesn't mean Danielle doesn't have troubles, too."

Walter Brennan was onscreen now, and Greta took a moment to watch his exit before answering. "Some people long to have someone who loves them to run home to."

Something in her voice caught Edie's attention. Edie gaped at her, beginning to have a inkling of understanding. "Your parents are gone?"

When Greta swung her gaze her way, the sharpness in those blue eyes was startling. "Gone, *ja*. Both. Since I am seventeen."

For a moment Edie didn't know how to respond. She thought almost guiltily of her kind, supportive, undemanding parents in Massachusetts. She hadn't been able to spend Christmas with them this past year because she was doing an off-off-Broadway production of *Heartbreak House*. They had been so happy for her, they hadn't given her any guilt for missing the holiday. And on the day after Christmas, her mom and dad and Douglas had comprised one quarter of the audience on what turned out to be the second night of a six-night run.

"I'm sorry. You must miss them," Edie said.

She shrugged. "I don't dwell. I am not an overly sentimental person."

No kidding. This was the woman who had threatened to send her cat to the shelter when it became inconvenient.

Threatened to, Edie realized. For the first time she wondered what Greta would *really* have done with Kuchen if Edie had stuck to her guns. As far as she could tell, Kuchen was one of the most pampered kitties on the planet.

Edie regarded Greta in silence for a moment. "Is that why you came here?" Edie asked. "To America, I mean?"

"*Ja*, I came here shortly after the accident." In answer to the curiosity in Edie's eyes, she added, "It was a car accident. I have an aunt in Cleveland, so I go there."

So how did she end up in New York? Edie wasn't sure she should ask questions. Greta probably didn't want to talk about it.

Still, she couldn't help commenting, "It must have been difficult, being so young."

Greta lifted her shoulders. "Life is not a luxury cruise, that's for sure. But I don't help, do I? I never do." She looked sheepishly at Edie. "I am sorry I said you sounded like Daffy Duck."

"That's okay."

"I am sorry for more than that. For those references."

"It doesn't matter now."

Greta gazed at her hard, obviously trying to ascertain how much of Edie's absolution came from pity. But did it matter? For whatever reason, a little of Edie's animosity toward her had seeped away.

"Thank you," Greta said.

Edie lifted her shoulders in mute answer. It seemed suddenly as if some kind of détente had been reached, yet all she felt was discomfort. "Aren't you going out tonight?" she asked Greta.

She made a face Edie couldn't interpret and flipped the channel to the Food Network. "No."

"Danielle said you've been home a lot this past week."

"That's right."

They watched the end of a barbecue special, and were halfway through "Emeril Live" when they heard Danielle's key in the door. Greta quickly snapped off the television with the remote and jumped up, almost as if she were as nervous as Edie to see what had happened with Danielle and her dad. They both gazed expectantly toward the door.

Danielle, looking pale, came in clutching a stack of white to-go boxes. "Hey, I brought ya'll dessert. Chocolate mousse cake and cheesecake with blueberries."

Edie dutifully took the boxes, which she put on the coffee table. Much as she wanted to devour that cheesecake, she kept her eyes on Danielle. "Thanks, I guess this is care of Judge . . . what *is* your name, anyway?"

Danielle sighed. "It's Porter."

Edie folded her arms. "Not Poitier?"

"I was going to change my name. Is that a crime?"

"No—but it does make me wonder if this isn't the most truth-deprived apartment in New York City. Doesn't anyone tell the truth about themselves anymore?"

Greta and Danielle stared dully at her.

Danielle sighed. "Well, never mind. It doesn't matter now *what* my name is. As far as my dad's concerned, I might as well have changed it to Mudd."

"What happened?"

Danielle staggered into the living room, dropped her purse on the floor, and flopped down on the love seat. "He tried to get me to go home."

"Natch. And what did you say?"

"I said no."

"And what did he say?" Greta asked.

If Danielle was surprised to see Greta showing an interest in her, she didn't comment on it. "He offered to buy me my dream car. In fact, he said he'd already ordered it."

"Hmph!" Greta said indignantly. "A car!"

Edie swallowed. Maybe Greta still didn't understand the American love affair with the auto. "What's your dream car?"

"A powder blue Mini with a white top," Danielle said, her voice breaking.

"Oh." That was some mighty cruel blackmail. Even Edie felt a little sick.

"I turned it down, of course," Danielle said. "I let him know that I want to be independent."

"Good!" Edie declared. "And he knew you really meant it?"

Danielle slumped. "Oh yeah!"

"Then what's the problem?"

"I made him understand so well that he is henceforth cutting off all funds from the Danielle charitable trust."

"You mean . . . ?"

"No money," Danielle declared, her voice beginning to fray with hysteria. "None. *Nada*."

"Oh."

Greta and Edie exchanged concerned glances. Silence settled

on them all like a shroud. It was as if something had just died, and that something was Danielle's bank account.

Poor Danielle looked as if someone had zapped her with a stun gun. "Now I'm going to have to find someone to give me a *job*. What kind of fool would do that?"

Edie laughed. "Oh, come on. There's all sorts of stuff you can do. You've had jobs before."

"Sure. Summer jobs working for friends of my parents. Paid internships."

Greta waved her hand dismissively. "Any idiot can make a living. You have nothing to worry about."

"Didn't you tell me you worked in a law office?" Edie asked.

Danielle shuddered. "I hated it. It was so boring."

Edie smirked. "Unlike waitressing, which is nonstop excitement. What did you do at this law office, exactly?"

"Well . . . I took orders every morning and ran down for cappuccinos."

"Hm. What about office work? Did you answer phones?"

"Not if I could help it."

"Well, you must have done something."

"Not really. I ran errands and typed."

"Bingo!" Edie exclaimed. "You can type!"

Danielle looked startled. "So?"

"So, that's a skill. We can go out right now, get the paper, and see what we can find for you. I bet there's all sorts of stuff, really. This town runs on secretarial work." Before Danielle could grunt with dread, she added, "And some executive secretaries get paid *a lot*." She shot a visual nudge Greta's way.

Greta managed to wipe the horror off her face. "*Jawohl!* You could be sitting on a land mine."

"Gold mine," Edie corrected quickly. "Besides, you've been cooped up here too much anyway. I bet you'll like having a job again. You'll get to meet people."

Greta snorted with laughter.

Edie tossed a glare her way.

Danielle, who had just been sitting there like a lump for several minutes, slowly began to perk back to life. "You're right. It *will* be better to get out. Like today, when I met Wilson."

Edie frowned. "Who?"

"Wilson Pickett. He's a musician . . . well, sort of."

"Wait," Edie said. "You met a musician today? Where?"

"Brooklyn."

"What were you doing in Brooklyn?" Edie asked.

Danielle blushed. "Well, I sort of caught the wrong train."

Edie shook her head. She knew she should have watched to make sure she went toward the right platform! "And you met this guy on the train?" She clucked maternally. "Oh, Danielle. That's lesson number one of life in New York: Beware of creeps trying to pick up women on public transportation! That's only romantic in movies."

"He didn't try to pick me up. And it wasn't on the train."

Danielle told them the story of following the cute, tall, red-headed guy into the falafel joint, and how they had spent part of the afternoon strolling on the promenade, then over the Brooklyn Bridge. Greta and Edie sat and listened, rapt. To hear Danielle tell it, the guy, Wilson, actually sounded like he was good looking, charming, and funny. And he'd taken Danielle's phone number and promised to call her the next day.

"Unbelievable!" Edie declared when the story was finished.

Danielle looked alarmed. "What?"

"You found a guy practically the first moment you stepped out of the apartment."

"There is something wrong with him," Greta guessed.

"Well, sure," Edie agreed, "but it's the ease with which she found him that's so astounding."

"Mark my words." Greta wagged her finger knowingly at Danielle. "There are no completely sane men here. You vill see."

Edie had to agree. "This Wilson guy might *seem* like a prince, but he's probably got a fatal flaw. They always do."

"He won't call," Greta predicted.

"Or you'll go out together sometime and bump into his parole officer," Edie said.

Greta grinned knowingly at Edie. "Or he'll start asking you if you are into foursomes."

"No kidding!" Edie laughed. It had been a while since she had been able to compare notes with someone. "How about this:

You'll get on his computer one night and discover he frequents Web sites for adult diaper fetishists."

Greta shook her head ruefully. "Or out from the blue he'll dump you for a naked midget."

"Or go to Uzbekistan," Edie said, growing depressed.

"Wait! Wait!" Danielle gaped at them as if they were both off balance. "Look, I don't *want* to go out with Wilson. He's just a guy."

They blinked at her. "But you said he was cute."

"And nice," Greta said.

"And impetuous!"

"You talked to him for three whole hours."

"He spent a whole afternoon with you," Edie gushed. "That's so sweet!"

"But I'm not that attracted to him," Danielle insisted. "He's cute, but he's just a friend."

Edie and Greta exchanged incredulous looks. "You're just going to let him go to waste?"

Danielle rolled her eyes. "Ya'll were just telling me that you were sure he was probably a closet sicko!"

"Well, yeah," Edie admitted, "but you've got to find out."

Danielle shook her head. "I didn't come to New York so I could settle for a guy like I could find just any ol' where. I want to go out with somebody really great. A go-getter. Wilson's the kind of guy you bring home to watch videos and eat pizzas."

"Grab him," Greta advised.

"Or someone else will."

Danielle laughed. "Someone else is welcome to him. It's not like there aren't a thousand other fish in the sea, guys."

Greta and Edie both gawked at her, then at each other.

"Have I been paddling around the wrong ocean?" Edie asked Greta.

Chapter 16

REJECTION

Two days later when Edie first opened the front door, she feared the apartment had been burgled. Either that or a retail hurricane had blown through. Shoe boxes littered the floor, which was so blanketed with tissue paper, she couldn't see the parquet pattern. Kuchen had squeezed herself inside a shopping bag and was stalking the clutter, her sizable rump twitching. There were clothes everywhere: On the couch. Draped over the Chinatown screen. Hanging on the opened balcony double doors. Hanging on the balcony itself. Summer dresses in shimmering silks, blouses, and shorts so tiny Edie couldn't believe a grown-up rear end could fit into them.

She inspected a price tag on a cap sleeved striped T-shirt with a tag from Barney's and let out a low whistle. Eighty-nine dollars? Good grief! If all this stuff was worth that much, they were going to have to take out apartment insurance.

Just then, snuffles came from the other side of Danielle's screen.

Edie froze. Should she say something?

"Danielle?"

The room fell conspicuously quiet. Edie tiptoed over the riches strewn across the floor and peeked over the screen. Her roommate's body was flung across the inflatable bed; her mouth was puckered in an attempt not to cry. Or to cry without making any noise.

"Danielle, what's the matter?"

She shot up to sitting and rubbed her palms across her soggy cheeks. "Nothing." Her voice was a reedy attempt at stoicism.

"C'mon. There must be something wrong. The apartment . . ."

"I'm sorry, Edie. I'll clean it up. I was just trying to . . . trying to . . ." Her breath sucked in a series of sobs. ". . . save myself!"

The floodgates opened, and all Edie could do was stand back and let Danielle cry it out for a moment. And could that girl cry! Streams of tears poured down her cheeks. Torrents, even. After a few minutes it became a little worrisome. Much more of this and Edie feared Danielle would float away on her blue rubber bed.

She couldn't imagine what had gone wrong. Danielle *looked* great. She wore a crisp navy-and-white striped linen sleeveless dress and stockings. She was shoeless, but Edie had seen a pair amongst the clutter in the living room, probably where Danielle had kicked them off after coming in.

"What happened?" she asked when the flood had abated a little.

Danielle swiped at her eyes with the nearest cloth, which was her bedspread. "What *didn't* happen?" She shot to her feet. "I was so sure of myself! Right off the bat I got this interview with a temp agency today. They wanted me to come in right away. So, you know, I was feeling pretty good. Pretty sure of myself. When I went with my dad to the airport, I was all, 'Put your wallet away, Dad, I don't need cab fare for the trip back. I can manage.' Ha! That's a laugh. I went straight to my interview, which was a . . . a . . ."

"A disappointment?" Edie ventured.

"A disaster!" Danielle started pacing, kicking aside shoe boxes in her path. "I met this woman, the personnel director, named Trina Schwartz. She was sooo judgmental and she just reeked of skank drugstore perfume—it was giving me a headache, I swear. She just kept looking down her nose at me, like I was this worm on the pavement."

"That's what people like her are paid to do."

"She acted like my resume was just worthless."

"Well, you did say your experience was mostly in vanity jobs."

Danielle stiffened defensively. "So? *She* didn't know that!

Trina Schwartz said she *might* be able to place me in a lowly clerical position, if I could score high enough on my typing test."

"You can type. You type all the time."

Danielle's lip trembled, and she lifted her fist to her mouth to compose herself. "Forty-eight words per minute."

"That's good!"

"With thirty-six mistakes."

"Oh. Not so good."

Danielle erupted again. "It was so unfair! They made me take the test on a typewriter. A *typewriter!* They probably pulled it out of mothballs just to mess with my head! I mean, what's the point? I'm so used to being able to go back and correct things, and what difference do a few piddly mistakes make anyway? As long as you get it right eventually."

Edie sighed. "So it was 'don't call us, we'll call you.' "

"Actually, coming from Trina Schwartz it was more like 'drop dead.' But I figured, *screw it.* One interview, who cares? I can interview with another temp agency. Besides, I'm a writer. Getting published is my goal, not some crappy temp job." She grabbed a manila envelope off the coffee table and thrust it at Edie. "Then I came home and *that* was in the mailbox."

Edie looked at the envelope addressed to Danielle in her own loopy handwriting and knew immediately what the package contained. It screamed rejection.

"Read it," Danielle said.

With no enthusiasm, Edie extracted the thin short story manuscript along with the rejection letter from an editorial assistant named Jennifer Poon. Edie smirked. What a name! Danielle could take consolation from that, at least. Jennifer might be doling out pain now, but she had probably received her own share of humiliation on school playgrounds growing up. Edie read the letter, which was turning down a story called *Hello, New York*. She could tell why Danielle was upset. These were not the words you wanted to greet you at the end of a hard day.

"She returned it so fast the ink barely had a chance to dry. I bet she didn't even read it."

Edie cast about for something positive to say. "At least they wrote you a real letter and didn't just send a form reject."

"I almost wish she would have just stuck in a slip! That at least wouldn't have been so brutal."

"There *is* some withering language in here," Edie admitted. There was no way to gloss over words like "trite," "cliché," and "facile." "On the other hand, look. It's this editor—this Mr. Picard—who's saying all the negative stuff. Jennifer Poon is being fairly encouraging, I think. And she's the editorial assistant, so they probably just tell her what to reject. She might have liked the story and is unable to say so. She seems to know you well. If she's ever promoted, she might be able to help you."

Danielle crossed her arms. "*You* read some of my stuff, Edie. Did you think it was any good?"

Edie swallowed. It wasn't that she'd disliked Danielle's stories; on the other hand, she could see where Jennifer Poon was coming from. Danielle was young, and her stories didn't have a lot of depth. They were just entertaining little yarns with some fun dialogue. "I thought they were cute," Edie said. "But I'm not that familiar with contemporary short stories. Maybe you should take a class or something. Get input that could actually help you."

Danielle let out a lengthy sigh.

It was then that Edie realized her roommate wasn't searching for honesty; she just wanted someone to stand up and salute the monumental pain she was going through. Edie, who felt like the rejection queen herself, could sympathize. She pushed the manila envelope aside. "This must have been an awful day for you. Your dad leaving, the interview, the letter. Someone should hand out medals for surviving days like this. A Purple Heart for crappy days."

Danielle shrugged; she looked very small amongst all her shopping treasures. Edie still couldn't figure out what the mess was all about.

"Let me make you a cup of coffee," she said.

Danielle exhaled listlessly. "It's too hot."

"Lemonade?"

"Well . . ."

Edie crossed to the kitchen, tossed some ice into two glasses, and splashed some lemonade into them. It was getting a little steamy out there. June was almost over. Still, even though the icky heat was on its way, she couldn't wait for July, when Aurora would be back from Toronto. She missed having her old friend to kvetch with.

"My day wasn't so great, either," Edie said, trying to channel Danielle's thoughts in another direction. "I had to go to Dr. Hanff again and get a crown fitted."

"And then you come home to"—Danielle surveyed the destruction—"this."

Edie doubtfully eyed all the stuff. "What were you doing?"

"Trying to salvage my Discover card. Now that I'm broke, I need to return enough stuff to bring one credit card down to a zero balance. The trouble is, my receipts are everywhere—I'm not very organized, I'm afraid. So I just pulled everything out and I'm trying to match what I bought at different places with the receipts I can find, and see if the stuff I need to return still has tags. . . ."

Edie frowned. "How much do you need to return to get a zero balance?"

"Four hundred and thirty-eight dollars' worth."

Edie gulped. She hardly bought four hundred and thirty-eight dollars' worth of clothes in an entire year. And Danielle had managed that and more—a lot more—in only two weeks!

That must have been some allowance Daddy was doling out.

Understanding the problem now, she eyed the loot with renewed interest. "What you need to do is pick out the high-dollar items and the really impractical stuff."

"If something were impractical, I wouldn't buy it."

Edie picked up a wispy orange bikini with little black James Bond silhouettes all over it. She quirked a brow at her roommate. "Danielle. I can almost guarantee you that you will never wear this."

"I *love* that! What if I go to the beach?"

"Then you'll probably want to run out and buy yourself a new swimsuit."

"But it was just sixty dollars."

"Good! Only three hundred and seventy-eight dollars to go." Edie bit her lip. "What we need is a big-ticket item. What's the most expensive thing here?"

Danielle searched through her treasures until her gaze alit on a shoebox. "Those."

Edie snatched up the box and looked at the sandals inside. She gasped. They were four-inch stiletto-heeled Pradas with multi-colored straps. "How much?"

"It doesn't matter," Danielle said, tugging at the box. "I'm not returning them."

Edie held firm. "How much?"

"Three hundred and seventy-nine," Danielle said under her breath.

The number hit Edie like a punch to the gut. Her fingers loosened just out of shock, and Danielle darted out of her reach with the box. Three hundred and seventy-nine smackers.

She *should* have let her pay six hundred in rent.

"Anyway, it doesn't matter how much they cost," Danielle said. "I put these on my Bloomingdale's card, not my Discover."

"You're going to have to pay that bill, too."

Danielle shook her head. "No, it's a new account—I got ten percent off my initial purchase!—and I'm going to get an extra thirty days to pay. Anything could happen in thirty days."

"Yes—you could be poorer than you ever dreamed. Take them back."

"You're heartless," Danielle said resentfully, but she stomped over and put the box next to the shopping bag with the bikini in it. "How will I ever get a job if I have to run around looking like a pauper?"

"You couldn't wear strappy stilettos to a job interview anyway . . . unless it was for a job requiring you to carry a beeper and call yourself Emmanuelle."

They labored for another half hour, whittling down Danielle's recent buys to a sleeveless dress, a couple of blouses, and two pairs of almost-practical shoes. The return pile was several times higher than the keep pile, which Edie deemed a personal triumph.

"Girl, you have a long day of standing in return lines ahead of you."

The doorbell buzzed, and Edie trekked down to the door. Without enthusiasm. At this point she wasn't expecting a lot of visitors. It couldn't even be a package delivery—an event that always perked her up—because she'd been too broke to order anything lately. (Yet now a little devil in her ear—with a distinctly Texas twang—was whispering something about opening a Bloomingdale's charge account. *Ten percent off the initial purchase . . . sixty days to pay . . .*)

It would be so easy to give in. She hardly ever charged anything, and she was still always strapped for cash. What good had it done her to be so frugal all her life?

Dear God. Danielle was getting to her. What was it about seeing the wretched spoils of someone else's shopping spree that made it so tempting to run financially amok, too?

When she unlatched and pulled the door open, she forgot all about her dreams of a wild spending jag. A tall guy with coppery hair was leaning in the doorway, holding two large paper cups with lids. And he was smiling at her as if he knew her.

"I'm here to see Danielle."

"Oh—of course."

"Let me guess. Edie?"

She laughed. There was just something about his face that brought that response. She didn't even have to ask who *he* was. "Wilson?"

He seemed surprised. "How did you know?"

"You're the only person Danielle knows in New York." Not to mention, this guy had the kind of face any woman would feel comfortable following into a falafel shop.

"Hope I'm not showing up at a bad time. I called earlier, but there was no answer at the number she gave me."

That was weird. Edie gestured for him to follow her up. "It's been a sort of rough day."

He snapped his fingers. "No problem. Crises are my speciality."

"I hope you mean getting rid of them."

He did. The moment he stepped into the apartment, the atmosphere changed. Gloom and anxiety lifted. He'd brought mochaccino milkshakes from the Last Drop, and gallantly offered to split his with Edie.

"No, thank you." She was busy inspecting the answering machine. It was turned on. "I can't understand why it wouldn't have picked up if you called," she told Wilson.

"Oh!" Danielle exclaimed. "It's probably filled up."

Edie gaped at it. *"Filled up?"* In the two years she'd had this particular machine, that had never happened.

Danielle started fiddling with buttons. "Sorry, I sometimes forget to erase my old messages. Well, a lot of the time I do. Anyway, on some of these things it's hard to tell if you're running out of space. You know how it is."

Edie was flabbergasted. The first time her machine had overloaded, and hardly anyone had called her in weeks.

A glass appeared under her nose. Wilson had split his milkshake with her after all. "Everybody needs punching up this time of day, and cold caffeine is just the ticket," he said.

"Speaking of this time of day . . ." Danielle raised a perfectly plucked brow in mirthful suspicion. "It's not even five o'clock, Wilson. Don't you ever work?"

He lifted his head proudly. "I'll have you know I've already played 'The Beer Barrel Polka' fifteen times today. *And* I'm working the graveyard shift at Ramsey, Lombard, and Gaines. I switched shifts with another proofreader."

Another night worker—a kindred spirit. "What are your hours?" Edie asked him.

"Five P.M. to one-thirty."

Edie immediately offered to return her half of the milkshake. "You need this more than I do."

He waved a hand. "I'll never miss it. We proofreaders swill coffee all night long. Ramsey, Lombard, and Gaines is hypertension central."

They all floated back to the living room area and plopped down on Greta's furniture—Edie and Wilson perched on the couch, and Danielle sprawled across the love seat with Kuchen.

The cat was purring up a storm and slowly began nosing her way toward the milkshake glass in Danielle's hand.

"So what's this I hear about a crisis?" Wilson asked.

Danielle heaved a dramatic sigh and unloaded her woe on him, detailing her day from when her alarm clock went off this morning to the moment Wilson arrived at their doorstep. Edie could understand why Wilson said crises were his specialty. The man was a wonder; the whole time Danielle was nattering on, he leaned toward her from the couch, his whole body tensed with interest. He occasionally laughed at Danielle, and even took a few sarcastic verbal jabs at the self-inflicted folly of her financial situation, but on the whole, he was a model friend/confessor. And his eyes never left Danielle. Not once.

He's already in love with her. Edie marveled at Danielle's luck. Wilson not only oozed compassion and "nice," he was really handsome in a sort of understated Eric Stoltzy kind of way. She was amazed Danielle couldn't see it . . . but she probably would. Men like Wilson never went unclaimed in New York City for long.

Edie tried to be magnanimous about the young potential lovers. After all, she had Douglas—or the idea of Douglas. He might have left her in a romantic limbo, but at least she had his apartment. Still, she went to sleep each night haunted by all the questions he'd left her with. What had happened? She knew they weren't exactly alike, but they had gotten along, hadn't they? Part of her wanted to take him at his word and believe that he was going to come waltzing back in their apartment door someday.

The realist in her told her she was dreaming.

"Forget typing," Wilson was telling Danielle. "Forget Trina Schwartz. It's simple. Become a proofreader."

Danielle shook her head. "I couldn't do that."

"Why not?" he asked. "The pay is good and there are plenty of jobs. That's one thing lawyers really excel at—cranking out paperwork through good times and bad. Banks use proofreaders, too—and they're never short of business, either. They're all parasites. You just need to learn how to be a parasite on the parasites."

Danielle mulled this over. "But don't you need special skills?"

"You have to know proofreader marks and a few other things, but that's a snap. I could teach you that stuff in a few hours. The dicey part is that you have to be a good speller."

Danielle brightened. "I can spell!"

"Really well?"

"I won the county spelling bee in eighth grade!"

"What about legal terms? All the firms give spelling tests, and they pull out their trickiest, most obscure words to weed people out."

"Bring it on! I soaked up all that junk at the law firm in Amarillo. I can spell 'jactitation,' 'ab initio,' and even 'abbacinare.'"

He beamed. "There. You're in like Flynn. And once you past your test with the agency, I can recommend you to the personnel office at Ramsey."

"How much does it pay?" Danielle asked.

"Well, it depends on your experience and what shift you take. The beginning day shift usually starts at fifteen dollars an hour, but tonight I'm earning $21.50."

Edie nearly fell off her seat. "Maybe I should stop waiting tables!" She frowned. "Except I *don't* know how to spell "abba"-whatever." She didn't even know what it meant. "I'm guessing it doesn't have anything to do with a Swedish rock group."

"*Abbacinare*," Danielle said. "It's a medieval torture method."

Wilson weighed in on the Abba-torture connection. "I suppose if a person hated the song 'Dancing Queen' enough . . .'"

Edie laughed. "Who would ever need to know how to spell that?"

"Sleazy people who like to win arguments by confounding people with arcane language," Wilson said. "Lawyers."

Danielle jumped up suddenly and did a zestful *Zorba the Greek* dance maneuver over to her shopping bags. "I'm gonna be a proofreader!" she singsonged as she skimmed along the line of her items to be returned. "Fifteen dollars an hour!"

"What are you doing?" Edie asked her, alarmed.

Her roommate blinked at her. "Fifteen dollars an hour? *Please!*

That means the cute bathing suit would only cost me four hours of work."

Apparently not even willing to consider the possibility of her chickens not hatching, Danielle dipped into a shopping bag and gleefully rescued her James Bond bikini.

Chapter 17

JULY

Aurora got back in town a few days later and called to tell Edie that she simply *had* to go to the Carnegie Deli.

She always did this. The minute she returned, even after a weekend in the Hamptons, she had to go running off to a New York City cultural (preferably food-related) landmark. Edie supposed this was her friend's twist on the traditional kissing-the-ground routine. Which, considering the things you saw on the sidewalks in Manhattan, was probably much smarter than putting her mouth anywhere near the pavement.

But part of Edie believed that Aurora just enjoyed watching *her* eat high-calorie foods. This was the routine: Aurora would talk Edie into ordering something typically New York—an over-stuffed, greasy pastrami sandwich, say—but then when the waiter came around to her, Aurora herself would order a coffee, protesting that, tempted as she was, pastrami just had *too much fat*. So Edie would end up gobbling down Aurora's artery-clogging homecoming meal under Aurora's wistful yet pitying gaze.

This morning it was a cheese blintz that she was eating for Aurora, while Aurora gulped black coffee and told her about Adrian Lyne and Ray Liotta, and how both of them agreed that Aurora was going to be the *next big thing*. Apparently Adrian and Ray were not shy about using the words "gorgeous" and "talented." And they were confident that Aurora's role in *The Mice Will Play* was going to give her *serious buzz*.

Aurora was on her third cup of coffee—*"Solid American diner coffee, God how I missed it!"*—before she remembered to ask Edie what she was up to.

"Who was that woman who answered your phone?" she asked, apparently peeved that there were strangers hanging around Edie's apartment.

Edie tried to remember who had taken Aurora's message. "Did she sound like she was from Texas?"

"No—more like Cloris Leachman in *Young Frankenstein.*"

"That's Greta."

Aurora's mouth went slack. "Wait a sec. You have *two* people living with you?"

Edie broke away from her blintz and explained in more detail what had happened in the past month.

"Oh! Oh!" Aurora shuddered. "I feel sooo guilty. I never should have left you. I should have told Adrian, 'No, I'm sorry. I *have* to stay in New York City and screen roommate candidates for my best and oldest friend.' "

"And sacrifice all that buzz?" Edie asked incredulously.

Happily, any sarcasm that might have just accidentally on purpose crept into her tone didn't register. "You obviously needed me," Aurora said. "It sounds like you found yourself two headcases."

"They're not so bad."

Her friend blasted out a laugh. "A Lone Star powder puff princess and a compulsive liar? Please! You don't have to put on a brave face for me."

"I wouldn't."

Aurora leaned back and started toying with a fork. In the old days, at this point in the meal (that she hadn't eaten) she would have lit up a smoke. Now that that activity was prohibited, she had taken to bending flatware. "What's become of Doug the lug?"

Edie lifted her shoulders. She didn't even bother defending him. "I have no idea. I occasionally see his byline in the *Times,* but I haven't heard from him since May."

Aurora clucked sympathetically. "I knew he wouldn't come back, but I didn't want to say anything."

"As I recall, you *did* say you thought he wouldn't be back."

"Did I?" She tapped her fork nervously, then laughed. "Well, good riddance! He really screwed you over."

Pride refused to let Edie believe that. Pride, and common sense. "I really don't think he meant to. I mean, we had just moved in together. And the job just fell into his lap. He could hardly refuse something like that when they just offered it to him out of the blue."

"Why not?" Aurora asked loyally. "Why should he traipse halfway around the world when he's got you here? Life is choices, and that rat chose his job over you."

Edie couldn't believe it. A few years earlier Aurora had left a boyfriend on the day he was going into the hospital for inner ear surgery because she had been offered a part in a music video filming in Florida. This was not a proponent of self-sacrifice and Tammy Wynette–style stand-by-your-man sentimentality.

"I wouldn't have wanted him to refuse it," Edie said. Partially lying, she knew, but still able to inject a smidgen of truthfulness in what she was saying. "If he had, and regretted it, he would have grown to resent me."

Aurora eyed her skeptically. "Very grown up of you to say so."

"What's next for you?" asked Edie, eager to change the subject. "Any new projects?"

"Not yet. Noel sent me something, but it was complete garbage." Noel Sprock was their mutual agent. (Or, as Edie was beginning to think of him, the Invisible Man.)

"Some dying daughter part in a cheesy Lifetime movie," Aurora was saying. "It had one of those names like 'A Cold Spring' or 'A Warm Frost' or something like that."

"That doesn't sound so bad."

Aurora clucked her tongue. "The part was *tiny*. The daughter—Carrie or Sherry or some name like that—dies at the beginning of the movie and the grandparents take custody of her daughter, who has some awful wasting disease. The part consisted of two pages of dialogue at the beginning of the script and a couple of wordless flashbacks later on. And I wasn't even like the physical description of the character. No way would I do something like that now."

Now, when she had *buzz*.

"I showed the script to Ray when I was in Toronto and he was with me all the way. He's so smart about stuff like this! You know what he told me?"

"What?"

"He said that when you're choosing scripts, you always need to make choices that will move your career *forward*."

"Which means . . . ?"

Aurora gaped at her as if she were dense. It was a look that said *no wonder I'm so much more successful!*

Or maybe Edie was just being paranoid.

"It means that you don't choose projects that are going to move your career backward," Aurora explained.

"What about side-to-side?" Edie asked.

Aurora skewered her with an impatient gaze. "Ray's really smart. You have to be to get ahead in the film business. And I'm telling you, after my hard work in *The Mice Will Play*, a part like Carrie-Sherry would really be beneath me."

Edie's brow puckered. Aurora might turn up her nose at it, but the role certainly wouldn't be beneath *her*. Why hadn't Noel sent her the script?

The waiter came by to inquire, brusquely, if there was anything else they wanted. When they hesitated, he slapped their check down on the table. This was just as well, Edie decided. An idea was forming in her mind, and she didn't want to give herself time to think twice. She goggled at her watch. "Oh! I didn't realize how late it was," she said, mentally calculating the fastest way to dash over to Noel's office. "I've got an appointment at eleven."

Aurora brightened. "It's so good to be back in the hustle-bustle again!"

Edie reached for the bill.

"My treat," Aurora said, challenging her.

"Don't be silly. You didn't eat anything."

Her friend drew back, smiling as if in surprise. "You're right! I almost forgot. I'm full just from watching you scarf down that *huge* plate of food. I can practically feel your blintz on my hips."

Edie grabbed her pocketbook and headed for the cash register.

"Thanks for the coffee," Aurora said when they were back out on the street. "I'm gonna have a get-together at my place sometime, if I can get it straightened up."

That meant she would never have a get-together at her place. "Great," Edie said, waving as they parted ways at the corner of Seventh Avenue. "Give me a ring."

"Or we could catch a movie!" Aurora yelled after her.

"'Kay!"

Edie's heart felt like it was pumping double-time. Maybe it was. The combination of July heat and midtown bumper-to-bumper traffic made her feel as if she were sprinting into an exhaust pipe. She'd always heard that cold weather caused the most deaths, but to her *this* was heart attack weather.

And it didn't help that her blood pressure was spiking with anger at the idea that Noel had forgotten about her. She was becoming so accustomed to accepting Aurora's meteoric rise, she'd forgotten that she herself was just as good an actress. Aurora had been lucky and hardworking, but she had also been good at minding her P's: pushiness and persistence.

Meanwhile, Edie had fallen into the worst trap for an actress—brooding on what hadn't happened in her career, instead of looking for the possibilities that might be out there.

As Ray Liotta—brilliant man—would have said, she hadn't been moving *forward.*

Artists Unlimited, the agency Noel worked for—which wasn't CAA by a long shot, but still respectable—was housed smack in the middle of Fortieth Street, in a gray stone building with windows that looked as if they hadn't been washed since V-E Day. The glass was brown and streaky. You'd think that people who lopped fifteen percent off of paychecks of Broadway regulars and minor movie stars could afford to get their windows cleaned once in a blue moon.

She took the elevator up five flights and pushed open the heavy wood door to the waiting room. "I need to see Noel," she announced to the woman sitting at the desk.

The woman's title was probably receptionist, but her job was actually akin to that of a doorman at a crowded nightclub. She wasn't there to receive people but to keep them out. Even the whiniest and the pushiest. "Do you have an appointment?"

"I'm one of his clients."

"Do you have an appointment?"

Edie figured she was here as an actress, so she acted. "Yes. Eleven o'clock."

The receptionist looked down at a book in front of her on which names and times were scrawled in tiny writing. "Your name?"

"Edie Amos."

The expected frown drew across the woman's face. "Are you sure it's for today?"

Edie didn't blink. "Of course. Isn't Noel here?"

"He's in . . . but he doesn't have you down."

"But I just spoke to him on the phone!"

Her nemesis drew back. "Oh! Was this recently?" She picked up the phone and called Noel's extension, but obviously he wasn't picking up.

"This morning," Edie lied.

"Just a moment." The receptionist got up and bustled toward the back offices.

That was all the opening Edie needed. She crept along right behind the woman until the moment when she tapped on Noel's door and cracked it open. At that point, Edie pushed in from behind.

Noel, who was sitting at his desk, thoroughly absorbed in his computer, jumped when he saw the two women enter his office. Edie felt her arms being seized by the receptionist, who was surprisingly strong. No doubt Artists Unlimited paid her dues at the Iron Man gym as a necessary business expense.

"Noel, I need to talk to you!" Edie called out.

"I'm sorry, Mr. Sprock!"

He leapt to his feet. "What's going on? *Edie?*"

"I need to talk to you about *A Late Frost*," she blurted out.

His face registered utter confusion. "About what?"

"I'll call security," the receptionist said, tugging Edie toward the door.

Noel laughed. "No, no—now, there's no need for that. I'm glad to see Edie. As always."

The grip loosened and Edie almost fell forward.

"Would you like some coffee?" Noel asked her.

"No, thanks."

"Well then, sit down." He tossed the receptionist an appreciative but dismissive glance. "Thanks, Kate. I think I'll be safe."

Kate scowled in Edie's direction and backed out the door.

Noel looked at Edie and shook his head. "Good grief!" he exclaimed in a show of befuddled amusement. In central casting terms, Noel was Stanley Tucci all the way, from the not unattractive male pattern baldness to his intelligent eaglelike brown eyes. "Am I Howard Hughes all of a sudden, that you have to break my door down to get to me? Just call, Edie."

"I called you twice a few weeks ago and I never heard back."

His brow furrowed into painstaking lines as he stretched his memory. "Really?"

"Besides, I was in the neighborhood."

He sat down at his desk and tapped a pencil against his Rolodex. "Well, great! What can I do for you?"

"*A Warm Spring,*" she said.

He squinted at her, clueless. "Come again?"

"I was just having brunch with Aurora and she was telling me that you sent her a script for a TV movie called *A Warm Spring* or something like that, for a character named Terry."

"Carrie," he said. "And the movie had nothing to do with warm springs or early frosts. It was called *Cruel April.*"

"Fine," Edie said. "Whatever. The point is, why didn't you think of me?"

He stiffened into a defensive posture. "Because it wasn't right for you."

"How could it be right for Aurora but completely wrong for me?" Edie asked. "We're the same age, same body type."

"But you haven't had the same experience," Noel shot back.

"She said the part was small . . ."

He shook his head. "It was actually a pivotal part, but believe me, you weren't right for it. Carrie was supposed to be ugly. She kills herself in the first scene."

"*Ugly?*" Edie regarded him with disbelief. "Then why would they want Aurora?"

"Because Aurora's almost a name. The director saw an early

cut of her playing the crazy girl in the Susan Sarandon thing, and he thought that if Aurora would do it, they would change the part to be not ugly. But nobody *knows* you. The casting director would take one look at your headshot and call me to tell me that you're not ugly enough."

She sank into a chair. Not ugly enough! Life was so unfair.

He leaned across his desk. "Edie, listen. I thought you were more mature than this. You can't get yourself into a twist over parts you know nothing about. That's no good."

"I just don't seem to be getting anywhere," she said, hating the whine in her voice. "I want to *do* something. Otherwise I feel like I'm just going to fizzle."

"Have you taken a class lately?"

She sighed. "I don't want to take a class. I want to work. I'll do anything—you know I will. Off-off-off-Broadway, dog food commercials, you name it."

"Okay. I can see you're motivated. That's good."

"It's not good if there's no work. Isn't there anything I can do to improve my chances? Should I lose weight, or get a new hairdo, or new headshots?"

"It couldn't hurt," Noel said.

Couldn't hurt? What encouragement!

That was the trouble with being an actor. There were no steps you could take to guarantee success. A person in a normal business got a degree, then a first job, then maybe did a few extra things to make himself look good so he could be promoted, and so on. But schools pumped out trained actors now like so many widgets from a factory. Thousands more than the world would ever need. And getting one job didn't necessarily guarantee you would get another—not when there were a hundred actresses for every available part. There were no night courses that would give you an edge, no dress-for-success seminars. There was only whim, and chance, and things you could do that *couldn't hurt.*

But that's the way it was. She hadn't decided to become an actress because she craved job security.

She stood up. "Okay, Noel. Sorry I busted in on you."

He followed her to the door and put a paternal hand on her shoulder. "Don't apologize for showing drive. That's what it takes."

She laughed. "What it takes to get you thrown out by security guards, you mean."

"I'll do what I can," he promised. "Have a little faith."

She eyed him doubtfully. Edie was beginning to suspect men told you to have a little faith when they secretly meant that you would most likely never lay eyes on them again.

Chapter 18

DAZZLED

Wilson nudged Danielle with his foot. "Hey! Wake up. We're almost done."

Danielle grudgingly fought her way back to wakefulness; she desperately needed something to prop her eyelids open with. She hadn't realized that she had dozed off over a brief for *Breyer v. Hampstead*, but neither was she surprised. It wasn't that she was that tired, it was that her job was that tedious.

She and Wilson had been slouched in chairs in an unused office at Ramsey, Lombard, and Gaines for hours now doing something called "double slugging." In a sort of spoken shorthand, one proofreader read aloud the editing and proofing changes marked on an original brief while the second proofreader followed on a printout of the corrected draft to make sure all changes were included. Welcome to Snoozeville.

She struggled to lever herself back up to sitting, but the sweaty backs of her legs were stuck to the chair's leather upholstery. The maneuver required more energy than she was willing to expend, so she just settled for stretching her arms. She made a mental note to wear a longer skirt tomorrow. If there ever was a tomorrow.

It was beginning to seem possible that today would never end. "What time is it?"

"Almost four."

She could have wept. "Over an hour to go?"

"The final stretch." He said this as if he expected the hour to fly swiftly and painlessly by, when to her it felt like an eternity yawning ahead.

"They should play music in this place." Danielle reached for her coffee cup. The half-dissolved non-dairy creamer was floating around the rim in clumps. The brew was so disgusting; at the same time, she couldn't get enough of it. "Either that or they should start putting amphetamines in the coffee."

"One hour," Wilson said. "And then a friend of mine asked me if I wanted to go hear his girlfriend's band."

This news made her ears perk up. Wilson knew so many cool people. She couldn't believe he'd only been in New York a year.

"It's a dance club called the Sixth Ring," he told her. "I can't vouch for how good the music will be, but I think you'll have a good time."

"Of course!" She always had a good time. (Except when she was working.) She managed to haul her carcass to a full upright position. She loved going to clubs! Her feet started tapping in anticipation. "I need to go home to change, though."

"Okay." Wilson was used to the drill. "That'll give your roommate a chance to glare at me some more."

"Greta?" Danielle laughed. "She's okay, really. She's just going through some . . . problems right now." She didn't actually know what Greta's deal was; it seemed that overnight she had transformed herself from cranky, compulsive partyer to TV-addicted catatonic.

Wilson looked mystified. "What kind of problems require a woman to sit on her couch with an enormous cat watching 'Iron Chef' all the time?"

"She doesn't watch it all the time."

"Right. Once I caught her watching 'Date Plate.' "

"She's thinking about taking up cooking, she told me."

"*Thinking* about it? What's there to think about? It's not as if the future of the world rests in the balance of whether Greta finally gets off her butt and makes a soufflé."

"I know. I guess she can seem a little odd at first, but she grows on you."

"Like a creeping fungus, I'll bet. I like your other roommate. The cute one. Edie."

Danielle squinted at him. He'd never said anything about Edie being cute before. "Really?"

"Well, I don't know her," he said quickly. "I just know she's easier to talk to than Greta."

"For a minute there I thought you had a crush on my roommate. Which would explain why you're always hanging around, I guess."

He stared at her, his lips curved in a vague half-smile. "Well, that would be *one* explanation."

She hated it when he would throw out some cryptic comment that would stop the conversation dead. Like he knew something that she wasn't catching on to. It was sort of annoying, though it was hard to be too annoyed with Wilson.

In the past few weeks he had introduced her, really introduced her, to New York. They'd done touristy stuff like Coney Island, the Cloisters, Chelsea Piers, and the Staten Island Ferry. He'd taken her to the big Steinway store and played Brahms for her. On July Fourth they had sat forever in the cool, dank dark of the penguin house at the Central Park Zoo, chattering about their lives over the loud echoing squeals of children.

He also introduced her to another New York, which included secret little places he'd found and wanted to share with her. One night he'd take her to what seemed to her like a hidden bar with a courtyard patio tucked away behind a brownstone, and then the next they would visit a great Polish place in the East Village. And he'd introduced her to people—old Juilliard classmates, people he'd met on jobs, and odd friends of distant cousins of acquaintances he seemed to effortlessly accumulate.

She felt as if Wilson had waved a Tinkerbell sparkle wand over her and now she was living the life of her dreams, in the city of her dreams. She sometimes looked up at the line of buildings around her now not with awe, but with fierce possessiveness. Maybe she only rented a tiny corner of Manhattan, but the whole bloomin' city felt like it was hers now.

She wanted to go on and on this way, but sometimes it seemed like Wilson had a little crush on her or something that threatened to end everything. Couldn't he see they were having fun just as they were? Did he really want to risk it all by embarking on a love affair that was—face it—doomed? She liked Wilson, really liked him, and was so grateful to him for coming along just when she needed a friend. But he wasn't what she was looking for.

The trouble was, she didn't want to hurt Wilson's feelings. She didn't want to reject him, and so she kept hoping that these occasionally uncomfortable little undercurrents would just die off eventually.

Like now. Wilson looked away, the moment passed, and things seemed normal again.

"Okay," he said. "Where were we?"

But she was already thinking about dancing, and what to wear. Honestly, she had never had so much fun in her life. Not even in college, and college had been a blast. Edie had been right about working. She *had* met a lot of people. And it wasn't all directly through Wilson. The law firm where they were working was huge—two floors of an old skyscraper on Wall Street. The really important lawyers and the partners worked "upstairs," which meant the eighteenth floor, as opposed to the seventeenth floor where the newer people and the hourly temp laborers like herself and Wilson worked. Even downstairs felt huge to her. Entire suites of offices like self-contained little worlds spun off from the green-and-beige-carpeted hallways. She'd talked to scores of people on the seventeenth floor, but she would bet money she'd only met an itty-bitty fraction of the horde who toiled around her.

She'd been on two dates with a fellow proofer named Brent, though by the end of the second date they had sputtered out of things to talk about and found they weren't even physically attracted, either; and she'd had a really hot date with a paralegal, Tom, who had been wildly flirtatious over dinner before he had excused himself to go to the restroom right after the main course and shot up, popped, or snorted something that made him completely crash. They were supposed to go to a movie, but instead Danielle spent ten minutes struggling to stuff Tom into a cab.

When they met the next day at work, he greeted her with a jaunty wink, as if she hadn't last seen him looking like a lobotomized mess. He didn't ask her out again, thank heavens.

But that was the thing she really loved about New York. You never knew *what* was going to happen.

In the past few weeks her life had taken on a few little routines, of course. Some proofers, eager to trade caffeine for alcohol, went out drinking after the shift ended, usually somewhere in Tribeca. And when she didn't feel like hanging out with those guys, there was always Wilson and their outings.

Her life, in short, had picked up big time. She hadn't written much lately, but writers needed a break every now and then, didn't they? Wilson had read a few of her stories and said they were entertaining, though he suggested she might want to go back to school in creative writing. Going back to school seemed to be his solution for everything. But Danielle had had it with school. She was gaining life experience, just like that vile Jennifer Poon woman had recommended.

She and Wilson had finally managed to buckle down and slug when the door flew open.

"Erin?" a man's voice called out.

Danielle glanced up and then did a double take. Poking his head through the door was the best looking guy working at the law firm. He was a lawyer, so she hadn't actually met him, but she'd seen him, all right. Seen him and drooled, probably like everything else female within his vicinity. He had classic looks— jet black hair, clear blue eyes, and a wide, gorgeous mouth. His nose was straight, his jaw looked like something chiseled by an old master, and he had a body so fit and perfect that you could detect muscles rippling under his snazzy Zegna suits. The man was so hot he steamed even in fluorescent office lighting. He could have been a model. Instead, he was here among them at Ramsey, Lombard, and Gaines, which seemed miraculous. Several times Danielle had found herself gawking after him as he walked down the hall, and then continuing to stare at the point at which he had disappeared from view. He had such powerful dazzle he seemed to leave a vapor trail, like a jet airplane.

But what she was staring at now wasn't vapor. And his incredible blue eyes were focused on her—giving her an up-and-down glance that sent a flush through her entire body.

Wilson, naturally, barely looked up from *Breyer v. Hampstead*. "Erin's not in here."

Danielle flashed a smile at the lawyer and parroted, "Not here." She had no idea who Erin was.

He returned her smile with one ten times as bright. "You're a new one, aren't you?"

Oh, God. He was speaking to her. She felt suddenly like a rabbit in front of an oncoming car. She knew she ought to nod or say "yes" or something, but she just sat there, petrified.

"She's been here a month," Wilson said, irritation evident in his tone.

The lawyer barely spared Wilson a glance. He kept that grin focused on her, where it counted. Where it was appreciated for the dazzling work of art it was. "Still a newbie! I've been wondering what's been missing in this office all these years. Now I know."

She felt as if she were going to have a heart attack. Was it possible to go weak at the knees when you were sitting down?

"Well!" he exclaimed in the awkward silence. "No Erin here. Wonder where she could be?"

"Somewhere else?" Wilson suggested helpfully.

The guy laughed and was about to disappear when some instinct made Danielle blurt, "My name's Danielle!" She probably would have brazenly yelled out her phone number, if she'd thought she could squeeze it in before the door shut.

The legal Adonis darted his head back in. "Nice to meet you, Danielle. I'm Alan Mara."

A sigh fluttered out of her. "Nice to meet you, too."

"See you around, I hope." With a wink, he disappeared.

Danielle sat holding her breath, her gaze fixed on the door. Alan Mara. The vapor trail had a name now.

Slowly, she sank back against her chair. When she could focus again, Wilson was eyeing her with something between disgust and astonishment. He shook his head. "What an ass!"

She nearly fell over. "Who? Alan?"

"*Alan?*" He mimicked her in a breathy voice with a way-exaggerated drawl that made her tense defensively. She didn't sound like that. "Yes, Alan. The guy's going to be sued for sexual harassment one of these days."

She laughed. Men could be as jealous of each other as women were. "What on earth for? All he did was introduce himself."

"Yes, and wink at you, and make some remark that was the equivalent of 'where-have-you-been-all-my-life, baby?' "

"So?"

"So, he's a lech."

"He's the best looking thing moving around here."

"And did you hear what he called you? 'A new one.' *One.* Like you were a new Xerox machine or something, here for his convenience."

"Oh, come on! He was just being nice."

"Sure. To *you* he was being nice."

She crossed her arms. "Maybe because I was being cordial to him, while you practically bit the man's head off." Even while she mouthed the prissy little words, she knew she was lying through her teeth. She and Alan Mara had just had a moment. A pre-lust, checking-out-the-goods moment. She knew that as surely as she knew that she would be plotting ways to throw herself in Alan Mara's line of vision from now till he asked her out.

A little thrill of the chase began to zip through her. Alan was so handsome it hurt, and he was probably rich, and he had to be thirty. Hot damn! A real master-of-the-universe type, and she had a crack at him.

"Danielle, don't be naïve. I couldn't care less what goes on in this office, and even I know that guy is bad news. He's probably slept with half the women here."

"That is pure speculation on your part! Also, it smacks of prejudice."

"Prejudice against whom? Vile contract lawyers?"

"No," she said, lifting her head, "against good-looking people."

He howled. "Now I've heard everything. Victimized for GQ looks . . . Pretty people of the world unite!"

"Admit it. You don't like him because he's handsome and rich."

"And glib and arrogant."

"Arrogance is epidemic in this place." It really was. Danielle had never seen so many self-important people gathered together in such a close space. If Ramsey, Lombard, and Gaines weren't a law office, you would swear it was command central for the Society of Swelled Heads. "You've never called anyone else here arrogant."

He gaped at her. Wilson was hardly ever at a loss for words, but right now he looked as if his tongue were in knots. "Can we please drop this conversation and get back to work?"

"Suits me," she said.

Every atom in her body felt fully awake, but she still had to struggle through the rest of *Breyer v. Hampstead*. It was hard to concentrate on misplaced commas when her mind was feverishly imagining her next encounter with Alan Mara.

Alan had been with the firm just short of four years. He had lunch out every day, never at his desk. (One alcoholic beverage, probably never more than two.) He took his coffee black, in the porcelain coffee cups and saucers that the muckety-mucks used. He was an equal opportunity office flirt: he bantered with every female in sight, old or young, fat or thin, married or unmarried. It was annoyingly democratic of him. He didn't seem to have a girl-friend—at least there was no one woman's name that appeared re-peatedly among his messages at the reception desk, where Danielle had taken to hanging out on breaks. Alan occasionally had a high-carb energy bar around four o'clock, and usually left the office by seven.

That was all Danielle could learn about the man in a week. It was distressingly little. And though she just happened to stroll past his office about twenty times a day, and started frequenting the water cooler nearest the men's restroom, she never bumped into him. Days ticked by and her frustration mounted.

She knew she should drop it. Her behavior was so juvenile!

She hadn't obsessed over a guy like this since she was fourteen, and she hated herself for it. *Stop*, she told herself every morning as she wedged herself onto the 3 train downtown. But her willpower was so shaky, she might as well have been trying to put out a barn fire with a teaspoon.

This weekend a cute guy she'd met at a club had phoned her but she hadn't returned the call. Her mind was fixed on Alan, even as she went through the motions of getting through the day. Sometimes to herself she would frankly admit that the guy was way out of her league and that she was better off watching him walk down the carpeted hallways from afar. But then the next moment the challenge of this magnificent, elusive prey would seize her again, and she would take to coming to work ten minutes earlier just to get an extra ten minutes per day of Alan-watching time.

But never more than ten minutes early. Any more than that would have seemed too obvious, to Wilson if no one else. Wilson was already becoming a little suspicious. A few days earlier he had caught her gazing down an empty hallway (that just happened to be the hallway where Alan's office was).

Wilson had shook his head mournfully.

"What?" she asked. A person couldn't be hanged for staring at air, could they?

He shrugged. "A depressing thought occurred to me."

"What?"

"That, best case, I'm going to be the guy you'll call in ten years to go out for drinks with when your husband is out of town."

"What—you predict that in ten years we'll be having an affair?"

He looked glum. "No. I predict that in ten years we'll still be *talking*."

She laughed. "In ten years you'll have met the woman of your dreams, someone who knows all about medieval law, or NATO, or musette orchestras of the 1930s. She'll have an accordion in one hand and *The Outline of History* in the other."

"You can't hold an accordion in one hand," he said. "And what will you be doing?"

A smile tugged at her lips. "Hopefully writing and living with somebody incredible."

If she could only get the incredible somebody she had in mind to speak to her again!

But nothing worked. Not arriving early, or snapping up her wardrobe with expensive accessories (charged . . . but it was important to establish a credit history, wasn't it?), or walking very, very slowly down hallways when she knew Alan happened to be in the vicinity.

And then, the next Friday evening as she was getting onto the elevator with Wilson to go catch a bite and a movie, he spotted her. He was walking by the elevator.

Their gazes intersected during that hesitation before the doors made up their mind to close. Alan passed, then stepped back, beaming at her. "Hey, doll!"

A week. She'd been waiting an entire week for *this moment*. And now, when it was her time to shine, she was caught so off guard that all she could do was lift a hand weakly and say, "Hey."

And then the doors slid shut.

Oh, God! Could she have sounded any dumber?

Wilson let out a breath in disgust. "Did you hear that? Doll! The guy thinks he's Dean Martin."

"I thought it was kind of funny."

She was soaring. Soaring, and kicking herself for not saying more. Even if there hadn't been time to say much anyway. What a dope she was, what an inarticulate hick!

"Funny that he would forget your name?" Wilson asked.

"He didn't forget my name. He was just being charming."

Wilson leveled one of those looks at her. Like the look he'd given her when she told him she thought Greta was probably a really fun person once you got to know her. "He's a wolf."

Some wolf! For an entire week he hadn't attacked the willing, fabulously accessorized sheep grazing at his very feet.

"You're so crazy, Wilson." Her voice was as cool as the proverbial cuke. "You've really let this Alan Mara guy get under your skin."

Those gray eyes of his looked almost sad. "You, too."

Uh-oh. Was she that easy to read, or had he caught her loitering in front of the men's room? She managed a laugh—though perhaps it was a bit too loud. "Give me a break. The guy has spoken to me all of two times. He barely knows I exist."

The doors opened.

"He knows," Wilson muttered sadly as they stepped into the marbled lobby of the office building.

Chapter 19

MORE CAREER ADVICE
FROM RAY LIOTTA

Aurora took a deep, bracing breath of sticky Manhattan air. "It's so good to be back, I can't tell you."

Edie didn't reply. Aurora had been back now for two weeks—more than enough time to reacclimatize. She hadn't been gone *that* long. And it wasn't as if she'd been filming in Calcutta. Not that Edie had ever been there, but Toronto to New York just didn't seem like that huge of a culture leap. The natives were probably friendlier there than here.

Plus, they were standing on line outside on an unpleasantly stuffy ninety-degree afternoon to get into a movie . . . mostly so they could sit in the air-conditioning. And the movie they'd wanted to see had sold out, so now they were going to have to settle for the latest Adam Sandler thing. A gravely high price to pay to be air-cooled for two hours, in Edie's opinion.

In short, this was not a moment that would make any sane person rhapsodize over the glories of living in New York.

Aurora just wants to remind me that not so long ago she wasn't *here. That she was off making a movie. . . .*

Thoughts like this had been creeping into her mind more and more, and she hated them. Jealousy was so childish! She and Aurora had always had their differences, their mutual ups and downs. There had even been a two-month stretch when they hadn't seen each other because of a stupid spat over fifty dollars (Edie now believed she'd been unfair and that Aurora—as she had claimed—

had actually forgotten borrowing it). But there had never been jealousy between them. A few pangs of envy, maybe, but more often genuine gladness at the other's success.

But now something really unpleasant was creeping into Edie's head, and what was worse was that she believed Aurora was actually fostering the little green monster.

But why would she do that?

The line was stalled, and Aurora turned to Edie. "So how've you been? You keep letting me run on about myself all the time. I'm dying to hear what you've been up to. When's the audition?"

There. See? Aurora cared about her. Edie didn't understand how she could doubt a person she had counted as a friend for so long.

Edie had an audition for a commercial coming up. It was nothing great. A Sudz detergent commercial . . . whoopee. But at least *she* had something to talk about for a change. Because things had felt so weird between them lately, she had refrained from telling Aurora about the scene she'd made in Noel's office that day after she'd left the Carnegie Deli. Now she spilled the whole story, in all its awful, embarrassing detail. (It seemed less awful to her now that she had an audition coming up.)

Aurora listened patiently, smiling at times, wincing at others. To Edie even those winces seemed rehearsed.

She knows all this already. Noel must have told her.

But Noel couldn't have talked about her to Aurora. That would have been unprofessional of him . . . wouldn't it? Edie wasn't sure about agent-client confidentiality, but she was fairly certain that it extended to not blabbing embarrassing stories to the client's best friend.

Except, perhaps, if that friend happened to be another client . . . a more valuable client . . .

Edie gave herself a stern mental shake. *Stop it.* God, she hated this. Seven months with no acting work and she was just turning into a paranoid wreck. Doubting her friend, her agent . . . what would be next?

Aurora tapped her fingers against her purse. It was an expensive little clutch bag, like the ones Danielle always carried. They looked precious and inconvenient, like something Jackie Kennedy would have carried. "I think Noel has been neglecting you," she said. "It's awful. And believe me, I like the guy . . . but come on. If *you're* having trouble getting work, he can't be doing his job."

Remorse swamped Edie. Had kinder words ever been spoken?

"You were ab-so-lutely right to stomp into his office like you did," Aurora continued. "I don't care what anyone says."

Anyone? She made it sound as if she had been talking this over with *lots* of people. But maybe she was just misinterpreting. . . .

"I'll bet you anything that's why you've got this audition. You lit a fire under him."

"I thought I needed to be more aggressive."

Aurora bit her lip, and it was almost as if she were biting back words she was afraid would be hurtful.

"What?" Edie asked.

"Well . . ." Aurora took a breath. "I was just going to say, you could give *yourself* a little nudge, too."

"What do you mean?"

Aurora's eyes took in Edie's face, and then snagged on her hair. "You need to do something that will make an impression."

"You mean about the way I look?"

"Exactly!" Aurora said, as if Edie had miraculously read her thoughts. As if her thoughts weren't written all over her face.

Instinctively, Edie reached a hand up to her hair—maybe to protect it from Aurora's skewering glance. "I've thought about getting a new cut—"

"You should!" Aurora said, pouncing on the idea. "What's this commercial?"

"Detergent. They're looking for hip and sassy soccer moms, Noel says."

"There—hip and sassy. Right now you don't look either of those things."

Edie's heart sped a little in panicked embarrassment. Aurora was right. She was so unhip. So *not* sassy.

"Well, maybe hip for 2001," Aurora allowed, "but you've got to move on. As an actor, your appearance is an important investment. It's like with any property. You have to keep making improvements or no one's going to be interested."

"You're right." Edie suddenly felt like a run-down tenement to Aurora's fabulous suburban split-level.

Aurora flashed her a reassuring smile. "I'll give you the name of somebody who'll make you look *great*. He's fabulous with color."

"You think I should change my color?" she asked, alarmed.

Her friend laughed. "If you're worried about being noticed, mouse brown isn't exactly the hue I'd choose."

Edie thought about this, and felt a pang. "I always go to Sarah."

The answer to that was a pitying look. "*Exactly*. That's why you should try Julian."

"But if I cheat on Sarah, I'll never be able to go back to her. She'd know someone else cut my hair."

"So?"

"So, I'd feel like a heel. It would be like that Dick Van Dyke episode where Rob goes to another dentist and Jerry Helper finds out."

Aurora was astounded. "Edie, this is your life. You can't sit around mulling over ethics you learned from sixties sitcoms. You'll never get anywhere."

"I suppose I could tell her I went out of town."

"Or you could just not go back to her. You probably won't want to after Julian. The most important thing is to make an impression. That's what Ray told me. 'Make them sit up and take notice.' "

It sounded like Ray was getting his ideas from sitcoms, too.

Edie sighed. "I guess my big fear is that I'll do everything I can to get noticed, and I'll still be a flop."

Aurora blinked. "Well, then you'll know."

"Know what?"

"Whether you're cut out to be an actress or not."

Was she kidding? "Are you saying I might *not* be an actress?"

"No! No! You're *very* talented. It's not that . . ."

In spite of the heat, Edie felt cold. In fact, her teeth were chattering. "Then what is it? I'm chronically unlucky?"

"No . . . but . . ." Aurora looked reluctant to say any more, but she forced herself. "Maybe you're *just not ready*. Everything happens for a reason, you know. Sometimes the stars align just so and a person has the right combination of looks, talent, and drive. But if that happened all the time, no one would seem exceptional."

Like her, she means.

"So it's all about fate?" Edie said.

"Fate, and hard work, and attention to appearance. You have to be poised to take advantage if all those stars *do* align. You have to be ready."

Oh, God, Edie thought in a panic. *She's right. I'm not ready. If my stars aligned now, I'd be so screwed.*

She reminded Aurora to give her Julian's number after the movie.

They bought their tickets and Aurora said she wanted to visit the concession stand, even though there was practically no time before the show started. In the end, Aurora got a bottled water, and Edie bought a box of Junior Mints that she proceeded to munch on furiously through the hundred previews and the commercials. Forget national scourges like homelessness and poverty. Commercials before movies were what brought out Edie's socialist impulses. Wasn't ten dollars a ticket enough for these people? How much profit did movie theaters have to make?

"Edie, you're grumbling," Aurora hissed at her.

Edie stopped grumbling but kept stewing. By the time they'd left the concession stand, the only two seats together had been in the front row. The screen was so close it felt as if it were bearing down on her. Her eyes already ached from staring straight up into Carrot Top's nostril.

Aurora shot an envious sideways glance at Edie's candy. "I love Junior Mints but chocolate always goes *straight* to my hips."

Edie bristled.

But it wasn't just the food thing. It was all the career advice, which seemed tailor made to make Edie a nervous wreck. First Aurora was telling her to change her hair, and then she was telling her that what really mattered was that the stars aligned properly or some b.s. like that. And that bit about not everyone being able to be exceptional—ha!

She was trying to help you. She said some nice things, too.

But what about the other stuff? And why should she listen to

Aurora when half the time it seemed as if she were trying to undermine her confidence?

Because she's successful, and you're not.

And that, unfortunately, seemed what their entire friendship was boiling down to.

Chapter 20

LUNCH

Wilson was short on cash again, so he decided to take an accordion day Monday and work the late shift. Danielle felt like an orphan. She struggled through three hours of proofreading in an overlit, frigidly cold room before her neck hurt, her eyes began to cross, and her urge to flee the building was just too powerful to resist.

She bolted from the long table and out the door, running for the elevator before she could think better of her decision. She dashed in at the last minute and found herself wedged among ten expensively suited people from the building, including Alan Mara. He smiled at her over someone's shoulder, and she smiled back briefly. Then it became necessary to assume the elevator position of staring straight ahead at doors everyone knew weren't going to open while the car was moving.

For the eternity that it took the elevator to creep down sixteen more floors, Danielle was almost certain that she could feel Alan's eyes pinned on her. She was standing two feet from him; what luck! It was tempting to believe that the silent voice of destiny had urged her to leave before her usual lunchtime. It was fated that she and Alan should be jammed in this elevator. Yet the only question going through her mind, perversely, was how she was going to get away from him. He was probably going to lunch with colleagues, or maybe meeting someone at a restaurant, and here she was going out for a forlorn sandwich by herself. She didn't want the man of her dreams to think she was a friendless geek.

She squared her shoulders, intent on appearing busily focused when she stepped off the elevator. Anyone looking at her was going to think she had an important errand to run. She would not glance back at Alan. She would not.

She couldn't help patting herself on the back for being very neatly outfitted, though. A loose cotton Norma Kamali jacket over a neat orange summery dress that she'd actually bought from a street market in Greenwich Village one weekend, and new white slingbacks with three-inch heels (hidden from Edie, her financial overseer). Her handbag—white with multicolored polka dots—matched her earrings (funky faux-bakelite plastic flowers). From her reflection in the steel double doors of the elevator, she stood out, *way out*, among the horde of black, gray, and navy blue all around her. She wasn't very Wall Street . . . but who wanted to be? She looked well put together and breezy. A girl who knew what she was doing and where she was going.

At least she could look that way, even if she didn't actually know.

The elevator stopped, the doors opened, and taking a breath, Danielle stepped out purposefully. Then the brand spanking new heel of her shoes met the newly polished marble of the lobby floor.

Slipped would be a kind word for what happened next. Fell on her ass would be more accurate. She could almost swear she heard the crack of her tailbone hitting the ground echoing across the lobby. Gasps went up all around her, and suddenly it felt as if a million arms were reaching for her.

"Are you all right?" at least five voices asked.

Who said New Yorkers were heartless? She was getting solicitude aplenty, just when she would have liked to have had the cold, cruel world ignore her. Just when she would have preferred to sink clear through the floor, actually. But no. *Now* she had drawn a large solicitous crowd. Now, when she was red-faced with humiliation.

"Do you need help?" an older man asked.

Danielle was still sprawled on the ground with her legs shooting out in front of her, when a strong hand locked around her arm. "*I'll* help her." With just a tug, Alan Mara lifted her to her feet as if she weighed no more than air.

She stood blinking in amazement, first at the ease with which Alan had yanked her inert body up from the ground (the man definitely worked out), and second by the fact that she was able to stand without excruciating pain.

"I'm fine," she announced to everyone. "Thanks."

The group of do-gooders filtered away quickly, except for Alan, who kept holding her arm. Just the touch of that firm hand was enough to give her duck bumps. She swallowed and forced herself to look into those blue eyes. So much for striking him with her air of downtown sophistication. He probably thought she was an ungainly chowderhead. A polka dot–pursed fool.

"Are you really okay?" he asked her.

How could Wilson have called this guy a wolf? Alan's eyes showed nothing but kindness and concern.

"Of course," she replied. "Except that I feel like an oaf."

His head drew back a little. "Because you fell? Everyone in the building has probably spilled across this floor at one time or another. You'd think the management in a building full of lawyers would be more worried about lawsuits. They ought to at least put down mats near the doors."

"I would probably trip over those." She frowned at her traitorous feet. "It was really the fault of these shoes, I think. They're new, and the bottoms are slick."

"They're slick, period," he said, admiring them. Then, she noticed, his gaze traveled a little northward and admired her legs for a moment. Gratification flushed through her. She cleared her throat.

"What?" he asked, looking into her eyes.

"I was trying to get your attention."

"You've got it. In spades." She could swear his blue eyes actually sparkled at her. "Where were you headed?"

"Oh . . ." She still felt a little dazed. "I was just going to grab a bite, but—"

"Good," he said, cutting her off. "Grab a bite with me."

"But—"

"No buts, I insist," he said, dragging her along with him as he strode toward the revolving doors. Outside he flagged down a cab and one stopped for him almost immediately.

A cab, she thought as he helped her in and she slid to the other side. She leaned back, savoring the pleasure. She hadn't ridden in one in weeks, not since the day Edie had lectured her about wasting money on taxis. Wilson was also a fanatical straphanger. All that deprivation now made her feel as if she were being whisked away in a chariot. As they sped past all the other schmucks on foot during their lunch hour, a gleeful smile touched her lips. *I did it*, she gloated to herself. *I'm out with Alan*. And all she had to do was fall on her butt.

The café he took her to was not overly fancy, but it had great atmosphere and a window that looked right out on the Brooklyn Bridge. She remembered when she and Wilson had walked over the bridge, on that day not so along ago when she had felt so lost. She didn't feel that way now. She didn't think she would ever be able to take this incredible city for granted, the way Edie, Greta, and other people seemed to, but she felt comfortable with it now.

"I have to ask," he said as they sipped at their drinks. (Zinfandel for her, scotch and soda for him.) "Where are you from?"

"Texas."

He smiled as if she'd said something funny. "*Where* in Texas?"

"Oh. Amarillo."

"I've never been there," he said. "But I've been to Dallas several times. I loved it there."

"You did?" He seemed like such an East Coast kind of guy.

"Well," he said, "it was a nice place to visit."

She laughed. "That's supposed to be my line. Though, of course, that's not how I feel. I wouldn't want to live anywhere else but New York now."

He drew back. "Ever?"

"I think there's enough here to keep me occupied for a few decades, at least. And for sure I know I can't go back to Amarillo."

"Why not?" he asked, tilting his head at her. "Have you fled the law?"

"No, just my overprotective family, a boring job, and a dull fiancé."

"Fiancé—that's interesting."

"Not really," she said quickly, dismissing the subject. The last thing she wanted to talk to Alan about was Brandon.

"What was your boring job?"

"Oh, I . . ." She felt her face go red. "Well, I had a job in a small law firm."

He tossed back his head, laughing. "Great. Now you have a boring job in a large law firm. You've really moved up in the world."

"This is just temp work, though. It pays really well. What I really want to be—"

"—is an actress," he finished for her.

She straightened. "No, a writer."

He seemed surprised. "I would have thought you'd be trying to break into show business. You're so pretty."

She took several gulps of wine, hoping the man wouldn't notice that she was completely on fire. The alcohol along with that word "pretty" was giving her a buzz, and she had to stifle the urge to giggle nervously. She thought about *Rudolph the Red-Nosed Reindeer*—the claymation TV special version—when the girl reindeer kisses Rudolph and he flies up into the air shouting "She thinks I'm cuuuuuuute!"

She felt like flying and shouting now. It was a miracle, really, that she was able to sit there, almost calmly, and say simply, "Thank you. One of my roommates is an actress."

"One?" Alan asked, alarmed. "How many people do you live with?"

"Just two other women. Greta, who's a dental assistant, and Edie, the actress. She does theater, mostly, and soap operas."

"And waits tables," he guessed.

She smiled ruefully. "That too."

The food came, and Danielle restrained herself from falling hungrily on the plate as she normally would. She felt ravenous, but she tried to imagine Miss Manners was sitting on her shoulder and managed to take small, ladylike bites of ahi tuna. Also, she remembered her mother's oft-repeated advice about the way to a man's heart: not through his heart, but through his mouth . . . as in, let him talk your ear off about himself. She put that advice to good use now.

She learned that Alan was the son of a Chicago doctor (a dermatologist) and that he went first to Cornell undergrad and then Yale Law School. He liked to travel, preferably to places where he could sail and get a tan. He also liked Hollywood movies, shopping, good food, and quiet Sunday mornings in his apartment. He didn't have a car but loved those Hummers. He hated pretentious bullshit, sushi, and anyone who wasn't nice to his mother.

He actually said that. "I can't stand people who aren't nice to their mothers. My brother's that way. Lives in Florida. Didn't even remember to send our mom a card on Mother's Day. You should have heard her voice over the telephone when she told me that . . ."

"Oh, how awful." Danielle experienced a pang of guilt over her parents, neither of whom she'd spoken to over the past few weeks.

He shook his head, then downed the last of his coffee, which they had both ordered in lieu of dessert. "Listen to me. I've talked your ear off, when I brought you out because I wanted to hear all about you."

Her heart jumped. He had? "Maybe some other time." Once the words were out she could have kicked herself. Did that sound like she was begging for a second invitation, or a date? She couldn't tell from looking into Alan's eyes whether he thought so.

He paid the check—scoffing at the very idea of going Dutch—and then they caught another cab back to the office. It wouldn't have been that far to walk, really, but it was probably just as well that they didn't, because the lunch had gone over an hour. She would have to make up some excuse for the temp supervisor.

As the cab pulled up to their building, she caught Alan gazing at her.

"I'm glad I was on that elevator," he said.

Her mouth felt bone dry. She just barely managed to rasp out a reply. "Me, too."

Was he staring at her lips? Was he going to . . . ?

But he didn't kiss her. He just leaned toward her and handed her a business card and a gold fountain pen. "Would you write down your phone number for me?"

Would she! Her hand felt so shaky, she could barely scrawl out the numbers. "You wouldn't mind if I used it soon, would you?" he asked, taking it from her.

Be still, my beating heart! She was too eager to even think of a wry answer. "Are you crazy? No!"

He sent her one of those devastating smiles, and for a moment she thought he actually might kiss her. Instead, he gave her an almost avuncular pat on the thigh. "Good answer." He yanked out his wallet and started counting bills to give the driver.

They didn't say much on the way back up to the seventeenth floor. Just chatted about the hours they worked, and how they dreaded going back for another afternoon of toil. Usual shoptalk kind of stuff. And when they parted ways, they did so wordlessly. He just sent her a quick wink.

When she sat back down at the long proofer's table, her whole body felt like it was shaking. She stared at the neatly typed motion in front of her but the sentences were all a blur. Her mind sifted through every word Alan had said to her.

But he'd been so nice to her. And not a wolf at all. That Wilson—some judge of character he was! She couldn't wait to tell him about her lunch with Alan. Although, on second thought, maybe she wouldn't tell him anything. If Alan didn't call her, it might be embarrassing. It would make her look like she had gotten her hopes up or something.

She wouldn't want anyone to think that.

Chapter 21

RECONSTRUCTING EDIE

Edie bolted through the apartment door, but she couldn't move fast enough to avoid detection. For fifteen blocks people she passed on the sidewalk had been swiveling to gawk at her. And why shouldn't they? Twice she'd looked into shop windows and jumped back in horror at her own reflection.

Danielle was chattering on the phone, but the handset nearly slipped out of her grasp when she saw Edie. Even Greta was roused out of her new vegetative state. "*Verdammt!* You scared me!" Her horrified gaze was pinned on Edie's head.

Meanwhile, Danielle was shouting into the telephone. "Can I call you back? Something awful's happened!"

That something awful was Edie's hair. It was a disaster. She had taken Aurora's advice and gone to Julian for color and . . . well, what she had *requested* was "something to give it a little more body." What she'd gotten was red, red hair and tight spirally curls. Little Orphan Edie.

She sprinted to the bathroom, faced the mirror, and groaned.

Danielle and Greta trailed after her, crowding in the doorway to gawk.

"What did you do?" Danielle asked her.

"What does it look like?" Edie asked in exasperation. Then she sighed. No sense begging for wisecracks about Irish setters and electrical sockets. "Don't answer that. Just bring me a bag to put over my head."

Why? Why had she done this? All her life she had been so sensible. Her hair had always been its natural color—good old washed-out brunette—tamed into unremarkable but simple straight below-the-shoulder cuts. She had told herself that it was because it made her more flexible, but now she suspected she had wisely been trying to avoid *this*. Hair experimentation disaster.

The phone rang. "I'll get it!" Danielle leapt for the portable handset she had just laid down. "Hello? Oh, hi, Wilson." Disappointment was thick in her tone. As she listened, she regarded the back of Edie's head with a quizzical frown. "Uh-huh. Say— can I call you back? Something's happened to Edie." She smiled. "No, nothing bad. That is, not *terrible*." She smiled encouragingly into the mirror at Edie. "Okay, talk to you *mañana!*"

She hung up. "That was Wilson." Her tone made it sound as if she'd just rung off from a conversation with the grim reaper.

"What's the matter with Wilson?" Edie asked. "You sounded like you were talking to a telemarketer."

"Nothing's wrong with him—he's just not Alan."

Alan. Mr. Fascinating. Alan the-straight-guy-who-loves-his-mother Mara. Edie had been hearing odes to Alan for days. He was gorgeous, he was charming, he was rich. The man was perfect in every way, in fact, except that he hadn't called Danielle when he said he would.

"Do you think he could have lost my phone number?" she wondered aloud.

Greta guffawed. "Oh, sure. It is lost in a drawer among a hundred other phone numbers."

Greta had heard the story of the lunch, too. *Everyone* had. Edie wouldn't have been surprised if Danielle had blurted out the story of her lunch with Alan Mara to the cashier at the Korean deli. Alan was her obsession, the dating prize of a lifetime, the white whale to her Ahab.

"Alan's not like that," Danielle said hotly. "I swear, ya'll are just as jaded as Wilson. He thinks that every phenomenally hot guy must be a womanizer."

Edie and Greta's glances met, but briefly. It was becoming obvious to both of them that they weren't in a good position to dish out dating advice to the little innocent from the country, since neither of them had had anything resembling a real date since Danielle had moved in. Meanwhile, *she* had been attracting men like flies. She seemed very deft at swatting them away, too. Despite her Lady Bird accent and her sweet, rattle-headed demeanor, it was increasingly clear that Danielle knew exactly what she wanted and could take care of herself. She was a ditz of iron.

Though sometimes Edie wondered. Twenty-three. She had done a lot of stupid stuff at that age. Maybe Danielle actually did need advice . . . but whether or not she'd take it was a whole 'nother story.

Danielle's dark brows beetled as she peered at Edie in the mirror. "Your hair isn't really *that* bad."

Edie clucked unhappily. Her spectacularly bad hairdo was probably the only thing capable of diverting Danielle's thoughts from Alan. "I told that Julian character I just wanted it a light shade of auburn—and what do I get? Bozo orange."

"The color is good," Greta declared flatly.

Edie sniggered. "Good if I had an audition to play Raggedy Ann, maybe." Instead, she had that damn hip young mom detergent audition. *Hip!* She could kiss that job goodbye.

"It is your haircut that is the problem," Greta said. "Why did a hairdresser do this to you? That look went out of fashion, I think."

"When was that look in fashion?" Danielle asked.

"Never," Edie said. "Not outside Barnum and Bailey clown college."

"I vill fix it."

They blinked at Greta, who seemed perfectly serious. Edie couldn't help it. She laughed. "Are you nuts? I just paid someone a hundred and sixty dollars to spend four hours making me look like a demonic Toni twin. Do you honestly think I'm now going to let *you* loose on my head?"

"Why not? I could not do worse, and for dead sure I would not charge you one hundred and sixty dollars. I won't charge a cent. You have audition tomorrow, *ja?*"

"*Ja*," Edie replied, utterly depressed by the thought. She might as well not even go, unless . . . She regarded Greta with suspicion. "What do you know about cutting hair?"

"I attend cosmetology school for three months," Greta said.

This was news. Greta in beauty school. Edie couldn't quite imagine it. "What happened after three months?"

"I dropped out."

Danielle gasped. "Just like Didi Conn in *Grease!* That was, like, my favorite movie of all time in seventh grade."

Edie squinted at Greta. "Why'd you leave?"

Kicked out, she guessed.

Greta shook her head, seeming to remember that period in her life with disgust. "I couldn't take it. All that talking! People get in the chair and chatter, chatter at you. Like just because you cut their hair you actually give a shit about them."

Nice, Edie thought.

Greta shrugged. "Then I hear you could make a good salary doing dental assistant's job. I figure that patients can't yak at me while I had my hands jammed in their mouths. So I borrow the money from my aunt and switch."

"But you know how to do hair?"

"Some. I do my own."

Edie inspected Greta's shaved head and was not impressed. The Annie Lennox look wasn't any more in than Bozo.

Impatiently, Greta grabbed hold of Edie's chin and ratcheted her head toward the mirror. "Look. You have good, strong bones. Why do you hide behind this mess?"

Greta's hand forced Edie's lips into a fish mouth. "That mess you're talking about is my hair," she managed to say. "I need my hair."

"I vill make it less mess."

Edie agonized for a moment. What could be worse than the hairy disaster now screwing out of her head?

Danielle was staring at them in suspense, her fist practically in her mouth. Then the phone rang again and she trotted after it.

Edie slumped in resignation. She had to do *something*.

"I don't want a buzz cut," she warned Greta.

Greta shook her head. "Of course not. Your bones are not *that* good."

Oh yeah. Edie could really see why customers would want to pour their hearts out to this woman.

Danielle didn't get off the phone again until after the shampoo-ing was done and Edie was perched uncomfortably on the toilet. Edie had refused to allow a mess to be made in her room or the liv-ing room, so they had fashioned a makeshift barber stool by topping off the toilet seat with a dictionary, a five-hundred-page hardcover bio of Laurence Olivier, and the complete works of Shakespeare.

"Who was that on the phone?" Edie asked Danielle. It would be good to be able to concentrate on something other than what Greta was doing to her hair.

"Some guy I met the other day at a proofreader happy hour. Jack."

"Don't you ever meet any women?" Edie asked her.

Danielle seemed surprised she would ask. "Sure, I guess. I met you guys."

Edie laughed. "Oh, right. Who could ask for anything more?"

"Keep still," Greta growled at her.

"Anyway, this guy wanted to go out to a movie," Danielle said, as bored as if the guy had asked her to a tractor pull. "On Saturday night."

"What did you say?"

"I said that I needed to work on my story."

In other words, she had lied. The sound of the clicking of Danielle's keyboard had been conspicuously absent in the apart-ment lately. "Danielle . . ."

Danielle stubbed her foot against the doorjamb. "Well, what if Alan calls and I'm busy on Saturday? I'd be crushed if I couldn't go just because I'd promised to see a movie with Jack. Or I would say yes to Alan and then have to call Jack and give him some half-assed excuse for canceling the date."

"But you wouldn't be stuck at home on Saturday night."

"It doesn't matter. I *could* stand to do a little work."

" 'Iron Chef' is Saturday," Greta remembered. "They are hav-ing special marathon of potato battles."

"See?" Danielle said. "There's plenty I could do here. I don't have to run around like a social butterfly all the time. It's kinda tiring, to tell you the God's honest truth." Giving it another mo-ment's thought, she added, "Anyway, Wilson's usually up to doing something last minute."

Poor Wilson. "Danielle . . ."

"What?"

"Not to sound like a mother hen, but don't you think you're being unfair to that guy?"

"Which guy? Jack?"

"No," Edie said, rolling her eyes. "Wilson."

"How? We're just friends."

"Does he know that?"

"Of course! There's never been anything romantic between us."

Greta frowned. "Who is Vilson?"

Edie swung her head around, only to have Greta forcefully pivot her forward again.

"Sit up straight," she reminded Edie.

Edie obeyed, but managed to swipe an incredulous glance at her.

"You *must* know who Wilson is," Danielle said. "He's in the apartment, like, all the time."

A faint frown clouded Greta's brow. "I don't remember . . ."

"Greta, you've sat there watching television with him while I've gotten myself ready. Tall . . . red hair?"

Edie's mouth screwed up. "Damn! I should have brought Wilson to the salon for a color match. Wilson red."

"*Ach!* I remember him now." Greta's lips pursed. "Sort of."

Danielle regarded her with amazement. "Wow. Your brain must be completely fried, Greta."

"I don't remember who comes by while I'm meditating," Greta said.

"You meditate while you're watching television?"

She lifted her shoulders. "Why not?"

"I'm not an expert or anything," Edie said, "but during meditation you're supposed to focus on one thing, aren't you?"

"So? My one thing is the television." She snipped off a huge hank of hair, causing Edie to shudder. Maybe she shouldn't argue with the woman while she was wielding scissors. "It is very therapeutic."

The phone rang, and Danielle was gone again in a flash. This time it was obvious there wasn't a mere Jack or Wilson on the other end of the line. Danielle's voice looped up into a Mitzi Gaynor perkiness that Edie hadn't heard in weeks, and she immediately darted behind her screen for a little privacy.

Edie was left with no alternative to dwelling on what Greta was doing to her. "How is it looking?"

"*Gut, gut.* Don't worry."

She hadn't been worried when she'd sat down in the chair in Julian's salon, either. She'd had complete confidence in Aurora's recommendation. Not that she could blame Aurora for a bad haircut . . . but *why the hell had she listened to her?*

This is what happened when you tried to slip out of your groove.

All of a sudden, letting Greta cut her hair seemed a reckless, dangerous act. Three months of beauty school. Was she insane? "Not too short, is it?"

Greta laughed.

Which was not exactly the sound Edie wanted to hear.

By the time the snipping ended and Greta had started blow-drying, Edie's nerves were jagged and her butt ached from sitting on Laurence Olivier.

Danielle rushed back into the bathroom. Edie hadn't seen anyone look so happy since Douglas had declared he was leaving her.

"Pay dirt!" she exclaimed triumphantly.

Greta turned off the blow-dryer. "Pay who?"

"That was Alan!" Danielle stopped bouncing when she saw Edie. "Omigod!"

That was it. Edie leapt to her feet, sending books flying. She stared into the mirror and . . .

She smiled. This was *not* a haircut she would ever have asked for. It was short. Very short. But not too bad. The red seemed less aggressive when there wasn't so much of it, and the curls framing her face looked airy and natural. It was a summery look.

"I like it."

Greta still didn't crack a smile. "You still are not finished. I am going to cut your neck. Make it tidier."

Edie nodded, shocked to find herself in agreement with anyone who wanted to cut her neck. "How did you think of this?"

Greta shrugged, replacing the books.

"I can't believe he called!" Danielle said, getting back to what she obviously considered the truly momentous topic of conversation. "We're going out Saturday—so you see, it was a good thing I gave Jack the brush-off."

Edie felt unequipped to make a pronouncement. The quandary of too many men clamoring for dates was not a problem she had been forced to deal with at any point in her life. "I guess."

Danielle spun gleefully. "He is *so* incredible. You guys aren't going to believe it when you see him." She gasped. "What am I going to wear?"

Greta snorted. "Maybe one of the outfits you've bought since you swore off shopping."

Edie had also noticed that Danielle had been slipping back into old habits. The girl was probably carrying more debt than Argentina.

But Danielle seemed unfazed. "I'm not talking clothes. I mean lingerie. I haven't bought anything like that since coming to New York. And I packed in such a hurry, all I really brought along was some stuff my mom had bought me on sale. Ya'll can't expect me to go off on a date with the hottest guy in all of New York wearing Sam's Club panties."

Edie wasn't as impressed by the date with the hottest guy in New York so much as by the idea of having a mother underwear shop for her. She struggled to remember but only came up with a vague recollection of the days when her mother would present her with a new surprise shirt, or some socks. Mostly Edie had had to plead to go to the mall and get what she needed. But Danielle's parents apparently had her needs planned right down to her underpants.

It was either appalling or impressive. She couldn't decide which.

When the buzzer sounded, they all three stared at each other. Who would drop in on them on a Wednesday night?

"It's probably Wilson," Danielle said in a funereal tone. "I can't see him now. He'll pester me about Alan." She clearly wanted to savor her triumph for a while.

"But what if it's not Wilson?" Edie wished Bhiryat would put in an intercom system, but of course that would be an over-the-top extravagance.

"I vill go," Greta offered.

She wasn't gone long, and when she came back up, she had a tall, handsome stranger in tow. Another man for Danielle, of course. This one was clean cut, with short brown hair and friendly brown eyes. He appeared to be in his mid-to-late twenties. He wasn't bulked up, but he still managed to look good in his shirt and tie tucked into his khakis. For a moment Edie wondered if this could possibly be the incomparable Alan Mara, but she dismissed the notion almost immediately. Danielle might be new to town, but even a twenty-three-year-old from Amarillo would know phenoms didn't wear Dockers.

Not to mention, judging from Danielle's blank expression, she obviously didn't have a clue who the guy was.

Uneasiness clouded the man's face as he confronted three women. He looked at Edie expectantly, taking in her hair and her terrycloth robe, and a smile broke across his lips. A really radiant smile, Edie noted with a subtle shiver of appreciation. The man might not be a phenom, but he was definitely above average.

He was also clueless. She nearly laughed. *He* didn't know who Danielle was, either.

She cleared her throat and offered her hand. "I'm Edie."

He shook it with a firm grip and stared into her eyes for a moment. When he spoke, his deep voice bore a familiar drawl. It was Danielle's accent, plus a little testosterone. "I'm Ross Johnson." Then he turned to Danielle. "I guess you must be Dani, then. I'm sorry I didn't call. I didn't have your number."

"Dani!" she exclaimed, clearly uncomfortable with the nickname. And the fact that a total stranger would be using it. "How did you get my address?"

He kept the smile on his face, even though this obviously wasn't the howdy-do he'd expected. "Well, see, your dad plays golf with my dad. And I was just home last weekend and we ran into him, and your dad asked me, when I got back to New York, if I could—"

"Check up on me!" Danielle howled in outrage. The offense electrified her. She turned to her roommates. "How do you like that!"

Ross Johnson recoiled a little. "Oh no, I'm positive he didn't—"

Danielle cut him off. "Believe me, you were sent here as a spy."

Edie immediately felt a surge of pity for Ross Johnson. He'd had no way of knowing he'd been dispatched on a thankless mission.

"That's why Dad didn't give you my phone number," Danielle said. "He knew that the moment I heard you were from Amarillo I'd hang up."

Edie swung on her. "You would not have hung up."

Danielle at least had the good grace to blush. "I'm sorry," she said to Ross. "I don't mean to be unfriendly, but my parents have been a little overbearing. They hate it that I've moved to New York."

To his credit, he appeared eager to excuse her rudeness. "Judge Porter did seem worried about you. . . ."

"Worried!" Danielle hooted. "All he's worried about is that he's lost control of his little girl. Now he's sending strangers after me. This takes the cake!"

Ross shifted uncomfortably. "He told me he thought you might like to hear a voice from home."

"Well, I'm sorry that you came all this way," Danielle said.

"It was no bother. I was on my way back to my apartment. I thought we might go someplace and have coffee."

"Oh, I don't think—"

Edie interrupted them. "How long have you been in Manhattan, Ross?"

"Oh, almost a year now. I've got a residency at the New York Animal Hospital."

"You're a vet?" What a dumb question! Who else would have a residency at an animal hospital?

She had to admit, the guy flustered her a little.

He smiled. "That's right."

How cool. Not just that he would be a vet, though she'd always found vets strangely appealing (they seemed to carry an automatic badge of compassion). It just seemed striking that this strapping Texan would be wandering loose in Manhattan, like something out of an old Frank Capra movie.

She felt her lips tugging into a grin.

Danielle was still tapping her foot. "Did Dad send any particular message for me?"

Ross pulled his gaze away from Edie. "Uh, no. Just said to tell you hello if I saw you. Like I said, if you want to go out for coffee . . ."

"No, thanks," Danielle said flatly. "I'm sorry, but you see, I've got this date tonight. He should be here in a few minutes."

Danielle was dressed in shorts and a T-shirt; not date clothes, obviously.

Ross's smile flattened and he looked around at the three women. His gaze fell finally on Edie's robe, and then her hair, and finally the disarray in the bathroom they were all standing in front of. "I understand. And on top of everything else, I seem to have barged in on a hen night."

Edie laughed. The idea of the three of them being hens together was almost ludicrous. "Greta was just doing a little damage control with the barber scissors. I had a haircut-from-hell day."

His gaze took in her hair now. "Looks good to me."

For some reason, the innocuous words sent a little thrill zipping through her. Which was nuts. Douglas had been gone so long, just having a guy speak to her was affecting her in weird ways.

Still, she felt like inviting him to stick around. No matter what he said, he *had* come out of his way. But she couldn't ask him to stay without exposing Danielle as a liar when her fictitious date didn't show.

"Tell you what," he suggested. "I'll leave my number for you, Danielle, in case you ever feel like chewing the fat. I know I still get homesick after a year."

"Really?" Danielle asked. "I haven't had a twinge of homesickness yet."

Edie wanted to smack her.

Ross wrote the number down on a business card anyway and handed it to her. "Just in case," he repeated.

Thankfully, Danielle managed a forced smile at the last minute, and at least showed a modicum of cordiality as she was shoving the guy out the door. When he was gone, though, she was huffing again. "I can't believe Dad would do that! He could have at least warned me that he was sending a spy."

"Wouldn't that have defeated the purpose?" Edie asked her.

Danielle wasn't listening. "And what kind of guy would just show up at a girl's apartment unannounced like that?"

Edie couldn't take anymore. She rounded on her, arms akimbo. "A *nice* guy," she said. "Maybe you've forgotten this, what with your obsession with the sex god of Manhattan, but *nice* is actually a pretty desirable attribute."

Danielle lifted her chin. "What's the matter with you?"

"Danielle," Greta said. "You were quite inhospitalable to that man."

Her jaw dropped. "That's a good joke, coming from *you*. When was the last time you were polite to anybody?"

"I cannot remember," Greta said. "I also cannot remember the last time anyone cared enough to check up about me."

"Oh, sure, you're completely alone in the world," Danielle muttered sarcastically. "Poor Greta!"

"Danielle . . ." Edie muttered in warning. She supposed Danielle didn't know that Greta *was* alone in the world. Or closer to it than either of them were.

Not that Greta needed Edie's help. She pinned a steely gaze on Danielle. "*Ja*, poor me. I was so popular for years, I never spent a night alone. So many good, good friends. I could call them any time of the night." She laughed bitterly. "Where are they now? Now that I don't go out to bars no more, I don't hear from anyone. Except my AA sponsor. She's a nice person."

The blood drained from Danielle's face. "AA?"

"That's right," Greta said. "Maybe if I was Danielle Poitier with friends coming out from my ears and phone ringing all the time, I could tell that nice lady trying to help me to get lost, too. Right?"

This was the first Edie had heard of AA. She'd known something odd was going on with Greta, of course . . . she just hadn't bothered to actually ask.

No wonder Greta had practically been comatose these past few weeks.

"I don't see what any of that has to do with my not wanting to go out with Ross Johnson," Danielle said. "Why should I? I don't even know the guy."

"I guess you never will," Edie said. "Not now."

Danielle looked from one of them to the other, obviously thinking they were ganging up on her, then tossed Ross's number to the floor in frustration. "Well, *you* call him, if you're so strung out over it. Then Ross Johnson can type up a little report and send it to *your* parents!"

She turned on her heel and flitted back to her screened-off cubbyhole.

Edie braved a glance at Greta, who was staring at the painted dragons on the screen and shaking her head. They traded annoyed looks.

"Come," Greta said. "I cut your neck now."

Chapter 22

WHEN SOMETHING FALLS
IN YOUR LAP

The director stared from Edie, to her headshot, and back again. Several times.

She was beginning to question the guy's mental sharpness. What was so hard to grasp? Edie had been updated. Her photograph had not.

"My hair is different." She hoped the nervous quaver in her stomach wasn't transmitting itself into her voice. She was beginning to feel a little sick, actually. Facing her were three middle-aged guys, the director and his "associates," perched on stools on the scuffed black stage of a television studio. They mumbled among themselves, but so far nobody had said more than hello to her.

Phil, the actual director, sat in the middle of the three. He was a thin guy of medium height. The guy on his left could have been his brother. His name was Jeff. She couldn't remember the name of the man on the right, but his name was probably the only thing about him she would ever be able to forget. One look and his image had been burned forever into her memory. Tight T-shirt over a beer belly. And everywhere his clothes ended, thick black hair sprouted—up from the crew neck of his shirt, on his arms, in the space between the legs of his jeans and the tops of his ancient black Reeboks. He wore thick glasses with unfashionably huge plastic frames. Glasses nerdy kids in her high school wore. They were so ugly that she was stunned someone still manufactured them.

Why there were three men there, she couldn't say. It felt like some kind of joke. How many jerks does it take to cast a television commercial?

After what seemed like ages, Phil looked her in the eye and smiled at her. "Your hair doesn't suit you, does it?"

She felt like weeping. Her hair! She'd never angsted so much about her head as she had in the past twenty-four hours. Why the hell hadn't she just left it alone?

Why on earth had she listened to Aurora?

"I, um, just got it cut. Believe it or not, it's better than it was."

Phil and Jeff looked sourly back at her headshot. The furry fat guy, however, guffawed loudly.

She felt like screaming. Were these people really going to humiliate her for the sake of a commercial? What was the point? They had fifteen other women sitting out in the lobby to play their sassy soccer mom in need of soap. At least one of them was bound to have acceptable hair.

Phil stood up and walked halfway toward her. "It's obvious that you're an accomplished actress, Edie . . ."

It was? He'd been so busy staring at her picture, she was surprised he'd even flicked a glance at her resume.

". . . so we're not going to have you read."

Her heart sank.

His tone turned artificially sincere. "Instead, Edie, I'd like you to tell me about a moment in your life when you felt *wonder*—when you saw something you never in your life expected to see. When suddenly *new possibilities*"—here he gesticulated like a cheap carny conjurer—"opened up for you. Do you understand?"

She nodded. He was asking her to show that she would be able to endow a box of Sudz laundry detergent with a sense of awe and wonder. She hated doing little improvs like this at auditions. In fact, she hated auditions, period. They were torture.

Why had she ever thought she wanted to be an actress?

"Tell me, Edie," Phil said, his voice oozing fake urgency. "Make me feel what you felt."

She closed her eyes for a moment, fervently praying her mind would glom on to something. For a split second she was frightened that she wouldn't even be able to come up with a moment of wonder.

And then one came to her.

She locked her gaze on Phil. "It happened last December. It was the week of that big ice storm, and hardly anyone was working. My boyfriend, Douglas, called me up one afternoon and told me he'd found something. He wanted to know what I thought. He gave me an address on West Thirtieth and told me to meet him there.

"When I walked up the street, I saw it was an apartment building. Four stories. Brick. Really beautiful, with ornate art nouveau railings on the outside balconies. I went up to the apartment number he'd given me, expecting to see your typical cramped one-bedroom . . . but it wasn't like that. It was huge! Two full big bedrooms and a bonus area, with high tin ceilings and an exposed brick wall. I didn't see the flaws then—the mildewy grout and the curling linoleum and the old peeling paint. I just saw how spacious it was, and how perfect it would be to live there with Douglas, who I realized at that moment wanted me to move in with him but hadn't worked up the courage to ask me. In an instant I visualized myself being so happy there. And it was only twenty-one hundred dollars a month! It was a like a miracle!"

It *had* been a miracle. But now, as she recounted the story, it felt like a tragic moment. *The moment I became delusional.* She finished with an exclamation, but she realized that her voice was tight—not just from nerves, but from the realization of how wrong everything had gone since then.

Phil was gaping at her blankly, while behind him his twin was nervously scribbling something on her resume to avoid looking her in the eye. Only the bespectacled werewolf seemed to be at all moved by her story. *He* was chortling.

"Twenty-one hundred a month!" he exclaimed. "What happened?"

Edie cleared her throat. "I moved into the apartment."

"With Douglas?"

"Yeah, but . . . well, he left."

Hairy guy seemed to think that was a real riot. "Apartments are harder to get than lovers anyway."

If furball here could say that, it was a sad statement on how hard up the women of New York City must be.

"Thank you so much, Edie," Phil said, interrupting them.

This was her dismissal. There was no smile of encouragement. No promise to get in touch with her agent. She picked up her shoulder bag and headed for the door.

The hairy guy stopped her halfway there. "Can you sing?"

"Roger . . ." Phil said impatiently.

Edie stopped. "I'm not Edith Piaf, exactly . . ."

The fur factory nodded knowingly. "But you can sell a song."

"Exactly!"

"Selling a song" was a euphemism used by actors who croaked their way gamely through musical numbers that their voices were not actually up to. The most famous song seller was Rex Harrison in *My Fair Lady*. His Henry Higgins had given false hope to millions of the vocally inept, which Edie was. But to tell a director that you couldn't sing for shit just wasn't done.

Roger, unfortunately, called her bluff. "Great! Sing 'Oklahoma!' for me."

She gulped. "Right now?"

"Sure. Just pretend you're Aunt Eller out on the porch."

It was on the tip of her tongue to ask if she should be a young, hip Aunt Eller. At this juncture in the miserable audition, she had a feeling that the man was just messing with her head. What was the point? The director obviously didn't want her.

On the other hand . . . What was one more little humiliation? Edie took a deep breath, threw out her arms, and bellowed the damn song with all the gusto she could muster. She even injected a little of Danielle's accent into her voice to give it some authenticity. She hadn't made it far past the bit about the waving wheat, though, when Roger stopped her.

He was laughing again.

"That was actually better than I expected."

He made it sound as if he expected her to sound as tuneful as a cement mixer. In which case, she couldn't have disappointed him by much.

She tossed her purse over her shoulder and exited through the small throng of waiting actresses huddled on plastic chairs. She knew part of the reason she wanted to cry was just because she had been so tense and now it was all over. But she would not start bawling in front of these people. She was not going to be so un-professional as to cry in front of other success-starved thespians. It was just an audition. For a laundry detergent commercial, for heaven's sake.

She would wait till she got back to her apartment to be unpro-fessional.

But right now her apartment seemed so far away. Not to men-tion, after that audition, just thinking about her apartment was giving her the willies. *The apartment!* What a dumb response to Phil's question! The man had so obviously been expecting her to rhapsodize over the first time she'd been to a play, or heard Beethoven, or seen a shooting star. He hadn't wanted her to nat-ter on about her twenty-one-hundred-dollar-a-month apartment.

She's blown it, blown it, blown it. And now she was doomed to spend the rest of the day tormented by *esprit d'escalier*, compli-ments of Sudz laundry detergent.

From Tenth Avenue in the upper fifties she trudged south through Hell's Kitchen and then east toward the theater district. It was hellishly hot, even in her casual cotton hip soccer mom clothes. As she neared her subway stop, though, she found herself stopped in front of the frosted glass door of a bar. "The Back Page" was etched in *New York Times*–masthead font across the glass. She used to meet Douglas here sometimes. Her heart felt so tight, she wondered if she could take much more today.

She decided to test it, and pushed through the door.

It was still afternoon, but the liberally air-conditioned bar was doing a healthy business. All the usual types she remembered from the old days were present: The businessmen with their coats draped over the backs of their chairs. Print journalists (recogniz-able by the absence of neckties) who sat talking at each other at a million words per minute. And of course there were one or two barflies, the guys who hadn't shaved in days who sat alone at the bar, looking straight ahead, seeing no one. They might look un-employed, but they somehow managed to scrape together enough money to piss away on a drink in the middle of the day.

She heaved herself onto a barstool and ordered a gin and tonic.

That's what she used to order when Douglas would bring her here. God, she forgot sometimes how much she missed him.

Thinking about Douglas, a familiar frustration welled up in her. Why had he just left her hanging like this? He hadn't called her since May. It was now mid-July. Didn't he care what hap-pened to her, to their relationship? Was he expecting just to come waltzing back into her life someday?

She prayed he would. Much as her little heart thumped when she looked at a guy like Ross Johnson, she wasn't doing hand-springs at the possibility of having to start dating again. Those first dates were murder. You never knew if you were going to have fun or be forced to endure a nightmarish four hours before you could make your excuses and go home. And you had to go through so many first dates before you finally found one person you were compatible with.

She went over that word. Compatible. It sounded so blood-less, so lacking in joy. Is that what she and Douglas had been? Compatible? She couldn't remember the last time *he'd* made her heart thump. She couldn't even remember why she missed him; sometimes it felt as if she just missed not being alone.

"Edie?"

She spun toward the sound of a familiar voice and found her-self looking into the eyes of Tom McCormick, a journalist buddy of Douglas's. "Hi!"

He settled down next to her. "I almost didn't recognize you. You look great! Your hair is different, isn't it?"

Different? Brunette to red, long to short. It amazed her that men could be so obtuse when it came to something any woman would have referred to as a massive change. "Yeah, I just got it cut."

"Fantastic! It looks really sexy."

"Thanks," she said. "I was just crying into my beer. Well . . . my gin and tonic."

"Love problems?"

Why would he ask that? He knew better than anyone that with Douglas gone, she had no love problems to speak of. "No, work problems. I just blew an audition, thanks partly to my hair, I think."

"Whoever it was must have crap for taste, then. You look incredible. You really do."

"You're looking pretty snappy yourself," she said, and realized that he did, actually. Tom had always been sort of handsome. Blond hair, blue eyes, square jaw. He'd come from the West Coast after college, and he and Douglas had worked together for years. "Are you still at the *Times?*"

"No, I'm freelancing now."

"That's good," she said before she realized she didn't know whether it was or not. "Isn't it?"

He shrugged. "I get to do more in-depth pieces. Right now I'm doing a story about alternative fuels. Not exactly glamour boy stuff like your old boyfriend, but interesting."

Her *old* boyfriend? She took a swallow of gin. "I haven't heard from Douglas in weeks." She couldn't bring herself to confess to months. "Have you?"

He shook his head. "Nah. Not since June."

A dagger pierced her heart. *June?* Douglas had contacted Tom McCormick, but not her?

"He's probably keeping himself busy," Tom went on. "Frankly, I always told him he was insane to want to go over there."

"To Uzbekistan?"

Tom smiled ruefully. "I think what he really was aiming for was the Balkans. You know, closer to the romance of Paris and Prague and Rome. Those assignments are like gold, of course. But he lobbied as best as he could."

"Lobbied," she repeated.

Tom laughed. "Okay, *pestered* would probably more accurately describe what he was doing. Sometimes I thought James—" He frowned. "You remember James, don't you?"

She nodded. James had been an editor of the Metro section.

Douglas had worshiped him. Or maybe he had just enjoyed sucking up to him.

"Sometimes I thought James would hit the roof if Douglas complained any more about wanting to be transferred to the international section so he could go to Europe. Old Douglas was always cornering him at parties and taking him out to lunches and then griping at him nonstop about how he wasn't being challenged. James used to yell at him, 'You want a little cheese with that whine, Doug?'" He shook his head and laughed at the memory. "James is hilarious."

Edie gulped down more gin. "I always thought the assignment in Uzbekistan had just sort of . . . you know . . . fallen into his lap."

"Ha!" Tom shook his head. "Believe me, nothing fell in Douglas's lap that he didn't spend months trying to tip over himself." He smiled at her. "I always told him he was crazy to want to leave the country when he had you here."

"Really?" she asked tightly. "What did he say to that?"

"You know Douglas. He'd just get so focused on one thing that he'd forget about everything else. That's just the way he is."

"Mm." She felt like she was going to throw up.

Tom put his hand on her arm. "Hey, are you okay?"

She swallowed. "I guess I'm just not used to drinking in the middle of the day. Plus that audition . . ."

"Sure," he said, his eyes flashing with concern. "And it's so hot out. Maybe I should catch a cab. I'll take you back to your place."

"I was just on my way to the subway when I came in here."

"A cab'll get you there much quicker. I was going downtown anyway." He smiled in the face of her doubtful expression. "Scout's honor."

The idea of cruising in a cab down Seventh Avenue while the hordes of people sweated it out on the steaming subway below was too seductive. She paid for her drink and then she and Tom left the bar together. In the cab, he slid over to the middle of the seat to give the cabdriver the coordinates of her apartment. Then he failed to slide back over to his window. His hand came to rest on her thigh.

She winged a hostile glance at him.

His brows raised. "Are you seeing anyone?"

She'd never noticed before how much he looked like John Tesh.

"No one seriously," she answered, unable to muster the courage to admit that she hadn't even been sure she had been dumped until she ran into him. "I'm not really interested in playing the field right now." She added pointedly, "Not interested *at all*."

Still the hand didn't move. Instead, it squeezed. "That's what all you women say when you've been unlucky. We could remedy that, you know."

God, he was practically waggling his eyebrows at her. She tried to stifle the urge to laugh and only half succeeded.

"There," he purred, "at least I've got you smiling."

"Yes, you have. If you keep it up, I'll be laughing in your face."

He leaned back, touching his shoulder to hers as he looked down into her eyes. "You should smile all the time. A woman's always prettier when she smiles, you know."

He needed to be thumped. "That's what my grandmother and a few annoying uncles used to tell me."

A deep chuckle rumbled out him. "Just think of me as a substitute uncle."

"Uncle Tom?"

He laughed, shaking his head. "You always had a great sense of humor, you know that? I could never understand how Douglas could get bored with a girl like you."

She went cold. "Did he say he was bored?"

Tom winced as if he'd just made a giant boo-boo, or betrayed some male *omerta*. "No, of course not. But when the guy announced that he was flying off to live two continents away, you had to wonder, didn't you?"

No, she never did. She had thought that maybe he didn't love her enough. She had thought that he loved his job more than her. But she had never considered the fact that he was *bored* with her.

Why had this never occurred to her? It wasn't as if she were so wildly egotistical as to believe that any man would find being with her all the stimulation he would need for a lifetime. She wasn't Aurora.

God knows she wasn't.

The cab pulled up outside her building. Tom reached for his wallet.

She shook her head. "Thanks for the ride, Tom. I think I'm going to go in and rest."

He looked offended. "I thought I could come up with you. See what you've done to the place."

Yeah, right. Like a vulture he was going to swoop in and pick at the sad little brokenhearted carcass that Douglas had left on the savannah before he'd decided to move on. Before he'd gotten bored.

"I have two roommates now."

"Two!" Tom said, appalled.

"They're probably home right now." Actually, late afternoon was one time when she could be fairly certain that the apartment would be empty. "I'm lucky if I ever get a moment's peace."

"Oh." His disappointment was palpable. That was one thing roommates were good for: Keeping wolves at bay. "Well, I'll give you a buzz sometime."

"Sure, Tom," she said, numb. "You do that."

As she had guessed, she did have the apartment to herself. But the emptiness of the place only added to her blue mood. She threw down her purse, flung herself onto the couch, and picked up Kuchen. The heavy weight and the loud purr were some comfort, at least. In fact, she had the childish urge to bury her face in all that soft fur and cry.

What was she doing with her life? Why had she ever thought anyone in his right mind would ever fall in love with her, much less stay that way?

Restlessly, she got up again and paced. It was just all the rejection that was getting to her. Rejection at auditions, and now—she realized belatedly—rejection by Douglas. He had been lying to her, letting her down easy. She saw that so clearly now. All those stupid words that she swallowed whole—that she and his job were just "temporarily incompatible." That the job had just fallen into his lap. Of course it hadn't. Of course.

She had two hours until she had to get to Geppetto's. Two hours. For the first time in her life, she would rather be waitressing than sitting alone with her thoughts. Not knowing what else to do, she stumbled toward the refrigerator. It was empty except for three different brands of diet soda, Snapple, milk, a tub of raspberry yogurt, and a take-out container of cold sesame noodles with Greta's name on it.

She stared in disappointment. What she really wanted was something sweet. Chocolate.

But in the end, she just made do with stealing Greta's noodles.

Chapter 23

HARPOONING THE WHITE WHALE

Danielle was sorry Edie had to wait tables and wasn't there to witness her moment of triumph when Alan picked her up at the apartment.

He looked so damn good. Different than he did at work. His hair was slicked back, and he wore some really sharp jeans and a brown leather jacket over a dark silky shirt. He was more casual than she had expected, but she wasn't in the least disappointed.

The outfit she had chosen, a silky summer dress with a low-cut back, he took in with appreciative eyes. "You look pretty."

Pretty. He always used that word. It seemed old fashioned, courtly. Dainty.

Greta loomed in the doorway of her room, impossible to ignore.

"This is one of my roommates, Alan," Danielle said, gesturing. "Greta, this is Alan."

The two nodded.

"How *ist* your *Mutter?*" Greta asked him politely, laying on an accent as thick as Colonel Klink's.

Alan, bless him, didn't seem to catch the sarcasm. "She's fine," he said, his tone laced with confusion.

Danielle glared at Greta.

Just having a little fun, Greta's glance to Danielle said. But to Alan she turned and smiled. "Forgive. It is customary in Germany to ask after family."

"I didn't know that," Alan said. "How interesting."

"Guess we should get going!" Danielle locked on to his arm and started yanking him toward the door. "See you later, Greta."

Greta fluttered her fingers in a wave. "Don't do a thing I wouldn't do."

"What would that be?" Danielle fired back.

Greta's laugh followed them out the door.

Back on the street they walked to the corner to hail a cab. "Where are we going?" Danielle asked.

"I want it to be a surprise." His smile would have taxed the resources of Con Ed. "Do you mind?"

In that instant, she wouldn't have minded if he announced that the night's agenda was a wade through the East River.

He gave the taxi driver an address in the east fifties and then settled down next to her. A surprise—how romantic! Instead of just settling for the *dinner and* . . . formula, he had really thought out in advance how to make this date special.

Unless the surprise was where he was taking her to dinner and what movie they were seeing afterward.

"I liked Greta," he said, breaking in on her thoughts.

It was impossible to keep the amazement out of her voice. "Really?"

He laughed. "She seemed . . . singular."

"Oh." She shrugged. "I guess."

He squeezed her hand. "But then, so are you. I should have guessed that you would know interesting people."

He thought *she* was singular? Suddenly, the word seemed magical to her. No one had ever called her that before. She liked it even better than pretty. It indicated individuality, maybe even depth. Of course, he'd also called Greta singular. Which would mean that they were both singular. But maybe he meant that they were singular in different ways.

"You know most of the people I know, I imagine," she said.

He looked startled by that statement. "I do?"

"Well . . . the ones I know in Manhattan, at least. Most of the folks I hang out with here are proofers."

"The temps at work, you mean?"

She frowned. *The temps.* That anonymous term was how the

lawyers probably thought about all the proofers who worked diligently all the livelong day cleaning up the errors riddling their documents.

"Maybe you don't know many of them by name," she said, "but you must know a few. Wilson, for instance."

He frowned. "That name doesn't ring a bell."

She was shocked. Wilson had been working at Ramsey, Lombard, and Gaines for over six months! "I *know* you've seen him," she said. "The first time you spoke to me, he was sitting next to me in that unused office."

He frowned, as if casting back in his memory.

"Red-headed guy?" she said, giving him a hint. "He was a little sarcastic that day, if I recall."

He shook his head, smiling at her. "Sorry. It's not ringing any bells. I guess I only had eyes for you."

Her stomach did a little flip. God, he was smooth. But smooth in a good way. He wasn't just hammy and glib . . . and despite what Wilson said, she didn't find him the least bit arrogant.

When the cabbie dropped them off on the Upper East Side, Alan took her arm. "Have you ever been around here? The next avenue over is Sutton Place."

She replied that she'd heard tell of it.

"But this is where we're going," he said, nodding toward the large apartment building right behind them.

"Is there a party here?" she asked.

"That's right. A private party."

The doorman nodded at Alan. (Another first—she'd never been in a doorman building.) In the elevator, they stood slightly apart while the car went up eight floors. "Here we are," he announced when the doors opened.

The gray-carpeted hallway seemed very quiet, almost somber. If there was a party going on here, it had to be a gathering of deaf mutes.

At apartment 8C, Alan took out a key and opened the door. When he switched on his lights, she was stunned. The room in front of her was modern, yet warm. There were several interesting lamps casting gentle light, aided in places by recessed lighting from the ceiling. On one wall there was a small glass-encased waterfall letting out a gentle trickling water sound. The furniture had that mod Euro look, but even she, an interior décor ignoramus, could tell the pieces were of incredible quality, probably fashioned from rare endangered tropical woods and buttery leather from Norwegian cows.

The apartment was empty.

"This is *your* place," she said, feeling vaguely foolish.

"For our first real date, I couldn't see going to a crowded restaurant and then a noisy club, or a movie where I wouldn't even be able to talk to you."

Then she noticed something that made her heart stop. On a table next to a sliding glass door that led to a small terrace, there were two place settings with an unlit candle between them. Through the door she could see a corner of the Queensboro bridge, its lights more than a fair replacement for all the stars that were unavailable to the residents of New York City.

A private, candlelit dinner for two. How romantic!

She whirled, practically bumping chests with Alan, he was standing so close to her.

"I wanted to be alone with you as much as possible." He touched her arm. "Is that selfish?"

Selfish? She was practically choking on the lump in her throat. "No!" she managed to blurt out. "It's exactly what I wanted . . . or would have, if I'd been given the choice."

His eyes twinkled down at her. "Good."

"And your apartment—it's so incredible!"

He shut the door and gleefully gave her the tour. "Of course, this room is what drew me to the place," he said, gesturing around the living room. "And the terrace, of course. But it's also got a pretty good little kitchen."

The kitchen had granite counters and sleek steel appliances. It was like a kitchen in one of those magazines her mother was always looking at for "ideas"—interior decorating tips she would never get around to using. The bathroom was done in Italian tile and had an old clawfoot tub and a separate shower stall in one corner. Alan opened the door to the bedroom, but she was too giddy to look much beyond the king-sized bed.

"Incredible," she whispered. "I thought my apartment was nice, but this makes it seem like a gopher hole."

He laughed. "I thought your place was charming. All the old-fashioned furniture."

"Greta's," she said.

A wall phone rang, and he answered it. "Be right down," he said into the receiver. He hung up and looked at Danielle. "Can you keep yourself entertained for five minutes?"

"Of course!"

"I'll be right back."

The minute the door closed, she circled back to the bedroom. Not that she was a snoop or anything, but you *could* tell a lot about people from their private spaces. And what she could tell immediately about Alan was that he was the neatest bachelor on the planet. Not a thing was out of place. The bedcovers were so tidy they could have passed military muster. There was nothing on his dresser but a comb. A small shelf on the wall held a few family pictures (he looked just like his dad) and five books. A few nonfiction books including a biography of Lindbergh, *The Sun Also Rises*, and something by Norman Mailer.

She frowned. That was not a satisfactory bookshelf. Five books? Whoever just had five books? There didn't seem to be any others around. She continued poking about, opening a door she assumed would be a closet. She was wrong. It was a textile ware-house. She stepped in, surrounding herself on three sides with suits and shirts and shoes, shoes, shoes. A little wire daisy wheel contraption sticking out of the wall had to contain over a hundred ties. The man was a clotheshorse! And he actually had the room (and the money) to be one!

Standing there, she honestly felt her heart swell. In this great big city of eight million souls, could it honestly be that she had found the perfect man for her, right off the bat? It seemed too fantastic to believe ... yet she couldn't imagine dreaming up a better guy than Alan. The words "too good to be true" came to mind, but she pushed them away. Why couldn't he be true? Perfect matches did exist in this world—love wasn't all fairy tales.

"See anything you like?"

The words jarred her out of her reverie. She hadn't heard a door . . . or footsteps. She turned, mortified. "I'm sorry! I wasn't snooping, I was just . . ."

Just snooping.

He grinned at her. "You've discovered my weakness. I'm a compulsive shopper."

"Me, too!"

"Then *you* can really appreciate my collection." As he took in his wearable wealth, his expression was one of adoration. And when he looked down at her, the expression didn't change. "I had a feeling you'd be my dream girl."

Her breath caught, and her mouth formed a shocked O. Had he really said that? Had the words "dream girl" really passed her dream man's lips?

He took her hand. "Come on. I'm starved."

He led her back to the window by the little terrace. Stacked on the table now was a small city of take-out containers. "Do you like Chinese?"

"Love it!"

The word "love" leapt so easily to her lips, she noticed.

He pulled out a chair for her and got her settled. "Let's see . . . we've got dumplings, Kung Pao shrimp, and Moo Shoo pork. All very messy and tasty. Oh, and wine?"

She nodded. "That would be wonderful."

He dashed to the kitchen and came back with a bottle of cabernet. "I'm not sure this is the correct choice, but it's the best I've got. I've been saving it for you."

She drew back in surprise. "You've only known me a week."

A sheepish grin touched his lips. "Well, I only bought the wine two nights ago."

"You really have shown restraint."

They settled down to some serious eating. When she took her regulation modest first-date portions that would have made a debutante's mother beam with pride, Alan heaped more of everything on her plate. When she said she couldn't possibly take seconds, he practically forced the last dumpling into her mouth with his chopsticks.

"You can't fool me. I've watched you at the office," he told her. "You're a three-snacks-per-shift girl."

She was amazed. He must have been watching her! Of course, his office was on the way to the hall that had the vending machine, which more than anything explained her sudden mania for Kit-Kats. But she thought she'd been spying on *him*.

When dinner was over, they talked some more, and another bottle of cabernet was produced. The conversation reached a lull after he'd told her a few anecdotes from law school, and Alan stood up.

"Entertainment time!" he said, pulling her to her feet. He made it sound as if they were going to do a conga around the living room . . . which would have been a challenge, given that the half-bottle of wine she'd just consumed was making her feel a tad light-headed.

Happily, he had something more sedentary in mind. He drew her over to the other side of the room, near the couch, and pulled open a curtain she'd assumed covered a window. Instead, he revealed a flat plasma screen television. Next to it stood a large armoire, and he started opening doors to reveal sound system controls. It was more hi-tech than any home entertainment system she'd ever seen. He pointed to a shelf of DVDs.

"Pick out something," he said.

"But you've probably already seen all these."

He shrugged. "I'm a movie-holic. I could watch my favorites again and again."

She was that way, too. She perused the shelf, which was chock-full of action pictures. Practically anything ever done by Arnold, Bruce, and Sylvester (except *Rhinestone*), plus a liberal smattering of Steven Segal, Tom Cruise, James Bond films, and Clint Eastwood. Buried in all of this was a copy of *West Side Story*.

She pulled it out and hummed the "One of These Things Is Not Like the Others" song from "Sesame Street." "Did someone give you this as a gift?"

He drew back in mock offense. "Why? Don't you think I can appreciate"—he read a quote off the box—" 'a thrilling musical masterpiece on film'?"

"I don't believe you've ever watched the whole thing."

"Then I will tonight, with you," he said.

He led her over to the couch and settled her in with another glass of wine and then began fiddling with the control levels. When the movie finally began, she had to admit that his investment in electronics had not been wasted. The sound coming at her was incredible, and the picture made her almost feel that she was in a movie theater. In fact, some of the movie theaters in New York had actually seemed *smaller* than this.

"This is wonderful," she told him as he eased next to her on the couch.

He draped an arm in back of her shoulder. "Cozy, isn't it? Sorry there's no popcorn, though."

As if she could eat another thing. Or even want to, when Alan was inches away from her, his body brushing hers. "I won't miss it."

And she didn't. The same couldn't be said for the movie, however. By the end of the opening credits, Alan was holding her hand, his thumb making rhythmic circles against her palm in time to "When You're a Jet." By the time Tony sang "Maria," they were locked in a kiss, and by "Officer Krupke," Danielle was flat on her back with Alan's erection pressing urgently against her thigh.

She just couldn't seem to help herself. One minute she'd been wondering how much makeup they'd used on Natalie Wood, and the next minute she was panting and pulling off Alan's clothes. His body was so incredible—muscular and hard, like a perfectly put together package just for her.

Straddling her, still half-clothed, he cradled her head with his hands. God, he was handsome. Just looking into his eyes was making her squirm with longing.

"I have something for you," he said.

No kidding. She almost laughed. But the earnest look in his eyes told her this wasn't some coy way of letting her know he was ready. "What?"

"A present," he said, almost shyly.

She squinted at him. "You mean, a real present? A wrapped-in-a-box present?"

"Uh-huh, and tied with a ribbon." He brushed his lips against hers. "Does that seem too pushy?"

Pushy? More like unbelievable! No one had ever given her a gift on a first date before. She nearly swooned from the romance of it. "I think it sounds wonderful."

He smiled like a kid. "Hang on, I'll be right back." He pushed off the couch and practically skipped toward his bedroom.

She lolled on the couch, half watching a big dance scene as she wondered what Alan could have gotten her. What? Her mind drew a blank. All she could do was wallow in the wonder of having found someone so wonderful, who was as attracted to her as she was to him.

When he came back, he tugged her gently up to sitting and presented her with a small red clothes box tied with a silver ribbon. "I hope it fits. I had to eyeball the size."

Of course! He was a clothes hound, after all. She laughed at the fun of it and pulled the bow off. After she'd opened the box and pushed aside the tissue paper, it took her a moment to realize what she was staring at. Lingerie. She picked up a wispy strip of pink lace and felt herself flush. He was giving her a *bra?*

Nominally it was a bra, though it wouldn't cover anything and it certainly wouldn't lend much support.

Danielle wasn't sure what to think. No man had ever given her a gift like this . . . especially on a first date. Wasn't it sort of strange? Or, at least, presumptuous?

Of course, maybe that was just her inexperience talking. And this did show that he had been thinking about her. That was nice, wasn't it?

"What do you think?" His eyes were shining eagerly.

She swallowed. "It's very . . . sexy."

"Look—there's something more."

She gingerly picked out another pink lacy item—a few mere straps of elastic, when you came right down to it. Of course they were matching panties, although she had to inspect them closely at first. It was weird. There were, like, three leg openings. She held them right up in front of her face and squinted at them for a good thirty seconds before she finally puzzled it all out. They were crotchless.

Alan leaned forward and massaged one of her breasts. "Ever since I spotted that little combo I haven't been able to think about anything else but seeing you in it."

"Oh." She didn't know quite what to say. He would certainly be able to see her *through* it. "Thank you."

He nibbled playfully at her earlobe, then whispered, "I'm ready for my fashion show."

Fashion show?

"You can change in the bathroom."

He stopped nibbling and touching. Now he was just waiting.

Fleeing to the bathroom sounded pretty good, actually. She gathered the box to her chest and stood up. Halfway across the living room she turned back and retrieved her purse and the half-full wine bottle off the coffee table.

In the bathroom, she closed the door, sank against the Italian tile on the wall, and swilled wine right from the bottle. Her thoughts were running amok. She'd been pretty sure they were going to have sex before he'd brought out the raunchy lingerie . . . so what was the big deal? Sure, the moment had turned from being a spontaneous expression of lust to a command perfor-mance, but so what? This was still what she'd dreamed about for weeks, this was what she wanted.

He'd bought her a sexy gift. He had been fantasizing about her. She should be thrilled.

Outside the door, she heard Alan moving around. The TV had been turned off, and now the sounds of soft jazzy saxophones drifted toward her. Mood music.

Don't be a fool, Danielle. You wanted adventure.

Resolutely, she set down the wine bottle and shed her clothes. Wriggling into the bra and panties didn't take long, so she did a little touch-up work, pulling a comb through her hair and swish-ing some Scope she found in his medicine cabinet. She had her hand on the door when she remembered her purse. She un-clasped it and dug inside until she'd found two key items, Chanel and a box of Trojans. She spritzed herself quickly and grabbed one—then, on second thought, four—of the foil packets. Unfor-tunately, she had nowhere to conceal them, so she supposed she would just have to carry them out like this in a foil prophylactic snake.

She gave herself a final check in the mirror. It was shocking how little it took to achieve a back-of-the-*Voice* sex ad look.

As she headed for the door, she really only had one regret: That underwear she'd bought at Victoria's Secret. She'd spent fifty precious bucks, thinking Alan might appreciate something sexy.

Chapter 24

GRETA GOES TO THE GYM

"**H**ey Mickey" was blaring from an unseen speaker, its peppy synthesized strains echoing all over the cavernous room. Greta hadn't listened to the song since she was a schoolgirl in Germany, when she'd thought it was cute. Which was yet more proof, as if any were needed, that eleven-year-olds had no taste.

She found the pulsing rhythm and squeaky lyrics nauseating, but she was not feeling so hot in any event. This was her second trip to Round-the-Clock Fitness. (Her first had been yesterday to fill out membership forms, which had seemed strenuous enough.) She had lifted weights. She had bicycled. Now she was on some elliptical doohickey, sweating and breathing—barely—in ragged wheezes. She hadn't yet experienced an endorphin high or the satisfaction of taking steps to get fit that they had assured her she would feel when she signed up for her membership. Instead, her body hurt, her head ached, and she felt like she was either about to have a heart attack or vomit. Possibly both.

This couldn't be good for you.

This was part of her improvement plan, though, and she needed to stick with it. Thirty was creeping up on her. She was going to be sober, nonsmoking, and reasonably healthy. She'd had her fun; now she was getting old and it was time to suffer.

"You have a great body!"

Greta wheezed through a few more rotations before she real-

ized someone had said something to her. The man on the machine next to her, in fact. "I beg your pardon?"

The man was wearing a muscle shirt tucked into loose shorts,
and elaborate Nike sneakers that made his feet look dispropor-
tionately large. He had dark hair with a balding spot on top and
wore a tidy little beard. What was he, some kind of health club
lech? It was Saturday night. What kind of losers exercised on
Saturday night?

She hoped he wasn't going to pester her.

"I bet you're a runway model," he said.

Greta almost lost her grip on the support bars. She didn't dare
let go of them for fear she would pitch over. "No, I am not."

"No? You *could* be."

That was a laugh. In fact she did laugh . . . which turned into a
juicy, hacking cough.

"I like your voice," the guy said. "You Russian?"

She was tempted to stop pedaling, so she could lean over and
strangle the guy. "I am German."

"What do you do?" he asked.

"Nothing that would interest you," she managed, wanting to
end the discussion.

The guy recoiled. "Okay, okay. Sorry I asked!" He faced forward again, his cheeks stained with red.

Greta huffed along. She had heard about these health clubs
being meat markets, but she had never imagined anyone messing
with her. If the guy *had* been messing with her. Maybe the man
was paying her a compliment—just being friendly, as Americans
would say—in which case she had not answered correctly.

And she had upbraided Danielle for being rude!

She was always missing connections, it seemed. She thought
perhaps it was because English was her second language. But now
she wondered if she was missing a getting-along-with-people
gene. She was not talented at communication. That was a hard
idea to accept, considering how long she'd spent trying to learn
how to speak English. Now she knew the language; she just
couldn't talk to people.

Make the effort to be nice, she told herself. *It won't kill you.* She'd done it with her roommates, and it had sort of worked. They didn't seem entirely awful to her now. There had even been a few moments of camaraderie. Then she'd go and do something like tonight when she'd made fun of Danielle's date.

She shouldn't have. She should try to be a better person. It was just so difficult to be better when you felt so cranky all the time.

She turned to the man. She felt dizzy. "*I'm* sorry."

He glanced back at her. "Huh?"

"I was rude. I'm sorry."

She was also feeling chilled.

The man stopped pedaling to look at her. "Hey. Are you okay?"

"No," she said. In fact, she felt as if she were about to faint. And then she did.

Maybe being nice *would* kill her.

When she came to, several health club employees in matching blue polo shirts were hovered over her, peering into her face. She moved a little and winced.

"How are you feeling?" one of the men shouted at her in that loud, precise tone people used with foreigners. The guy on the elliptical must have told them she had an accent.

She wondered what had happened to that guy. He wasn't there now.

"Okay," she lied. "I feel okay."

She was in an office, nowhere near the workout area. Someone— or several someones—must have carried her out. The image of men heaving her long, sweaty body through that maze of machines, no doubt drawing the stares of everyone in the club, made her skin crawl. It wasn't the first time she'd made a spectacle of herself, of course, but it was the first time she'd done it sober.

"Can you stand up?"

"Of course." She stood up, fighting wooziness, and discovered that her ankle was killing her.

"You might have twisted your ankle a little during your fall."

"Yes, no doubt," she said.

The man who had spoken, a short, stocky fellow with thick short brown hair, regarded her with a concerned expression. "Would you like us to call an ambulance?"

She barked out a laugh. "No, I am fine."

"If you'll recall, you signed a paper when you joined declaring your understanding that we could not be held liable for any accident you suffered on our machinery, so long as that machinery was properly maintained."

Oh, for God's sake. Were they worried she was going to sue them? "It was me not properly maintained."

The three of them exchanged looks of relief. "Well, then . . ."

The meaning was clear. Now that they were assured she was not going to slap a lawsuit on them, she was free to hobble off into the sunset.

"Thank you for your help." She recalled that after she had signed the paper agreeing not to sue them, she signed another paper agreeing that she would be able to get a full refund on her dues if she was not satisfied with the club within the first ten-day period. "I would like now to cancel my membership."

When that was all taken care of, she limped down the street toward home and was surprised by the things she'd never noticed before. The uneven places in the sidewalks that she was apt to trip over; the oppressive shadows thrown by the taller apartment buildings; and the fact that there was a bar on almost every block.

At least, that's how it seemed. All the bars were packed, too. She had pressed her nose against the windows of a few of them and stared enviously at all the happy people inside. Smiling. Laughing. Drinking.

She stopped at one now. Delia's. Why had she never noticed this place before? It was two blocks away from the apartment . . . just two blocks. The inside was a long, narrow room with a bar lined with stools extending as far as she could see toward the back wall. Next to the wall there were two-person tables. A comfortable, intimate little neighborhood meeting place.

God she wanted to go in.

She looked up the avenue. Two blocks. All she had to do was face forward and keep shuffling her feet homeward.

But she couldn't move. She was paralyzed. It hadn't been a good night. Sweating a lot, fainting in public, limping home . . . this is not how she expected to spend the evening. She'd imagined herself jauntily bustling around. The new healthy her.

So much for that. The new her felt even worse than the old her. All her efforts seemed so pointless. What good had shutting herself up alone for weeks on end done her? She wasn't having any fun. She could worry all she wanted about getting old, but what good would it do her to be healthy if she was just going to be alone and pathetic? She had heard once that the good died young because they realized being good was no way to live.

She stared longingly into the bar. *Those* people were happy.

An empty stool beckoned her. Her willpower unraveled like a badly knitted sweater.

Fuck it. She wasn't thirty yet. Besides, she was thirsty. Just one vodka tonic, and she'd make it home in time for the "Iron Chef" potato marathon.

Chapter 25

THE MORNING AFTER

Greta didn't wake up so much as crawl on her hands and knees over broken glass back to the land of the living. Every atom in her body groaned in protest. Her head was pounding, her muscles screamed in agony, and her left ankle throbbed. She risked blinking open one eye against the terrible sunlight pouring through the window and discovered herself crammed into a sleeping position across the couch; her neck was curled into a painful crick and one leg, an anarchist, dangled off toward the floor. She was sharing her place with Kuchen, who felt like a furry bowling ball pressing on her bladder.

She picked up the kitty and dropped her to the ground, where she waddled a foot away and contentedly stretched out on her back under the coffee table. Greta closed her eyes and tried to forget that she had already been assaulted by daylight.

No memory of when or how she'd gotten home came to her. Why was she on the couch instead of her own bed? The only thing she understood completely was the noxious mixture of aching head, feeble stomach, and crawling skin. The symptoms were unfortunately familiar to her, as was the sour, cottony taste in her mouth.

Footsteps came toward her. They sounded unnaturally loud and hollow, like sound effect footsteps in an old radio program. "Good, you're awake!" Edie said.

Good? To Greta, consciousness felt like a tragedy.

She squinted up at Edie, who loomed over her wearing a T-shirt and jean shorts. That meant that it had to be pretty late. After waitressing on Saturday nights, Edie wasn't usually fully functional until after noon the next day.

"Can you talk?" Edie asked her, as if she were a choking victim.

Greta made a stab at pushing herself up to sitting. Halfway there she abandoned the effort and propped herself up on her elbows. "My head has split."

"I made you something for that." She went to the kitchen and then came back again, which in Greta's messed-up head seemed to take either an instant or an eternity. A glass of reddish fluid appeared in front of her. Greta's stomach threatened an unpleasant outcome to any endeavor at consumption.

"No, thank you," she said, swallowing.

The glass was shoved closer to her. "Go ahead, it'll do you good."

She wrinkled her nose. "What's in it?"

"Don't think about that. Just drink."

Tentatively, she took the glass and sniffed it. It was tomato juice mixed with no telling what else. She gulped it down.

"I didn't know we had tomato juice in the refrigerator," she said, after assuring herself that her stomach wasn't about to send her lurching for the bathroom.

"We didn't." Edie dropped down onto the adjacent love seat. "I went to Food Emporium this morning."

She'd made a special trip to the store just to put together a hangover cure? Greta felt curiously touched. "Have I been on the couch all night?"

"Yup."

"What about my room? Is it empty?"

Edie's eyes clouded in confusion. "Of course."

"*Gut.*" That was one thing to be thankful for. Greta had a vague recollection of flirting with some guy at that bar. It wouldn't have been completely unprecedented, unfortunately, if she had found him in the apartment this morning.

Edie cleared her throat. "Are you okay?"

Greta flopped back down on her back. "Sure. Fine."

"You were in pretty bad shape last night."

"I had a vodka tonic. Or maybe seven of them."

Edie's lips curled into a commiserating smile. "Vodka tonics. The Lays potato chips of mixed drinks."

"Potato chips?" Greta asked.

"You can't drink just one," Edie told her.

Greta still had no idea what she was talking about and she was too queasy to care. "So I was here when you came home?"

"Actually, you were in the bathroom."

Ugh. "I'm sorry."

"I tried to get you into your bedroom, but you kept muttering about 'Iron Chef.' What happened to your ankle?"

To the best of her ability, Greta recounted what had happened at the gym. She wasn't sure she could convey the desperation she felt afterward, standing outside that bar.

Now she felt even worse. She felt like a failure.

But how could she expect a perfect little person like Edie to understand that? "I blew it. Now I don't know what to do."

"Start over," Edie told her. As if it were obvious. As if it were so simple, too.

"I don't want to. I'm so tired."

"Then what *do* you want?"

That was what she couldn't answer. She wanted to turn around and find herself just like everybody else, she supposed. So that she wouldn't feel like something apart from everything else. Was that too much to ask?

"You have to start over," Edie said. "Everybody falls apart some-times, but that doesn't mean you have to give up completely."

"*Ja*, I see. I would be throwing the baby out with the dishwater."

"Right." Edie frowned. "Or pretty close to right."

The front door was flung open. Greta flinched, then looked up to see Danielle planted in front of them, absolutely beaming. Greta had forgotten all about her and her big date. Danielle was wearing the clothes from last night, the dress a little wrinkled now. "Hi, ya'll!"

"Hi," Edie said. Then, since Danielle was clearly dying for someone to ask, she added, "How did it go?"

Danielle twirled around like a little kid in her Easter dress. "I'm in love!"

Greta flopped her head back on the cushion, feeling nauseous again. She wasn't sure she was up for this.

"That was fast," Edie observed.

Greta listened to the loud clop clop of Danielle's feet as she headed for the fridge. Her footsteps seemed to shake the earth, like those dinosaurs in the *Jurassic Park* movies. "I knew I was in love with him weeks ago. I just didn't want to think it. I didn't want to hope. It would have been too overwhelming."

"Is this overwhelming emotion reciprocated?" Edie asked her.

"Of course!" She came back slurping contentedly at a Diet Coke.

Edie's lips pursed, and she looked over at Greta. "Did you meet him?"

Him? Oh, the lawyer creep. Greta nodded. That seemed like another lifetime ago.

Danielle nipped over to the couch and squeezed in next to Greta's feet. "Wasn't he yum?"

Greta couldn't begin to say what that was supposed to mean. "He was very handsome. A real studded muffin."

Danielle's jaw dropped. "Omigod—he's, like, a sex god. I mean, really. If you thought he was good looking when he picked me up last night, you should see him without his clothes."

"Uh, Danielle . . ." Edie hitched her throat. "You *really* don't have to go into anatomical detail."

Danielle laughed. "Okay, I'll shut up." She flushed, then flopped backward, sighing dreamily. "I never knew life could be like this! I mean, every single pore in my body feels alive, excited. Have either of you ever felt like that?"

Edie grunted noncommittally.

"Every single pore in my body wants to throw up," Greta said.

"And it isn't just Alan," Danielle twittered on, ignoring them. "It's everything. I've always heard how awful your twenties are, and about what a grind being single is—but honestly, I think it's great! This is the life! I think I could be single forever!"

She chugged down about a third of her soda, oblivious to the hostile stares coming her way.

"What did you and Alan do?" Edie asked. "Besides the obvious, I mean."

Danielle, lost in thought, hummed absently.

Edie shot Greta an exasperated glance. "Ground control to Danielle!"

Danielle jerked her head toward her. "Huh? Oh! We went to his place and ate Chinese food."

Greta frowned. "Some date!"

"I know it sounds peculiar . . ."

"It sounds cheap," Edie said.

Danielle gasped. "Oh! But you should see his place. It's *incredible*. He's got a giant living room with the most incredible television setup, and a gourmet kitchen, and a little terrace with a view of the Queensboro Bridge."

"Huh." Edie was as reluctant as Greta to succumb to the rhapsodic view of this man and his apartment. "Didn't you guys do anything besides eat Chinese food?"

"We sort of watched *West Side Story*."

"Sort of?"

Danielle blushed furiously. "Well, we didn't get very far."

"Good grief! This rich lawyer lured you over to his place, stuffed you full of takeout, then attacked you on the couch during a video?"

"It wasn't like that," Danielle said defensively. "He didn't *attack* me. God! You make it sound so sleazy." She crossed her arms, and Greta noted a strange expression pass over her face. But in the next instant, it was gone. "He was really sweet. Really. You have no idea."

"He just sounds too good to be true," Edie said. "I guess I've been disappointed so often, I can't wrap my mind around the fact that Mr. Perfect exists."

"I couldn't believe it, either," Danielle said. She frowned at Greta. "Are you okay? You look sort of green."

"I am fine," Greta said automatically.

Danielle smiled. "That's good! Today, I want everybody to be happy." She floated back over to her little room behind the screen.

Greta eyed Edie. "Did I say anything about happy?"

Edie shook her head. "God, I feel like a complete pill. Like someone's cranky, finger-wagging aunt. I'm getting defensive about other people's relationships. Everything seems doomed. Everyone who's happy seems delusional. What's come over me?"

Greta closed her eyes and thought for a moment. "Realism," she said.

Chapter 26

WORKING

Alan took Danielle out to dinner—to a real restaurant this time, she had gloated to Edie this morning—and at the end of the date he gave her a box and told her to open it when she got home. Then he extracted a solemn promise from her to wear whatever was in the box to work the next day. At that moment, standing in a streetlamp's glow and staring into those incredible blue eyes, she would have done a swan dive off the top of the Chrysler Building if he'd asked her to.

The gift was another box of lingerie—he seemed to have a little fetish about it—but this was more elaborate than anything she'd ever owned. Danielle had sat on the edge of the tub for ten minutes this morning just trying to puzzle out what went where. It took her another twenty minutes to wriggle, squeeze, snap, and button herself into the corset–panty–garter belt combo. Alan had even thoughtfully included thigh-high stockings for her. The corset was made from soft pink satin with black lace overlay and edging, so that she looked trampy and old fashioned at the same time. Nostalgically raunchy. If the Gibson girls had been into pole dancing, this is what they might have worn.

Where did Alan *get* this stuff?

She supposed it did feel sexy to have all these straps skimming around her thighs, but what good would feeling sexy do her if she was going to be hovering over legal documents all day? Also, a worry started forming in the back of her mind that this was just the beginning of something that could get out of hand. Corsets and undies were one thing . . . but what if Alan started asking her to wear cheerleading uniforms and skimpy nurse outfits?

Where was a person supposed to draw the line?

Greta pounded on the bathroom door. "Danielle! Are you still alive?"

Startled, Danielle whisked on her robe and opened up. "Sorry."

Greta looked her up and down. "You had drowned, I thought."

Danielle wondered if Greta could detect anything weird about her shape. The corset squished in her waist and smashed her breasts toward her collarbone. "How could I drown? I was taking a shower."

Greta blinked at her. "I was giving you a joke."

"Oh, right," Danielle said, scurrying away. Greta could be so odd!

In the privacy her screen afforded her, Danielle puzzled over the portable clothes rack that now stood at the foot of her bed. For a laugh, to wear over Alan's ensemble she chose a loose-fitting, high-necked knit jersey dress in navy blue that her mother had bought her from the Talbot's catalog. It was about as sexy as an all-weather coat. But if she was going to spend her day being pinched by her underwear and limiting her fluid intake, then Alan could at least be forced to exercise a little imagination.

She arrived at work early for her shift and breezed toward the coffee room. Alan had obviously been waiting for her, because when she passed by his office, the door opened, his hand darted out, and he yanked her inside.

Behind the closed door, he pulled her into his arms for a long, wet kiss. A few brief pecks were all they had dared exchange at work before now; kissing there still felt dangerously forbidden.

"Are you wearing it?" he purred eagerly.

She grinned. "What do you think?"

He looked her up and down, and blurted out a laugh. "Is the Hefty Bag company making women's clothing now?"

She stepped back and did a comical catwalk strut for him. Her efforts were rewarded by a low-volume wolf whistle. Then he strolled over to his desk, leaned back against it, and pulled her to him again, so close this time that she was straddling one of his legs.

"Alan!"

He reached under the hem of her skirt and then skimmed his hands up her thighs until he could snap her garters. Then he kissed her so hard and for so long that she started to feel light-headed. She could also feel his hard-on.

"Come here," he said, taking her hand. He sat in one of the leather chairs across from his desk and pulled her, facing him, onto his lap. "Take off your dress."

The blood drained out of her cheeks. *"What?"*

"I want to see you."

"Here?" Her voice was a squeak.

He nodded toward the door. "It's locked."

"But someone could come by . . ."

"Nobody knows I'm in." He leveled his sexiest grin at her. "What are you, chicken?"

Yes, she was. Also, she wasn't accustomed to stripping in office situations.

"All I want is a peek," he said, reaching up and rubbing his knuckle lightly across her breast. Desire flamed through her so predictably, it would have been depressing if she didn't want him so much. "I dreamed about this all night."

Oh, God. When he looked at her like that . . . when he touched her . . . something inside her just shattered. Maybe this was what love was—doing things for someone that you'd never in your life dreamed of doing.

She didn't want to be a prude. Everybody had little fantasies they wanted to indulge in. What had she come to New York for, if not a little excitement? You couldn't have excitement without risk, could you?

Taking a breath, she slowly gathered her dress and pulled it over her head. She dropped it to the floor, draped her arms around his neck, and shook her hair out.

There was nothing disappointing about his reaction. His eyes feasted on her for a few moments, and then he skimmed his fingers along the lace edge of the bustier, down across her stomach, to her thighs. "You're gorgeous," he whispered. She shivered.

Mm . . . Okay, she could see now how this outfit could have its appeal. She bit her lip, and had to hold herself back from grinding against him.

He kissed her again, hard. She heard the quick yank of a zipper, and felt him wriggling underneath her to push down his pants and get into position.

She pushed back, panting. Was he crazy?

"Alan—this is Ramsey, Lombard, and Gaines!" There were lawyers wandering these hallowed halls who had presented cases before the Supreme Court!

He grinned. "I know. That makes it all the more fun."

"But we work here—it would be so unprofessional. . . ."

As if sitting in a guy's lap in "Gunsmoke" undergarments wasn't stretching the code of office behavior enough.

"I want you so much, Danielle. I can't think of anything else. . . ."

"But . . ."

He moved his hand to her panties and slipped a finger inside her.

She gasped.

"You're so beautiful," he whispered. "I can't believe how lucky I am."

He was lucky? Oh, God. "Alan . . ." She swallowed. She couldn't believe she was arguing with him. She couldn't believe she could even think semi-coherently while he had his hand inside her. But *here?* "I-I don't think . . . I don't know if even two of us could get this corset off."

"Who wants it off?" he asked.

In the next moment he pulled her down onto him, penetrating her. Heat flooded her and she let out a bleat of surprise.

"Sh . . ." Alan whispered. He put one hand over her mouth while the other firmly cupped her left buttock. "Just be still and let me do the work."

For the next few minutes the only sounds in the world were their heavy breaths, the squeak of Alan's butt against the chair's leather upholstery, and the whirring of a distant Xerox machine. Danielle couldn't say she was turned on—she was still too stunned, too nervous. And shouldn't he have waited for her permission?

Of course, she had been writhing in his lap in a skimpy outfit. . . .

Alan seemed positively electrified by the verboten activity, however. It was the second time in her life, Danielle realized as he groaned in muted ecstasy beneath her, that she'd had sex without even taking her underwear off.

Afterward, he kissed her and helped her scoot back into her dress. "You're a dream come true," he said, nuzzling her neck. "Did you know that?"

She looked into his blue eyes, and though she'd felt panic-stricken ever since he had pulled her into the office (and would have been more so if she'd known what he had in mind), she felt in that moment that if he asked her to, she'd toss her dress right off again. She even forgave him his pushiness. After all, what did it matter? Work hadn't really started yet . . . and it's not as if he'd asked her to pull a Monica Lewinsky on him while he talked on the phone with a client. They'd just had a little innocent office chair sex. What was the harm in that?

When he looked at her it felt as if her whole body was ablaze. She was putty in his hands, but it didn't seem to matter, because he was obviously just as crazy about her. Sure, he had this little underwear obsession . . .

He gave her a quick parting kiss. "I've never enjoyed being at the office this much."

"Me neither." She left his embrace reluctantly and floated toward the door.

"Danielle?"

She turned. The look in those blue eyes was devastating. "Yes?"

"Keep Friday night open. I want to take you somewhere really special."

Her heart did a somersault. "All right."

He sent her a parting wink.

In a daze she stepped out into the hallway and almost smashed right into Wilson. Her friend stopped, bracing his hands on her shoulders and smiling at her in greeting.

Slowly, though, as he inspected her face, then took note of whose office she had just come out of, the smile faded. Danielle's cheeks felt fiery as dismay, almost disgust, registered on his face.

"What are you doing?" he said in a whisper so violent it was almost a hiss.

"What do you mean?"

He rolled his eyes. "For God's sake, Danielle, go into the bathroom and look. Your lipstick is smudged."

Reflexively, she lifted a hand to her lips. There had only been the corner desk lamp on in Alan's office. He probably hadn't noticed.

She hurried toward the area where the break room and the ladies' room were located. Wilson was right on her heels. "Are you fooling around with Alan Mara now?"

She cringed. "Why don't you get a bullhorn and announce it to the whole building?"

"Well?"

By the little kitchen that housed a coffeepot and a mini-fridge, she rounded on him. "I didn't know I needed your written consent."

He groaned. "Danielle, *at the office?*" He stared at her lips. "It looks like wild suction-mouthed beasts attacked your face."

Alan's kissing could be quite a workout.

"And your hair's mussed," he said. "I can't believe you would let him take advantage of you like this."

That was more than she was willing to take, even from a friend like Wilson. "Who do you think I am? Some impossibly naïve virginal hick? I know what I want,"—she suddenly realized that she was almost shouting, and lowered her voice—"and what I want is Alan. I'm crazy about him, and he feels the same way."

"About you and how many others?"

"*No* others! God, why are you so mistrustful of him? He's been nothing but nice to me, and gentlemanly."

Wilson laughed.

"He hasn't done a thing I didn't want him to," she insisted.

Unbidden, her thoughts flashed back to ten minutes ago, when he'd thrust himself into her. That hadn't exactly been against her will, though. After all, she'd been half-dressed in the guy's lap.

And then a thought occurred to her, one that made her go cold. *We didn't use a condom.* Of course not. She hadn't gone into his office prepared for action. Now she was going to have to go beg for a morning-after pill somewhere. And—oh, God. Tests.

"Danielle?"

Wilson's voice barely penetrated. She felt so light-headed and foolish. *But I can trust Alan.* He looked healthy—and he was so crazy about her. He wouldn't hurt her.

"*Danielle?*"

"What?" she asked, peevishness in her voice.

"You barely know this guy."

The words startled her. Could he read her thoughts now?

She went on the defensive. "I barely knew you and I went rambling around Brooklyn with you. Was that wrong?"

"There's a difference."

"What?" she said. "What's the difference?"

He looked almost at a loss for words. "Do you really have to ask?"

No, she didn't. She didn't because her mind was already whirring with the problem of having to find a good doctor in the next few hours. She felt a headache coming on.

While the pressure built in her head, Wilson seemed so irritating that she wanted to shake him . . . and it looked like he wanted to do the same thing to her. It had been wrong, she saw now, to depend so much on Wilson these past weeks. He obviously thought he deserved to hold some sort of sway over her. He wanted to suffocate her, just like Brandon.

"If you think I have such terrible taste and judgment," she said, "I don't know why you even want to hang around me."

Two splotches of red stained his cheeks. After a moment, he muttered, "Me, either," and then turned into the coffee room.

Regret and relief battled in her for a moment as she looked at him with his back turned to her, but she realized this was not the place, and probably not the time, to work through little friendship problems. First off, she had to unsmudge her face. She had work to do today, which would be difficult enough since she knew Alan would be popping into her thoughts constantly. Along with other worries.

Anyway, if that was the way Wilson wanted to be, fine. She didn't need him hovering over her like a spare conscience.

Chapter 27

HOT SHOTS

Edie stacked a pile of stuff next to her bedroom door. She should have probably taken the junk into her room to get it out of the way, but things were crowded enough in there.

Greta peered over the couch at her. She had gotten home early and was already in her post-work zoned-out mode. "The Naked Chef" was on. "Vot are you doing?"

"Oh, just getting rid of some things."

Greta must have caught the overly casual quaver in her voice. "Things?"

Edie cleared her throat and nudged the pile of Douglas's possessions with her toe. "It's so crowded in here—especially for Danielle. I thought we could shed some dead weight."

Greta pushed herself off the couch and made her way over. She poked into a box of mostly old sporting equipment. Hand weights and a basketball and a few old books. "Whose is this?"

"Actually, it belongs to the guy who used to live here." She added quickly, "I'm sure he won't be using it anymore, and you can get money for some of these things. On eBay and places . . ."

And what she couldn't sell, the passersby on West 30th would be welcome to. Douglas was a liberal. He believed in charity.

"*Ach so!*" Greta said, laughing her approval. "So you are selling the asshole's belongings."

"Exactly," Edie admitted, a wicked grin breaking across her

face. "Danielle said I could use her computer to eBay a few things."

"*Was ist das?*" Greta zeroed in on something in the pile and pulled out a case.

"What?" Edie frowned. "Oh—that's an oboe."

She actually felt a little guilty for selling it, since it was practically new and hadn't been cheap. Then again, she wanted to make a few bucks here. After her discussion with Douglas's old buddy Tom, she decided that Douglas's three-month storage payment had run out.

Greta snapped open the latches and inspected the instrument with something close to reverence. "Beautiful!"

Edie tilted her head. "Do you play the oboe?"

"*Ja*, some. When I was young." Greta looked at her, noting Edie's surprise. "My parents owned music shop and gave lessons."

"Would you like it?" Edie asked her. "I wasn't sure I was going to sell it."

Greta shook her head. "No, I could not! It is Buffet. Very fine." And yet her blue eyes were shining covetously.

"Just noodle around on it if you want," Edie said. Though she feared she might regret making the offer. When Douglas had tried to play the oboe, it had made an ear-piercing racket that had the neighbors complaining to Bhiryat.

"*Danke.*" Greta took her treasure back to the couch and began putting it together.

"Say." Edie remembered finding something earlier. She went to the bathroom and brought back a couple of strings of metal to show Greta. "I found it on the floor in the bathroom. What is it?"

She watched as Greta held the thin chains up. There was a clasp . . . and a thick chain and two chains coming off of it . . . and two circular chains attached to those . . .

"It's a bra," Greta said.

"No way."

"Sure." To demonstrate, Greta slipped the chains over her shoulders but couldn't fasten the clasp at her back. It wouldn't reach. But the thing did fit her like a bra. The cups were nothing but two circles, but clearly that was the idea. "See?"

"Wow. That's sort of twisted, isn't it?" Edie asked.

Greta looked down, misunderstanding. "No, I have it on correct, I think. Except it should not be worn above a T-shirt."

Edie frowned. "It must be Danielle's. Who'd have thought our bard from Amarillo would own something this kinky?"

Greta waved a hand. "I had a friend into bondsmen."

"Bondage?"

"*Ja.* She had one of these. Also matching G-string."

G-chains. All this time Edie had thought Danielle needed sheltering. "You'd think it would pinch . . ."

Greta pulled the thing off and looked at it critically. "How can someone be so small when she eats like a herd of goat?"

"Must be the Diet Coke," Edie said, taking it from her. "Do you think I should put it on her bed?"

"Sure, why not?"

"Because she might not want us to have seen it."

Greta, who was already back to fiddling with the oboe, glanced up at her as if she were crazy. "Why?"

"Well, because . . ." Edie fumbled for an explanation.

"What are we, her mothers?" Greta asked her. "I don't care what she does with this guy. She obviously thinks he's some kind of a hotshit."

"Hotshot."

Greta looked perplexed. "What are you talking about?"

"The expression is 'hotshot.' "

"Are you trying to make my brain crazy? For years I hear this expression all the time. Hot shit."

"Right, but if it's a person, he's a hotshot. It's a completely different thing."

"But I didn't want to say 'different.' I meant that Danielle's boyfriend is a hotshit. What is a shot? What would that mean?"

"Well . . . I'm not sure. I guess it has something to do with guns or the old west or something. Maybe because a guy who could shoot well could swagger around town. Hotshot. It's also the name of a spray that kills bugs. Surely you've heard of that?"

Greta shook her head pityingly. "You make less sense every time you open your mouth, Edie. Why would I call Danielle's boyfriend bug spray?"

Edie was out of answers. Maybe Greta was right, anyway. Who cared what Danielle was doing? They were just her roommates. "Okay, I'll just put this . . . thing . . . on her bed. Or maybe on the floor next to it so she won't think we found it."

That Danielle! Two months out of Amarillo and she'd found a rich boyfriend and was having sleazy fun. She was out buying trampy sex gear, while the only piece of clothing Edie had purchased this summer was a new crisp white shirt for waitressing.

Which reminded her, she needed to hurry to make it to work on time. She finished tidying up the to-sell pile, threw on her work clothes, and hurried out of the apartment. On the staircase she heard an odd sound coming from behind the door she'd just closed. Actually, it wasn't odd, but beautiful.

That was what an oboe sounded like?

Damn. Greta really could play.

On the street outside the restaurant, Bhiryat was showing off a new carpet to some of his cronies. When he saw Edie, his smile widened and she thought for a moment the man was going to run over and throw his arms around her. "Edie—look! Our Douglas has sent this lovely present to the restaurant."

She looked down at the rug. It was gorgeous—a handwoven wool rug in rich hues of red and blue. "He sent this to you?" she asked. "Just now?"

"Yes! Isn't it lovely?"

Douglas had sent the *landlord* a rug, but not her? The voice in her head was building to a screaming whine. No doubt he'd sent Bhiryat a chatty letter, too, but her pride wouldn't allow her to ask about that.

"Such a wonderful tenant! So thoughtful!"

Edie seethed as she stared at the rug. Damn. She bet *that* would have brought a lot on eBay.

She was a little late for work, but managed to get there before any customers arrived. Geppetto's big rush came around six-thirty, when the pre-theater diners came in. Nevertheless, Nick, her boss, was annoyed. "Whatsamatta?" he blasted at her while she tied a white smock apron over her white shirt and black plants. The waitstaff all looked like penguins rushing around a

Disney set. "You get amnesia and forget where the restaurant was?"

"Sorry, Nick," she said, grabbing wineglasses to put at all the place settings. "I was working in the apartment and lost track of time."

"Lost track of time? What kind of excuse is that?"

"It's not an excuse. I was just telling you the truth."

"I don't want the truth. I want people here on time."

She felt like cracking a Chianti-bottle candleholder over his head, but managed to stop herself. *I was late*, she reminded herself. *Of course he's mad.*

It was this year. It had begun great, turned to disaster, and never recovered. She was becoming irritable and irrational, and if she didn't watch out, she was also going to become unemployed.

And would that be a tragedy? Maybe if you weren't a waitress, you would be forced to grow up and get a real job.

Edie accidentally knocked a salad fork off a table and had to run to get another one. Any job would be just that—a job—she reminded herself. Because her real vocation was acting.

Is it? A little voice inside her head taunted her. *How can you be an actress if you never act?*

But I do act, Edie said. *I was in that play last Christmas. Most actresses have their ups and downs. Edie Falco waited tables in between jobs before she landed* "The Sopranos." *She was almost forty.*

And if she hadn't landed "The Sopranos," *she would have ended up a forty-year-old waitress. Not everybody gets lucky.*

I will, Edie thought.

That's what everybody thinks.

Edie turned and slammed into Sam, who dropped a handful of plates. The noise had Nick swooping down on them immediately.

"It was my fault," Edie said. "I zoned out."

Nick practically howled. "Zoned out? Is that professionalism?"

Sam laughed nervously, but was obviously relieved that Edie was taking the heat. "C'mon, Nick. It's three plates."

Nick pointed his finger at Edie. "Twenty dollars. Tonight. Outta your tips."

She nodded. "Okay, okay." Over six dollars apiece for white

Mikasa salad plates seemed a little steep, but she just wanted to diffuse the tension.

"Professionalism!" Sam sneered in a whisper when Nick was safely out of earshot. "As if either of us want to be professional waiters!"

She smiled up at him. "Have you had any luck at auditions lately?"

He rolled his eyes. "No—but I have discovered a place that does catering jobs. You should try it. It's a good way to earn extra money, and it makes you feel less dependent on Simon Legree . . . er, I mean, Nick."

For the next few hours she tried to focus her thoughts on the tasks in front of her. It was a Thursday night and reasonably busy, so she didn't have too many free moments to brood. Then around ten fifteen they got another spike in customers from the theaters letting out. Coming from the kitchen with a tray of lasagna, out of the corner of her eye Edie saw two new customers seated at one of her tables. She delivered her dinners then retrieved two menus for her newcomers.

"Good evening," she said.

The man and woman reached out for the menus, but for a moment their arms remained extended in the air, unmoving. All three of them were gawking at each other.

Her new customers were Aurora and Noel.

Noel was the first to speak. "Edie! What a surprise!"

Edie's cheeks felt hot. "Welcome to Geppetto's," she said automatically, then laughed. She didn't feel like laughing, though. She was going to have to serve dinner to her best friend and her agent? Could life get any more demoralizing than this?

Aurora took a menu, then grabbed her hand excitedly. "I didn't know *this* was where you worked!"

Didn't know? How could she not know? Edie whined about Geppetto's all the time.

"Geppetto's in the theater district," Edie reminded her. "I've been here since January."

"Oh! Right!" Aurora frowned. "I knew it was some Italian place, but I forgot the name."

Edie wanted to strangle her. Why, why, why did they have to

come to *her* restaurant? She was already at low ebb—watching these two out on the town together was not going to perk her up.

"Noel just took me to the Maggie Smith show," Aurora said. "You've *got* to go."

"I'm dying to." Envy spiked in Edie's chest. She loved Maggie Smith. *She* wanted to see Maggie Smith. *She* would have to go some Saturday morning and stand in the half-price TKTS line in Times Square and pray she lucked into a seat for the sold-out limited run. She certainly wouldn't be escorted into a hard-to-get orchestra seat by her agent.

"She was spectacular," Noel said. "So funny." He and Aurora glanced at each other and then started laughing, obviously at some little bit of remembered stage business performed by Dame Maggie.

Edie ground her molars. "Want some wine?"

"Ab-so-lutely!" Aurora exclaimed. "We're celebrating."

"It must have been a really good play."

Noel and Aurora laughed again. "That's not what we're celebrating," Noel said. He was staring at Edie's hair. "Aurora's going to Italy."

"Rome!" Aurora's face was a triumphal beam. "Parker Posey pulled out of a part in a Sam Mendes movie, and *I'm in!*"

Edie's stomach churned. "Congratulations!"

"And guess who else is in it?"

She tried to bite her tongue, but blurted out, "You mean you aren't star power enough for Sam?"

Aurora chuckled. "No seriously, are you ready?"

"Sure. Knock me out."

"Meryl Streep!"

"Wow."

"*And* Al Pacino!"

"That's incredible." *Please shut up*, she wanted to tell Aurora. *Shut up while I still like you.*

"*And* Ewan McGregor!"

Edie was afraid she was going to be sick. "What," she quipped, "did Tom Cruise have to pull out, too?"

Aurora swung toward Noel, her brow furrowed in confusion. "Was Tom Cruise ever cast in the movie?"

"I think she was joking," Noel explained.

"Oh!" Aurora laughed playfully. "No, I'm just going to have to make do with Meryl, Al, and Ewan. Isn't that fantastic?"

"Sure is!" Edie was smiling so hard, her mouth was beginning to hurt.

"Unfortunately, I'm going to be playing Al's daughter, so I won't get to fuck him."

Noel looked at Edie and laughed a little nervously. "How have you been, Edie? Your new look is fantastic—very mod."

"Isn't she cute?" Aurora said. "I sent her to Julian—he's a miracle worker!"

She made it sound as if it would take a miracle to make Edie look cute. Or maybe that was being overly sensitive.

But was it? Deep down, Edie finally got the feeling that Aurora decided that she really didn't need to take Edie's feelings into account anymore. She had bigger things to worry about now.

Like Al and Meryl and Ewan. . . .

"I'm fine," Edie said. "Keeping myself busy . . . waitressing."

Stop whining! Be an adult about this. A professional . . .

A professional waitress, she thought dismally.

"Great!" Noel said.

Edie cast a glance over to another of her tables, where the patrons were looking restless. "Excuse me. You guys study the wine list and I'll be right back to take your orders."

She fled, and had to keep her hands in her apron pockets as she took orders so the customers wouldn't see them shaking.

She got through the ordeal as best she could, keeping track of orders and requests, refilling coffees and drinks efficiently, ignoring Aurora's bubbling about *bella* Italy. *Don't be jealous*, she told herself. *Don't. You'd be happy, too, if you were rubbing elbows with movie stars and flying off to Rome.*

She delivered meals to two tables at once—first to Aurora and Noel, and then to a larger table of what appeared to be tourists from the Midwest. When she lay the last plate down and got out the Parmesan grater, one of the midwestern women looked up at her with *that look*. It was the distressed-diner look. Sitting in front of the woman was a heaping portion of fettuccine Alfredo. "I ordered the primavera," she told Edie.

Edie's heart sank. It couldn't be that she had mixed up the orders at this table, because everyone else seemed perfectly happy. She had just screwed up and given the kitchen the wrong order.

"Oh . . . I'm . . ." She flicked a glance over to the other table. Aurora, who was yakking away about Ray Liotta again, was sitting in front of a big steaming plateful of pasta primavera. Before she could think twice, madness seized her.

"Just a little mix-up!" Edie grabbed the plate of fettuccine, rushed it over to Aurora's table, and swapped it for the primavera. "Sorry about this," she whispered before dashing over to deliver the primavera to the tourist. She was just getting everyone cheesed when she heard Aurora clear her throat.

"Um, Edie . . . ?" Aurora called. "Could you come over here?"

Edie smiled apologetically at the tourists. "Excuse me."

Aurora was staring open-mouthed at her pile of pasta and white sauce. "This isn't what I ordered."

Edie nodded apologetically. "I know. I'm sorry."

Aurora's mouth dropped open, and she looked at Noel and then back to Edie. "Well, then . . . ?"

"There was a mix-up. I was one primavera short at the other table, so I volunteered your meal."

"You mean you screwed up, so now I don't get my food?"

"You get food—it's really good fettuccine, much better than the primavera. And even better yet, it's on the house."

Which made three plates and one meal out of her tips tonight.

Aurora's mouth gaped. "But I don't *want* fettuccine Alfredo, free or not."

"For God's sake, Aurora, can't you just do me this one favor?"

Noel chuckled uncomfortably. "Hey, I've got an idea—"

Aurora cut him off. "This sauce is pure fat!"

"So?" Edie shot back. "You never eat any of your food anyway."

Aurora's voice rose. "I do when I'm hungry, which I am right now, and I'm certainly not going to slurp down this mess of cheese and cream when I have to be on a movie set in five days' time!"

Growling impatiently, Edie grabbed the plate to take it back to the kitchen.

"That would go *straight* to my hips!" Aurora huffed.

An evil, evil force suddenly gripped Edie. That was the only explanation she could think of later. But at that moment, she wasn't thinking at all. She was just quaking. Aurora's coming here had unleashed a Pandora's box of suppressed rage inside her.

"Really? Let's see." Edie lifted the plate over Aurora's head and dumped it over.

Her action sucked all the air from the room. Conversation died. Waiters stopped in midstep. Glasses raised halfway to mouths froze, and forks dangled before parted lips. The only thing moving in the entire room seemed to be the globs of pasta dripping down from Aurora's hair and shoulders. The decorative sprig of curly parsley was stuck on her hair.

For once Edie was glad Geppetto's served large portions.

"See, it *didn't* go to your hips," Edie assured Aurora sweetly. "Like everything else, most of it has just gone to your big head."

Chapter 28

NEWS

Greta was acting weird, even for Greta. Danielle could hear her in the kitchen, where Greta hardly ever spent any time, making a ton of noise. Pots and pans clanged against each other and onto the burners on the stove. Cabinet doors and utensil drawers slammed open and closed. Even the sound of ingredients being yanked out of the fridge seemed unnaturally loud.

Screwing up her courage, Danielle stuck her head around her screen. "What's up?"

"Nothing," Greta said curtly.

Danielle was a little stunned by the mess on the counters and ventured closer to inspect what was going on. For all the time Greta spent watching the Food Network, Danielle had never seen her actually cooking before.

Of course, there had been those awful muffins. . . .

She wrinkled her nose. "What're you making?"

"Cake!" Greta reached into a cabinet and set off a bakeware avalanche.

Danielle rushed over to help her pick things off the floor. Greta's face looked incredibly red. It wasn't that hot in the apartment. Late August had brought a cool snap, and now, during Labor Day weekend, the days were actually pleasant. You could take deep breaths again.

Greta looked like she needed to take a real deep breath.

"You need any help?"

That question brought a braying laugh. "Why? You think I can't make a cake?"

Remembering those muffins, Danielle forced herself to lie. "No—no, of course not. I was just trying to be helpful."

Greta snorted.

If *that* was the way she wanted to be about it, well fine. "I'm going to get the mail."

It usually came around ten-thirty, and it was past that now. Danielle ran down to the landing, where she discovered a letter waiting for her in their box. She took her time going back up to the apartment, reading the note from her mom as she went.

The message, which started out cheerily enough, turned odd around the second paragraph.

My friend Inez told me this morning that she'd heard Brandon had gotten married last weekend. Can you imagine? He eloped with Bev! Oh, I wish you two had never had your little lovers' spat.

She had never been able to convince her mom that she and Brandon hadn't had some quarrel that had precipitated her breaking off the engagement. She would never believe that Danielle had just looked into her future and yawned.

If you ask me, Bev decided to nab Brandon by hook or by crook, since she knew he would naturally be inclined to wait for you till you came home again. I'm just sick about it.

Oddly enough, Danielle wasn't feeling too well herself. Brandon? Married? To *Bev?* She'd just broken up with him three months ago!

No wonder Bev hadn't called her lately!

Her face felt as hot as Greta's had looked in the kitchen. But there was nothing to be upset about. She should be happy for them. Brandon had found Bev, and she'd found Alan, and *voila*— everyone was happily-ever-aftering. Danielle could even take pride in all of this. She'd practically orchestrated it all. That just proved she'd been right to break off the engagement, right to leave Amarillo.

And yet . . .

What had ever happened to Mr. "You're-the-One"? How long

had it taken him to decide that Bev was "The One"? Or did he simply think of Bev as "The *New* One"? The fickle fool—were fiancées interchangeable widgets to him?

She frowned. The new one. Alan had called her that when they'd first met.

Well! There was no sense making comparisons between Brandon and Alan. The two men were as different as a coyote and a poodle. She certainly didn't feel bored looking at her future with Alan.

Alan was wonderful. She could say this categorically and with no reservations, because her recent trip to the gynecologist had revealed her to be spic-and-span, pregnancy-free, and in tip-top health. All her fears and all those ominous rumblings from Wilson had been for nothing.

She returned to the apartment with her mother's letter tucked into her pocket.

Edie was up now, her face still bearing sheet wrinkles, her hair mussed from sleep. She looked draggy and annoyed. She'd had a catering job the night before and probably hadn't gotten in till late. She glared at Greta.

"What are you doing?"

"Making a cake," Greta told her sharply.

Danielle felt as if she should pull Edie aside and warn her against crossing Greta's path, but Edie didn't so much as spare her a glance.

"Before noon you have to make a cake? While people are trying to sleep?"

"I wanted to make it this morning," Greta said. "This afternoon I go to a movie."

Edie looked past her to the mess in the kitchen and groaned. "And naturally you'll run out of time to clean up before showtime. Jesus wept, Greta. If you wanted a cake so badly, why didn't you just go buy one? You probably spent more money buying all the different ingredients than a cake at the bakery would cost you."

Not to mention, Danielle was tempted to add, the bakery cake would be edible.

"I want to make it myself."

"Well, I'm tired of listening to you make it," Edie snapped. "What do you need a cake for today anyway?"

Greta put her hands on her hips and yelled in reply, "Because it's my birthday! Okay?"

That shut Edie up.

Danielle rushed forward. "Happy birthday, Greta! What's the damage?"

Her enthusiastic well-wishing met a withering gaze. "What?"

"How old are you?"

Greta took a breath. "I am thirty goddamned years old, and if either of you makes one smartcrack about my age, I will smack you with a spatula."

Edie and Danielle exchanged looks.

"You meeting friends at the movies?" Edie asked her gingerly.

"Why do you want to know?"

"Just curious. I was also wondering what you were going to see."

"I am going to Museum of Modern Art to see a Fritz Lang movie in German. By myself."

"What's the movie?"

"*M.*"

"Wow. Going to see a movie about a child murderer on your birthday," Edie said. "That sounds like some fun."

"No English for two hours—that is my fun. Happy birthday to me."

Greta turned her back on them to resume her cake making operation, and Danielle suddenly felt very sad for her. She looked at Edie and said, pointedly, "Did you still want to go for coffee?"

Edie's face filled with confusion. She was apparently sleepy enough to wonder if perhaps they had talked about going out together, which they hadn't. Danielle just wanted to get away from Greta for a moment.

"You were going to have coffee with me and tell me what you thought of my new story," Danielle said. Edie squinted at her some more until Danielle started twitching her head toward the door and mouthing "Let's go." She gave her every facial clue short of winking at her.

"Oh!" Understanding dawned on Edie's face. *Finally*. "Sure, let's go get coffee."

Some people just weren't at their tack sharpest in the A.M.

Chapter 29

PREPARATIONS

"**I** think we should throw Greta a party," Danielle said.

Edie, who had been about to take a bite of scone, put it back on her plate. She wanted to savor it anyway. This was the first time she'd splurged on breakfast out since she'd lost her job (translation: thrown her job away) at Geppetto's.

"A party?"

The very idea of a party was antithetical to her mood. Ever since that awful night when she'd dumped food on Aurora, she'd been wandering around feeling as if she had blown everything. She'd even pissed off her best friend in an eruption of petty jealousy. Actually, it had been her Krakatoa of emotional outbursts.

She felt so alone now. Aurora hadn't answered her phone calls so she could apologize, and probably never would. Edie couldn't blame her. And her agent probably thought she was a lunatic. She would probably have to start looking for new representation— someone who wouldn't know that underneath her calm exterior lurked a food-fighting maniac struggling to break free.

She didn't know if she could ever make things right again. Maybe she should just embrace the gloom, like Greta.

"You seriously want to have a party?" she asked Danielle, without enthusiasm. "Today?"

Edie had planned on keeping herself busy. She had to go to the post office at some point. Some of Douglas's old punk CDs from college had fetched good prices on eBay.

Danielle made a distressed face. "You saw her! She looked so sad standing in there all grumpy and making her own birthday cake. And then going to a movie by herself! She's too proud even to ask one of us along."

Edie frowned in thought as she took a sip of cappuccino. "Maybe she doesn't want us along. Maybe she wants to be alone."

"On her birthday? Come on!"

"She obviously didn't even want to tell us it *was* her birthday," Edie reminded her.

"Of course. No one likes to blurt it out. And you know Greta, her first reaction to everything is defensive."

This was true. "Even if we did have a party, who would we invite? I don't know any of her friends. Except Asgarth, and it still feels like we just got rid of him."

"She doesn't seem to have any friends," Danielle said.

"There are her AA people, but I don't know where she goes to meetings. We couldn't round any of them up."

Danielle obviously wasn't one to let something like a lack of well-wishers deter her from throwing a birthday party. "We'll just have to introduce her to people."

"That would be less like us throwing her a party than inflicting one on her."

"So? She needs to have a little fun inflicted on her. She never does anything anymore."

"Anyway, it's such short notice," Edie reminded her. "And it's Labor Day weekend. Who could you and I drag in for this thing?"

"I know tons of people!" Danielle said.

That was depressing. Danielle hadn't even been in New York for three months yet.

"So do you," Danielle told her. "You can ask people you worked with, and friends you went to college with. Ask that guy you used to work with."

"Sam?"

Actually, she still worked with Sam; after the debacle at Geppetto's, he had convinced her to take catering jobs with him until she found something better.

"Right! Tell him to come and bring everyone he can round up."

"Just fill the place up with warm bodies, you mean."

"Exactly! And while Greta's at the movies, we can run and get food . . . we'll need lots of food . . . and a few decorations. And we *have* to get her a present."

Edie still had misgivings, but she thought about Greta being alone, without family, no presents . . . God, that seemed awful. "I guess we could give it a shot."

"Yay!" Danielle dove into her muffin. "What can we get Greta? I have two hundred whole dollars on my Lord and Taylor charge card."

Edie frowned at her. "Since when do you have a Lord and Taylor card?"

Danielle ducked her head. "Since I *really* needed a new outfit for when Alan took me to the Hamptons."

That reminded her. "What about Alan? Aren't you two going out tonight?"

"We hadn't made definite plans, but I expect him to call. I'll just ask him over." She brightened. "You've never even met him, have you?"

"No." Alan had picked Danielle up from their place on their first day, but since that time the two had always met at his place.

"Then tonight's the night! Alan'll be great. He loves parties."

"Well, that's one guest we can count on."

"I can invite Wilson, too—and he can call out his cavalry."

Edie frowned. "Where's Wilson been recently?"

Danielle shifted uncomfortably. "You know, just working and so forth. He's such a granny! He doesn't think I should be going out with Alan." She sighed. "But I bet he'll come to the party. He likes you."

Edie didn't give much credence to that. She'd only met Wilson a few times, and those times he'd always had his eyes glued on Danielle.

"It's funny. I got the weirdest news today," Danielle said.

"What?"

"Brandon got married."

Edie's jaw dropped. "*Your* Brandon? The dull guy? Brandon with the good golf score?"

"Exactly. He ran off with Bev—my best friend. Well. My best friend back home."

A long-ago conversation came back to Edie. "The woman he told you was irritating?"

"Exactly. I worry about him. He was so in love with me! Or so he said. Why would he marry Bev three months after I left? He's setting himself up for failure."

"Maybe not. Maybe it was love at second sight for him and Bev. Anyway, you can't blame a drowning man for climbing on the first life raft that floats by."

Danielle harrumphed again. "He ought to at least make sure it doesn't leak before he starts paddling for shore."

"You're lucky you have a hundred others waiting in the wings."

"Hardly," Danielle said. "But I'm happy just having one."

Yeah, Edie thought sadly. *I'd be happy with that, too.*

Though she was slowly purging Douglas from her life, she hadn't made much headway toward reentering the romance market. Tom McCormick had called her, but she didn't want to go out with him. Even if he weren't semi-sleaze, he reminded her of her Douglas days. So he became another person she'd X'd out of her life.

It felt as if all she'd done was push people away recently.

She couldn't think about Aurora without mixed emotions. Sam swore she was better off without Aurora (Sam had never liked her), but Edie wasn't so sure. Aurora was fun to talk to. They had a history.

She was beginning to feel like she had no history. How could you be twenty-seven and feel so cut loose from everything?

"All right, I'll call Sam. He'll come if he's free." Edie said, trying to lighten up. "He has a roommate, too. Louis."

"See?" Danielle was all enthusiasm. "The apartment's filling up already!"

She and Danielle spent the next hour at the coffee shop taking turns using the phone. They called up everyone they could track down through information. They left detailed invitations on answering machines and with roommates. They *invited* the roommates. Danielle decided to make up a flyer for the party and post it at the law office for the people working the weekend shift.

"Just saying 'free food' should bring the proofers in," Danielle said.

"The actors, too," Edie said. She had found a few acquaintances from shows past who were in town.

After their phoning was done, they set off for Lord and Taylor to charge a present. Shopping with Danielle was dangerous, Edie discovered. She seemed to run from department to department, falling *absolutely* in love with something in each place. Edie dug in her heels, but they still bought perfume, a shirt (black, of course—Greta's favorite color), a decorative needlepoint pillow that would go great with Greta's couch, and a gift bag that they filled with hair doodads, funky socks, a rhinestone collar for Kuchen, and all the samples they could wheedle out of the clerks at the cosmetics counters. They nearly maxed out Danielle's card and put a healthy dent in Edie's Visa, too.

To her surprise, Edie didn't feel a single pang of shopper's remorse. She had that eBay money coming in, after all. And by three o'clock she was as jazzed for the party as Danielle was. They hit the grocery store on the way home. It had been forever since Edie had done anything more than cruise prudently through the aisles with a handbasket. Now she was manning an actual cart and tossing in two-liter bottles of soda and supersize bags of potato chips, huge ready-made party trays, and tubs of dip into her cart with abandon. Neither of them had any idea how many people would show up tonight, but they were prepared to clog the arteries of half the people in the New York City phone book.

They crept up to the apartment, wanting to make sure that Greta had left. She had. In the kitchen was the homemade chocolate cake on a crystal cake stand. They went over to inspect it. Edie hadn't been sure what to expect from Greta's attempt at baking. Probably a lopsided, gloppy mess, or a burned failure.

Instead, they stood in front of a perfect three-layer cake, chocolate, iced elaborately with two little chocolate rosebuds.

"Wow," Danielle said. "How'd she do that?"

Edie was fingering a box of birthday candles, but hesitated to spoil Greta's handiwork. "I'm not sure. Maybe you *can* learn to cook off television."

Danielle touched her finger to the very bottom of the cake and scooped up some icing. Tasting it, she let out a happy groan. "That's not Duncan Hines."

Edie didn't know what to think. The homemade cake on the crystal stand—did Greta have some little ritual she didn't want them to interfere with? The stand was probably an heirloom from her family. Perhaps her birthday was a time when she liked to be alone and think about her parents and her home back in Germany.

"Maybe we're doing the wrong thing," she told Danielle.

"Why?"

"I'm not sure . . ."

"Well, there's no way we can uninvite all those people now," she said.

"No."

And two hours later, it seemed like every single person they had called was there. Greta was still gone, but Edie and Danielle broke out food and drink for everyone to keep them occupied till the birthday girl arrived. There were so many people there, in fact, that no one heard Greta's footsteps on the stairs. When she walked in, she simply found her apartment full of people and made her way to find Edie in the kitchen.

Edie was making sandwiches. Apparently when you told people "free food," they wanted real nourishment and not just a handful of chips. When Greta's shadow loomed, she was expecting just another greedy guest. "We're almost out of turkey," she barked, assuming that the person at her elbow was Danielle.

It wasn't.

"I would not eat that pressed crap anyway," she heard Greta declare. "What is going on here?"

Edie spun on her heel. "Greta! Happy birthday!"

"You said this already this morning."

Edie waved Danielle over, and when Danielle saw who had arrived, she let out a shriek. "Here she is! The birthday girl!"

A wave of people—none of whom actually knew Greta— flowed toward the kitchen. "All together now!" Danielle yelled. A natural born cheerleader, she slapped a cone-shaped birthday hat on Greta's head and led the group in a cacophonous rendition of "Happy Birthday." The whole way through, Edie watched Greta for signs of volatility. She seemed to be in shock. The smile stuck on her lips was feeble, and the rest of her was so immobile, she might have been cut from a slab of granite.

It wasn't till the song was over and the whoops and claps of the guests had died down that Greta turned back to Edie. "Was this your idea?" she demanded.

Uh-oh. Edie swallowed. "Mine and Danielle's." She wasn't going to take the rap alone.

Danielle came forward dutifully and for a moment Greta just stood there looking at them, red faced and quaking. Then she lunged, hooking a long arm around each. *"Danke!"* she said, sniffing. Tears stood in her eyes. She squeezed the air out of both Edie and Danielle. *"Vielen Dank!"*

Danielle looked at her nervously. "What's that mean?"

"It means thank you very much," Greta translated.

Chapter 30

FOR HE'S A JOLLY
GOOD FELLOW

Of course it was odd, being the center of attention. And she felt so foolish for crying in front of all these people that it had been a little hard for her to mingle at first. All she could think was that she had spent twelve—no, thirteen—birthdays in America, and this was the first surprise party anyone had ever thrown her. It was like a Hollywood movie—everyone gathered around her and singing their foolish songs about her being a jolly good fellow, which made it sound as if she were a transvestite.

After mingling a bit, she wedged herself onto the balcony, out of sight, to eat her sliver of cake. She wished she could enjoy herself. Really enjoy herself. Maybe she should have told her roommates that this would be an exceptionally difficult day for her. It would still probably be a good idea to warn them that for the next few weeks she might be gripped by the periodic urge to kill them.

She felt bad now for screaming at Edie and Danielle this morning. Especially after she opened all the things they had bought for her. She had not had such a birthday since she was a little girl. And really not even then. Her parents had been very down to earth people, not given to extravagance. They would have frowned at all her roommates' gifts . . . all except the free samples.

Someone put his foot through the window to climb out on the balcony. That foot almost landed on her cake plate. *"Passen auf!"* Greta shouted.

"Oh, excuse me! I didn't see you out here."

She looked up into a face she recognized. Vaguely. In any case, the man seemed genuinely sorry to have upset her. She felt a little bad for yelling at him. "It's okay. There's room enough for two, if we suck on our breaths."

It would have helped if they were both normal sized, but this guy was tall, too. He squatted down next to her and smiled a pleasant smile. "Happy birthday."

"Thank you."

"Were you surprised?"

"*Ja*, very."

"Pleasantly?"

He looked so doubtful, it was almost as if he knew her. She laughed. "Yes, it was nice of them—of Edie and Danielle. You know them both?"

"Of course!" He crossed his arms, regarding her as if she'd said something odd. "Well . . . I guess I should correct that. I thought I knew Danielle."

For a moment they just stared out at the lights across the street, where a couple of brownstones were wedged in between two larger buildings. You could see in through some of the windows, at people watching television, or walking through their kitchens unaware that they were being spied on. In one window, though, there was a man with his chair pulled up, staring across the street at them.

Greta nodded at him. "Look. We're his TV."

"I wonder if he wishes he were over here, having fun."

The words surprised her a little. "Are you having fun?"

His brow pinched in thought. "I'm trying to."

"*Ja*, me too. It's not working very well. What's wrong with you?"

"It's a love problem. What about you?" He smiled impishly. "Despite the fact that you're not getting any younger."

"I quit smoking today."

His jaw dropped. "On your birthday? Are you insane? You should at least have waited till tomorrow."

"Today, tomorrow, what difference? I alternate feeling like killing someone, jumping off this balcony, and eating chocolate. I ate two boxes of bite-size Butterfinger candy at the movies. I am revolting."

"What on earth made you decide to quit smoking on your birthday?"

That was a good question. It seemed so clear to her before. She was going to be vice-free by the age of thirty. Now thirty was here, and she wished she hadn't been quite so precise with her roadmap. "It has to be sometime. I don't want to be a hacking, coughing old lady."

She didn't want to be passing out on exercise equipment for the rest of her life, either.

"Are you doing anything?" he asked.

She didn't understand the question. "I am not smoking, that's what I am doing."

"But what about hypnosis, or acupuncture, or patches?"

"No. I am eating the turkey cold."

"Sounds like you're doing a great job," he said, smiling. "You know, 'Birthday Bloodbath!' would be a hard headline for the *Post* to resist."

She laughed. "How about 'Chocolate-Eating Birthday Blimp Explodes on Balcony!'"

The beginnings of laugh wrinkles appeared at the corners of his blue-gray eyes. "Even better. Have you ever tried to quit before?"

"Sure. I quit six times before this. Once I lasted twenty-six hours." Though, to be truthful, twelve of those hours she had been sleeping.

"Impressive! How long has it been now?"

"Twenty-one hours."

"You're closing in on your record."

"I will be fine if I can just make it to sleep time." She frowned. "If I *can* sleep."

"You should tell everyone to go home."

"They all seem to be having fun."

He laughed. "The point is for *you* to have fun—and you're out here. Don't you like talking to people at all, Greta?"

"*Ja*, very much. Only . . . it is hard to describe. I speak English very good now, but I still don't understand things. I miss jokes."

"No one tells you jokes?" he asked, completely mistaking her meaning. He obviously thought she had a hankering to hear one. "I can remedy that! Here . . . Did you hear the one about the dyslexic agnostic insomniac?"

"No . . ." She shook her head in confusion. "The *what?*"

"He stayed up all night wondering if there was a dog."

"I don't think—" She was going to explain that he had misunderstood her, but the punch line hit her belatedly and she laughed. "That is terrible."

"I've got a million of them!" he said, brightening.

"One is enough."

"Damn—I thought I was really cookin'."

"I don't know any jokes in English."

"Do you know any in German?"

She thought of the rusty old jokes from her childhood, then stopped short. "Do you speak German?"

"Not a word," he said.

She blinked at him, mystified. "Then why would you want me to say one?"

He shrugged. "I don't know. Why don't you teach me German?"

She drew back. "What, now?"

"Sure."

"You're crazy! It is not easy, you know."

"Okay, then just teach me a little something. Teach me to say happy birthday."

"*Herzlichen Gluckwunsch zum Geburtstag.*"

His eyes rounded. "Isn't there a simpler way?"

"It *is* simple," she told him. "*Herzlichen.* That's the 'happy' part."

"Hairtsleeshen!" he mimicked.

"*Gut!*"

She took him through the whole phrase, word by word, until he was completely fluent in "happy birthday."

"Feeling better?" he asked.

"Oh yes. I haven't thought about smoking in ten minutes."

"Great. What are you thinking about now?"

"Not smoking."

He stared across the street at the man who was still looking at them and thought for a moment. "If I left for a little bit, you'd still be here when I got back, wouldn't you?"

"I have nowhere else to go," she said.

"Promise not to go berserk while I'm gone?"

"You ask a lot," she joked.

He straightened up. "I'll be right back."

When he was gone, Greta felt unaccountably lonely. And regretful. He seemed so funny and nice. Why had she rambled on about smoking to him? Who cared! And all that talk about chocolate and killing party guests! He probably thought she was a lunatic.

Oh, well. It didn't matter. He seemed like a nice young guy—not her type. That is, she wouldn't be his type. Plus he said he had woman troubles, so he was probably already in love with someone else.

But it had been nice to talk to someone. And he'd seemed interested in her. Really interested.

But maybe she just wanted to believe that. She was lonely, that was all.

Danielle darted her head out. "Hey! Having a good time?"

"Yes, thank you."

Danielle's dark brows drew together in an expression of doubt. "You don't look like you are."

"I am okay. I am meditating, you know." She inhaled deeply. "Breathing."

"Oh! Where did Wilson go?"

"Who?"

Danielle frowned. "*Wilson*. You were talking to him forever out here."

"That was your Vilson?"

"Of course! Greta, you know Wilson."

No wonder he seemed so familiar! "I guess I never really looked at him."

"Where did you chase him off to?"

Greta lifted her shoulders. "I don't know. He just took up."

"Rats." Danielle puffed out a breath. "Did you notice who's not here?"

"Ben Affleck."

Danielle rolled her eyes. "No—*Alan!* What do you think could have happened to him?"

"I have not expent much thought on it."

"He said he'd be here."

"Maybe he's working."

"On a Saturday night? Not likely!" She huffed. "Oh, well. Maybe he'll be here later."

She flitted back inside. Greta stared at the apartments across the street, battling disappointment. *Wilson!* No wonder he'd been so friendly. He knew her.

And that was it. He was just being friendly. That love problem he had hinted at—it was Danielle he loved, she was pretty sure. Everything male seemed to love Danielle. Greta couldn't see the attraction, but maybe she let out low-frequency mating calls, like an elephant. Whatever. If you weren't male, it was discouraging.

Greta decided she'd been antisocial enough and climbed back inside. It was hard to talk at parties, she discovered, with no smokes and just a tepid ginger ale in her glass. She could sniff alcohol in the air, but if people were drinking, Edie had obviously told them to keep it discreet. She was grateful for that. Grateful and resentful. This business of living healthy was the pits. What if she lived to be ninety? That startling thought made her do some rapid calculations. If she lived to be ninety, that meant she had sixty years of stimulant-free existence looming ahead.

And that was the best case scenario.

She met more friends of Danielle's, but her gaze kept straying toward the door. *Wilson said he'd be back*, she kept thinking.

But he was probably just being polite.

She tried to put him out of her mind, so she was surprised when, about fifteen minutes later, someone grabbed her arm. "*Herzlichen Gluckwunsch zum Geburtstag*, Greta."

She turned and looked into Wilson's blue-gray eyes and couldn't help the smile that spread across her lips. "You're back!"

God, she sounded like a fool. Like she was so glad to see him.

He didn't seem to mind, though. "I brought you a present." He tugged her toward the balcony again and handed her a white plastic shopping bag. "The nearest drugstore was closed, so I had to go down to Fourteenth Street."

"You should have not bought me anything," she protested, practically yanking the bag out of his hands. He'd gone out for a present? For her?

"It's not much."

She peeked down into the bag and drew back in surprise. "Nicotine patches?" Three boxes of them!

"Just trying to keep you out of the headlines," he said.

If he had brought her flowers and candy, she wouldn't have been more touched. Which made her wonder if she weren't going a little out of her mind. "That is very kind of you."

"Here," he said, taking out a box for her and unwrapping the cellophane. "Start with one of these." He actually pulled out a patch and put in on her arm. The care he took made it seem like a tender, loving gesture. "There," he said when he was done. "If you murder anyone now, it won't be on my conscience."

She wasn't sure if it was the burning sensation on her arm or the wry expression on his face, but she felt better already. She also felt a strange sensation in the pit of her stomach. Almost as if she wanted to kiss this man.

This *nice young* man, she reminded herself. A guy like this was okay for Danielle, but a complete mismatch for her. What's more, someday he and Danielle would probably get together. She didn't want to step into what was bound to become a sticky situation.

Even if Danielle didn't deserve such a nice guy, she thought a little resentfully.

"Would you like to go for a walk?" he asked her.

"A walk?" It was already past midnight. "Where?"

"Anywhere. Down to the Village, maybe, or even farther. Have you ever been to Wall Street at night?"

She laughed. "I've hardly been there during the day."

"Then come with me. You won't believe it—it's like a ghost city."

Her feet itched to head for the door, but she hesitated. "It's my party."

"And you can fly if you want to," he said, smiling.

She puzzled at that. "What?"

"Nothing, I was just being goofy, which unfortunately isn't rare." He held out his hand to her. "Come with me."

Cautiously, she slipped her hand into his and felt comforted by the gentle pressure as he squeezed it. "You won't regret this," he promised.

They were just slipping out the door when Danielle scampered toward them. "Wilson!" She stopped and her eyes locked on their joined hands. "Where are you going?"

"Just out for a little."

"But I've hardly had a chance to talk to you!"

"We won't be gone long," he assured her.

Down on the street, Greta shook her head at him. "You lied to her. A walk down to Wall Street and back? That could take forever!"

The night air was almost brisk, and they walked quickly, their long strides a near perfect match. "Sorry, but I just didn't feel like negotiating the terms of our outing with Danielle," he said. "She should know that the world occasionally revolves around other people."

Greta cut a glance toward him. "Is it now revolving around you?"

He smiled. "I was thinking *us*, actually."

Us. She didn't like the sound of that.

Or maybe the problem was that she liked the sound of it too much.

Chapter 31

WHERE WERE YOU?

On Monday Danielle steamed down the hallway as quickly as her dignity and her four-inch heels would allow. When she woke up this morning, she had decided that she was simply going to ignore Alan . . . or at least pretend that she hadn't actually noticed his absence from the birthday party. But by the time she had an arm jutted through three people so she could cling to a pole on the crowded subway to work, she was feeling ornery and more convinced that she should not let this pass. He had stood her up. Where she came from, that was called rude behavior.

By the time she was actually in the hallway outside Alan's office, she was swollen with indignation. She rapped on his door and at the sound of his voice, slipped in and marched all the way up to his desk. Her breath was coming in heaves.

He grinned at her. "Hey, doll. Whassup?"

His flippant greeting made her see red. He could call her *doll*, just as if nothing had happened? She crossed her arms. "What happened to you?"

His brows pinched together. "I wasn't aware that anything had happened. I feel okay."

"I meant on Saturday night."

"What was Saturday night?"

"I had a party!"

He snapped his fingers. "That's right. That thing at your apartment for what's-her-name."

"It was a birthday party," she said through gritted teeth. "For *Greta*." Did he really not remember the names of her room-mates?

He laughed. "Right. Greta. How'd it go?"

"Fine!"

"Well . . . good." He tilted his head, eyeing her as if she were a ticking package on his doorstep. Which wasn't that far from the truth. "So what's the problem?"

"The problem is that you said you would be there!"

"No, I didn't."

"Yes, Alan, you did. I told you Saturday afternoon about the party and you said, and I quote, 'That sounds fun.'"

"It *did* sound fun, but I didn't make a solemn vow to attend. And, unfortunately, I couldn't make it." He shook his head in wonder. "Is that why you look so angry? Because I couldn't even make it to the birthday party of some woman I barely even know?"

"She's my friend."

"She's your roommate—you told me you don't even like her all that much."

"Yes, I do."

"Well, then your change of heart has been a recent develop-ment." He stood up and drifted around the desk, smiling at her. He gathered her into his arms, where she stood unresponsively. "I didn't know it meant that much to you. Don't you think I would have been there if I had?"

She lifted her shoulders. She wanted to let him off the hook, but she wasn't so sure she should. Something told her Edie wouldn't be a wimp about this. And Greta would have punched his lights out by now. Or told him to go to hell.

Greta probably wouldn't have spent two months playing dress-up doll, either.

Not that Greta was her role model or anything.

Alan took her chin in one of his hands and lifted her gaze up to his. His blue eyes sparked. "You're not going to let this business about a party come between us, are you?"

He seemed genuinely upset at the prospect; her heart tightened. He was worried that she would break off the relationship. He *was* sorry.

"You could have called," she said.

"I *should* have," he agreed.

For some reason, she hadn't expected him to be so conciliatory. Maybe she *was* blowing a little thing all out of proportion. Missing a party? In the big scheme of things, how big a deal was that?

"I'm sorry if I acted like a shrew just now," she said. "I thought maybe you had stood me up on purpose."

"You think I'm a fool?" He chuckled. "Why would I want to jeopardize this incredible thing we have?"

She lifted her hands to his shoulders. "I wasn't sure. I was worried."

"You must have no faith in me."

"Yes, I do," she said quickly. "I'm sorry—it was just the first party I've thrown in New York. I suppose I wanted to show you off to people."

He bent down and kissed her. "I'm the one who should want to show you off—and I intend to. How about going with me to a play next weekend?"

Her heart skipped. God, how could she have spent a day so angry over nothing? "I'd love to!"

"I hoped you would. That's why I bought the tickets already." He smiled, even blushing a little.

Was that sweet, or what? She stood on tiptoe and kissed him.

His hands roamed down her body. He lifted up her skirt and broke off their kiss to look down. "Sweet Jesus, where did you pick up those?"

He was speaking of her less-than-sextastic underwear. She smiled. "At an outlet mall in West Texas."

Alan dropped her skirt hem, practically shuddering. "I should go over to your apartment if for no other reason than to purge your drawers of anything Hanes."

She laughed. "You should come over anyway."

He let her go and returned to his desk chair. "I hope I can. It would be great if I could rid my desk of all this crap and just take a few days off."

That was her exit cue. "I'd better let you get back to it, I guess."

"Catch you later," he said.

"Lunch?"

A shadow passed over his face. "Not today. I've got an appointment."

Disappointment pricked her, but she tried to let it go. "Maybe tomorrow, then."

As she left his office, she was floating. He was taking her to a show! Even as she had been brooding all day yesterday, he had probably been buying the theater tickets for their next date. How could she have been so panicky?

After about thirty seconds, however, her euphoria began to dissipate. He'd blown her off Saturday. He had. And yet in his office, she had apologized to *him* for being pissed off.

There was something not right about that. . . .

She headed to the coffee room, where there was just one other proofer, a relatively new woman named Carol, standing by the coffeemaker. Danielle had been waiting to get a chance to get to know her a little.

"How's it going?" she asked, taking in the woman's trendy tweed outfit, which managed to look both conservative and incredibly sexy. Carol had really cool clothes. Plus she wore thin rectangular-shaped glasses in tortoiseshell frames. They were so cute, Danielle almost wished she were nearsighted so she could go out and buy a pair herself.

Stirring half-and-half into her coffee, Carol sent her a meager smile. "Fine."

"Did you just start here last week, or were you on another shift before?"

"I just started."

And that was all she intended to say, apparently.

Well, you couldn't squeeze blood from a turnip, Danielle thought to herself as she turned to get her own coffee. As she was pouring, something cold hit her back.

"Oh, oh, oh! I'm soooo sorry!" Carol yelled.

Danielle straightened too quickly, and spilled coffee down her front as she twisted to see what had happened.

But all she had to do was look at the little open carton in Carol's hand to understand. Somehow, she'd managed to spill half-and-half down Danielle's back. What an oaf!

Danielle sputtered and reached for paper towels to blot away some of the damage. Luckily, this was not a new outfit. She hadn't had a chance to really do any fall shopping yet. On the other hand, she liked it, and the dress was yellow and would show everything.

"Can I help?" Carol asked.

Danielle backed away instinctively. "That's okay, I think I can handle it."

"I'm really sorry."

"It's no big deal . . . just a coffee stain." *Just practically irremovable*. "And milk stains."

"I feel just awful!" Carol said miserably. "DKNY, isn't it?"

It was, Danielle thought, still a little steamed. Now her DKNY was KO'd from her wardrobe.

Wilson swung into the coffee room. When he saw Danielle, his eyes bugged. "What happened to you?"

"I spilled on her." Carol hung back looking distressed as Wilson tried to pat Danielle's back with napkins. "I guess I'd better get going," she said finally. "It was nice chatting with you, Danielle."

"Uh-huh," Danielle said.

She'd had time to wonder how a person standing still behind her could manage to spill something through an old-fashioned carton with a spout. It didn't even seem physically possible.

"That woman must be an incredible klutz," she said.

"What, just because she spilled something on you?" Wilson asked, surprised.

"Einstein couldn't have figured out the physics behind that spill."

"Anyone can make a mistake," Wilson said.

She frowned at him. He wasn't exactly going over the top with sympathy. Also, she remembered that *he* had pulled a disappearing act on her this weekend, too. "What happened to you Saturday night?" she asked. "Or should I say Sunday morning?"

He smiled as he tended to his own little coffee-pouring ritual. She'd always thought it odd that he preferred non-dairy creamer to milk. Too bad Carol didn't prefer it, too. "Greta and I walked."

"Walked where?"

"Down this way, actually."

"On foot?" she asked, aghast. "No wonder Greta slept all day Sunday!"

His eyes lit with interest. "She did?"

There was something about the curiosity in Wilson's eyes that made her feel uneasy. "Well . . . she sleeps a lot anyway. She never does much, really. Just watches food shows or plays the stupid oboe."

"She plays the oboe?" he asked excitedly. "She didn't tell me she was musical."

Oh, for heaven's sake.

"Did you talk to her last night?" he asked.

Danielle nodded. "Of course. We aren't Benedictines."

"Did she say anything about me?"

"Not that I recall." His disappointment was palpable. Danielle suddenly felt as if she were going insane. "Wilson . . . you're not developing some kind of crush on Greta, are you?"

He stared at her blankly. "What if I were?"

She nearly choked. "It would be a disaster, that's what!"

"A disaster for whom?" Wilson asked.

"For both of you, frankly." She laughed. "Greta is a nut, you know that."

"No, I don't. And if that's what you really think about her, I'd say you don't know the first thing about her."

He sounded almost offended. *Over Greta!*

"I know she's tough—she'd eat you alive," Danielle warned. "Just the idea of you chasing her is insane."

"That's your opinion," he said, turning for the door.

"Wilson, wait!" She grabbed his arm, and he stiffened. "What's happened? Are you trying to get back at me or something?"

The look he sent her made her immediately regret having said that.

She bit her lip. "I only meant . . ."

"I know what you meant," Wilson replied. "And all this time I thought maybe you were just oblivious to how I felt about you.

But I guess all along it just suited your vanity to have someone dangling after you."

"Oh, come on. That's crazy!"

"Is it?"

He turned and left her.

She frowned, her back twitching in discomfort from the way her dress was sticking to it. What an awful day. And it wasn't even nine o'clock yet.

But at least I've got Friday night to look forward to, she thought. *At least I've got Alan.*

Chapter 32

SILLY, DISGUSTING LOVE

Edie had never realized how damned annoying it was to be surrounded by so many disgustingly happy people. Suddenly everything seemed to be sunshine and lollipops in her apartment . . . for everyone but her. *She* was dragging around like something leftover from "Mary Hartman, Mary Hartman."

As she put on her uniform for her catering job, she could hear Greta and Wilson in the kitchen. They were just getting started making some elaborate Japanese dinner they had seen on television—a bunch of dishes involving weird ingredients like taro root and kimchi. They had come in from shopping with two bags of groceries, Asian noodle bowls from Chinatown, and his and her matching aprons. Now they were giggling like fools as they clattered around the small galley kitchen calling each other Greta-san and Wilson-san.

Hilarious.

Meanwhile, ten feet away, Danielle was getting ready for her latest date with the studded muffin and was apparently trying to drown out Greta and Wilson with some twangy country music cranked up to a volume that rasped on Edie's nerves. It wasn't just that the keening whine coming from Nashville divas these days seemed to have a distinct chewing-on-tinfoil quality; Danielle compounded the problem by singing along in the same slightly off-key howl that she also used to sing along to Jewel and a million unknown dance bands that she was always dragging in CDs of.

They were all in love, though in entirely different ways. Like those irksome country singers, Danielle never stopped announcing that she was head-over-heels, way gone, crazy for her no-good man. (Edie supplied the no-good part.) Greta, on the other hand, was in full-tilt denial. Asked if she and Wilson were dating, she would bark something at you indicating that you were either crazy or just dumb as a bag of hammers. For weeks she and Wilson had been hanging out, but she never tired of reminding Edie that Wilson was just a nice guy—too nice for his own good—who was being friendly to her through a rough patch. As soon as he started graduate school, Greta speculated, he would have better things to do with his time. He would meet some sexy graduate student and that would be that.

Meanwhile, school *had* started, and Wilson was at their place during all his precious free time, which couldn't have been much, between classes and temping and earning cash in the subways. The guy had to *really* want to see Greta.

Greta wouldn't have admitted his devotion to her for all the world; at the same time, whenever they were in a room together, she positively glowed. Edie was only now getting used to the sound of Greta's laughter—not the dry, raspy cackle of the old days, but a sharp, helpless kind of laughter. The giddy kind of laughter that Edie remembered from slumber parties and late nights in the freshman dorm.

Edie folded her black apron and put it in her leather shoulder bag; she was armed and ready to report for duty. When she ventured out of her bedroom, Wilson and Greta were in the kitchen, bickering over a smelly fish wrapped in butcher paper.

"You just leave it like it is, Greta-san," Wilson was saying.

Greta's eyes bugged in horror at the fish. "Do not Greta-san me, Vilson. I refuse. I do not want my dinner staring at me with those shriveled, cooked eyes. Disgusting!"

Wilson picked up the flounder and began to make it sing "Smoke Gets in Your Eyes."

"Stop!" Greta shrieked, trying to duck away.

As always, Edie found herself staring at the two of them in

amazement. Tonight she was joined by Danielle, who was decked out, made up, and bejeweled for her big date. A generous aura of Chanel Number Five clung to her. She shook her head, almost as if ashamed of the spectacle they were making of themselves. "Unbelievable," she muttered under her breath.

She punched off her music. Even with the sudden onset of silence, Greta and Wilson didn't turn around.

"See ya'll later!" Danielle called to the kitchen.

The two would-be chefs turned, waved, then went back to arguing over their fish.

"Let's go," Danielle said. In the stairwell, she turned to Edie. "Wilson must not like graduate school as much as he thought he would. Otherwise I doubt he'd be hanging around here so much, don't you?"

"I don't think school has anything to do with it. I think he's in love with Greta."

Danielle looked astounded. "That's so crazy! He's just got this weird infatuation going."

"So . . . isn't that what love usually is? A weird infatuation?"

"They aren't anything alike," Danielle argued. "And if you want my opinion, they probably aren't even physically attracted. They've only even kissed a couple of times."

Edie wasn't surprised so much by the revelation as by the fact that Danielle and Greta had been exchanging girl talk. "Greta told you this?"

"God no. Wilson did."

"Well, it's none of my business," Edie said.

"Mine, either," Danielle admitted quickly. "Only I would hate to see Wilson with a broken heart. He's really, really sweet, don't you think?"

Edie just smiled. *If he's so sweet, why didn't you fall in love with* him *instead of that creep you're trotting off to meet?*

Danielle gasped at her watch. "Oh, I gotta run. Can I drop you somewhere? I'm going to get a cab."

A cab! Edie shook her head over that. Danielle was just a lost soul.

"No, thanks. I'm walking over to Grammercy Park."

"'Kay—bye! Have fun!"

Edie frowned as she watched her scamper toward Broadway. Did she *look* like she was going to have fun? Danielle obviously hadn't noticed that she was dressed for a night of passing out small things made of cheese.

As she approached the brownstone where the job was located, she spotted Sam crouched by the iron fence of the private park, smoking his final pre-work cigarette.

Actually, he spotted her. "What's the matter, dewdrop?"

She worked up a smile. "Nothing. I'm just the last single person in New York, that's all."

"No, you're not." Sam spoke quickly and with authority. "Louis is."

This news surprised her. "Louis, your roommate? I thought he was keeping you awake with loud, exuberant sex."

"The whoopee days are over. Suzanne flew the coop and Lucky Lou has morphed into mopey boy. Now I have to listening to him moaning when he's *not* having sex, which for some inexplicable reason I find even more repulsive."

Edie was amazed. "I thought they were so happy."

"I've come to realize that even the happiest couple is just one nasty spat away from loneliness."

"Sam Shearing, philosopher," she mused.

They stood in silence for a moment as Sam tugged thoughtfully on his Camel. "Hey, hold the phone!" He snapped his fingers, and she could almost see the lightbulb switching on over his head as he looked at her.

Edie could guess what he was thinking, and she wasn't pleased. Sam wanted to play matchmaker. "Oh no."

"Why not?" Sam whined. "You just said you were lonely."

"No, I said I was *alone*. There's a big difference."

He exhaled sharply. "You're lonely, or you wouldn't have been whining about being alone."

"I wasn't whining."

"I *saw* you drooping down Lexington. Your chin was dragging the sidewalk." He touched his hand to her chin. "See? It's all scraped."

She batted his hand away playfully. "No, Sam. Me and your roommate? That just doesn't seem right."

"Why not?"

"For one thing, I couldn't spend the night in your apartment with you there."

"Why not?"

"*Please*—knowing that you would be regaling your coworkers the next day with stories of what kinds of noises were coming through the walls?"

"Couldn't you just be quiet?" he asked.

"See? You're already annoyed."

He stubbed his cigarette butt beneath the heel of his Kenneth Cole and began to beg in earnest. "Please, Edie? It wouldn't even be like a blind date, because you two have met."

"Barely."

"Barely counts. And you guys would have tons to talk about. You both are experts on theater *and* soaps."

Louis had piled up money writing for "Guiding Light" for a few years, then quit to devote himself to playwriting. He was also the only person Edie knew who was a paid dramaturg, a sort of theater company researcher.

"Think about it," Sam said. "You two have so much in common."

"Like what?"

"Well . . . theater."

"You and I have that in common, too," she pointed out. "That doesn't make us couple material."

"But he's more intellectual, like you."

That was a howler. "Come on, Sam. The last book I read was *Merv*, the autobiography of Merv Griffin."

"That's because of the company you've been keeping."

"Lately I've mostly been hanging around you."

"Exactly. In college you were brainier. And just think of it— Louis could tell you more than you wanted to know about practically every production of *Blood Wedding* that had ever been staged. He's a real authority on Federico Garcia Lorca."

She arched a brow at him. "How could a girl resist?"

"Okay, but if that's not incentive enough, he's good looking."

This was no lie. Louis was a tall, lumbering Minnesota boy with curly blond hair and green eyes. He was certainly better looking than Tom McCormick, Douglas's old work buddy, who had called Edie again a week ago. She was ashamed to say that she had actually been tempted to accept. Yes, he was a jerk, but he was a jerk who would have sex with her.

But Louis wasn't a jerk. In fact, she couldn't think of a thing to say against him, except that he was on the rebound. And hadn't she told Danielle that rebound relationships weren't necessarily disasters?

"All right," she said, finally relenting. "I'm game."

Sam hugged her. "Oh, you wonderful thing! You don't know what a favor you're doing me. This is *just* what Louis needs to perk himself up and forget that skanky Suzanne."

A few nights later, Edie had herself a date. The entire day preceding, her spirits alternated manically between giddiness and depression. It felt great to be in the swing of things again—to be part of the single throng. She dusted off her diaphragm and spent an hour tearing apart her clothes closet in distress. Even worrying about what to wear suddenly seemed like a luxury problem. Then, when she wasn't watching out, despair set in.

She hadn't been on a first date in almost a year—not since she'd first gone out with Douglas. How depressing was that? A year . . . and she was right back where she started.

Out in the living room, Wilson and Greta were making music together. A really warped version of the Beatles' "She Loves You" wheezed loudly through the apartment with Greta on oboe and Wilson on his accordion.

"Hey!" Wilson shouted, spotting Edie. "You look great!"

"Thanks."

"This must be a really fancy catering job tonight, huh?" Danielle said, poking her head around her screen to look.

Edie frowned and looked down. After months of being sick of having to wear penguin waitstaff clothes, for her date she had chosen a black shift dress with black boots, set off with a black-and-white scarf. She had obviously fallen into a fashion rut. "Actually, I'm going out."

Danielle's face registered shock. "Wow! Who's the fella?"

Edie provided a thumbnail sketch of Louis.

"That's great! It's about time you had some fun," Danielle told her. "You want to share a cab? I'm going uptown to meet Alan."

"No, thanks. Louis will be coming by in a few minutes." *Some men actually pick up their dates*, she wanted to add, but refrained.

Danielle shrugged. "'Kay. Have fun!"

"Thanks."

Danielle must have met Louis at the door and let him in, because he knocked on the apartment door a few moments later. He was wearing vintage herringbone pants, a brown shirt and tie, and a really sharp jacket. He looked handsome, if a little ill-at-ease. "Am I late?" he asked. "Ever since Suzanne dumped me, I just can't seem to get places on time. It's like nothing really matters anymore."

She wasn't sure how to respond to that last statement. "No, you're just on time," Edie told him. "Nice outfit."

"Thanks, it was a gift from Suz—" His voice hitched. "You know."

"Oh."

The jam session had stopped and Greta and Wilson were peering at them curiously. Edie made introductions.

"I've been thinking of taking up a musical instrument," Louis said, poking curiously at the plastic shell of the accordion case. "I've been thinking it might help me with my chronic depression."

Edie smiled. *Off to a great start!* "Ready to go?"

"Oh," Louis seemed reluctant to move. "I guess."

It's seven-thirty, she thought as they descended the stairs single file. They were going to go to a movie and to dinner after. *That means only four hours to go. Maybe three, if I eat fast. . . .*

As she opened the front door, a guy was pressing on their buzzer. When she looked into his brown eyes, she recognized him immediately as Ross Johnson. Judge Porter's Texas spy.

Edie had almost forgotten about him. "Hello!"

He jumped. Apparently, he hadn't expected to be blitzed before he'd even rung the doorbell. "Hi," he said, smiling. His brown eyes gave her a once-over that made her pulse rev. "Don't you look fine."

"Thanks." *Not that my date has noticed.* Ross peered curiously over her shoulder at Louis, and she introduced them.

"Nice to meet you," Ross said.

Louis agreed that it was nice to meet him, too. Then they all fell silent.

"I guess you came by to see Danielle," Edie piped up. *God only knows why,* she might have added. "She just left."

"Left?" he asked.

"On a date."

"Oh." If he was disappointed, he didn't show it. He kept staring at Louis.

Damn, Edie thought. If Louis weren't there, she might have asked Ross up to the apartment, or maybe even out for coffee. Not that she knew him at all—except that he was Judge Porter–approved. But coffee with Ross held a lot more appeal than a night on the town with the chronic-depressive world authority on *Blood Wedding.*

"Well, I won't keep you," Ross said, backing away from the threshold. If he'd been wearing a Stetson, he would have tipped his hat at them. "Just thought I'd drop by for a visit."

"I'll tell Danielle you were here," she said. *If you really want me to. . . .*

He didn't look like he cared whether she did or she didn't. It was weird. After his last drop-in fiasco, why wouldn't he have called before coming by?

After he was gone, Louis shook his head. "Is he in love with your roommate?"

She considered this as they went down the stairs and started down the street. "I don't think so." How could he be? Frankly, she was surprised to see him again at all.

"I get it," Louis said, his voice sounding even more morose than usual.

"Get what?"

"He came by to see *you,*" he guessed. "That's why he was looking at you that way."

"What way?" she asked, aware that she sounded just a little too eager.

"Like you were some precious, unattainable object."

She laughed. "You've got to be joking! I've only laid eyes on the guy once, and that was months ago."

"Well, maybe I'm wrong," Louis said. "That wouldn't surprise me. I seem to have very bad instincts for romance."

"I'm not exactly razor sharp in that department, either."

"Right." Louis nodded. "Sam told me about your getting dumped by that other guy."

Thanks, Sam.

Had Ross been looking at her that way? She felt oddly giddy at the possibility.

"I guess that's one thing we have in common," Louis said.

She focused on him with effort. She hadn't been listening to him very closely. "What?"

"We're both losers at the game of love. Dumpees. I guess that gives us one thing to talk about at dinner. . . ."

"Mm."

If those weren't words to make a girl's heart go pitter-pat, what were?

Chapter 33

HALLOWEEN

"You'll never take me seriously, will you?"

Given the fact that the question was asked by a guy in a parrot suit, Greta should have laughed. God knows Wilson had made her laugh more in the past two months than she had in the entire lifetime leading up to her thirtieth birthday. But Greta knew instinctively that he didn't want her to laugh right now. Not really.

"Your feathers are crooked." She straightened the elaborate papier-mâché headdress that they had wasted an entire weekend slaving over. It fit his head like a skullcap, except that it was bulky and covered with both painted-on and real feathers.

Wilson snapped his beak into place. "You didn't answer my question."

She couldn't help it; she giggled. She couldn't remember giggling since she was ten.

Knowing he had her hooked, Wilson struck an offended pose. He crossed his arms, which were weighted down with feathered attachments, and shifted from one yellow high-top sneaker to the other. The rest of him was clad in green shorts over a bright red one-piece thermal underwear suit.

"I can't believe you're actually going to walk the streets in that," she said.

He refused to break character. In fact, he seemed to fluff up all the more. "Why not?"

"I give up." She refused to play along anymore. She grabbed her long black coat and snapped her eyepatch into place and glared at him through the one eye left available for glaring. "We will be late for the party."

This was the first time Wilson had seen her whole costume put together. He let out a low wolf whistle. "You are one sexy buccaneer."

"Oh, sure."

"I mean it. Put you and Captain Hook and Long John Silver in a lineup, and you'd be the hands-down winner for Miss Pirate America."

"You are insane," she said, grabbing the box of saltines they had run out to the deli for when they decided they needed a prop. "We go?"

He wasn't budging, so she tossed him the crackers, thinking maybe it would be better if he didn't have his hands free. These waning moments in empty apartments usually turned into long necking sessions, which she knew she should be trying to avoid but at the same time couldn't seem to resist.

"Where did you get those boots?"

She had found her old knee-high purple suede boots in an old box. "I went through a Prince phase in my teens. These are a souvenir."

"You never throw anything away, do you?" he asked admiringly.

That was just the problem. Everything he said to her seemed admiring. It puzzled her almost as much as it flattered her. She was so accustomed to people treating her either as a delinquent (her poor aunt and uncle) or a burnout (everyone else), that having an admirer—a sane one—threw her completely. In Wilson's estimation, everything she did was great. Even when she was in a foul mood, he didn't seem to take it personally.

She hadn't had as many foul moods lately, though, since Wilson had been around.

It was all so confusing. Ever since her birthday she had the feeling that she was in a dewy Hallmark card kind of world, tumbling laughingly down a hillside that would inevitably end with a nasty thump. She kept trying to catch herself, to stop before things were too out of control. But she just couldn't seem to. She liked him too much.

"Things—I try to hold on to things," she told him carefully. She wished words could come with flashing warning lights. "People I am not so good with."

He considered her answer, and for a moment she feared a scene. The he tilted his head. "Okay. If you aren't so good with people, how are you with sea chanties?"

Her brows drew together in confusion. "What?"

"Sea chanties," he repeated. "Damn! We should have been practicing."

They left the apartment and headed down to the West Village, where one of Wilson's friends was having a party. The guy's apartment was in the basement of a brownstone. He apparently hadn't expected as many people to come as he got, because the place was packed. People had to yell to be heard over music and the sound of other people yelling. Greta still felt ill at ease among revelers, though Wilson did his best to help her adjust. During any kind of social function he performed the duties of a combination nursemaid/butler, constantly ensuring she had a fresh glass of something nonalcoholic in one hand and something sugary or salty to eat in the other.

Usually at these parties with Wilson, she felt like the odd man out, but tonight she actually recognized people. "I think I have met all your friends, maybe," she said in astonishment. It was miraculous. Wilson knew so many people.

"Maybe most of the ones in New York City," he said. "I can't wait to take you to North Carolina with me."

"North Carolina?" She laughed uncomfortably.

He smiled back at her, though a little uneasily. "Sure, why not?"

She had heard all about his big happy clan down south. Surely he really didn't intend to take her there? She would probably fit in about as well as a bag lady at a cocktail party. *This is why I shouldn't be with him*, she thought. *This is why we're all wrong.* She didn't know how to put it into words. They went together about as well as Jimmy Stewart and Courtney Love.

Her chest felt tight. It was so unfair. Why couldn't she be someone else, someone better?

"You look pale," he said. "What's the matter?"

She shook her head.

From out of the blue, he produced a bowl of candy-covered nuts. "Chocolate bridge mix?"

She should leave him alone, she thought as she so often had. Just quit answering his calls. He had school and lots of friends and . . . well, he wouldn't miss her. He'd find a little chipmunk of a girl like Danielle (a Danielle who liked him back) and he'd be happier.

Except that whenever she seriously considered the prospect of never seeing him again, she felt like this. Like all the air was slowly being squeezed out of her.

"Dance?" he asked her, keeping things moving along as smoothly as a cruise director.

"Okay," she said.

They fought their way through the stationary section of the room to the part that was moving. Greta hoped that dancing would make her feel better, but it didn't. Whoever was in charge of the stereo had put on a slow, pulsing music that wasn't really suitable for wild abandon or even slow dancing. About all you could do was undulate around your partner and think about sex, which was really disturbing when your partner was not just completely wrong for you, but also wearing a bird suit.

She made a correction in her mind. It wasn't Wilson who was all wrong. It was her. She'd lived at the edge of excess for years, never holding down friends, or lovers, and barely managing to hold on to her jobs. She wasn't the sort of person a nice guy like Wilson could depend on. Once he got to know her, he would realize this.

That's what usually happened, wasn't it? You got to know someone, and then one or the other of you grew tired of the other, and then it was over. But she couldn't see herself growing tired of Wilson . . . she could only see him wanting to end it, but being too nice to. And there she would be, the old German crone who had gotten her claws on a sweet southern boy.

Poor Wilson. He was younger, more naïve. He couldn't see that they were doomed.

He leaned toward her. "What's wrong?" he yelled over the music.

She stared at his beak, feeling as if her heart were breaking.

"You need a drink?"

She could have cried. *Did she need a drink?* Was he joking?

"Hang on—I'll get you something." Wilson turned and loped off toward the kitchen.

The moment he was out of sight, she hunted down the host and screamed in his ear, "Thank you for the party! Tell Vilson I have to leave!" Then she slipped out the door and clattered up the small flight of stairs to street level. She was halfway down the street when she heard Wilson hailing her. She quickened her pace. If she could just get to Sixth Avenue, then she could disappear into the subway.

"Greta!"

Behind her, someone laughed and slurred, "Look—a parrot chasing a pirate!"

It was dark, but as she approached Sixth Avenue she could tell it was jammed. She remembered what was going on and her heart sank. Halloween! The Village Halloween parade. An endless procession of weird costumes and guys in drag. People were bunched up five-deep on the sidewalk, gawking.

Wilson caught up to her and took her arm. "Greta! Where are you going?"

"I don't know," she bit out. "Home?"

She hazarded a look at him. The hurt in his eyes pierced her. *Better to see that hurt now than later. . . .*

"Don't you know the worst way to dump a guy is to leave a vague message at a party and take off running?"

Her eyes stung, and she looked away from him again, toward a line of guys marching down the Avenue of the Americas in tight red sequined dresses and Marilyn Monroe wigs. "I didn't know what to say."

"Try to think of something," Wilson said. "The worst is having no explanation—just to be tossed out for no reason. So tell me

I'm a jerk, or an idiot, or that I have persistent halitosis . . . anything."

If only it were that simple. "I can't."

"Then *what?*" he asked, flapping his wings in frustration. "Why won't you take me—us—seriously?"

"Because it couldn't last," she said.

"How do you know?"

"I know. We sleep together a few months, one of us gets bored—you, probably—and then we break off. *Das Ende.*"

He gaped at her in frustration. "That's it? You won't sleep with me because you're afraid that at some point in the future we'll break up?"

"*Ja.* Exactly."

"You know that's nuts, don't you? If everybody thought like you did, nobody would ever sleep with anyone. We should send you over to the U.N. You've discovered the remedy to world overpopulation."

She shook her head. "I am not for you, Wilson."

He rolled his eyes. "Please don't start in with the older-and-wiser routine. You're all of thirty—not fifty. And I'm twenty-five, not some pimply teenager. And okay, you've had some problems and your life hasn't been a bed of roses. No one is requiring you to do penance."

"You are in school."

"*Graduate* school."

"You are tender hearted. Sentimental."

"And you're *not?*" he asked incredulously. "Take a hard look at yourself, Greta. You might see a world-weary burnout, but what I see is a brokenhearted wreck so sentimental she's been dragging a houseful of furniture around with her for ten years because she can't bear to part with her parents."

"I told you . . . those are things," Greta muttered.

"What about those emotions you tried to pickle all those years? Were those things?"

"Shut up, Dr. Freud," Greta said. "Look at yourself. What are you doing? You are rebounding from Danielle. She is what you really want."

"No." He stepped forward, his gaze intense. "She's not. Anyway, I can't be on the rebound from her because I was never *with* her."

"Still . . . You were wild about her."

"*Was.* Don't you get it? For months I've only thought about you. *You're* the one I'm wild about now, whether you want to believe it or not. You and your sad eyes and your morbid humor and messed-up past and the way you call me 'Vilson.' *That's* what I think about—well, the part I can talk about on a public street, at least. I love you."

His words stopped her cold. Loved her? Was he insane? "Have you left your senses?"

He nodded.

Oh, God. This was terrible. Because she felt insane, too.

Gently, he pulled her into his arms, where she knew from experience she fit disturbingly well. Wilson pushed his beak up to the top of his forehead. "I love you, Greta," he repeated. "If it makes you any happier, I tried not to. For weeks I tried to mimic your gloom. I've tried to ferret out all the downsides, too . . . but there are only three that I can tell."

"What are they?" she whispered.

"My one roommate and your two. We'll *never* have any privacy."

She laughed, pressing herself gently against him. It was awful how much she loved him just at that moment. Really awful. "You see? We are doomed."

"If you insist," he said, lowering his mouth to hers. He kissed her, and as their lips and tongues and bodies began to intertwine, she felt heat coiling up inside her. It was so unlike her to kiss a man like this out on a crowded street. *Get a hotel room,* she'd always growled at nauseating lovebirds on the street.

But she was too far gone to care.

Besides, this was the one night of the year when a parrot could ravish a pirate in public and no one would bat an eye.

"Let's go to my place," Wilson said.

"My place is closer."

"But . . ."

"Edie is working and Danielle is with the jackass."

That settled it. Wilson took her hand and they wove across the street through a crowd of people tap-dancing to old B-52s music. The strains of "Rock Lobster" followed them as they ran down the steps to the subway, laughing.

Chapter 34

LOOK WHO'S HERE

The day after Halloween, Danielle was working the afternoon shift, so she actually had a few morning hours of peace before having to stick her head back into the meat grinder. She let herself into the apartment and made a beeline for the kitchen, clutching a Krispy Kreme bag.

Some awful mornings could only be remedied by donuts, and this was one of them.

Last night she had expected Alan to surprise her—either by taking her off to a round of Halloween parties or by having a fun evening at home indulging his fetish. It would have been an appropriate moment for him to break out the bunny suit. Instead, he had stunned her by announcing he was exhausted from work and needed to catch up on sleep. So they'd had a few slices of pizza, watched some television, and then gone to bed.

And that's when things had gone very, very wrong.

The memory of what an idiot she had been slammed through her anew, and she felt suddenly as if she could cram all six donuts down her mouth at once. It would take that kind of sugar glaze infusion to calm her down. She started making coffee, but her hands were shaking, and she kept remembering those awful words she had said to him.

"I love you, Alan."

Okay, maybe it wasn't such an awful thing to say by itself. It was the way she had said it, though. She had blurted the phrase out—opened her mouth and spilled it—when they were still sweaty from sex.

And how had Alan responded? He had taken her face in his hands, sent her the sweetest smile, and said, "You don't know how great that makes me feel."

She had fallen asleep with a dopey grin on her face . . . and popped awake at six A.M., brooding. Okay . . . he felt great that she loved him. But didn't he love her, too?

He hadn't said so. *Why* hadn't he said so? His answer had been so noncommittal! So damned inconsiderate when you came right down to it. In her experience, it was standard operating procedure to say "I love you, too." Unless, of course, he didn't love her.

How could he not love her?

One thing was clear. He didn't love her enough to lie and say he loved her. She would have preferred a lie. At least then she wouldn't be sitting around worrying about whether he did or he didn't, and why he didn't, and how she could love him so much if he didn't love her.

She shoveled five scoops of coffee into the filter and then slammed it into place.

And another thing. This underwear business had to stop. She hadn't worked up the nerve to tell Alan this . . . she'd wanted to wait until they were on solid footing . . . but she *hated* thong panties. Really. What was the point? He seemed to think they were sexy. God knows, she was all for sexy. But she wasn't asking *him* to trade his comfy boxers for butt floss.

She took a shaky breath, then exhaled.

The underwear thing was just a side issue. She *loved* him. And he didn't love her. That was the crux of the matter.

Or maybe, *maybe*, he was one of those guys who couldn't express his feelings very well. Maybe he was just reticent about telling her how much she really meant to him.

But how could that be? How could a man be so frank about *everything*, right down to what kind of bikini wax she should get, and then not be able to mouth the words "I love you?"

He didn't love her.

Damn it, damn it, damn it! She couldn't even wait for the coffee to brew. She reached into the bag and practically swallowed a

donut whole. It took a moment for the sugar to work its therapeutic effect.

Fortified by greasy, sugary dough, she was ready to embrace the
delusion again. He did love her. She knew he did. She wasn't an
idiot about these things. Hadn't she known all along that she and
Brandon weren't meant to be? Surely, surely, her instincts couldn't
be so haywire now as to make her fall in love, really in love, with a
man who was just really looking for a free lingerie model.

She understood people. That's why she was a writer.

Or had been a writer . . . until she had stopped. So she could
spend more time with Alan.

The coffee was done, so she went through the ritual of getting
her first cup of the morning ready. By the time she had stirred the
milk in, she had a plan of action in place. She would make herself
unavailable for one weekend. It might even take two weekends,
but that would be all to the good because she could really get
some work done on her latest story. She had been ignoring her
writing too much lately. Ever since . . . well, ever since she'd
found better things to do.

But now she would get back on track.

And at the end of a weekend—or two, if necessary—Alan
would realize that he loved her.

The creak of Greta's door opening startled her. It was after
nine-thirty—way past the time when Greta usually went to work.
Danielle poked her head around the open kitchen doorway. What
she saw made the blood seep out of her veins. "Wilson!"

He jumped back, his blue eyes wide. "Danielle! We thought
you were supposed to be with the jack—I mean, the boyfriend."

"We?" she repeated, feeling sick. *Please God, don't let Wilson
and Greta have become a we!*

But they so obviously had. Wilson's hair was smashed on one
side of his head and his clothes were rumpled . . . but not as rumpled as they would have been if he had actually slept in them.

"Oh no," she moaned.

He strolled right past her, sniffing. "Did you make coffee?"
Just like that. As if he belonged here!

He picked up her donut bag and peered inside. "Is that a
raspberry-filled I see?"

She attempted to snatch the bag back, but he raised it above his head, playing keep away. "There are six donuts in here."

"Five!"

"So? You can't eat them *all*."

"Watch me."

He shook his head. "I couldn't let you do it," he said, popping the raspberry jelly donut in his mouth. "You would never forgive me."

"I'll never forgive you now," she said, watching the red jelly seeping down his chin.

He smiled. "Why are you in such a temper this morning?"

"Why are you in such an annoyingly good mood?" She winced. "Don't answer that. I don't want to know."

He laughed. "Look who's acting like a prude all of a sudden."

"I am not."

"Yes, you are. Just because I spent the night with Greta you're jumpy as a cat."

If only that were the only reason. But Greta and Wilson together did make her uneasy. He was supposed to be *her* friend, but she hardly ever saw him outside of work anymore when he wasn't with Greta. He had abandoned her.

"Just remember, I warned you," she told him.

"You were wrong. I've never been happier."

She sighed. Poor Wilson! What was he doing with his life? "It can't last."

"How do you know?"

"Because as far as I can tell, Greta has hardly managed to keep any friends since she's come to America. And that's been over a decade."

"It's different now."

She shook her head and slurped angrily at her coffee cup. "We'll see."

"What's that supposed to mean?" he asked, his tone growing a little angry.

A tiny sneer pulled at her lips. "Listen to you—so defensive! I didn't notice that you were shy criticizing *my* affair."

"That's because I knew that was the extent you were going to get out of Alan Mara—an affair."

Her cheeks felt hot. That was not what she needed to hear this morning. "And how long do you think you'll last before Greta gets tired of you?"

"I don't care," he shot back. "I don't care, and do you know why?"

"Why?"

"Because if it only lasts a month, or a week, I'll be better off for having been with her. I'm better off because the day I met Greta was the day I stopped thinking about you!"

Tears stung her eyes. *Why did she ever come back here this morning?* "Those are nice words, coming from a friend!" She was shouting, and she didn't care.

"At least I'm being upfront with you," he replied hotly. "At least I'm not treating you as if you were just someone to be used and taken for granted!"

She put her hands on her hips and squared off with him. "When did I do that to you?"

He blasted a laugh right down into her face. "When did you not?"

"WHAT THE HELL IS GOING ON HERE?"

They both swiveled in surprise. Standing at the entrance to the kitchen was Edie, looking frazzled and red faced in her terrycloth bathrobe. "Jesus H. Christ, what is this, 'The Honeymooners'? What are you two screaming about?"

Danielle stepped back. "I'm so sorry, Edie. I forgot you were home."

"We weren't thinking," Wilson stammered guiltily.

"No, obviously." Edie squinted at Wilson. "What are you doing here?"

"Greta and I came back here after the party."

Edie's mouth formed a knowing O, and she glanced at Danielle. Initially, the look expressed the same astonishment that Danielle felt that of all people in the world, Greta should be on the receiving end of Wilson's sweet lovin'. But Edie was also checking Danielle for another reaction.

Danielle could feel her face turning red. *She thinks I'm jealous, but I'm not. I'm just . . .*

Jealous.

Wilson wasn't the kind of man who would tell you "That's nice, dear," if you confessed that you loved him. If she had fallen in love with him, she wouldn't have been sitting around eating donuts and wondering whether he loved her back.

"From the sounds of things, I thought you two were having a lovers' quarrel. I figured I needed to come out and referee, and maybe guard poor Kuchen from flying objects."

Wilson and Danielle exchanged sheepish looks.

Edie poured herself a cup of coffee. "So . . . I guess a lot happened last night."

No one answered until Danielle grabbed the Krispy Kreme bag off of the counter and held it out for Edie. She was willing to trade her treasure for a little peace. "Maybe it would be better if we all stopped talking and just ate donuts."

Chapter 35

BACK ON THE BOARDS

"**R**oger Hackett wants you to be a member of his theater company."

Edie couldn't believe what she was hearing. At first she'd thought this was a prank. After what had happened with Aurora, she had assumed she would have to start looking for another agent. It had been a while since she'd spoken to Noel. She certainly wouldn't have guessed he'd be calling her with such incredible news.

Incredible, except . . .

"*Who?*" Edie asked.

"Roger Hackett," Noel repeated.

Roger Hackett, Roger Hackett. Edie filtered the name through her memory and came up blank. She didn't even know anyone by the name of Roger.

"You know him," Noel prompted. "You must. He said he'd met you recently."

The only people Edie remembered meeting lately were catering waiters and a few of Danielle's friends at Greta's birthday party. None of those people were theater directors.

"You really impressed him, apparently."

"He didn't make much of an impression on me. I don't remember him."

"That's okay. Just pretend you do when you meet him at his studio in Jersey tomorrow."

"Wait." She knew there had to be a hitch. *"Jersey?"*

"Hoboken," Noel said. "Listen, I told you this wasn't Broadway, or even off-off-Broadway. He runs a company that does programs for industrial trade shows. But the pay's better than what you were getting for *Heartbreak House.*"

"Joy. That means I'll almost be making enough to starve."

Of course, now with her two roommates, she might be able to live just from her acting pay. *That* would be incredible! The first time she'd be living an apron-and-menu-free existence since "Belmont Hospital" had killed her off.

Noel gave her the address where she was supposed to meet this guy tomorrow at noon. "He says it's just a formality. To meet you again and go over the script a little."

She still couldn't believe this. Apart from being an industrial thing in Hoboken, with some crackpot director she couldn't even recall, it seemed too good to be true. This could be a good omen for her career—a turning point. Maybe her run of miserable luck was over now. Goodbye, troubles! She would look back on this year and shake her head that things had ever been that bad. These would be the lean times she would harken back to when she was sitting in the guest chair on Jay Leno.

Maybe she would even meet someone through the show. Her relationship with Louis had lasted half an evening. Conveniently, she had developed a stomach virus from what she could only conjecture was a tainted box of Junior Mints, so they had skipped dinner. To the mutual relief of both.

Noel cleared his throat. "Oh—I told this Roger character you could dance." He paused anxiously. "You can, can't you?"

Edie swallowed. "Sure, if you count two years of Lil' Princess ballet school in Springfield and Intro to Tap at NYU."

"That's great! You'll be great!" Noel sounded suspiciously like Mama Rose pushing her daughter onto the stage at the strip joint. "Give me a buzz and let me know how it turns out tomorrow."

"Will do," she promised.

She hung up the phone, relieved that there had been no mention of plates of fettuccine or even a word of Aurora. Then she felt a pang. She *missed* Aurora. Aurora would be the one she would call to celebrate with. Now there was just Kuchen . . . and the news only interested her when Edie brought out her foil bag of kittie treats.

Once the initial elation wore down, she sat staring at Greta's Picasso poster and absentmindedly petting the cat. Roger Hackett. Dancing. *What was going on here?*

When she finally met Roger Hackett after having wandered around lost in Hoboken for half an hour, she had to bite back a groan. He was the fat, furry guy from the Sudz audition! The jackass who had made her sing "Oklahoma!" on her way out the door.

This was the guy who wanted her?

Nevertheless, she plastered on a game smile and poked out her hand. "It's nice to meet you again."

He was wearing the same thick glasses. Another tight T-shirt gave the world an impressive view of his gut, only now he had an unzipped hooded sweatshirt over it. She'd lay money that the zipper would never make it over that beer belly.

They sat down on two metal folding chairs in a row of fifteen that lined the wall of the dance studio. There was a mirrored wall with a ballet bar across from them. "I guess Noel wasn't kidding when he said you wondered if I could dance."

He seemed thrilled that she had brought it up. "He said you could, but I never believe what agents tell me. Can you?"

"I know a little tap."

"Excellent! Let's see."

She looked around. There wasn't a piano nearby, or even a boom box. "You want me just to dance?"

"Sure! We're a little low-tech here, but I've always found that it inspires creativity." He gestured for her to stand up. "Do a time step for me . . . how about that?"

She eyed him doubtfully. She had dressed in loose clothing, but she hadn't worn dance shoes. Her time step was performed in street shoes.

It didn't matter. Roger seemed delighted. "Oh, that's terrific!"

She frowned at him. It wasn't terrific. She knew next to nothing about dance, but everything she did know confirmed that she was no twinkle toes. Was he some kind of a nut?

Or maybe—repulsive thought—he liked her and was going to stick her into this show in hopes that she would sleep with him. Though it seemed improbable that even a guy like Roger would think an actress would be so desperate to get ahead that she would try to sleep her way to the top of the industrial trade show world.

Just to test him, she was prepared to sacrifice herself. "I can do a waltz clog to 'Take Me Out to the Ballgame.' Would you like to see it?"

"Love to!"

She took a deep breath and began. She could barely sing and could barely dance. Put the two together and each skill seemed to diminish exponentially. Somewhere in heaven, Bob Fosse was weeping. But she put on a show for Roger, giving it her all and smiling like some desperate two-bit vaudevillian. She even ended with a flourish, clicking her heels together and then thrusting out her arms to her one-man audience.

Roger rose from his chair. You would have thought he had been visited by Gene Kelly's ghost. "Amazing! That's *just* what I'm looking for."

Okay. This was creepy. She put her hands on her hips. "Roger—I hope you don't think I'm being too frank here, but I'm just trying to understand. You're looking for a *mediocre* singer/dancer?"

"Exactly!" he said, still smiling delightedly.

"Oh." For some reason, even though she'd known it herself, having someone else confirm she was mediocre wasn't exactly thrilling. Though at least this way she knew Roger wasn't an insane person posing as a director. He was just a director who thought she was an insane person posing as an actress.

And she *knew* he wasn't angling for sex. He definitely would have lied in that case.

He sank back down and patted the seat next to him, beckoning her. As he spoke, he mopped his sweaty brow with an old handkerchief; her dance had evidently taken it out of him. "Noel told you we are putting on an industrial, right?"

She nodded.

"The show we're working on is for the national convention of nutrition counselors, which is going to be having their convention at the Marriott in December."

"Nutritionists," Edie repeated. What did singing and dancing have to do with nutrition?

"Yes. And then in January, we're booked to travel through school districts in New Jersey. It's going to be an informative, half-hour musical show involving twelve performers representing the different groups on the food pyramid. You will be a vegetable."

Look enthusiastic, she ordered herself. *Act like Danielle during her second week in New York.* "That's great!"

"Actually, I had the show all cast, but when someone had to drop out, I couldn't help thinking about you. You've got just the wry humor we're gonna need."

Great. I'm going to be vegetable comic relief.

"Now, here's our working script." He handed her a brad-fastened Xeroxed manuscript. "When you read it, I want you to look closely at the role of the fava bean."

She took one look at the title, *Follow That Carb!,* and forced herself to nod and smile. "How cute!"

Money. That's why you're doing this. *Also, it's experience. Any experience is good experience.*

Though *Follow That Carb!* looked like it might be the exception to that rule.

"I know the fava might not read like a *big* part," he said, "but I think you could do a lot with it. Just imagine yourself—singing, in costume. Comically. You'll be the Ado Annie of legumes. Got me?"

"Gotcha." She forced herself to add, "I can't wait to start!"

He handed her a schedule. "All the rehearsals will be held here until we can find a better space."

"Great!" she said.

He guffawed at her hard-fought enthusiasm. "You'll be hilarious."

All the way back on the PATH train, her emotions took wild swings. One moment she was elated beyond all reason at being in a show, any show, even if she had to portray a bean, and the next she was contemplating the chances of her dying peacefully in her sleep before she had to don a foam fava bean costume in public. For the first time, the odds of succumbing to a painless, early death were much too slim for her liking.

It didn't help when she flipped through the script and discovered that her part consisted mostly of stupid puns. *"Where have you bean all my life?"* *"How long has this bean going on?"*

What would she tell her parents? *"Mom and Dad—I invite you to view the glorious result of four years of intensive study."* She shuddered. One good thing was that for the first time in her life she was grateful not to have a boyfriend. There was one less loved one who would witness her humiliation.

What did a fava bean even look like? She'd have to swing by Food Emporium on her way home and buy a can for reference.

Back at the apartment, her announcement generated a lot of excitement. At least with Danielle.

"That's so terrific!" Danielle shouted at her, but her expression immediately changed from elation into a pout. "I wish I had time to celebrate, but I'm supposed to go over to Alan's." She thought for a moment, then brightened. "Why don't you come with me? We could all go out together."

Edie demurred. "Oh no."

Danielle drooped with disappointment. "Why not?"

"I've never even met Alan."

"So? You could tonight! I've told him all about you."

Edie shook her head. "Danielle, have you ever thought maybe there's a reason Alan doesn't want to meet your friends?"

"He *does* want to meet you. He told me so."

"But he never comes by here," she said. "He doesn't go out of his way because he knows you will."

Danielle frowned. "You mean he thinks I'm a pushover or something."

Greta snorted and Danielle rounded on her. "You're a fine one to criticize anyone. You've got your mitts on the sweetest guy in town."

"I don't know what you mean, 'my mitts.' But I do not use Vilson, if that is what you mean."

"His name is *Wilson*," Danielle said, "not Vilson."

"He does not mind Vilson."

Things had been a little tense between those two since Halloween.

After Danielle left for Alan's, Greta got up and joined Edie in the kitchen. "Congratulations."

"Thanks, but to tell you the truth, it's sort of a weird setup. It's an industrial, and the director seems really strange. . . ."

"Strange, how?"

"Well, I'm not quite right for the part, but he seems to think I'll work. At first I thought he was hitting on me—you know, tempting me to his boudoir with dancing fava bean roles."

"This is not the case?"

"I don't think so." Edie shook her head. "I don't get it."

"A director hires you for your personality and you don't get it?"

She laughed. "Maybe you're right. I've had such a rotten year actingwise—everythingwise—that I guess I'm beginning to buy into the old Groucho Marx theory of not wanting to be a part of a club that would have me for a member."

Greta listened and nodded. "You vill be making money, though?"

Edie nodded. "Enough to get by on if I'm careful and stay on a strict prison camp–style diet."

"Then you should be glad and not worry. You are that much more an actress and that much less a waitress."

"I guess."

"And you will be meeting new people. Making contracts."

"Contacts."

Greta frowned at her. "*Ja*, what I said."

* * *

At Edie's first rehearsal with the cast of *Follow That Carb!* she met the rest of the cast and the choreographer, Jimmy. Jimmy didn't seem as thrilled by Edie as Roger was, and he didn't bend over backward to hide his feelings.

"I hope you're a quick study," he said after the first hour of rehearsal. "You'll have *a lot* of catching up to do."

As far as Edie could tell, the whole cast was as bemused as she was to be found in this situation, and they had been at it longer than she had. They never tired of calling themselves by their food names. There was a ham, an egg and a milk carton, a French bread loaf (a Maurice Chevalier impersonation—some people had it so easy), a carrot, an English pea, a tomato, a banana and a pear, Edie's fava bean, a sugar cube, and a stick of butter.

She struck up an immediate friendship with a guy named Damon, who was playing the carrot. "Don't let Jimmy rattle you," he said to her after her first day. "The way he carries on, you'd think that he was choreographing a Rockettes show."

"I have a thick skin," Edie said, lying.

Everyone couldn't wait to see the costumes, which they were certain would make the show better. Or less bad. Or something.

Costumes would at least be a change from running around in sweats with Jimmy teaching them torturously hackneyed routines. Roger just sat back and laughed at them all. One got the feeling that they could have vomited in his living room and he would have told them they were ready for the Great White Way. Roger, Edie discovered, was more an impresario than a director. He had discovered a niche for educational theater productions, which he got off the ground with state grant money. *Follow That Carb!* was, much as it made Edie shudder to think of it, the taxpayers' dollars at work.

Despite everything, Edie couldn't help feeling pride at being back in a show, no matter how lame. Now when she ran into old friends from school, she could tell them that she was working. During rehearsals actors always complained that the shows they were in were disasters . . . nobody needed to know that in her case, the description was actually true.

No one needed to know anything, she decided, except that she was in a little production company out of town. The words "fava bean" need never be mentioned. She was a working actress again—not a waitress.

Chapter 36

THANKSGIVING TURKEY

Danielle supposed she had all sorts of things she should be really grateful for this Thanksgiving. She hadn't married Brandon, she wasn't gathering dust in Amarillo, and she wasn't entirely alone at the Alexander Hamilton residence hotel.

Still. She had a few complaints. First off, there was Alan; the one time he decided that he desperately needed to buckle down and work *would* be on a national holiday. Danielle had been so disappointed when he told her, she'd been dragging the ground the two days since. It would have been so great to spend the day at his place, stretched out on his couch. At least she wouldn't be in her apartment feeling like a fifth wheel.

Her second gripe was the fact that Greta and Wilson were doing most of the cooking for the big feast at the apartment, which meant that they were having an eel stir-fry instead of turkey. Danielle loved turkey. The idea of going through an entire Thanksgiving without her mom's traditional comfort food menu of turkey, sage dressing, Kentucky Wonder beans, mashed potatoes, and pumpkin-praline pie almost brought her to tears. She would even miss her great-aunt Julie's lime Jello salad with its weird layer of cream cheese and candied fruit. She felt so far from home.

She felt so *lonely*.

How could that be? Wilson was there, and Greta and Edie. An African American guy named Damon, the carrot in Edie's show, had come over early to watch the Macy's parade. It was the first time Danielle had ever experienced watching an event on national television that was actually taking place a few blocks outside her window. Later Edie's friend Sam and his boyfriend were supposed to drop by for dessert. They obviously hadn't been told that dessert was going to be caramelized beet and coconut surprise.

Right now, Damon and Edie were in a hot debate over how some dance step in their show was supposed to go. Back and forth they went, doing a spin and then a weird tap step. They wanted Danielle to decide the matter for them. "Which looks better?" they asked, as if she were Twyla Tharp or something.

Danielle could detect no difference between what the two of them were doing. "Um, I'm not quite sure . . . maybe if you did it again?"

She suspected they would keep it up all day if she asked them to. The two were completely obsessed with their show. Poor things. It sounded like a real dud . . . but she supposed it beat working. Seeing them reminded her of how excited she used to be about writing, how caught up in her stories she would become. It had been ages since she'd touched her computer.

Maybe that's what she should do today. . . .

She sighed. How could she? There were all these people around.

"Maybe I should call Alan," she said.

Damon and Edie looked over at her. "Does he know tap?" Edie asked.

Danielle rolled her eyes. Some people were so one-track minded. "No, I was just wondering if maybe he had changed his mind about coming. You know—maybe he thought he had more work than he actually did and is just sitting around bored."

"Then why wouldn't he call and say he was coming over?"

"He'd be too proud to." Danielle had thought of that a hundred times—had even imagined him ringing the doorbell out of the blue, to surprise her. Obviously, that wasn't going to happen. "He would worry that it would be an imposition, after he'd already turned down the invitation." She had her hand on the phone, but hesitated. "You think I should?"

"No, I don't, frankly," Edie said.

"Why not?"

"Because he won't show up, and then you'll just feel worse for having pestered him."

"But what if he *does* want to come?"

"He won't." Edie's look had a dollop of pity in it. "Danielle, don't you see what you've got here? You've got a can't-be-bothered guy."

Danielle sent an uncomfortable glance Damon's way. She really didn't want to discuss her ratty boyfriend—who wasn't really a rat except in the eyes of her roommates and Wilson—in the presence of a stranger. Damon took the hint and ambled off toward the kitchen to see how the eel was coming along.

"What do you mean?" Danielle asked Edie.

"A can't-be-bothered guy is a guy who wants to sleep with you, but doesn't want to meet your friends, your family, go to any of your parties, or participate in any function not initiated by or directly benefiting him."

Danielle tensed. Then she exhaled a long breath and took her hand off the phone. The can't-be-bothered guy description fit Alan to a T. "I'll call him later."

Wilson and Greta came out of the kitchen with Damon, laughing. They seemed so happy, Danielle felt a pang of jealousy. Wilson was the very opposite of the can't-be-bothered guy. He loved to be bothered. He would go out of his way to help a friend; he would certainly never leave his girlfriend languishing in her apartment on Thanksgiving. Wilson and Greta had gotten up at the crack of dawn this morning and braved an arctic chill that had blown in overnight to go look at the Macy's parade floats being inflated. That sounded like so much fun, so romantic in its own way.

Not that she actually wanted to be Wilson's girlfriend. He wasn't her type.

She only wished he was.

Now all of them, even Greta, were doing a tap step from the vegetable show—a regular chorus line. Danielle watched them from the couch, wondering how it could be that she felt so detached from all the fun. Maybe she was just hungry. The smell of frying eel wasn't helping any.

Suddenly, she bolted off the couch and headed for the coat-rack.

"Where are you going?" Edie asked.

"Out," she said as she bundled into her wool coat with the fake fur collar and wrapped a scarf babushkalike around her head. "Don't wait for me."

The cold wind seemed to brace her as she made her way to the east side and then caught the Lexington Avenue train uptown. On the way to Alan's apartment she stopped at their favorite Chinese restaurant. She might not be able to take Alan turkey, but at least she could bring him some Kung Pao shrimp.

A wave of apprehension hit her as she swung into his building. What if he'd gone to the office? What if he was so busy he wouldn't be glad she came for a visit? It was possible he would be angry for the interruption. Alan was basically good natured, but he had his moods.

She smiled at the doorman, who recognized her and smiled back. His name was Mel and he lived in Queens. She liked Mel better than the weekend guy, an old spidery man who glared at her as though she were a slut every time she got into the elevator with Alan.

"Is Alan here?" she asked.

"He expecting you?"

She lifted her white plastic takeout bag with the pagodas on it. "I'm bringing the feast."

He laughed. "Traditional American dinner."

He waved her past with a curmudgeonly smile, and she felt more upbeat as she was riding in the elevator. *His doorman likes me.* (One of them, at least.) Mel obviously thought they were a serious item, even if all her friends remained skeptical.

Not that she needed validation from a third party . . . but it did make her feel better to know that not everyone was looking at her as if she were a naïve, deluded female being used by the wolfish contracts attorney.

She knocked on Alan's door and then seemed to wait an eternity. She hoped he wouldn't mind the interruption, and for a split second she considered leaving the Chinese food on the floor by his door. But what if he never saw it and ended up with Kung Pao shrimp going bad in his hallway? He'd hate that.

The next time she knocked, the door jerked open with startling quickness. Alan blinked down at her as if he couldn't quite believe his eyes. He looked tired, poor thing.

She held up the bag. "Surprise!"

His eyes didn't leave her face. "You didn't call."

"I wanted to surprise you."

"I wish I had known you were coming," he said. "I'm sort of busy . . ."

A toilet flushed in the apartment. Danielle frowned. "Are you working with somebody?"

"Yeah."

An interior door opened and Danielle saw a shadow pass behind Alan. Then she stood on tiptoe and was able to bring the shadow into focus. It was Carol, the proofreader from work. The lethal lactose girl.

For a frantic, confused moment, Danielle had the desperate thought that they *were* working together. Maybe Alan had just needed something proofread. . . .

But before she could fully latch on to that notion, she was forced to dismiss it. Nothing about proofreading legal documents would require Carol to be wearing Alan's bathrobe.

"Don't fly off the handle," he warned.

The odd thing was, up to that moment, she hadn't had the presence of mind to fly off the handle. All her thoughts had been concentrated on the fact that everyone had been right and she had been wrong, and now she was going to have to crawl back to Chelsea, sadder but wiser.

But now that he mentioned it, she *did* feel like flying off the handle. She pushed past Alan, who didn't put up much resistance. Or maybe anger had given her the sort of superhuman strength usually reserved for hot martial arts babes in TV series. She strode into the middle of Alan's living room, hands ringing the plastic bag in her hands, itching to be ringing Carol's swanlike neck instead.

Then she looked down at the coffee table and was unable to

give Carol another thought. Lying on the glass top was a familiar red box with silver ribbon—the signature of Alan's favorite lingerie store.

He was already giving Carol underwear?

Her lip curled and an insane energy coursed through her. What an ass! What a pathetic . . .

What a pathetic idiot you've been, Danielle Porter.

She stood, heaving breaths, wondering how to get out of there. Carol was in front of her and Alan was behind her. She felt that the moment called for a speech, or a gesture. But words were beyond her. What good were words when she wanted to flatten Alan and hop up and down on him until he was just a stain on the carpet?

She looked down at the bag in her hand and an evil thought came over her. Stain. Kung Pao shrimp. It'd be a shame if it got all over the nice buttery leather of Alan's sofa, wouldn't it?

She unknotted the bag and started digging through the little cardboard containers. The first was the rice, and she chucked it away. Rice sprayed all over the floor.

Alan let out a pained bleat. "What are you doing!"

She found the right container, opened it, and held it over the couch. She felt the same insane energy coursing through her that Edie had described when she'd hurled pasta at her friend. With one slight difference. Edie bitterly regretted her action. Danielle knew she never would. "Happy Thanksgiving, Alan."

Enjoying the horror in his devastating blue eyes, she slowly dumped sauce and shrimp all over the couch.

"You little bitch!" he said, clamping down on her arm and jerking her away.

Too late, she was happy to see. Carol was already taking gazelle leaps toward the kitchen to get a towel, but by the time she got back the shrimp sauce would have penetrated irreparably. A crazy grin pulled at Danielle's lips.

"That couch cost me four thousand dollars!" he screeched at her.

She eyed him triumphantly. "You're a lawyer—sue me."

"Don't think I won't!"

"Don't think I won't go right up to your employer and tell him you've been using your office as a boudoir for screwing proof-readers."

Carol gasped, and Danielle turned to find the woman frozen, the towel in her hand.

"Oh, for God's sake," Alan growled.

Danielle smirked at Carol. "You didn't really think you were the only one, did you?"

Alan's hands clamped down on Danielle's shoulders. "Just get out." He turned her and propelled her toward the door. He practically pitched her out on her ass like a saloon bouncer. "And I thought you were so sweet!" he snarled. "A little southern dumpling. You're really just another graspy urban female running around with your claws extended."

She laughed. *Sweet?* He'd thought she was a pushover is what he meant. And now he was disappointed to find out that she wasn't. Not anymore. "You don't know how great it makes me feel to hear you say that," she said sarcastically, mimicking what he'd said when she'd told him she loved him.

She wasn't sure he caught the allusion, though. He slammed the door in her face too soon for her to tell.

Chapter 37

THE REDUNDANT FAVA

It was hard to believe such a dumb show could take so much out of you, but by the end of the first day of dress rehearsal, Edie felt ready for her last rites. For days everyone had been eagerly anticipating the arrival of the costumes. "It's going to make all the difference," people kept saying, as if they believed that if the actors actually looked like food, the inane show would make more sense.

And the costumes did add something to the show. In Edie's case, her costume added about twenty pounds. She was encased in a big rubber fava bean, with taupe colored tights and ankle boots with taps on them rounding off the look. She was ridiculous, she was hot, and she was seized with certainty that the director—and especially the choreographer—didn't like what she was doing.

The fava bean was a difficult part. Everyone admitted that. She wasn't a sexy tomato or a nervous sugar cube. Aside from having the worst costume (she didn't even look like a fava bean so much as a mutant black-eyed pea) she had the fewest lines and the crappiest song—a duet with the bread loaf to the tune of "Friendship." Roger had changed the words so that the "perfect blendship" in the song now referred to the complete protein achieved when you combined a starch and a legume. It was labored, and the combination of Maurice Chevalier French bread and wisecracking bean was less than inspired.

Roger, who had been so appreciative of her lack of musical

theater skill during her audition, suddenly sat sober faced as she lumbered through the rehearsals. Even after Jimmy the choreographer had worked with her privately, she clearly was not up to the level of the professional dancers in the cast.

"Look," Roger said, pulling her aside after one number, "I know you're not primarily a dancer, but can't you copy Damon?"

"I've been working with Damon."

His brow creased.

"Damon, who studied dance for years," she reminded him. "At Juilliard."

Roger rubbed his furry face for a moment—a moment in which Edie could actually feel her small supply of confidence seeping out of her body like air from a punctured tire. "Ah— right. Well, do your best!"

Her singing was not much better, and that also proved a sore point with Roger. He came up to her during the dress rehearsal as she was trying to wipe sweat away from her body with a towel. "That was great, Edie," he said. "But could you try to be a little more Merman?"

More Merman? She wasn't Merman at all. She thought she was doing well to croak out the song as well as she was. "I'm belting as best I can," she told him. "You said you wanted comic relief. . . ."

He nodded. "Of course! That's *just* what we want." He frowned. "Is that really the best you can sing?"

It had been a dismal day, and it didn't get better.

At the end of rehearsal, Roger called her over as everyone was filing out of the dance studio. He wore an uncharacteristically grave expression, and the few people around her shot her alarmed looks. She almost laughed at their bug-eyed concern. What did they think, that she was going to be fired?

As if she would even care!

Roger clamped his paw around her arm and led her over to a folding chair. They sat down. He seemed to be pondering how to start for a moment, his lower lip jutting out in thought.

"Edie. Your character isn't projecting."

That was a shock? He smothered an actor in a rubber suit and he expected her to be right on the money the first dress rehearsal?

"It's the costume," she said.

He nodded almost eagerly. "Of course. The costume is a *disaster*, but it was the best bean I could find within our budget, you see."

"It's sort of swallowing me."

His eyes oozed understanding. "I could see that."

"I just need to make a few adjustments," she said. "If I move a little farther upstage during my number . . ."

He lifted his hands and started waving them to stop her. As if she were a car about to run him over. "No need for that. I'm cutting that song."

Cutting her duet? For weeks the prospect of performing it before a real audience had made her bolt up in bed at three A.M., hyperventilating. Yet now she felt a sudden possessiveness toward it. If she didn't have a number, then what was the point of her even being in the show?

Reading her mind, he announced in a pained voice, "Edie, I'm cutting the fava."

It felt as if he had punched her in the stomach. "You're firing me?"

He winced. "I *hate* that word, don't you? It doesn't even make sense. Firing. What has fire got to do with it?"

Well, it felt as if her face were on fire.

"The English have a better expression—they say someone has been 'made redundant.' I prefer that. *Follow That Carb!* just doesn't need the fava."

She was still stunned. "What are you talking about? I represent the legume—the vegetable protein!"

He nodded as if this had occurred to him. "We've got the English pea, luckily. We'll have to work something in for him . . . but it will work."

God, he'd thought this all through already. He'd probably known he didn't want her since the moment she appeared in her costume. Maybe even before.

"It has nothing to do with you, I assure you," he said.

"Nothing except that you're changing your whole show because you've decided I'm not right for the part."

"No, no—your performance was fine. I could see that you were trying your hardest."

Great. She'd been trying her hardest and she still wasn't up to snuff. *That* was depressing.

Her gaze turned toward the door; she longed to make a getaway.

He clapped her on the shoulder. "I'll keep you in mind for future shows."

Right.

He must have read her expression. "I know this hasn't been the best experience for you, Edie, but you can't let yourself get discouraged. You have to wait for your moment."

He was trying to be nice, Edie knew, but his words triggered a sort of panic in her mind. What if this—this awful show—*was* her moment? And she'd blown it?

"In fact, I'm working on an American History overview show," Roger said, "which is going to require a female who can double as a pioneer and Eleanor Roosevelt. Can you do Eleanor Roosevelt?"

For a moment, she thought of singing "Oklahoma!" for him in the flutey Eleanor Roosevelt voice that she had perfected during a studio performance of *Sunrise at Campobello* in college. But she didn't have the heart for it. Deep down, she knew that she wanted this to be the last time she saw Roger, or any of the cast of *Follow That Carb!* She felt awful about Damon . . . she sort of liked him . . . but she didn't think she could stomach being around someone who was carrying on as a carrot when she couldn't hack it as a bean.

"I'll work on it," she promised Roger.

On the PATH train home, she felt so small. She probably had "loser" written all over her face. Worse, Aurora's voice rang in her ears. *Maybe you just aren't ready. . . .*

Edie snorted. Right. She wasn't *ready* to play a vegetable in a crappy industrial show?

They fired you, didn't they?

But it was all about luck. She'd just had bad luck. The part was no good, and the costume . . .

A good actor makes the most of the parts that come to him.

But some things you can't overcome. A rubber costume . . .

It wasn't the costume. It was you.

It *was* her, she realized. She had thought the show was beneath her, but in the end—for whatever reason—she hadn't been able to cut the mustard. In the past year there had been a convergence of circumstances that made her realize that she was deficient in more ways than she had ever imagined. She couldn't hold on to things—not boyfriends, not friends, not even dumb jobs.

How had this happened?

She stumbled home, all the while wondering if she should even go back there. If the apartment was empty, she would feel lonely and sorry for herself. She would wonder how she could have lived nine years in a city of eight million people and still have no one to talk to. If there were people there, she would feel crowded and want to hide in her room, which would clue people in that something was wrong, which would lead to her having to tell them what had happened. Then she would feel even worse.

Bhiryat accosted her as she was putting her key in the lock. "Where is Douglas?"

She frowned. Was the man losing his mind? "The paper sent him away." Maybe spending too long in the tandoor had baked his brain cells.

"Yes, I know that very well," Bhiryat replied. "But *where* is he?"

It wouldn't do to tell Bhiryat that she had no earthly idea where the guy whose name was on his apartment's lease was. "Tashkent."

"Uzbekistan!" Bhiryat shook his head. "I will pray for his safe return."

She blinked at him. "What?"

His face paled. "You have not heard?"

"No!" she practically shrieked. "What's happened?"

"There was bombings there today. The pictures are all over CNN."

With a shaky hand, she undid the lock and flew up the stairs. The apartment was empty. She dashed to the couch and hunted for the remote but a frantic pawing around magazines and under cushions produced nothing. Finally, she saw its buttons peeking out from under Kuchen's fur. She yanked the remote away and turned on the television.

Non-news channels flashed by irritatingly as she surfed frantically for CNN. Who watched all this stuff? Shopping channels and home decorating and reruns of "Touched by an Angel" . . . Didn't people have better things to do with their time? Didn't they realize that the world was in crisis?

All the while her thumb was moving, a creeping awareness grew in her that something wasn't right in the apartment. It wasn't just that no one was here . . .

Kuchen. She hadn't moved a muscle when Edie had unwedged the remote out from under her.

Edie jerked her gaze toward the cat, who was sprawled out with her four legs sticking straight out. Her heart began to thump uncomfortably in her chest. *Kuchen!*

She gingerly reached out a hand to touch the kitty, prepared to draw it back quickly if she felt anything cold and stiff. The kitty felt cold, but she didn't seem dead. Not exactly. Or not yet. She didn't respond to Edie's touch except to quiver a little.

Edie shrieked and jumped up. A vet. She needed to get to a vet. But what vet? As far as she knew, Greta hadn't taken Kuchen to the vet since she'd moved in. And *where* was Greta? She looked at the clock. She should be home from work by now, if she was coming home. Probably she was at Wilson's, or out with Wilson.

Edie found Wilson's number and dialed it, but his roommate said that he and Greta had gone out to a movie.

She lunged for the Yellow Pages. There had to be a vet around here somewhere . . . but how would she get an appointment? Was there an emergency hospital?

Her finger jittered through the listings and finally came across the New York Animal Hospital on York Avenue. Of course! It was to hell and gone from where she was, but she would get there.

She stuffed Kuchen's inert furry bulk into the plastic carrier and dashed down to the street. Without thinking twice, she flagged down a cab. After what seemed like an eternity crawling through crosstown traffic and then driving to the Upper East Side, she was dumped off in front of a huge building that looked like . . . a hospital. It even had an entrance that looked like the ambulance entrance to a hospital. She frowned.

She walked in and was stopped and given reams of paperwork to fill out. *Just like visiting a real doctor,* she thought with irritation. Only while she was filling them out . . . what little she *could* fill out, she was stuck on a wooden bench in a waiting room that was filled with miserable-looking people with cat carriers and ferrets wrapped in towels. Dogs whimpered and barked at each other, and a cockatoo in the corner intermittently released ear-piercing squawks. The place reeked of antiseptic over pet urine, and if the tension in the room wasn't enough, a mounted television was blaring "Emergency Vets" on Animal Planet.

Have a little reality with your grim reality?

When she had filled in all the vital information she could, Edie took her paperwork to the front and was told to sit down again and wait. So she gazed up at the television, like everyone else was doing, and watched as a bulldog named Q-Tip was treated for an obstructed bowel. When Q-Tip didn't make it, his tragedy seemed to absorb all the oxygen from the room.

The woman next to her, who was holding a quivering miniature dachshund, began to cry.

Edie felt the same way. She began counting the people in the room. Twelve. And they had all gotten there before her. In her carrier, Kuchen still appeared to be in a semi-coma.

Edie's teeth chattered. *Please hang on, Kuchen. Please don't die. . . .*

She didn't think she could stand it if, on top of everything else that had gone wrong, she couldn't save Kuchen.

When Edie felt as if her body had pleated into an accordion shape from slumping on the bench from hours of waiting, her cat's name was finally called. Edie jumped up and hauled Kuchen into the examination room, where a tech helped pry her out of the plastic carrier.

When they were done, the tech frowned at Kuchen's considerable mass spread across the stainless steel examining table. "This cat is"—she cast about for the right word—"fat."

"We've had her on a diet for three months."

"Has she lost any weight?"

"No," Edie admitted. What did that matter now?

When the vet came in to examine Kuchen, her brows pinched. "This cat is *quite* overweight."

Edie felt like screaming. This cat wasn't just overweight, she was in a coma! You would think *that* would be of the utmost concern right now.

"How long has she been like this?" the vet asked after probing around the semi-conscious body.

"I'm not sure . . . she was like this when I got home. I wasn't able to contact my roommates. . . ."

She felt foolish, neglectful. They had all been out when Kuchen needed them.

"Her blood pressure and temperature are too low," the doctor said. "I'm going to run some blood tests and give her fluids. If she doesn't perk up after some observation, we'll do an EKG. Also, we'll put her on a heating pad and try to warm her up."

"Okay. Should I . . . ?"

"We'll need to observe her overnight."

Edie was given instructions to pay a deposit on her way out and to call in the morning. As she gave Kuchen a last pat good-bye, she had tears running down her cheeks. She felt awful just abandoning her here in this cold place, with strangers. What was she going to tell Greta?

She hurried down the hall where the cashier was, wiping tears from her eyes. Someone was behind her, so she had to resist the urge to bawl outright. What a day. Fired from her job . . . her ex-boyfriend caught in a war-torn country far away . . . her cat dying . . .

"Edie?"

She turned and discovered Ross Johnson standing there holding a chart out to the receptionist. They blinked at each other in mutual surprise. He wasn't dressed like a vet—he had on his coat and looked ready to get out of there.

She tried to pull herself together as best she could, and prayed she had her mucous under control. "Hi. I forgot you worked here. I had to leave my cat . . ." Her voice went tight, so she stopped short.

He frowned in concern. "Is she okay?"

"No . . . that is, I'm not sure." She tried to explain as best she could and simultaneously paid a bill that would have staggered her if she weren't so upset already. They probably counted on emotional turmoil to blunt the sticker shock.

Ross took her arm. "Come on, let's go see her."

Edie sagged with relief. "Could we? I mean, would it be okay for me to go back there?"

"Of course," he said.

They went back to where a bank of large cages was set up with kitties and other small animals in resting. Kuchen was already sleeping in one.

Ross studied her chart while Edie stuck her fingers through the bars and petted Kuchen. "If she looks puffy, it's because they've given her fluids."

"She's sort of puffy anyway," Edie admitted. At least *Ross* hadn't called Kuchen fat. She listened to him as he basically repeated what the other vet had said, although it felt good to hear a second opinion.

"Hopefully, Kuchen will feel better in the morning," he said. "I'm a little worried about you, though."

She looked up at him in surprise. "Why?"

"Don't take this the wrong way, but you look as though you could use a drink."

She smiled. "I could use something."

"How about having dinner with me?"

She drew back. She hadn't realized it until just now, but it was almost ten o'clock and she hadn't eaten a thing since lunch. She'd been so worried, she'd assumed the churning in her stomach was just nerves.

They walked to a Thai place nearby. It occurred to Edie that she should probably inform Ross that Danielle had broken up with her boyfriend, a fact she had managed to pry out of Danielle a few days after Thanksgiving. It hadn't made sense to her that Danielle was hanging around the apartment over the holiday weekend. She hadn't even done any Friday-after-Thanksgiving shopping, which seemed a sure sign that something was wrong. While Edie couldn't say she was surprised at the bust-up with the jerk, she still felt a little bad for Danielle. Maybe now she wouldn't be so touchy about Ross getting in contact with her.

"I don't know if you've thought about Danielle lately . . ." she began as the waitress brought their spring rolls.

"Actually, I haven't," Ross said bluntly. "She made it pretty darn clear she didn't want to be bothered the first time we met."

Edie couldn't think of much to say in Danielle's defense about that night. "But when you came back later . . ."

Two dark red blotches stained his cheeks. "Well, I've got a confession to make. I was actually there to see you."

"*Me?*" she squeaked.

He ducked his head, embarrassed. "I liked you when I met you at the apartment. That's why I didn't call that night when I came by again. I wasn't sure I had your name right, and I would have felt like a fool calling up the apartment and asking for Danielle's cute roommate."

Edie blushed. "I wish you had! Maybe then I wouldn't have spent that horrible evening with Louis."

"Your boyfriend?"

"He's not my boyfriend," she clarified quickly. "We just went out that once. He'd recently broken up with his girlfriend and needed a shoulder to cry on."

"What happened to him?"

"He and his lady love got back together again. I think a night out with me gave him the nerve to go begging her to take him back."

Ross laughed. He had a slow, lazy chuckle that she found incredibly appealing. Well, everything about the man was appealing. And he'd actually called her *cute?* To her face? That one compliment seemed to lift a day full of woe from her shoulders.

"Do you like horseback riding?" he asked out of the blue.

"I have no idea," she said. "I've never done it."

His jaw went slack. "Never?"

She shook her head.

"Didn't you ever go to camp?"

"Oh, sure. Drama camp. The only horses were sound effects offstage during our Shakespeare production."

He laughed. "Would you like to try it? Say, this weekend?"

He was asking her out on a date? Even after he'd seen her a

weepy wreck at the animal hospital? She couldn't say yes fast enough. "I'd love to!"

She would probably break her neck. But then, remembering her recent reentry into the ranks of the unemployed, she consoled herself with the fact that her neck wasn't actually worth that much at the moment.

Chapter 38

STARTING OVER

"You've been a legal proofreader for four months?"

"That's right." Danielle could anticipate the next questions; the skin on her forehead began to crawl into a gathering of worry lines. The LegalProof woman she was interviewing with was a no-nonsense sort, with big iron gray hair, a mouth that seemed to be permanently pursed into a frown, and small, skeptical blue slits for eyes. (The better to weed out candidates who had foolishly slept with coworkers at their last jobs, Danielle thought nervously.)

"What firms did you work for?"

"Just one. Ramsey, Lombard, and Gaines."

She didn't even want a new temp agency, but she couldn't make herself go back to Ramsey, Lombard, and Gaines; and if she didn't go back, she would have to explain to someone at her current agency why she didn't want to. And she couldn't afford not to work.

For almost a week she had sat in the apartment in a mental funk. It was as if she'd turned into Greta during her Food Network meditation phase. She'd had breakups before, but she'd never felt so *burnt*. She didn't want to go to work and face everyone. She didn't even want to venture outside the apartment, where the world seemed to have turned wet and cold and wintry overnight. Christmas was coming, but who cared? For the first time, she couldn't work up much excitement over the holidays—she had no money, for one thing. She had put off making her reservations to go home because she worried if she went home feeling this way, she would never come back.

So she'd just been sitting on the couch, dithering over what to do next; most of the time she hadn't even had Kuchen to cuddle with. That really made her feel that the fates had ganged up on her.

Of course, if you'd just listened to your friends' warnings, you might have avoided this so-called fate. . . .

The personnel woman fixed a penetrating stare on her. "Was there a problem that made you want to leave Ramsey, Lombard, and Gaines?"

Danielle had rehearsed this part. Carefully. "No, another proofreader told me that LegalProof was a better agency than the one I was working for before."

The woman attempted a smile, but those lips remained firmly turned down. "I see. You just wanted a change."

"Slut," was the undeniable subtext of that comment, Danielle was sure.

After further interrogation, her employment at LegalProof was approved pending confirmation of her references, and Danielle was given another clipboard full of forms to fill out. Social Security number. Contact information. Emergency numbers. She hated filling out forms. If you judged by the newspapers, privacy was dead and everyone knew everything about everybody. Couldn't all these temp agencies tap into some Big Brother database—the one that knew what DVDs you'd rented in 2002—and get her social security number there instead of wasting her time?

Someone plopped down next to her. "Danielle?"

It was Jack . . . Jack whose last name she couldn't remember. She hadn't seen him, hadn't even thought of him, since that night he'd called for a date and she'd turned him down because she was hoping to hear from Alan. Back in the golden age, as she was now beginning to think of it. "How's it going, Jack?"

"Okay. What are you doing here? I thought you were a Proofreaders, Inc. gal."

"I heard the pay is better here."

"It is. I've been working for them for a year."

Now that she took a real gander at him, she was surprised to find that he was actually pretty good looking, in that sort of Josh Hartnett frat boy way. Why hadn't she noticed this before?

Because you were too blinded by lust for the lingerie king. . . .

"You haven't been to a happy hour in ages," he said. "Where've you been?"

She tried to evade a real answer by putting on a saucy little smile, though it didn't feel quite natural anymore. She hadn't flirted with anyone new in ages. Maybe her hinges were going rusty. "You know . . . just out and about."

"We hardly see Wilson anymore either. I thought maybe you two had gone exclusive, but someone told me he's seeing some Swedish babe."

"She's German."

"Yeah, that's it."

"She's my roommate."

His expression was tinged with surprise and maybe a little awe. No doubt he imagined Wilson had lucked his way into an urban harem. "Serious?"

"Wilson and I have never dated," she told him. "We're just good friends."

His expression turned to pity—obviously thinking she was putting a brave face on a dumped-girlfriend situation. "That Wilson," he said, shaking his head.

"No, really," she said. "Actually, I was seeing someone for a while, but it didn't work out. Now I'm kicking up my heels again." Actually, propping them up on the coffee table and watching "Law and Order" reruns would be more accurate, but who needed to know? She flipped her hair in what she hoped was a fetching manner.

Jack smiled. "That's great."

"So what are you up to these days?" she said, nudging him.

"Actually, I've taken up martial arts . . . like the rest of the world, it seems." He chuckled. "Kung fu."

She was sorry she'd asked. Was there anything more boring to hear about? Still, he was cute. And martial arts was kind of sexy. She loved those Chow Yun Fat movies.

"Maybe we could get together for drinks sometime," she said, going out on a limb. "Catch up."

He shifted uncomfortably. "Oh."

Something was wrong. Or maybe he just thought she was coming on too strong. Danielle's face felt hot and she tried to backpedal. "Just for a drink."

"The thing is, Danielle, I'm seeing someone right now."

Her smile froze, and she could feel the egg splattering all over her face. *Don't make an idiot of yourself!* "She doesn't allow you out by yourself with friends?" she countered. "That sounds like a pretty tight leash."

Her stab at diffusing the situation was somewhat successful. He laughed. "Hey—we're having a Christmas party next week. Why don't you come? A lot of people you know will be there, and you could meet Jen."

"Jen's your gal?"

He flushed slightly. "She's really great. She knows all sorts of people in publishing. You're a writer, aren't you?"

"Well . . . a not-so-successful one."

"You should meet her. It would be great to see you there."

"Sounds fun. I'll see if I can make it," she said, injecting just enough doubt into her tone to make him think that somewhere there was a day planner with her name on it, full of appointments and heavy dates.

He took the pen from her clipboard and scrawled down his address and phone on the LegalProof bylaws sheet that the personnel lady had handed her. It was full of dire warnings against things like wearing cut-off shorts and not showing up to work. The sad thing was, there were probably a lot of people who needed those warnings.

When he was done, Jack gave her a brotherly pat. "It's just a drop-by-and-eat-finger-food party. But if you don't show, I'll take it personally."

She smiled, grateful for his kindness, which she had a sneaking suspicion she didn't deserve. "Thanks, Jack. It was good to see you."

When he was gone, she felt temporarily buoyed. *See there, you shouldn't feel depressed. You still have friends in this town. You belong here.*

One love affair gone sour didn't mean the world had come to an end.

Chapter 39

EDIE'S CLANDESTINE SORT-OF LOVE AFFAIR

Everyone was home when Kuchen came back. The little carrier door was opened and the kitty waddled out to huzzahs and many of her favorite crab cake–flavored treats.

Danielle, who hadn't seen Kuchen since she went to the hospital, kneeled down and gave the mostly indifferent animal a huge hug.

"Oh, you sweetie!" Danielle cooed to the animal, who appeared most happy to see her furniture again. "What an amazing recovery."

Not so amazing, Edie thought, when you considered all the marvels of modern science put through their paces in the effort to make Kuchen better. That cat had undergone more sophisticated medical tests than most people receive outside of the Mayo clinic. She'd had multiple blood workups, an EKG, and had undergone three sonograms. Not to mention, she'd had a flock of vets and vet techs watching her every hiccup for four days and five nights.

When Edie had come back from the hospital that first night, Greta had nodded knowingly when Edie explained the condition she had found Kuchen in. "She has small heart problem. I give her heating pad, it goes away."

Small? "Greta, that cat looked like she was about to die! It's much worse than just a *small* problem."

Four days later Edie received the diagnosis: A slightly irregular heart valve and unexplained drop in blood pressure.

The treatment: Fluids and two days on a heating pad.

The bill: $785.00.

"I vill pay it," Greta offered. "I have it."

But Edie couldn't let her pay the whole amount. *She* had insisted Kuchen undergo the thorough testing; it was only right that she should pony up the cost. At least most of it. Even if she had to take out a bank loan.

She and Greta finally agreed to halvsies, and Greta put Kuchen's heating pad out in the bathroom for easy access in the next emergency.

Part of the reason Edie didn't feel so stung by the whopping bill, she knew, was because of Ross. If it weren't for Kuchen's attack, she might never have seen him again. And that was a possibility too unbearable for her to contemplate now that the man seemed to occupy all of her waking thoughts. For the first time in a few eons, she wasn't worried about the future—or wallowing in her own mental muck. Ross had even taken the sting out of being fired.

In fact, on their horseback riding date, she had confessed the whole sad tale of *Follow That Carb!* to him, halfway worrying as she did so that no man would want to be associated with a woman who couldn't even hold down a job as a dancing legume.

Instead, Ross laughed and looked at her with what almost seemed like admiration.

Edie had been focusing all her concentration on staying astride the old sway-backed plug Ross had picked out for her at the New Jersey stable where he rode. But now she hazarded a glance at him. "What?"

"I've never met a genuine has-bean," he said.

She groaned. "That's awful!"

He smiled apologetically and looked so sexy that she would have forgiven him a thousand bad puns. "I'm sorry. I just can't see the tragedy here. That show was a waste of your time. In the long run you'll be much better off going to auditions and looking for something else. You'll see."

He made being fired sound so *positive*. Why hadn't she been able to look at it that way?

"Some day you're going to be on Broadway, and I'm going to

be there on the opening night, cheering you on. You won't even remember your aborted stab at plant life."

Would that his prediction should come true! Having Ross in the front row of her life, most of all. He was so nice, so funny . . . so seemingly available.

She wondered what was wrong with him.

After their ride, which was only notable for the fact that Edie didn't break her neck as she had expected, they cleaned up, returned to the city, and went out for Chinese. Edie's fortune read *Posterity is just around the corner.*

"Do you think that's a misprint? Shouldn't that be *prosperity?*" She added quickly, "Not that I'm picky. I'll take either."

"It's an omen. You're a hair's breadth away from success."

She leaned toward him. "What does yours say?"

He lifted his little white slip. "A stunning red-headed actress is going to come into your life."

Edie's jaw dropped. "No kidding!"

He laughed. "Actually, yes. I made it up."

Damn! If that had been his fortune, Edie had been ready to embrace superstition in a big way. Still, it was sweet that he'd made it up. "But I'm not a real redhead," she confessed.

"Is anyone?"

"Wilson is."

He tilted his head. "I wouldn't call him stunning, though."

She laughed. "That's because you haven't seen him playing 'The Lonely Goatherd' song from *The Sound of Music* on an accordion in the Hunter College subway station."

They ambled back to Edie's apartment, where Ross dropped her off at the door—at her own insistence. Danielle was probably over the idea that Ross was a spy, but Edie didn't want to risk ending the evening with a confrontation. She didn't want to share Ross, period.

She *did* want to end the evening with a kiss, however, and panicked when Ross escorted her to the door and then stepped back to go. A flash of urgency swept through her. *He was just going to walk away?* She'd thought they'd had a great time together. Had she misjudged? Was he not attracted to her?

If he wasn't, why had he called her stunning at the restaurant?

Did she have black bean sauce on her chin?

She was straining to think of some lame excuse to see him again—something to do with Kuchen, she thought frantically—when he took two steps forward again and pulled her into his arms. She sagged against his chest with a combination of lust and relief.

"I've got to kiss you," he said in an irresistible raspy drawl.

"And I've so gotta let you," she whispered before his mouth descended on hers.

He had incredible lips. She had been scoping them out all day—furtively, she hoped—and had imagined he'd be a good kisser. She had underestimated. Warmth, pressure, not too much tongue—everything was just perfect.

Yes, her life might have fallen to pieces in every other respect, but this made up for it. It made up for the loss of her job, and her fight with Aurora, and even the fact that Douglas had abandoned her. When she was with Ross, those problems fell from her shoulders.

She was so euphoric that for once she wasn't even tempted to wonder how long something this good could last. She'd postpone pessimism for a while. At least until they had slept together. (That usually was when the troubles began. . . .)

But by their third date she was beginning to wonder if they would make it that far. He never put a move on her beyond the traditional goodnight kiss. What was up with that?

Was there a problem? Was he gay? She considered asking him out for drinks with Sam. Sam could always be relied upon to make a definitive gay/not gay pronouncement in the time it took to down half a martini.

The next weekend, on their way home from a movie—a long Christmas season Oscar contender drama that Edie had spent distracted by thoughts about sex—Ross stopped and turned to her on the street. It was chilly outside, and they were huddled in coats, puffing little clouds as they breathed. He bent down and kissed her. "If I take you back to your place, will you ask me in this time?"

Her heart skipped. Then it thudded. "My place?"

One of his dark brows crooked. "What's wrong with that?"

"My two roommates," she said. "Plus Wilson, who practically qualifies now as a pro bono resident."

"Too crowded?"

"I wouldn't mind if it weren't for the Danielle issue. . . ."

His eyes widened in amazement. "You still haven't told her we're going out?"

She shrugged helplessly. "It hasn't come up. And poor Danielle—she still seems so distraught. She broke up with her dream guy."

"*So?*"

"So, do you know how it feels to believe everyone in the world but you has someone?"

He pulled her to him for a hug. "You're sweet, you know that?"

She laughed. "You're the first person who's called me *that* since my grandmother."

He let out a long sigh. "Those roommates . . . You weren't just using them as an excuse, were you?"

"An excuse?"

"Not to sleep with me."

Edie gulped. There was no way to play this cool. "Don't *you* have an apartment?"

He looked doubtful. "So-called. I have a studio. It's about the size of a matchbox. With both of us in there we'd hardly be able to move around."

What was he expecting they were going to do? "Even at my most exuberant," she assured him, "I'm hardly a Flying Wallenda."

She couldn't believe she'd said that!

But he seemed glad that she had. "Then you just stay right here while I go lasso us a taxi."

And she loved him so much in that moment that she didn't even bother to lecture him about throwing away money on cabs.

Chapter 40

A NOT-SO-SILENT NIGHT

Wilson insisted on a tree. Greta had resisted right up to the moment he dragged a spindly Douglas fir through the apartment door. Then she threw herself into the decorating of it with him. They went out shopping for cheap ornaments, and spent a weekend personalizing a few dozen plain Rite-Aid Christmas balls with glitter, beads, and fringe. She strung popcorn and went to several places just to get the right kind of tinsel. To add to the festive mood, she and Wilson had worked up "Rockin' Around the Christmas Tree" as an oboe-accordion duet.

Danielle heard that song so many times, every time the first notes played she had the Pavlovian reaction of wanting to go shoot an elf. It seemed especially grating the night she was getting ready for Jack's party. She should have felt especially happy this night. With her first LegalProof paycheck, earned through weeks of toil at a bank, she'd been able to splurge on a new dress.

But even new clothes didn't lift her blue mood. She tried telling herself that she could meet someone—lots of people met their future spouses at Christmas parties, she'd read somewhere—but she couldn't help thinking about Alan, who was probably out with Carol. And Brandon, who no doubt was celebrating with Bev. Everyone in the world seemed to have a love life except her.

And maybe Edie. But Edie was being so mysterious these days, who knew *what* she was up to.

She was just finishing the last touches on her face when *that song* started up again. "Rockin' Around the Christmas Tree," take two thousand and ninety-three. Danielle's entire body went rigid.

"Would you *please* play something else?" she screamed out from the bathroom.

The apartment fell silent. Blessedly silent, even if it did make her feel Scroogelike to admit it.

"Any requests?" Wilson called back after a moment.

Her brows pinched, and she darted her head out the door. Wilson was sitting alone on the love seat. "Where's Greta?"

"She went out for eggnog."

Danielle ventured out, and Wilson let out a long wolf whistle as he took in her new outfit. She felt a flutter in reaction to the appreciation in his eyes.

He dragged out an old Billy Crystal imitation. "Dahling—you look mahvelous!"

"Thanks." She felt herself blushing, even though it was just Wilson.

No. It wasn't *just Wilson.* Right now she couldn't think of anyone whose opinion mattered to her more.

Anyway, it seemed like weeks since anyone had said something nice to her.

She crossed to the love seat and plopped down. "I can't believe it's almost Christmas."

"Are you going home?"

She shrugged. "I suppose so, if I can find some kind of econo-jet service."

"You should make reservations soon or be prepared to fly standby."

She couldn't bear thinking about it all.

"What's the matter?" he asked.

She sighed. "I'm not sure. I think I've lost my enthusiasm for everything."

"Oh, come on." He gave her a friendly punch in the arm. "It can't be that bad."

She looked into his eyes and suddenly felt tears well in her own. He was so kind. More than kind. He was wonderful in every way, and good looking to boot. She laughed at the idea that she had at first declared him cute, or not quite her type. Since when was wonderful in every way not her type? *How* could she have possibly thought Alan was preferable to Wilson? Wilson was just as handsome. In his own way. She loved Wilson—had almost from the first moment. She just hadn't loved him with the pulse-pounding, heart-in-her-throat way she had loved Alan.

But now her heart was in her throat. Now, when it was too late.

His expression turned pained when he saw her crying. "Danielle, for heaven's sake, what's the matter?"

"I've made a mess of everything," she said, sniffing. "I just wish I could go back."

"To when?"

"To . . . I don't know. Last summer. Back when we were hanging out together. I wish I could go back and . . ."

She couldn't say it. She looked into his eyes, hoping he could read her feelings. How could he not?

"What would you do differently?" he asked.

She took a deep, shuddering breath. Here went nothing. "When you told me that you feared that we'd just be buddies in ten years, I'd say that I hoped we'd be much more than that."

After the words left her mouth, it felt as if her blood were pounding in her ears. The room was so suffocatingly silent, there didn't seem to be any air left.

Wilson's eyes narrowed. "Why are you telling me this now?"

Her hands balled into frustrated fists. "Why do you think? Because I'm in love with you!"

"Danielle . . ."

She put a hand on his thigh, which seemed to strangle his words. She might have thrown her arms around him, but there was a ninety-six button Hohner piano accordion between her and his chest. "You can't tell me that you don't feel the same way," she said.

He stared at her long and hard, making her squirm with discomfort.

He couldn't, could he?

"Yes, I can," he said finally. "I don't feel the same way, because I'm in love with someone else."

She snorted. "Greta?"

He picked up Danielle's hand and returned it to her own lap. "That's right."

"Oh, come on," she said.

"Danielle, *where have you been?* The time I've spent with Greta has been the happiest of my life. Do you think we've been play-acting? Do you think that now that you've suffered a little setback, we're supposed to bust up what we have to make way for your latest whim?"

The front door slammed shut downstairs and Danielle jumped off the love seat. She could hear Greta in the hallway. "All right," she whispered. "You don't have to be nasty about it."

He stood, too, and unstrapped his accordion. When he laid it on the couch it let out a discordant wheeze. "Greta's your friend," he told her.

You should be ashamed of yourself! Wilson didn't say it, but it was written all over his face. He thought she'd betrayed Greta. Danielle wished she could vanish.

The door flew open and Greta blew in, her cheeks rosy from the cold outside. She carried a bag. "Look what I found—*soy*nog. No dairy." She proudly produced a carton. It was a few moments before she realized that something seemed amiss in the room. "What is wrong now?"

He shook his head and took her arm. "Nothing, nothing. I just don't know if I'm up for eggnog-flavored soybean product."

"It's so good for you!"

"Right now I feel like a chocolate éclair at Figaro's would be the best thing for me."

Her face lit up. "Really?"

He took the eggnog carton from her and tossed it to Danielle. "Drink it in good health." He reached for his coat on the back of the couch.

Greta looked suspiciously at Danielle. "What is wrong with you?" she asked. "What is going on here?"

"What's not?" Danielle shot back.

"Don't mind her," Wilson said, tugging Greta toward the door. "She's just got pre-party jitters."

When they were gone, Danielle felt like collapsing. The *last* thing she wanted to do now was go to a party. She didn't have the heart for it. She felt deflated, foolish. *How* could she have said those things to Wilson?

He was right. He was Greta's boyfriend—and she'd just blurted out that she loved him. Just like Greta didn't even matter. She didn't know if Greta was actually her friend or not, but she couldn't deny she felt guilty. When she walked around the apartment, she looked back more than once, expecting a trail of green slime to be following her.

She couldn't stay in the apartment. What good would that do? She would just brood. At least by going to the party she would be getting on with her life.

She grabbed her coat and pocketbook and was headed out the door when the phone rang. Huffing, she stopped to pick it up, even though she was pretty sure it wouldn't be for her. It hardly ever was anymore. Her popularity days were as gone as disco.

"Edie?" a voice asked. The connection was a bad one; the man might have been calling from a street pay phone.

"No, this is Danielle."

"*Who?*"

"Edie's roommate," she explained.

There was a long, staticky pause, as if the caller couldn't quite take in the fact that Edie would have a roommate. "Is Edie there?"

"Well, no." Duh. Didn't he think she would have put her on the phone if she had been there? Or did the guy think she enjoyed stilted conversation and staticky silence?

"Do you know where she is?"

"Not exactly," Danielle said.

Edie had been scarce around the apartment lately. Danielle knew that she had been doing a lot of catering jobs to cover Christmas and Kuchen's medical bills. But she had no idea what had happened to her tonight.

"What the Sam Hill does 'not exactly' mean?" the guy on the phone said.

Sam Hill? She nearly laughed. She hadn't heard that expression since leaving Amarillo. "It means I'm not sure."

"Well, when she gets in, will you tell her Douglas called? It's urgent."

"Douglas." Where had she heard that name before? Probably an actor friend of Edie's. Those theater people were all such leeches. "Okay."

"Tell her I'm coming in on American from Baltimore at nine. To LaGuardia. I got bumped off the direct from Paris."

As if Edie would care about this schmuck's travel woes. "Okay, will do," she said, signing off.

An unexpected visitor. The guy probably needed somewhere to crash and was calling Edie at the last minute. Nice! No wonder he'd been so silent and stunned sounding when she'd announced that Edie had a roommate. He was probably calculating how much less space there would be for him.

He had no idea.

She was feeling slightly better by the time she was in a taxi headed for the East Village, where Jack lived. She had to push the incident with Wilson out of her mind and move forward. The night was cold and drizzly, so she tried to focus on something positive, like that statistic about however many women it was who found husbands at Christmas parties.

Or maybe that was *weddings* . . .

Oh, well. It wasn't as if she wanted to get married or anything. Only she didn't want to be single forever. It was too nerve-wracking. How had Edie and Greta stood it for so long? They had to be gluttons for punishment or something.

Jack's apartment was a one-bedroom on the third floor of a bare-bones row house. His block buzzed with little restaurants and coffeehouses; a few businesses on the street had closed for the night and showed only their graffiti-covered steel burglar doors. It was so cold the air felt like ice going into her lungs. Danielle was glad to get off the street and felt that old pleasant zip of party anticipation as she climbed the stairs of Jack's building; she felt even better when she saw the crowd in his apartment. Milling about were some folks she recognized from work and proofreader happy hours, and she fell right in with them.

"What have you been up to, Danielle?" a proofer named Skip was asking her. He appeared to have drunk a lot, and a cigarette smoldered forgotten in one hand, its long ash looking as if it might drop to the floor at any second.

She shrugged and took a big swig of scotch and soda. Skip wasn't bad looking. She'd always thought so. She just hadn't cared until now. "Not much," she said. "Just writing, mostly, in my free time."

"Oh, that's right! You're a writer." He gave it a snooty pronunciation. *Write-uh.* "Jack's gal works with writers. Don't you, Jen? Jen?"

He was drunker than Danielle had thought. Forget whether he was good looking. He was a sloppy drunk.

A pretty Asian woman appeared. "What are you yelling about, Skip?"

"I got a little Texas gal here who wants to be a *write-uh!* Tell her how to do it, why don't you, so she can quit her day job and become the next Ernestine Hemingway."

The woman named Jen laughed and turned to Danielle. "*Don't* listen to him. Are you really from Texas?"

Danielle nodded.

Jen lit a cigarette and took a deep puff. She exhaled on a laugh and looked at the crowd gathered around them. "No offense, but that is *not* my favorite state. For months I was dealing with some crackpot kid who kept submitting *the most awful* stories."

Everyone laughed and leaned forward. All except Danielle, who seemed to have frozen. Jen. Jennifer . . .

"She changed styles so often you never knew *what* was going to show up in the mail. You just knew it was going to be bad. I guess she thought because she could type, that made her a writer."

It can't be, it can't be . . .

Skip put his arm around Danielle. His ash splattered over the toes of her boots. "Jen's an editorial assistant at the *New Yorker.*"

Danielle's heart beat like a rodent's. This was a nightmare. She needed to escape, fast, but her feet were anchored to the floor by shock and the rest of her was anchored by Skip's drunken bulk draped over her.

"Finally, I had to start making up stories so I wouldn't feel so guilty for rejecting this girl all the time. So I invented an editor— Mr. Picard, like the captain on "Star Trek"!—and told her he had read her stuff and *he* thought all the nasty things about it. What a dope! She had a really weird name, too—like some movie star."

"Nicole Kidman?" Skip asked, then blasted out a laugh at his own little joke.

Jen rolled her eyes. "No, it was an old name. Poitier! Like Sidney Poitier, only this woman's name was . . ."

Danielle twisted frantically. The door was ten million miles away.

Unfortunately, her movement seemed to mentally rouse Skip. His eyes bugged and he jabbed his cigarette hand toward Danielle. "Say, Danielle—isn't *your* last name—"

"Danielle!" Jen said, finally remembering it. "That's it! Danielle Poitier."

When she put together what Skip had just said, Jen's mouth dropped open.

Everyone stopped short, and a thick silence descended on the room.

Afterward, Danielle couldn't remember how she got out of there. It didn't seem to matter. It wasn't a situation you could get out of gracefully. She just retreated, quickly, through the cigarette smoke and thick silence and the heavy feeling of every person in the room following her every move. Tears stung her eyes, but she kept them in check by sheer force of will.

Not until she was on the street again, where the drizzle had turned to sleet, did she allow herself the luxury of letting a tear or two drop. But she couldn't bring herself to really weep. She was still just too stunned.

I guess she thought because she could type, that made her a writer. . . .

Oh, God.

Of course it was true. That's why it hurt so badly. She *wasn't* a good writer. She had sensed that for months. Edie had read her stuff and told her that she needed to study writing. Wilson had said much the same thing when she showed him a few stories. It wasn't just being wrapped up with Alan that made her stop writing, it was the feeling that she wasn't getting anywhere with what she was doing. That she was just typing.

The word made her wince. But wasn't that true? Her work didn't make her any more a writer than being able to hop up and down would make her an Olympic gymnast. She hadn't done any real hard work or study. She'd just assumed being published would come easily to her, because everything else in life had seemed to.

But these days nothing seemed to come easily except humiliation.

She didn't even bother with a cab but slid her way home through the ice. Tiny bits of snow flurried through the air now, mixing with the sleet. In the distance, the Empire State Building spire was lit up in red and green; even that made her feel no enthusiasm for her first snow in New York. She wondered if she would ever feel enthusiastic about anything again.

When she got back to the apartment, the place was empty. Oddly enough, she would have welcomed company. Edie, Wilson—anybody. Even Greta and Wilson together. Even Greta and Wilson together playing "Rockin' Around the Christmas Tree." She didn't want to be alone.

But she had no one to call. All the people she could have called in a pinch had just seen her completely humiliated at Jack's apartment. No doubt Jennifer Poon was giving them the real lowdown on exactly how lousy her stories were.

How was she going to face those people again?

She went to the message machine, which was blinking, and half listened to a message for Edie from that Douglas guy, who was rambling on about airports and being evacuated. He was *so* self-important and irritating sounding, she had to turn the volume to zero before he was finished. Then she went and flopped on her bed.

This was it. Last June she'd said she wanted to be published, have lots of friends and a fabulous boyfriend after six months in New York. But after six months, she had no boyfriend, couldn't face her friends, and had learned that when it came to writing she was just a sad little wannabe. She had as much chance at being published as one of the Olsen twins had at winning an Academy Award.

New York! She didn't belong here, that was the thing. She must have been mad to move here. What was the big deal about living in a city that couldn't even pronounce "Houston" right, where getting any little thing done was a huge hassle, and no one had tasted good barbecue or had even *heard* of Frito pie? She hated New York. It was crowded and cold and expensive. The people were vain and smug and really just as provincial as they were in Amarillo, when you got right down to it.

Amarillo. It *hadn't* been so bad, had it? She had just been immature. She hadn't been able to appreciate its good points, like . . .

She frowned.

Well! Like the fact that it was home, for instance. Her parents had a great house and probably hadn't paid half for their mortgage what she was paying for rent for something that *wasn't even a room!* It was just a cubbyhole. No wonder she felt so tense all the time. She had about as much room to move around in as Kuchen did in her cat carrier. Her parents had tons of space, and a swimming pool, and a big yard with prairie dogs in it. Nature! It was all right there; you didn't have to go to a park or a botanical garden or an Imax theater to experience it.

She wished she knew someone who understood how she felt. Someone who wouldn't sneer at her for feeling a little homesick.

She bolted up. As a matter of fact, she *did* know someone. That guy who'd come by last summer . . . what was his name? Something westerny sounding. Hoss or Ross or something.

Ross Johnson—that was it!

In the next ten minutes she turned the apartment upside down in search of the little business card with the phone number scrawled on it that she had discarded five months before. The needle in this particular haystack finally turned up in the kitchen in the back of the silverware drawer. Danielle snatched it and ran for the phone as if it were a lifeline.

Ross Johnson . . . He was really handsome, if she remembered correctly. Not that she was calling for a date or anything. She just needed someone to talk to . . . and if he happened to ask for a date . . .

Well. Nothing wrong with that, was there?

She dialed Ross's number. His answering machine picked up.

Damn! Would nothing go right this night?

At the sound of the beep, Danielle realized she needed to think of something to say. Something that didn't sound like she was on a self-pity jag. In other words, a lie. "Hi, Ross! This is Danielle. You probably don't remember me. Danielle Porter from Amarillo, a fellow transplant? I'm sorry it's taken so long to get back to you . . ." She couldn't help giggling self-consciously here. So long? Who the hell was she kidding? "I know it's been ages. I just found your card here . . ." She winced. That made it sound as if she would have called anyone whose card she'd found. Or that she had a million cards floating around her apartment. "And I re-membered how nice you were to come by that time, and I won-dered if you'd like to go out sometime. Just for a drink, you know?" She waited, almost wondering if he was standing by the answering machine, trying to decide whether to pick up. If so, the decision was apparently no. "Okay, well, give me a ring some-time."

She blurted out her phone number and hung up. Fast.

Calling a stranger. What a dumb idea. All she and Ross shared was a town in common. A town she wasn't even particularly fond of most of the time. That just showed how desperate she was.

God, she hoped he called back.

She stumbled back to her bed and collapsed facedown. Lordy. Being a loser really took it out of you, apparently. She was ex-hausted.

She must have dozed off for a while, because the next thing she knew, a door shut somewhere and she heard voices. Edie and someone else.

"See?" the strange—but disconcertingly familiar—voice asked. "Empty."

"They could come back, you know."

"So, we shut the bedroom door."

Edie laughed. "Anyone could guess you live alone. You have an odd expectation of privacy."

"You don't have any?"

"Haven't had for over six months. Greta's okay, but if Danielle's in the apartment, she's in your face *all the time*."

Danielle's fist went to her mouth. Her skin felt feverish. Should she say something?

What, and be in her face? a little voice asked angrily.

"She doesn't really have much of a room, so it's not really her fault—not the way, say, leaving towels on the bathroom floor is. Which she does all the time, by the way. What a slob! You can always tell the ones who grew up with maids."

Danielle just stopped herself from gasping. *Was Edie trying to insinuate that she was pampered or something? Her? Ha!*

And when had she ever mentioned their housekeeper, Albina, to Edie?

"I only met her once, of course, but she did seem a little spoiled."

Okay, Danielle thought, trying to piece it together. *I know this guy. No wonder he sounds familiar.*

In fact, he sounded almost as if . . . She shook her head. She thought he sounded like he was from Texas. But that was impossible. The only person here she knew from Texas was Ross Johnson.

"*A little?*" Edie guffawed loudly. "Well, she's better than she was. When she arrived she was like a little Amarillo princess. Her daddy was giving her *an allowance.*"

She and the guy shared a big chortle over this. Tears blistered Danielle's eyes. How dare Edie talk to someone about her this way! She could have almost imagined it from Greta . . . but Edie? She'd thought Edie was her *friend.*

"But you know, I didn't bring you up here to talk about your damn roommates . . ." the man purred.

"Would you like something to drink?"

"No."

"Well, what do you want?"

"Guess." The sounds of a small tussle ensued.

"Ross!"

Ross? Danielle gulped. It *was* Ross!

Edie was going out with *Ross?*

She slapped her cheek. And she'd just called him! What was *that* going to look like?

Like I was trying to make the move on both my roommates' boyfriends in one night . . .

Suddenly, the apartment went very silent. As if the two people were aware they weren't alone, and knew Danielle realized that they knew.

An interminable silence gripped the room, during which Danielle could imagine them pointing toward her screen and mouthing her name in wide, exaggerated lip movements. Finally, Edie called out in a small voice, "Danielle?"

What else could she do? Danielle took a deep breath and stood up. "Yep, it's me. The spoiled one."

Edie's face was as red as Danielle's felt. "Omigod. I didn't know you were here."

"Obviously!"

Edie was clearly distressed. Not that her pain comforted Danielle any. "You should have let us know . . ."

"What, and missed hearing what you really thought about me?" Danielle couldn't look Ross in the eye. God, please let her have left that message on the wrong answering machine. Maybe Ross had moved . . .

But no. The greeting had been in his voice. Which is why he had sounded so familiar tonight when she was eavesdropping.

"Danielle, what you heard . . ."

She couldn't take much more. Seriously. She wished there was a way you could just self-destruct in situations like this. An evaporation pill to instantly put yourself out of your self-inflicted misery and disappear. Instead, she couldn't stop herself from opening her mouth and making herself look a little more prickly and foolish with every word that came shooting out of her lips.

"It's how you really feel, obviously."

"I'm sorry—I was just running my mouth." Edie lifted her arms in a helpless gesture. "I thought you were going to some party."

"I did."

"Why are you back so soon?"

"Because I humiliated myself!" Danielle regurgitated the entire story, sparing no embarrassing detail. "And then I came back here, and I actually called Ross, because how was I to know you were going out with him? Nobody tells me anything!"

She was shaking by this point, and Edie stepped forward to calm her down. "Who cares what some woman, Jennifer whatever-her-name-is, thinks?"

"*I* care!" Danielle howled. "What if I told you that you

shouldn't care that you've been a failure as an actress for an entire year?"

Edie drew back, a wounded look in her brown eyes. Danielle could have kicked herself. Her and her big mouth!

"Actually," Ross said icily, "Edie and I were just out celebrating. Her old soap wants her back."

" 'Belmont Hospital'? But I thought they killed you."

"They decided I had a long-lost twin. Anita."

"Oh, Edie!" An overpowering emotion surged through Danielle. At least something was going right for *somebody*. "That's great! That's really great. I'm so happy for you!"

She started crying. Blubbering, actually.

And at that moment, Greta and Wilson *would* come in and see her in hysterics. "Vot happened?" Greta asked.

"Danielle had a sort of bad night," Edie said. "And then she heard that I got offered a part on a soap."

"But that is fantastic! Excellent!" Greta cried. She shook a finger at Danielle. "Are you crazy that you can't be happy for your friend? Are you really that selfish and spoilt?"

"Greta, it's okay," Edie said.

"No, it is not. She is too much."

"But, Greta—"

Danielle shot to her feet. "Don't *you* pile it on, too."

"Why not I pile it on?" Greta asked, sneering. "To spare your precious feelings? Were you thinking of me when you attacked Vilson tonight?"

Oh, God. Danielle darted an angry glance at Wilson; she felt utterly betrayed. "You *told* her?"

"She could guess something had happened, Danielle."

"Of course I could!" Greta roared. "I walk in and you are both red faced, and Vilson can not get out soon enough."

Edie moaned her disappointment like a solo Greek chorine. "Oh, Danielle!"

Danielle's face was on fire. "All right! I made a dumb, impulsive mistake!"

"You acted like what you are," Greta yelled at her. "A selfish brat!"

"*Brat?*" Danielle squealed. "What have I ever done to you?"

Besides try to steal her boyfriend, she meant.

Apparently, Greta had been waiting a long time to light into Danielle, because she seized the moment with the gusto of an old Viking sacking a village. "You treated me like a friend until I started being interested in Vilson. As soon as I stepped into your territory. And then you acted like I was not good enough for your precious boyfriend—who before you wouldn't even give the time in a day."

"I just—" Danielle didn't know what to say.

"You just expect everything to go all your way all the time. *Spoilt!*"

Danielle couldn't listen to any more. She lunged at Greta. She hadn't been in a girl fight since fourth grade recess, but she managed to hold her own. Greta might have had a size advantage, but Danielle was scrappy. And mad.

"You little spoilt brat!" Greta said, yanking at hanks of Danielle's hair.

It felt as if her scalp were on fire, and Danielle lashed back, kicking at Greta's shins. *"You . . . giant . . . German . . . meanie!"*

"Oh, for God's sake!" Edie jumped in to pull them apart. But pretty soon they were balled up like a nest of moccasins, going at it. Danielle didn't even know how long the brawl lasted, she only knew that at some point, she heard Wilson screaming at the top of his lungs.

"Cut it out!"

Just as quickly as it had started, the fight ended. With a little help from Ross, Wilson extricated Edie from the claws of Greta. God only knows why *they* were fighting . . . but Greta had lost a shoe.

Wilson smiled at them with exaggerated patience. "*Ladies*, you have a visitor."

Everyone turned to the door, where some guy in a navy blue overcoat was standing with a large duffel bag by his feet.

Edie gasped. "Douglas?"

Douglas! Danielle slapped her hands over her cheeks. She had forgotten all about his messages.

The man looked as mad as he was perplexed. "Visitor, hell," he told Wilson, offended. "This is *my* apartment."

Chapter 41

HE'S BAAAAAAACK . . .

"**W**hat are you doing here?" Edie asked, astounded. She was still breathing hard from the roommate sparring match; at first she'd half believed that she had been clunked on the head and her eyes were deceiving her. After all this time, was she really staring at Douglas?

He put his hands on his hips. "You *would* need to ask that question, since you never seem to be home. Didn't you get any of my messages?"

She blinked. "Messages?"

He rolled his eyes. "I gave them to some woman. Danielle."

Edie looked over at Danielle, who had been shrinking back ever since Douglas had announced himself. Apparently, she'd forgotten to mention something. . . .

"No, I didn't get them," Edie said. "I haven't been home, like you said. For some strange reason—I don't know, maybe it was the six months of silence from out Uzbekistan way—I wasn't really expecting to hear from you."

"You don't need to be sarcastic."

"I'm sorry, I just don't feel like I should have to apologize to you for having a life."

"What a life! I come home after nine months away and find you involved in what looks like a dry run for a mud wrestling show. Who are all these people—and was that woman on the phone telling the truth when she said she lived here?"

Edie grabbed Danielle's arm and dragged her forward. "This is Danielle," she announced. "And the woman at your left is Greta. They're my roommates."

"Roommates!" Douglas squeaked. "Holy Moses—who told you that you could start renting rooms?"

How she managed to refrain from wringing his neck would forever remain a mystery. Jerky little pipsqueak! "Did you think the half of three months' rent you left was going to last all nine months, Douglas? Didn't you ever once since May wonder how I was doing?"

"Of course I wondered!" he said. "I even sent Bhiryat a rug to keep him buttered up for you."

She laughed. "Oh, thanks. You might have put pen to paper and explained that twisted motive to me. Or, hey—here's an idea! You could have *called*."

"Do you think I've been idling around in luxury hotels?" he argued. "I've been *working*. It's not an easy job being a foreign correspondent in a country where there's revolution fomenting."

"Oh, that's right. I forgot about your *job*. The one that just so happened to fall into your lap." She paused for effect. "The one Tom McCormick informed me you had been begging for for months!"

He blanched. "Tom told you that?"

"Yes, your buddy Tom, who you spoke to *after* you last spoke to me. I suppose I should be glad that you were able to take time from your taxing job to speak to *someone*."

"Edie . . ."

She was right up in his face now. "Don't Edie me. You lied, Douglas. You *wanted* that job and you went after it, and you were too afraid to tell me that you were leaving me forever if you could manage it. What happened? No better opportunities presented themselves, so you decided to come back here to me?"

"I decided to come back to New York, not to you."

Ouch.

Okay, maybe she'd asked for that. She could almost hear the giant sucking sound as everyone tried to retreat from the fight. Danielle had already slipped from Edie's grasp and disappeared, and Greta and Wilson were backing toward the door. Only Ross stood sturdily beside her.

"And what business do you have lecturing me?" Douglas asked, his gaze cutting periodically toward Ross. "You obviously haven't been gathering dust while I've been gone."

She lifted her head. "No, I haven't. Douglas, this is my boyfriend, Ross Johnson. Ross, this is the jerky ex-boyfriend I've been telling you about."

Douglas had been extending his hand to Ross, but when Edie's words registered he retracted it. "Nice homecoming!"

"This isn't your home now, Douglas. It's mine."

"My name is still on the lease, isn't it?"

"Yes, but I've been living here. I've fixed it up."

"With all this junk?" Douglas said, gesturing around at the furniture. "It looks like set leftovers from 'The Munsters.' "

"Hey!" Greta yelled at him. "Watch it."

"I'm back in New York, Edie," Douglas said, ignoring Greta, "and I'm not going to go hunt down another apartment because you and a bunch of flaky women have decided it's yours when it's not. My name is on the lease."

"Flaky!" Edie said, hands fisting at her sides.

"Bhiryat will stand with me on this."

Edie wanted to scream—mostly because she knew he was right. Bhiryat had been keeping a vigil for Douglas, and now that he had returned, the landlord would no doubt be thrilled.

"What? You want to kick us out tonight?" Edie asked him.

He rolled his eyes. "Of course not. Stay the night here, by all means—I'm going to a hotel. This has been some homecoming, Edie. Thanks a whole darn lot."

He picked up his huge duffel. As he was leaving, though, he spied something on the coffee table and let out a cry. "My oboe!" he shouted. "Has someone been messing with it?"

"Someone's been *playing* it," Edie said. "Which is more than you ever did."

He glared at her. "I'll talk to you tomorrow."

When he was gone, they all stood silent for a moment.

"Oh, Edie . . . ?" Danielle said in a small voice from behind the screen.

Edie grunted.

"Douglas called."

Edie laughed through the tears welling in her eyes. She was furious. And embarrassed that all these people were witness to her official breakup with Douglas. And shocked that she could feel so little except anger for someone who had once meant so much to her.

Greta and Wilson came out of the kitchen, where they had been hiding since Edie and Douglas had started arguing. "We are going out for a while," Greta said.

"Sure," Edie said. *Abandon me*, she thought irrationally. "You might want to start thinking real estate solutions, though."

"*Ja,*" Greta said. "That is just what I was telling Vilson. We need a solution."

Edie looked at Wilson. "You spend more time in subway stations than any of us. Do you know a good one for sleeping in?"

"Hopefully, it won't come to that," he said.

"I am not so sure," Greta said. "Douglas looked very angry."

Edie nodded. "And he doesn't even know about eBay yet."

In contrast to the awful scene the night before, when Edie awoke the next morning she felt as if she were floating in a dream. Someone was kissing her, and that someone was Ross. He planted a noisy high-suction kiss on her cheek, coaxing a groggy laugh from her.

Then she opened her eyes, looking out at the room she loved, in the apartment she loved, and felt something pierce her heart. She was going to have to find a new place.

She groaned and attempted to pull the covers back over her head, but Ross stopped her. He was propped up on one elbow, his incredible body uncovered from the waist up and very tempting. The corners of his deep brown eyes crinkled a little in concern. "What is it?"

"I hate to move," she said.

He laughed. "Is that what's been eating you?"

She squinted at him. "How do you know anything's been eating me? We've been asleep."

"Wrong. *I've* been sleeping. I don't know what it was you were up to. I woke up three times to the sound of your teeth grinding."

"I'm sorry. I hate having things up in the air."

"Then let's make a decision," he said. "Move in with me."

She sat up, stunned. "Serious?"

"Of course."

Her heart pitter-pattered double-time as she looked into that adorable face, those come-hither eyes. Now they were beckoning her to go live with him and be his love . . .

. . . in his tiny studio apartment.

She sighed and fell back against the pillows. "It would never work."

"Why not?"

"Well . . . for one thing, your apartment isn't even big enough for half a person, much less two people."

"Have you decided to take up acrobatics after all?" he asked, grinning.

"No, but I occasionally like to stretch my arms out—which, as we both know, is a physical impossibility at your place."

"Okay, we'll find somewhere bigger."

"Then we'll *both* be inconvenienced," she told him.

"Edie, it's not an inconvenience for me. I'm not emotionally attached to my shoebox—er, apartment. And we're both making enough that we can find somewhere pretty nice. Maybe on the Upper East Side, close to where I work. That would be an improvement, wouldn't it?"

She closed her eyes and tried to imagine domestic bliss in the east 60s. She and Ross getting up in the morning and strolling out for coffee and expensive baked goods, hand in hand. It wasn't a painful prospect.

Yet a sharp doubt nagged at her. What was it?

Oh, yes. *Douglas*. The man she'd been so over-the-moon happy to be moving in with less than a year before. What had become of *that* happiness?

She sighed. "I can't."

He didn't bother to mask his disappointment. That was one of the things she loved about him: there were no macho save-face games with Ross. "Why not?"

"Because we've only known each other a few weeks yet. It's just too soon. If we start rushing, it might spoil everything."

"How do you know?"

She thought frantically. She didn't know, of course. It was just a hunch. A hunch backed by experience. "I don't know if I can explain it. It's like rushing onstage before the stage manager gives you your cue."

He quirked a brow at her. "Aren't you going a little 'drama mama' on me here? If you just don't want to . . .'"

"But I *do* want to. Just not now."

He sighed. "Then we've got to find you a new place. Pronto."

A light knock sounded at the door. "Edie?"

It was Greta. "Yeah?"

Greta cracked the door and poked her head in. "I'm sorry to bother you, but we haff a slight problem."

"Good! That's *just* what we need."

"It's Danielle. She has disappeared."

Edie sat up straight and exchanged a troubled look with Ross. "Disappeared?"

"She left this note," Greta said, coming forward. Then she stopped. "I am sorry—I did not realize you were so naked."

Edie pulled a sheet up to ensure her modesty. "It's okay." She took the proffered note and scanned it. It was in Danielle's handwriting, all right, with its rounded, loopy letters. It was short and simple and perplexing.

Ya'll: I'm sorry for all the trouble last night. I'm sorry for all the trouble I've been for months, actually. I guess maybe I am spoiled. Anyhow, it's time for me to go back and start all over. I'll miss ya'll like heck, but I guess that's life. I'd wake you up and say bye, but I've created enough embarrassing scenes to last a lifetime. Thanks for the memories (most of them . . .). Danielle.

Edie looked up at Greta. "What do you think?"

"I think I should not have yelled at her last night. I feel bad now."

"Well, she did call you a giant German meanie. There are limits."

"*Ja*, but I *was* mean. Like kicking the dead horse when she is shot."

She understood what Greta meant. Too well, she was afraid. "We all went a little nuts last night. Besides, Danielle's a big girl."

"Where do you think she has gone?"

"She says in her letter she's going to 'go back and start over.'"

"She can not go back to Amarillo," Greta said.

Edie was a little surprised that Greta would take that position. "You always thought that was the best place for her."

"But now she would just be running away," Greta said.

Just then Wilson came into the bedroom, aka Grand Central Station. He held a notepad with writing and numbers scrawled all over it. "Okay—you're in at eleven o'clock."

Edie frowned. "In where?"

"I have a friend who's a super," Wilson said.

"Oh." She slumped. Greta had already abandoned her.

"Don't you want to go look at it?" Greta asked Edie.

Edie perked up. "Me?"

"All of us. It is three bedrooms."

Chapter 42

STICKING

Danielle heard the knocking on her door and sat up with a start, sloshing water all over the floor. Not that it mattered. The vinyl tiles in the bathroom had been so warped for so long that the floor resembled a dry, cracked riverbed.

She had been asleep for . . . how long? Her skin was soft and pruny and bore the sweet detergenty smell of Mr. Bubble. She jumped into her bathrobe and skittered out into the bedroom, creaming her shin against the metal bed frame. She hopped the rest of the way to the door.

"Who is it?" she called out. Of course there was no peephole. That would have been considered a frill.

"Who do you think?" a familiar voice yelled through the wood.

Danielle drew back. *Greta?*

"And Edie, too," Edie said.

How did they find her?

"Are you going to open up?" Edie asked her.

Danielle flipped the lock, opened the door, and stepped back. Greta marched in first, followed by Edie, who was wincing as she took in the hotel room's décor. It relied heavily on mustard yellow and green.

"What a shit hell!" Greta exclaimed.

"How did you find me?" Danielle asked. "I didn't say where I was going in my note."

"You said you were starting over," Edie explained. "Where else could you start but the Alexander Hamilton residence hotel?"

Greta was nosily inspecting the contents on the counter in the bathroom. There was a bottle of Sleep-Rite sleeping pills and that half-used bottle of Mr. Bubble. "What the hell have you been up to?" she asked, looking at the tub with its filmy, pinkish water.

Danielle blushed. "I, uh, fell asleep in the tub."

Her old roommates looked astounded. "How?"

"I was so upset, I took a few sleeping pills and I just"—she shrugged—"fell asleep."

"With Mr. Bubble?"

"It was cheaper than Calgon at the drugstore."

Edie shook her head. "You shouldn't have run out while you were so upset."

"What could I do? I knew ya'll didn't want me around anymore."

"What are you talking about? Of course we do."

"That is why we're here, numwit," Greta said.

Having Greta of all people here *and* being so nice to her (for Greta) was humbling beyond her wildest dreams. "I don't know how you can even speak to me after last night!"

Greta rolled her eyes. "You made a mistake. Mostly, you make a fool out of yourself. Also, I can forgive you because Vilson says he told you off."

She winced at the memory. "Yes. He did. He said he loves you."

Greta drew herself up. "There! See? I can afford to forgive a stupid little jerk like you."

Danielle didn't bother defending herself. Stupid little jerk was a step up from the names she'd been calling herself. "Forgiving is one thing. Why would you want me around?"

"I'm not sure," Greta said. "I think you are almost like family now—I did not choose you, but I feel something for you. You should not run away or hide yourself because you feel foolish and ashamed. You will get stuck in a butt that way."

"Greta's right," Edie told her. "If you go to ground every time you hit a snag, you'll never get anywhere in this town. It's full of snags."

As if she didn't know *that!*

"So what do you say?" Edie asked. "Are you with us?"

"You mean Douglas didn't kick us out?"

"Oh yes. We're history as far as Thirtieth Street is concerned. But we have a new place to go look at. A friend of Wilson's is the super. You have to come check it out."

Danielle felt like weeping, she was so grateful to them. She never imagined that they would come after her. She hadn't even expected to ever see them again, to tell the truth. She'd really meant she was going to be starting out from scratch, back in New York like last summer, knowing no one.

Only this time she wasn't going to make all those mistakes. And she was going to really figure out what she wanted to do, and not just float. Maybe she'd follow Wilson's advice and go back to school.

"Vell?" Greta said impatiently. "Are you coming?"

"Are ya'll sure about this? You're not just being nice? After everything that happened . . . and with Wilson . . ." She looked up at Greta, feeling tears stinging her eyes. "I wouldn't blame you for hating me. That's the problem. I'm so sorry."

"Vilson said nothing happened. I believe him. It is over now, and nothing like that will ever happen again."

"How do you know? How can you trust me?"

"Because you know I will kill you if it does."

Danielle chuckled nervously. "That's comforting."

"I fly from the handle too much. It is my drawback."

Edie looked at her watch impatiently. "Get dressed," she ordered Danielle. "We've got to be over there at eleven."

"Where?"

Edie smiled. "I think you'll be pleased."

Danielle couldn't help feeling a lift. They really wanted her! They didn't hate her. At least not enough to forgo having her for a roommate. That was something.

She hopped to it and threw on a pair of jeans and a lambswool sweater. "One thing I'm confused about," she said as she yanked on a pair of boots.

"What's that?" Edie asked.

"How did you know I wasn't going all the way back to Amarillo?"

Edie laughed. "Oh, that was easy! You couldn't have."

Danielle shook her head. "I'm not so sure about that. I was pretty upset last night."

"Haven't you looked outside?" Greta asked her.

Danielle headed over to the window. She looked out and gasped. "Snow!"

It had been snowing last night on her way over, but she had expected it to melt as it had a few times before this fall. But this time it had stuck—Manhattan was in full winter wonderland mode. Danielle's heart swelled. Even though her hotel just looked out on a grubby street in east midtown, it was like a picture postcard this morning. The sidewalks were virtually empty, and only a few determined cars plowed their way down the streets.

"It was practically a blizzard. The airports are all a mess. I knew you weren't going anywhere."

"It's so pretty!" Danielle exclaimed.

"We'll have to walk, of course," Edie said. "We'll never get a cab."

Danielle laughed. "I'm so sure you were really about to run down to the street and take a taxi."

"I'm a new woman now," Edie said, clearly still pleased with her news. "My role on the soap should allow for a few cab rides."

"That's right!" Danielle had forgotten about "Belmont Hospital." "Wait till I tell my mom! She'll watch you every day. Does being a long-lost twin pay well?"

"A lot better than being an unemployed fava bean."

There was no exposed brick. No tin ceiling. No balcony.

But it wasn't bad. Not bad at all. And it was only $2450.00 a month, which they could afford now that Edie was raking in good dough. She got dibs on the largest bedroom. And this time Danielle would have a real room, one with a door. And there was a bigger kitchen for Greta and Wilson when he came over to cook. And the living room was spacious and had three tall windows, which Kuchen would really love.

And best of all, the apartment was in Chelsea. Really Chelsea this time. The Last Drop was just a block away. They wouldn't even have to find a new laundry.

"It's perfect." Edie was in awe. Maybe her luck really had changed now. New job, new apartment, new guy.

"Positively perfect," Danielle agreed. She couldn't wait. She could buy some real furniture now. And she had a closet—with a long clothes rod that she was just dying to fill. She could start over, but this time she wouldn't be starting alone.

Greta could only see perfection in the layout. There would be a little more privacy this time. And the big kitchen was a plus. But at that moment, what she couldn't bring herself to believe was that the best thing about the apartment was that she would be sharing it with Edie and Danielle.

Her friends.

She wasn't just desperate. She wasn't resorting to some lame, last-ditch plan. She was going with what was logical—to live around people she actually gave a damn about. She didn't like to think about how long it had been since she'd done that. She was just grateful she wasn't running anymore. That somehow, improbably, she had set out to make her life a little better and had actually succeeded.

"Well?" The super, who knew Wilson from an early temp job moving furniture, looked at them impatiently. He wore a thick jacket and a baseball cap, and his young, tough attitude was just as Wilson had described.

"We'll take it!" they all said at once. Edie began to fish through her wallet for the money they had all taken out of the ATM on the way over. It included the money to bribe the super into accepting Kuchen. He seemed pleased to have his palm so liberally greased.

And he was doubly impressed by their references. His eyes popped at the list of names they handed to him, just in case he was still sitting on the fence. "Robert DeNiro? I *love* that guy! *Raging Bull* is, like, one of my favorite movies. And—Jesus!—you actually *know* Springsteen?"

"Greta's cleaned his teeth," Danielle said.

The super regarded them all with new respect. "When do you wanna move in?"

They looked at each other, smiling.

"Would right now be too soon?" Edie asked.